BATTLESTAR GALACTICA ™

BATTLESTAR GALACTICA™

A R M A G E D D O N

RICHARD HATCH
AND CHRISTOPHER GOLDEN

A New Novel Based on the Universal Television Series
Created by Glen A. Larson

BYRON PREISS MULTIMEDIA BOOKS
NEW YORK

POCKET BOOKS
NEW YORK LONDON TORONTO SYDNEY TOKYO SINGAPORE

An Original Publication of Pocket Books

Pocket Books, a division of Simon & Schuster, Inc.
1230 Avenue of the Americas, New York, NY 10020

A Byron Preiss Multimedia Company, Inc. Book

Byron Preiss Multimedia Company, Inc.
24 West 25th Street
New York, NY 10010

The Byron Preiss Multimedia World Wide Web Site Address is:
http://www.byronpreiss.com

ISBN 0-671-01169-3
First Pocket Books hardcover printing August 1997
10 9 8 7 6 5 4 3 2
POCKET and colophon are registered trademarks of Simon & Schuster, Inc.

Edited by Howard Zimmerman
Associate Editor Steven Roman
Cover art by Luis Royo
Back cover photo by Ron Sorensen
Cover design by Steven Jablonoski
Interior design by Kenneth Lo

Printed in the U.S.A.

For Mom, Dad, and my son Paul for your continuing belief in me and supporting me through all these years, especially the rough times.

Thanks to: Glen Larson and Universal Studios for developing such a heartfelt, entertaining and inspiring show; Ed Kramer; Barry Solomon; Rob Liefeld and Matt Hawkins; Lisa Crane; my girlfriend, Sophie La Porte; Byron Preiss and Howard Zimmerman for providing me with this opportunity; Steve Roman; and Chris Golden, who was an absolute pleasure to work with.

—Richard Hatch

For Mom and Peter, with love

Special thanks to Howard Zimmerman, Steve Roman, Lori Perkins, Glen A. Larson, MCA/Universal, Richard Hatch, and the entire cast of the original *Battlestar Galactica*.

—Christopher Golden

1.

B_{LIP.}

The Scarlet Viper's scanners had picked something up. Another ship, or the system they sought? A second after the soft alert tone notified Apollo, the scanner blossomed into a laser-constructed three-dimensional image of their destination. Binary 13 was a dual-star system in which each sun had several orbiting planets. The gravitational tides of the two stars wreaked havoc upon many of those worlds.

"Starbuck, I have Binary 13 on scanners," Apollo observed.

No response.

"Starbuck?"

"Sorry," a scratchy voice grumbled over the commlink. "Caught me during sleep period. We there?"

"I was wondering why you'd been so quiet," Apollo admitted. "Didn't you have sleep period just before we launched?"

"Sure, but I spent two cycles playing pyramid at the chancery on the *Rising Star* just before that. When I lose I drink grog. No problem there. But I got lucky. I scored a perfect pyramid and used my winnings to buy ambrosa. Now I feel like I've got crawlon webs in my brain," Starbuck said.

"Serves you right," Apollo replied without rancor. "Now I'll pretend I didn't hear that. I'd hate to have to report you for launching while altered."

Starbuck didn't respond. He didn't need to. Apollo might shake Starbuck's pogees a little, that was expected, but he also knew that there was no way Starbuck would ever go out on any mission, or even patrol, while intoxicated. Apollo was confident of his own abilities, but one on one, in individual battle, there wasn't a better pilot in the fleet than Captain Starbuck.

"So, what have we got?" Starbuck asked.

"Binary 13 system on a narrow vector just ahead. We want Ochoa, the only habitable planet in the system. It's the furthest out from either star, and the gravitational pull of the two has created a helix orbit. Ochoa orbits first one star, then the other, in completing a single rotation. Not unique in the galaxy, but certainly extraordinary," Apollo explained, fascinated by the holographic display before him.

"So even this outermost planet is within the gravitational range of both stars?" Starbuck drawled.

"Yes. But it's in a protracted orbit, forty or fifty yahren, and the planetary core appears stable."

"Stable? How can we be sure? Just because the seismic readings are zero-zero at the moment doesn't mean it'll stay that way. Are we really going to land on a planet that could be about to enter a cycle of geological upheavals?"

"Nothing on the scanner suggests that," Apollo interrupted. "And we need whatever the planet can offer by way of food and fuel and mineral deposits. It's a recon trip, Starbuck."

There was a momentary pause before Starbuck grumbled, "Recon missions don't usually mean risking my neck."

"You risk your neck every time you flirt, or play triad with the cadets, or cheat at pyramids, or launch that antique Viper for that matter," Apollo said.

"That's different," Starbuck sighed. "I'm a Warrior, not an idiot. There's no way, as I see it from my limited knowledge of science, that Ochoa could *not* be unstable.

"Oh—and I've had about enough of you mocking my ship,"

Starbuck added. "She's kept me alive this long, and I don't need a shiny new toy."

Apollo grinned. When the fleet had begun building Azure-class Vipers, Starbuck had held on to his ship. Recently, the first Scarlet-class starfighter had rolled off the line and been presented to Apollo. Starbuck was next in seniority, but still wouldn't have anything to do with it. He let the tech crews service his antique and update its systems when necessary, but that was it. Starbuck may have matured over the years, at least somewhat, but when it came to that Viper he was like a little boy. No other ship would do.

"Send a narrow-beam message to the *Galactica*; tell them we've reached the Binary 13 system and are going to do a recon orbit of Ochoa before landing. Just to be sure its safe," Apollo instructed. He studied the holo-map that still shimmered before him, as well as the readouts visible on the interior of his helm's energy shield.

Until it was put on, a Warrior's helm was open at the face. When it was donned by a pilot, however, a barely visible energy shield would be activated, sealing the face and the breach around the neck.

Not only did the helm offer a visual readout, or info-scroll, which offered a constant flood of data, but it provided commlink to the fleet and to other Vipers. The helm had a rebreather/filter function, which allowed regular breathing in any environment with even a trace of oxygen.

A Warrior's helm was almost as necessary in battle as the Viper itself.

After consulting both data sources, Apollo realized that an orbit around Ochoa would require a slight course correction. He tapped his navi-hilt to the left. So long had he and Starbuck flown together that Apollo didn't need to communicate the course change. Starbuck compensated simultaneously and continued his report to the *Galactica*.

The narrow-beam message was sent as a coded deep-space signal. All long-distance communication was beamed this way, scrambled on one end and de-scrambled on the other. The comm officer on the *Galactica* would hear Starbuck's voice, or the computer's closest approximation of his voice, since the de-scrambling of the comm-signal was automatic.

"All right," Starbuck said, his voice a bit tinny inside Apollo's helm. "Let's get this recon taken care of so I can get on with my long-delayed furlon. I saved up some cubits after that last game to buy a bottle of ambrosa for myself and Cassiopeia."

"It's been fermenting for six hundred yahren, Starbuck—another ten centons isn't going to make a difference," Apollo said, rolling his eyes. "Any additional instructions from *Galactica*?"

"No, but Athena said to tell you not to waste time. Apparently the commander's feeling ill," Starbuck reported.

"What? What's wrong with my father?" Apollo asked, instantly alarmed. As vital as Adama had always been, and despite being the most strong-willed Warrior in the fleet, Apollo had ever been an overly concerned son. And if Athena was worried...

"Athena didn't say," Starbuck replied. "Just asked that we cut the feldergarb, do the job and get home. I'm sure Adama's fine, Apollo."

Apollo didn't answer at first. After a moment, without any enthusiasm whatsoever, he mumbled his assent. Then he pushed his anxiety away and focused on the mission. A simple one, the type of recon he and Starbuck had pulled hundreds of times. Every Warrior in the fleet had flown these missions; they usually came up empty. But you never knew.

"We've still got ten or fifteen centari before we reach Ochoa," Starbuck noted. "It might as well be a parsec, for all the readings I'm getting on the planet. You faring any better with your new toy?"

Apollo was slightly chagrined. His Scarlet-class vessel didn't seem to be getting any more precise readings than Starbuck's antique. In fact, the scanners showed almost nothing at all. No mineral readings, no lifeforms of any kind, on a planet that they knew from long range scans was habitable. And certainly, they were close enough now for more specific readings. It was almost as if...

"Starbuck," Apollo snapped as suspicion grew, "I think we're being jammed."

"Oh, come on, Apollo, we're in the middle of nowhere," Starbuck groaned. "You just haven't had a good solid dose of paranoia for a couple of yahren, and it's getting to you. If there were any advanced sentient races, never mind space-faring civilizations, in the Binary 13 system, we would have picked up their communications on long-range scan from the fleet."

"*Not* if those communications are being purposely shielded," Apollo said. "Computer, scan the atmosphere of Ochoa, then a system-wide scan of Binary 13 for non-stellar interference."

"Don't jar my chips, Apollo," Starbuck warned. "This mission was supposed to be like walking the daggit. And there isn't any stellar interference, because the Vipers would have screened the stars' own natural radiation before it became a problem."

"I know that, Captain," Apollo snapped. "But unless Ochoa has become a dead planet in the last few centons, someone or something is blinding our scanners. I want to know who, and why."

Apollo gripped the navi-hilt and tilted it slightly forward. He felt the weight of the additional thrust, and the engines hummed behind and beneath him. Their vibration was never a distraction, more a comfortable, lulling resonance. When a pilot was on edge, that buzz offered a confirmation of the power at his or her disposal, both in the engines and in the turbolasers.

"I've got Ochoa in my starfield," Starbuck reported.

Apollo looked up from the Viper's flatscreen and he could see the planet, green and brown, at the center of the starfield ahead. Space, as seen from a Viper's cabin, was only the starfield visible through the canopy.

"I see it," Apollo replied. "Less than four centari until we reach orbit. It's too late to make a less conspicuous approach. If there's somebody down there, and we've got to assume there is, they've already got us locked."

"Yeah, but we've no way of knowing if they're hostile. They could be jamming us for defense. They probably think *we're* going to attack *them*. Let's not be hasty, here," Starbuck warned.

Blip.

Apollo scanned the laser readout on his helm's face shield. Even as he read, the Viper's holo-system generated a more detailed map of Ochoa's surface. The planet was rich with mineral deposits. It was practically overrun with vegetation—though whether it was edible or not was a question the computer couldn't resolve. Ochoa had veins of tylium that the scanners indicated were nearly pure, far more stable than the diluted element they'd been using for decades to power the fleet.

There were also massive clusters of lifeforms in hundreds of locations, as well as one enormous technological or industrial center. Just as Starbuck had predicted, there was no stellar interference. Their instruments had been blinded, albeit temporarily, by quite specific design. The jamming signal was being beamed from a techno center near the farther of Ochoa's rotational axes.

"Starbuck?" Apollo asked over the commlink.

"I've got it," Starbuck responded, all Warrior now with no time for sharp comments about the efficiency of his archaic Viper.

"Yes, but what is it?" Apollo wondered aloud. "We've got to assume they're hostile. Computer, scan for other starships within the Binary 13 system. Then broaden scan to include as much of this sector of the galactic quadrant as your instruments will allow."

Letters and numbers flashed by Apollo's eyes. He ignored his helm and stared anxiously out at the starfield, glancing down at the Viper's flatscreen every few heartbeats.

"What are we waiting for?" Starbuck urged. "Let's take a closer look."

Apollo knew he was right. They weren't under attack. By every rule of conduct, everything they learned at Academy, they ought to do a flyby as planned, get an idea what exactly was down on the surface of that planet. But it just felt...wrong.

"I don't like it," Apollo said.

"I don't like it either, Apollo, but it's our job," Starbuck teased.

"That's not what I mean, Starbuck. It's something more. I sense danger, hostility. That and...familiarity. They know us," Apollo said, trying desperately to put his portentous feelings into words.

"I thought you were done with that mystical feldergarb," Starbuck snapped, on edge.

"It's not feldergarb, and it isn't mystical. It's all purely scientific, exercising the mind to expand its power, its acuity. I don't claim to understand it completely; it takes decades of study, but I'm learning. And I know what I sense," Apollo stated flatly.

"We've got to warn the fleet," he added. "But we can't send another transmission without taking the risk that they'll track the signal back to the *Galactica.*"

Every muscle in Apollo's body was taut, energy buzzing all through him. He ought to have been afraid, ought to have been frantic, but his mind had never worked that way. He functioned best when the stakes were highest.

They were rapidly approaching the surface of Ochoa. Apollo was about to speak again when laser blasts erupted all around them, lighting up the starfield just ahead and to either side of his Viper. He blinked away spots, as if he'd stared too long at tylium fire.

"Frack!" Starbuck roared. "Cylons!"

Cylons! Six yahren without a single skirmish—so long that the fleet had almost begun to allow itself to hope that it had finally escaped Cylon tyranny. Apollo's heart sank. He'd sensed them, close by, but had denied the prescient awareness because he couldn't believe it was true.

But it was, and hazardously so. Cylon laser fire burst in startling, glorious colors to all sides. Apollo's Scarlet Viper took a tangential blast on the right wing, but the starfighter's shields shrugged it off. A direct hit wouldn't be so harmless. The laser blasts would have been beautiful if they weren't deadly.

"I've got twelve of them on scanners, Starbuck!" Apollo said. "Coming straight for us. Return fire!"

"What do you think I've been doing? Lords, Apollo, we're outnumbered pretty badly," Starbuck growled.

The phalanx of Cylon fighters approached at top speed. Each ship was an extruded oval, slightly bent at each end—a sliver moon seen dead on. Apollo gripped the navi-hilt and thumbed the right side button, arming the targeting system. His helm was linked to the ship's systems, but he looked past its readouts, paying sole attention to the Viper now; he had to trust his ship.

The targeting system locked onto a fighter, showing him a pattern of fire that would destroy two with one burst. He thumbed the left side button, and turbolaser fire arced from his cannons. Two Cylon fighters exploded into shrapnel. Even as he took aim again, Starbuck knocked out a third.

Three down, nine to go.

"Yeah! That's a relief!" Starbuck cried. "The Cylons certainly haven't improved on their skills as pilots or warriors!"

"Don't get cocky!" Apollo ordered, then realized what a useless thing that was to tell Starbuck, of all people.

The nine remaining Cylon fighters fired on them one more time, then Starbuck and Apollo had flown through the holes they'd blown in the phalanx of fighters.

"Okay, we've got a minute to breathe and circle around...or we can just take off," Apollo observed. "What do you want to do?"

"You're the lieutenant commander, buddy, you tell me," Starbuck noted.

"Why is it you always offer your opinion when nobody asks for it, and clam up when someone does?" Apollo mused.

"Just part of my charm," Starbuck answered. "This way you can't blame me if you make the wrong decision."

Apollo glanced at the Viper's flatscreen. Scanners showed the nine Cylon fighters turning to pursue. Now Starbuck and Apollo would have to max-out their Vipers to stay ahead of Cylon weapons fire.

"Let's do our job," Apollo decided. "A full-thrust flyby, not orbital—just enough to get a read on Ochoa's mysterious little village, and then we're out of here."

"Not the choice I would have made. I guess I should have spoken up," Starbuck grumbled.

"You had your chance," Apollo retorted. "Now, *go!*"

The Cylons were gaining, but still out of range. Side by side, the two Vipers closed in on Ochoa, making a high pass above the planet. Apollo waited breathlessly for his scanners to offer a readout of the base below. Waiting, waiting...

"Come on, come on!" he snarled.

Blip!

"Got it!" he shouted. "It's a Cylon base, all right, and no base stars on the scanners. Got to be a colony of some kind!"

"Great, now let's get out of here," Starbuck said without enthusiasm.

The nine Cylon ships had gained on them as Apollo held back, waiting for his scanners to examine the base. Now he pressed his navi-hilt forward, picking up thrust.

"Divide and conquer, Starbuck!" he ordered.

"Gotcha, buddy," Starbuck answered. "And if it works, I'll share that bottle of ambrosa with *you* when we get back!"

Simultaneously, Starbuck banked left and Apollo rammed his navi-hilt to the right. The Vipers peeled away from one another in opposing arcs. Ochoa was silent below them. Apollo saw no more launches on his scanners, and he hoped that meant these were the only Cylon fighters the planet had for protection. It wasn't likely, but after six years, he didn't know if he was any expert on current Cylon tactics.

The Cylons fanned out to follow them, finally splitting into two groups—five after Starbuck and four after Apollo. The maneuver was going just as planned, and practiced, so long ago in the Academy. The realities of space flight required such tactics. Head-on space battle ended in microns; one pass and it was over. By then, you and your enemy were too far away for the battle to continue. Without an atmosphere to provide friction, it took a significant expenditure of force to re-vector the ship's momentum.

But when Warriors were determined to do battle, and patient, the fights would go on, long pass after long pass. Colonial Warriors were trained to use themselves as bait to set up the enemy for their fellow pilots.

Starbuck's Viper circled around and Apollo's Scarlet-class ship mirrored the move in the opposite direction. Moments later, they were revectored and facing one another.

The two Vipers raced toward each other. Instead of slowing, Apollo thrust the navi-hilt forward, triple-pulsars spouting gouts of blue-white tylium fire. A klaxon alarm signal blared inside the ship, warning of imminent collision.

"Alarm off!" Apollo barked, head splitting with the noise. "It isn't like I've fallen asleep in here!"

He gauged the distance between his ship and Starbuck's, watching through the cockpit canopy as the archaic Viper filled his field of vision. He could see Starbuck's face, see the grin that was spread across his friend's features, and the fumarello clenched between his teeth.

"You're not supposed to smoke in your…"

"Now!" Starbuck cried.

Apollo whipped the navi-hilt to the right at the precise moment that Starbuck did the same. His Viper trembled as the two starfighters passed within metrons of one another, belly to belly, their hot-plasma wake jostling both ships.

"Take 'em down, Captain!" Apollo crowed.

"Yes, sir!" Starbuck roared.

The Cylons had been out of range a micron earlier and not gaining quickly enough. Now they were all unexpectedly face to face with a Colonial Viper. The Warriors had a split-micron advantage. Apollo barely paid any attention to the targeting system; he simply strafed the entire starfield in front of him with turbolaser fire.

One Cylon laser blast passed so close to his canopy that it blackened a small area. A torrent of turbolaser fire ripped across four of the Cylon ships that had pursued Starbuck, and Apollo winced and shielded his eyes from the violent explosions. His Viper did a small jump, rocked by the shock wave.

The fifth ship was there, in his sights. He fired again, obliterating the fighter, unable to avoid flying through the wreckage.

But the Cylon ship had gotten off a last volley before it exploded. To Apollo's rear, Starbuck had taken out three Cylon fighters, and had only one remaining, when that laser blast—the one Apollo had been unable to stop—pulverized Starbuck's apex pulsar, which flared and then went dark.

Apollo turned hard, but it was too late. As he craned his neck to see out one side of his canopy, Starbuck's disabled starfighter skewed to one side, his last turbolaser blast going far wide of the final Cylon attacker.

Then the two ships collided in space.

The Cylon fighter was destroyed, some of the wreckage clinging to Starbuck's barely surviving Viper. Apollo continued his turn, watching in horror, bile rising in his throat as Starbuck's ship began to glow and burn. The momentum of the collision had thrust it down into the atmosphere of Ochoa.

Gravity had a stranglehold on the crippled ship.

Blip!

Apollo glanced at the readout inside his helm. Another entire phalanx, a dozen Cylon starfighters, had launched from the base on Ochoa. Any micron, they'd be on him.

He looked out at the green and brown planet and saw the flaming remains of his best friend's starfighter burning through Ochoa's atmosphere. Even if Starbuck had survived the collision, even if he lived through the fire—all of which was possible given the Viper's safety features—there was no way he would survive a crash landing from the upper atmosphere of the planet.

Starbuck was dead, or about to die. Apollo could do nothing but watch him go. Nearly twenty yahren earlier, he had lost his only brother to the Cylons. Now he had lost Starbuck, a man who was closer to him than any brother could have been.

When the klaxon went off in his Viper, signaling the Cylon fighters' rapid approach, Apollo turned his ship out into space and retreated, full thrust.

He would fly a course that would not track back to the fleet, and then change direction when he was a safe distance from Ochoa's scanners. He had to get back and warn the *Galactica*.

In the vacuum of space, within the silence of his starfighter, Lieutenant Commander Apollo wept...and mourned.

2.

THREE WEEKS LATER:

Vapor supply vents cycled warm oxygen into the room's pre-fabricated atmosphere. Not fresh air. For the most part, only Warriors on recon ever got fresh air, when they happened to go planetside on a habitable world. The rest of the fleet's citizens thought of "fresh air" as the naturally derived oxygen generated by the plant life on the Agro-ships. There were even scheduled visits for just such a special treat. Fresh air.

The vents were quiet, but in the horrible silence of Athena's vigil, they seemed to rumble loudly. Somewhere there was another sound, a rhythmic clicking noise that she recognized as coming from her father's antique time device, called a clock. It was the one thing he had salvaged from the ruins of their home on Caprica.

The only other sound in the room was her father's labored breathing.

Adama was dying.

In a hard, uncomfortable chair beside his bed, Athena, his only daughter, sat stroking his hand. Adama didn't respond. He had drifted in and out of unconsciousness during the weeks after the first cardiac seizure, rarely recognizing or acknowledging the family gathered around him. Then it had gotten worse.

Roughly thirteen centons ago, Adama had a second seizure. Not long thereafter, and about twenty centari before he fell into a profound coma, Adama had opened his eyes and smiled, his mind working with sparkling clarity for the last time.

Just as she sat by him now, Athena had been with Adama then as well. Apollo had also been there, along with his adopted son, Troy.

"This is…very painful," Adama had admitted, not surrendering his smile. "I'd like to be moved to my quarters, if I may. Please don't concern yourselves with me. Your responsibilities are to the fleet. Only know that I love you all very much."

Apollo had stood, watching their father with furrowed brow. Once upon a time, he might have allowed this moment of clarity to give him tremendous hope. But he had grown to be a more realistic man over the yahren.

"Boxey," Adama had whispered, and Troy had perked up immediately. His grandfather was the only person in the fleet who could call him by his childhood nickname and get away with it.

Troy knelt by Adama's bedside.

"Yes, Grandfather, what can I do to ease your pain?" Troy had asked, and Athena had loved him more than ever for the gentle urgency of the question. Apollo had taken the seal of marriage with Troy's mother, Serina, before the woman had died tragically. But Adama and Athena loved Troy as if he were their own blood. And Apollo positively beamed whenever the young Warrior was in his presence. Troy just had a way of making everything all right. Athena prayed that Adama felt some of that comfort as Troy held his hand.

"Ease my pain?" Adama had repeated in wonder, then winced as the next inexorable wave swept over him. "Only promise me this. One day, you may yet command this fleet. For now, swear to me an oath that you will dedicate your life in service to the Lords of Kobol, as I have, as my children have. Only with the wisdom of Kobol can the fleet be saved."

Weeping, Troy hung his head and swore the oath. Adama tousled his hair as he had done since Troy had come into their family at the age of six.

There was silence then, save for the hum of machines, the low talking of doctors and techs in the med-center, and the agonized moaning of a patient somewhere else in the center.

Athena felt something nudging her fingers, and she looked down in surprise to see that Apollo had reached out for her hand. She took it, looked up and saw him staring back at her, eyes glistening with tears. She squeezed his fingers in her own and they clasped hands with an intimacy they had not shared since their childhood.

Without any warning, Adama's eyes grew dull and began to roll back. His smile grew impossibly wide, and he made a sound that Athena had thought at first must be choking. Then she realized it was a deep throaty laugh.

"Father?" she had asked, alarmed by the frantic sound of her own voice.

"The light has come, Athena. The Lords have come. Kobol is so close now. I hear their voices," Adama whispered.

Then he was still. The smile slipped slowly from his face and his eyelids lowered to a slit. Enough for him to spy on them, if he were pretending.

But this was no pretense. His coma would soon result in death.

As he had requested, Adama was moved back to his quarters, where he'd lain in coma for the past thirteen centons...Athena by his side all the while. Apollo and Troy had gone to meet with Tigh, who, during Adama's illness, was the President by Proxy of the ruling Council of Twelve, known officially as the Quorum. The fleet was in an uproar, panicked, desperately in need of leadership now that their guiding light, the wise man whose vision they had all followed, had been struck down.

Stop thinking that way, Athena instructed herself. *He isn't dead yet.*

She caught herself in that thought and was sickened by the one word, *yet*. But it was true. It was only a matter of time now.

"Oh, father, I miss you already and you're not even gone," Athena whispered, her chest constricting under some terrible, invisible weight.

She stroked the white, thinning hair from his brow, the rough salt-and-pepper of the beard he had grown not even a yahren ago. Her memories of him, of her mother and Apollo and Zac—of them as a family—were crushing her. She had learned to live with Zac's death, and her mother's as well. She knew she would come to live with the loss of her father in time. But the thought of him not being there in her future, not beaming proudly down upon her when she finally made colonel, or took a husband, or gave him a grandchild of his own flesh and blood....

"Lords, no," Athena snarled, and stood from her chair.

She turned her back on her father and glanced around his spartan private quarters. Athena had never understood why his rooms were so featureless, when the man himself was so wonderfully colorful, warm and charismatic. Perhaps, she realized, it was because all that had mattered to him, other than his children, had been destroyed on Caprica during the obliteration of the colonies eighteen yahren ago.

The white walls were unadorned. The only personal items in the bedroom were holo-images of Apollo, Troy and Athena herself. And Starbuck, whom Adama had taken in as an orphan so many yahren ago and raised as part of the family.

Unbidden, an image popped into her head: Starbuck enjoying one of his wretched fumarellos, smoke swirling about his head like a tainted halo, blue eyes twinkling with mischief. And he, as well, was now dead. Gone forever. She felt as though her heart had been withered by all this death, the eradication of love and happiness from her life. All she had left was Apollo, and they had not truly been close since he had left their home on Caprica for the Academy all those yahren ago. The sense of competition had been too great, though it had never blossomed into any real hostility. She loved her brother, but wasn't sure she really knew him.

Athena felt isolated, alone.

"Enough!" she hissed, cursing herself for selfish indulgence. She *wasn't* alone. Adama was still here, perhaps in pain. Dying. He needed her. Could he hear her? Did he know she was there with him? The questions themselves were heart wrenching.

"Oh, Father, I don't want you to go," she whispered, kneeling on the floor next to him and clutching his hands in her own. They were cold, but not lifeless. She could feel his pulse in the veins of his hand.

Ever so softly, in a quavering voice, Athena began to sing to her father. It was a lullaby that her mother had crooned to her every night in their hillside home on Caprica. She hadn't thought of it in ages, but she remembered every word.

Athena lay her head down on her father's chest, and in that uncomfortable position, after centons of anxiety, she finally fell asleep.

Athena.

It sounded like her father, and for a moment her heart leaped with joy. But as she drifted up out of the misty land of dreams, Athena knew it could not be Adama. He was in a coma, he was....

"Apollo," she said, lifting her head from her father's chest, looking up at her brother, who had entered to stand over them.

"I'm sorry," she mumbled, wiping sleep from her eyes. "I guess I...I was dreaming about Father. He was telling me stories, his favorites, the legends of Earth and the Thirteenth Tribe. Tucking me in bed the way he used to do and promising that everything would be all right."

For the first time, Athena noticed the strain on her brother's handsome face. His eyes sparkled as always, but there were tears in them now. His strong chin and chiseled features, so like Adama.

"What is it, Apollo, has something else..." she began.

Then she felt the stillness of her father's chest, where her hands still lay, felt the cold of his stiff fingers beneath her touch.

"...No..." she muttered, and stared up at Adama's face. His eyes were open, an expression of wonder now frozen forever in place.

"Father, no!" she cried.

Apollo laid one hand on her shoulder and softly spoke her name. She grasped his hand, pulled herself to her feet and embraced him with a ferocity born of grief and loneliness. Her brother, her best friend, the only family that remained to her.

As they held one another, offering comfort that only siblings can give, it occurred to her that Adama's death would have a terrible impact on the fleet. Morale would suffer. Politics might tear them apart; the entire motivation of the fleet would be in question. Many people would look to Apollo for leadership, but as she held him, Athena had to wonder if he was up to the task.

And what of those who did not want Apollo to lead them?

In dying, Adama had taken with him all the stability he had offered so courageously, so effortlessly, during life.

"Oh, Apollo," she whispered through her tears. "What are we going to do without him?"

The room seemed wrong to Apollo. Too familiar, too filled with memories of his father: military and philosophical debates. Despite its lack of ornamentation, it was too warm a place for this to be happening.

Not that Adama should have died some glorious Warrior's death—his life had been glorious, his legacy as commander enough—but it should have been in some dreary, poorly lit med-unit, or instantly on the *Galactica's* command deck. There was some added horror to the idea that such a terrible event should take place in those benevolent surroundings.

"*Sssh*, Athena," he said, trying to offer comfort though his heart was shattered. "He wouldn't want us to grieve, not Father."

"You're right," she agreed, wiping tears from her eyes, moving herself away and looking up at him. "He'd want us to go on, to rally the fleet, to stand against the unrest that has sprung up since he fell ill.

Our people need guidance. But I don't know if…"

Athena faltered, and sighed heavily.

Apollo's lips pressed tightly together and his eyes narrowed. A tear slipped down his left cheek as he stared at his sister.

"He was very proud of you," Apollo told her.

Athena laughed softly. "Wish he'd told me," she answered. "We always knew *you* were his pride and joy."

"You're wrong, Athena," Apollo said urgently. "I was a pilot, and too brash for my own good. But you're a soldier, and a born diplomat, and Father admired that in you greatly."

Athena smiled and hugged him close again. Apollo squeezed his eyes shut, prompting another tear, saddened that Adama's death had been necessary to return this intimacy to their relationship.

"I love you, Brother," she said, pushing her lush brown hair away from her face, her eyes as deep and commanding as their father's had been.

"I love you, too," he replied.

"So, shall we go out and do his will?" Athena asked, obviously taking control of her emotions with a show of strength and confidence.

Apollo hesitated.

"What is it?" Athena asked.

"I know I said we shouldn't mourn, that we should save our grief for another time," he explained. "But maybe a little while longer. I don't want to leave him…just yet."

Apollo looked at his father's face, really looked at it, studying the lifeless eyes, the flesh which seemed almost artificial, for the first time since he'd come into the room and realized Adama was dead. Apollo felt paralyzed.

"He's already gone, Apollo," Athena said gently, and it was his turn to smile. He'd tried to be the stalwart one, the older brother, but now Athena comforted him.

"We have our duties," she added.

Apollo nodded, broke their embrace and reached across to gently close Adama's eyes.

"Rest now, Father," Apollo said. "Your great burden has been lifted."
Side by side, the children of Adama left their father's quarters and
went out into the *Galactica* to bring the news of his death.

It was Caprican tradition that the immediate family of the deceased
would gather before the funeral to pay their final respects in privacy.
In Adama's case, immediate family had a broad definition. His son
and daughter were there, of course, and his adopted grandson. But at
the urging of both Athena and Apollo, several others had also been
invited. President Tigh was there, as was Boomer. And Cassiopeia
attended with her and Starbuck's daughter, Dalton.

Athena smiled at Cassie as they moved away from the casket
together. She had spent a great deal of time nurturing her jealousy at
Cassiopeia's hold over Starbuck. Yet she had never begrudged the
other woman the fondness that Adama had for her. After all, Adama
was Athena's father. As kind as he might be to Cassiopeia, there was
no competition there. No contest.

"I loved him very much," Cassie said softly as they went out into
the corridor together. "My own father never gave me half the support,
understanding and encouragement that Adama did. I'm sorry he's
gone, Athena. If there's anything I can do, please let me know."

"Thank you," Athena replied, then purposely and bluntly changed
the subject. "I'm told Dalton was allowed to graduate Academy early.
That makes her the youngest Warrior, the youngest pilot, in the history
of the fleet. She broke Troy's record. You must be very proud of her."

Cassiopeia smiled, chuckling softly.

"Very proud," she said. "Boomer and Sheba tell me she's the best
student they've ever trained. But they let her graduate early because
she cleaned out every cubit the other cadets earned or begged from
their parents, playing variations on pyramid card games they've never
even heard of. They *want* her to leave."

"Sounds like she takes after her father," Athena said, her smile
bittersweet.

Neither of them knew what to say after that. The silence grew uncomfortable. Athena suspected they were both grieving for whatever they had lost when Starbuck died. But that was the question, wasn't it? What did she really lose?

"Just before he went out on recon, Starbuck told me he was taking two weeks of the furlon he'd saved up and spending it with you," Athena said without accusation. "I suppose part of a rogue's appeal is that he never knows when to keep quiet."

The discomfort grew. Cassiopeia frowned, as if Athena's words had stung her, and glanced away. When she looked back, there was an uncharacteristic anger in her eyes.

"Starbuck was Dalton's father, Athena," she said sternly. "If we were going to spend time together, as a family, it didn't have anything to do with you. And as for what it might have led to, we'll never know now, will we?"

Athena was taken aback by Cassie's vehemence, but the woman wasn't through.

"You know, I ended things with Starbuck a long time ago. When you and he began to share quarters, I was happy for both of you, and for myself. I had moved on. If you're bitter now, maybe you should remember that Starbuck asked you to marry him, but *you* refused the Seal. You threw him out of your quarters! You have no right to question his actions, nor his reasons, now that he's dead!"

Cassie turned her head away, as if somehow embarrassed that she had said so much. Dalton and Troy came out of Adama's quarters and both women urged them to continue on to the funeral, insisting they would be along presently. Athena and Cassiopeia looked at each other a final time, and Cassie turned to march after her daughter.

"Cassiopeia?" Athena whispered.

Cassie glanced back at her and waited.

"I loved him," Athena said. "I know you did, too, but I loved him so very much. I just...I couldn't trust him."

Athena lowered her eyes. A moment later, a gentle hand lay on her shoulder and she looked up to see that Cassiopeia had tears in her eyes. They both did.

"Let me tell you something," Cassie said quietly. "Starbuck was in love with me, and I with him, off and on for eighteen yahren before he died. He cared for me, I know he did, and the spontaneous, adventurous Starbuck was mine to have and hold, to love...to leave.

"But the real Starbuck, the man he was at his core, the courageous and giving person beneath the facade, that man always belonged to you. That's why I left him to begin with, those yahren ago," Cassie finished.

Athena stared at her incredulously.

"Maybe he wasn't always *in* love with you, Athena," Cassiopeia said, "but he loved you deeply. He told me once that from the moment he came to live with your family, after his parents were killed, from the moment he first laid eyes on you, he loved you.

"Neither of us ever won his heart entirely," she observed. "I don't know if any woman could have. But there isn't any reason for our rivalry to continue, is there? Starbuck is dead, Athena. I don't know if we'll ever really be friends, but I do know we've both lost something. Now you've lost your father as well, and we've all lost our commander. I think it's time to move on, don't you?"

"Yes," Athena agreed. She held out her hand, and the two women clasped one another's wrist firmly. "My father was very fond of you, Cassiopeia. I thank you for coming and...for speaking your mind."

Cassiopeia walked on toward the funeral chamber. Athena waited for her brother and the others to emerge from Adama's quarters. Though she felt somehow relieved by her conversation with Cassie, she could not ignore a tiny spark of dread that burned within her. So many deaths, so many endings, and Adama's funeral still to come.

Endings.

Athena yearned for some kind of beginning.

As the mourners began to gather for Adama's funeral, Apollo suffered their regrets and kind words with all the grace and courtesy that was demanded at such times. His public face was grim, sad and proud. But his was a private pain, only slightly eased by the genuine warmth of the others who had gathered to mourn, and of the fleet itself.

He felt the current of emotions, sensed it like a whisper in the shadows. As a being descended from the pure blood lineage of the Lords of Kobol, he had greater access to certain areas of the brain than other humans. At least, that was how Adama had explained it ten yahren ago, when he had first revealed their lineage to Apollo. They were sensitive to emotions: hope, fear, joy, frustration...grief. It had made Adama a better commander, a more compassionate leader. It was a gift, his father had said, but not necessarily a pleasure.

Command. It was on his mind a great deal now, and the source of a terrible quandary. Even if he were chosen to fill his father's post, Apollo wasn't certain he could, or wished to. He had worn his Warrior's uniform to the ceremony rather than mourner's clothing and received several curious stares because of it. But somehow it seemed the proper way to remember Adama, not in some ceremonial finery.

Command.

Apollo had watched his father his entire life, and knew the toll command could take on the heart. Command meant sending Warriors to face death, in all probability watching them die. That knowledge had caused him to avoid intimacy from the moment he arrived at Academy with Starbuck to begin their training as Warriors.

Starbuck. Lords, how Apollo missed him. He'd been the counterbalance of Apollo's life. When they'd entered Academy together, Starbuck had already been a maverick and was as popular as he was wild. Apollo, who was quickly appointed cadet captain, firmly divorced himself from the other cadets. Nobody understood their friendship, and Starbuck himself did not understand Apollo's logic. If it weren't for Starbuck's insistence, Apollo might never have become friends with Boomer.

Yet, it was his father, not Starbuck, who finally made Apollo see the tragedy of his logic. Avoiding intimacy might prevent certain emotional hardships, but without question, it created others.

"Love and compassion are not liabilities," Adama had told Apollo, "but strengths upon which to draw. A Warrior has nothing to fight for if he does not allow himself to love, and be loved in return."

President Tigh now stepped to the rostrum at the head of the funeral chamber, and the echoing whispers from the gathered mourners dissipated. As the memory of his father's wisdom slipped away, a bittersweet smile spread across Apollo's face, even as a single tear stained his cheek.

"An era has passed," Tigh announced, standing just above and behind the casket that held Commander Adama's remains. Tigh had been voted President of the Quorum in an emergency meeting less than a centon after Adama's last breath.

"I served beside Adama for more than twenty-five yahren," President Tigh said. "Even when I retired from active duty and took my place on the Quorum, I looked to him as a source of knowledge and wisdom. His life was an inspiration, his faith in the Book of the Word unshakeable. Adama was an example of courage, of valor and ingenuity, of calm in the face of adversity, and more than anything else, of perseverance."

Tigh swallowed painfully and cleared his throat, deeply affected by the moment. It was a day he had always prayed he would not live to see. He looked out at the starfield through the enormous window at one end of the funeral chamber. Adama's casket lay on a conveyance that would slip it into a launch tube, to be set adrift in space.

Where he belongs, Tigh thought. He turned his eyes from the stars and the bittersweet thoughts they brought to mind.

"Goodbye, my friend. May the Lords of Kobol raise you into the light, if only so that they may benefit from your wisdom as we have these many yahren," Tigh said, eyes moist. "You will be missed."

Unable to bring himself to say more, he raised a hand, signaling that he was through. To his right, Apollo and Athena stood with Troy. Behind them, Cassiopeia wept openly, holding her daughter Dalton for support. Tigh didn't think he had ever seen Cassie cry. But no other being had ever shown her the kindness that Adama had. Tigh knew that. It had not been unusual for the man.

Apollo's squad was there with him: Boomer and Sheba, Jolly and Zimmer, all of them. They stood at attention, honoring the commander with their loyalty and their respect. Their uniforms sparkled with buttons and clasps of polished sylvanus.

As Adama's casket slipped down the conveyor, Tigh collected his thoughts, preparing himself for the rest of his pronouncements—some of which the Quorum were likely to be quite angry over. Locked in a launch tube, the casket rocketed out into deep space. Tigh heard a hitching breath, and looked over to see that Troy was crying as well. Sheba stepped forward and laid a hand on his shoulder.

Tigh cleared his throat. He straightened his shoulders and ran a hand unconsciously over the balding patch on the crown of his head. He was the only Leonid—the only Quorum member hailing from the planet Leonis—ever to serve as president of the Council. He wanted to make his people proud.

"We are at a crossroads, my friends," he said, his words carried to the fleet over the unicomm, which broadcast his holographic image. "A time no less important to our continued survival as a people than the days after the Cylons destroyed our colonies eighteen yahren ago. The questions now are the same as they were then: where do we go? Who will lead us?

"To be truthful, I cannot imagine any man, or woman, fulfilling the duties of fleet commander with the sagacity and fearlessness Adama always evinced. But Adama is gone. You must, each and every one of you, have many questions. Who will replace Adama as commander, I imagine, is foremost among them.

"With few exceptions, the last eighteen yahren have been spent with one battlestar commander leading the fleet, as it should be in a state of war," Tigh acknowledged.

"For the moment, the Quorum has revoked the state of war and assumed command of the fleet. Before the issue of Adama's replacement as commander of the *Galactica*, and, possibly of the fleet as a whole, can be addressed, the Quorum must, by law, vote for a

Caprican to take Adama's seat at the council table.

"An actual vote will not be taken for some time, as it is deemed advisable that we examine all nominations for this position before making any appointment," Tigh continued. "The same is true for the position of commander. There will be many individuals to consider, many arguments to resolve."

He saw the surprise on the faces of all those gathered, most of whom glanced toward Apollo. The assumption that Adama's son would be commander was a natural one, but the Quorum had many dissenting voices. Some felt that Capricans, or more precisely, Kobollians, had held authority over the fleet for too long. Others simply felt Apollo was too unpredictable, and too stubborn, to be commander.

Nobody denied his fighting skills or his courage; it was his ability to lead that some had questioned. Tigh didn't doubt Apollo for a moment. He was his father's son. But a diplomat he was not. He had offended most of the Quorum members with his bluntness at one time or another. And his considerable ingenuity had always been over-shadowed by that of his father.

"However," Tigh continued, "we cannot allow the *Galactica* to go on during these lengthy debates without a commander. The hierarchy must be preserved. To that end, with the authority that is mine as president of the Quorum, I have decided to appoint an interim com-mander for the *Galactica*, who will be responsible for any and all mil-itary operations within the fleet."

For the first time, Tigh smiled.

"I'm sure it will come as no surprise to anyone that I am appoint-ing Lieutenant Commander Apollo to this position, until such time as the Quorum votes otherwise," Tigh concluded. "Thank you all. May the wisdom of Adama continue to guide us for generations to come."

Apollo raised his eyebrows, surprised that Tigh had not consult-ed him before making the announcement. He wasn't completely cer-tain he wanted to be commander, nor if he was the best candidate for the position.

Athena smiled and put a hand on her brother's shoulder. She leaned over and kissed him lightly on the cheek. As she withdrew, she experienced an odd sensation. It took her a moment to identify it as jealousy. Not that she thought Apollo would be anything less than exemplary as commander. Rather, it was that although she was lieutenant colonel, and second in command of the *Galactica*, Tigh had not even consulted her about his choice. Nor, apparently, had he even considered her for the job.

3.

IN THE WAKE OF THE COLONIAL FLEET, but far enough behind that even the longest range scanners would not pick it up, a Cylon base star stood near motionless in space. Its engines were cold. The monolithic structure had slid into place twelve centons earlier, and now kept vigil for any signs of human presence.

There had been humans nearby recently. One had even crashed a small ship on the distant outpost of Ochoa. Since news of this minor conflict had arrived, the hunt for the last bastion of humanity had heated up considerably. The surviving human pilot had retreated on a heading that would have taken him from Ochoa directly to where the base star now lay.

But there was no sign of them.

"I'm not at all surprised!" Baltar sneered, looking down his nose at Lucifer, the Cylon who had been made his aide after the massacre of the colonies.

"May I remind you, Baltar, that this destination was your choice?" Lucifer inquired.

Baltar merely sniffed in his direction. He despised Lucifer. Not as much as he hated the rest of the Cylon Empire. The mindless drone Centurions were essentially a hive mind, responsive to the Cylon Imperious Leader, a mysterious figure whose intelligence seemed light years beyond others of his kind.

Baltar was the scourge of humanity, the greatest traitor the species had ever known. Nearly two decades earlier, he had been advisor to the President of the Quorum. He had organized a peace treaty with the Cylons, after nearly a millennium of warfare. But it had been a trap, a prelude to the defining victory for the Cylons. Or it would have been if not for the atavistic survival instinct and sheer luck that Adama seemed to have. The arrogant Kobollian commander had gathered up refugees, not only from his home planet of Caprica, but from all the Colonies, and fled across space. Baltar had been ordered to destroy this last vestige of humanity, but had been thwarted at every turn.

In the time he had been among them, Baltar had been able to determine that there were three kinds of Cylons. The Centurions were not completely mindless, but almost helpless without the constant guidance they received from the Imperious Leader. There was the Imperious Leader himself, of course. Then there were Cylons of Lucifer's ilk, those who functioned at a higher level. Lucifer had, in fact, told him that when an Imperious Leader died—the Cylon lifespan was extraordinarily long, more than two centuries—a new leader was chosen from their ranks.

Which only made sense. The idea that a leader could come from the moronic Centurion caste was ludicrous.

"Well, now what do you propose?" Lucifer asked, the transparent skull on his cyborg head flashing with the sparks of his contemplation. Normal brain function, cybernetically enhanced. Amazing, really, Baltar had always thought. But then, normal brain function for whom?

There was so much about the Cylons he still did not know. They had gone to great lengths to make certain this was so.

"It's simple, really," Baltar replied haughtily, a tone he had always taken with the Cylons. "We'll go to Ochoa and interrogate their prisoner."

"I'm afraid that's impossible," Lucifer noted smugly. "Ochoa is in a dual star system, Binary 13. The planet has become unstable, and will soon be ripped apart by the dual stars' gravitational pull. It is being evacuated as we speak."

Baltar stepped down off his high seat of command, boots clacking on metal floor. He stalked the empty space as if caged, hands behind his back because he thought it made him look regal. Finally, he spun on Lucifer.

"In that case, you will have the prisoner brought to us. Immediately," he ordered.

"By your command," Lucifer replied.

Baltar bristled. When any other Cylon said those words, it was an absolute. When Lucifer said them, he always sounded almost...amused. Baltar hated him.

Lucifer went to Baltar's chamber door, and it slid apart to reveal three Cylon guards, two silver and one the golden color of Centurion captains. Their entire bodies were plated with armor. Where the eyes of any humanoid would be was a thin horizontal screen, upon which a small red light blipped back and forth. Some kind of visual scanner, he imagined, linked to the cyborg brain. But this was yet another secret he...

"Just a minute," Baltar hesitated. "I did not summon you. What are you doing here?"

"Oh, yes, please do tell us," Lucifer cooed, turning to his fellow Cylons with a twist that made his robes flutter around him.

"By order of the Imperious Leader," the Centurion captain said in an electronic monotone, "the human known as Baltar is to be removed from command of this base star, effective immediately."

"What?" Baltar cried, fear leaping into his heart. If he was relieved of his command, he knew it could mean only death. "You don't have the authority to..."

"By order of the Imperious Leader, Baltar," Lucifer chided him. "I'm sorry, but you'll have to step down. Centurion, what does the Imperious Leader suggest be done with Baltar? Or has he left the decision up to us?"

"Baltar is to remain aboard the base star as an advisor," the golden gleaming Cylon replied. "Lucifer is now in command of this base star."

"No!" Baltar shouted, enraged. "I'll not have it, do you understand? I'm the commander here and I order you all to leave my chamber at once! At once!"

He ought to have been relieved. He knew that. The death order had not come, after all. But still...Lucifer in command and he a mere advisor? The very thought was nauseating!

Lucifer sighed. Baltar had never heard another Cylon sigh, and it always disturbed him profoundly. For the first time, he recognized the tone of it, the weary patience of a pet owner training his new daggit.

"Baltar, if you're going to make things difficult, we'll have to detain you until you learn to behave yourself," Lucifer said, the red lights of his eyes seeming to flare brighter with menace.

The Centurions moved to snare the human.

"No!" Baltar shouted. "No. I will be most pleased to be at your service, Lucifer."

He had never spoken words so revolting. But if he had any chance of survival, he could not allow them to make him a captive.

"Excellent," Lucifer said. "Centurions, see that the human captive on Ochoa is brought to me with great haste."

"By your command, Lucifer," the three Centurions intoned, then turned and left.

"Ah, alone at last," Lucifer said. "Now, what shall you advise me on, dear Baltar?"

The Cylon turned and stepped slowly up to the high seat of command. When he turned and sat, head swiveling to look down, Baltar could barely contain himself. Lucifer's face was emotionless, as always—a subtle reminder of the limited emotions available to the Cylons—but his silent mockery brought Baltar to the edge of a homicidal rage.

And there he remained.

A lone figure strolled in contemplation along the Garden Path, a public area aboard the food cultivation vessel *Agro-3*. The dome of the ship showered stellar-light down upon the solitary stroller. Lost in thought, mind occupied with weighty concerns, the walker started at the sound of a voice.

"Your life need not trouble you any longer," the low, insinuating voice promised in a whisper. Accompanied by the sound of laughter, a spectacle took place without notice on board *Agro-3*. An unnatural flame erupted spontaneously, and a human life ended in a silent blaze of murder.

A military reception in honor of Commander Adama was held fifty centari after the funeral in the rearmost officers' club, the one Troy's grandfather had favored most.

So much time had passed. Troy took a long pull from his tankard of grog and watched his fellow Warriors speaking quietly but pleasantly amongst themselves. So much time.

He'd been six yahren old, and his mother still called him "Boxey," that horrible night when the Cylons swept out of the sky and decimated everything on the surface of Caprica. The other colonies had suffered just as badly, in some cases worse. But he hadn't been on one of the other colonies.

Troy still remembered that night, and still had horrible, restless dreams about it. Cylons. They'd taken his father, and eventually, half a yahren later, his mother too. But even at the age of six, he'd known what he wanted to be: a pilot like Apollo.

Not because he had always wanted to fly a Viper. Not because he so loved and respected Apollo that he wished to follow in his footsteps, though that was certainly a part of his desire. His most fundamental reason for becoming a Warrior, at the time the youngest Warrior ever to graduate from Academy, was quite simple.

He wanted to kill Cylons.

Troy believed he was the only person in the entire fleet to be disappointed when the Cylons seemed to have forgotten them. He had finally become a Warrior, could go out and take them on nose to nose, ship to ship, could pay them back for his parents, and for sleepless nights, and so much else. But they had disappeared.

When Apollo returned without Starbuck, heartbroken at having been unable to save his friend, Troy was distraught. He wished he could bring Starbuck back, yes. But he was glad the Cylons had reentered their lives. Starbuck's death was only one more thing to make them pay for.

"Troy! Over here!"

He looked up to see who was shouting his name at such a solemn event. Dalton, of course. She was so beautiful, with her mother's blond hair and twinkling blue eyes, and her father's confident, knowing grin. She swaggered with a pride he'd never known in anyone. She was only seventeen, a bit too young for him, but he found himself falling for her anyway.

It might have had something to do with the fact that she had beaten his record at the Academy. It was official now. Ensign Dalton was the youngest person ever to graduate Academy and become a full-fledged Warrior.

The attraction was odd for him. Troy had known Dalton since she was birthed, had taken care of her many times during her childhood. He had tutored her in language skills during numerous learning periods. There had never been any question that he was fond of her. But this was something...else.

"Come. Here," she commanded. Troy rose from the table where he sat alone, dropped a cubit for the servitor, and carried his tankard over to where Dalton stood laughing, surrounded, as she usually was, by other pilots.

Troy had always stuck pretty much with the family: father and Sheba, whom he'd been hoping would enter the Seal together for a decade; Boomer; Starbuck and Aunt Athena; Cassiopeia and Dalton. Tigh. Grandfather, of course. They weren't all related by blood, but he still thought of them as his family.

Dalton was surrounded by younger pilots, the new breed. Some of them, Dalton included, had never lived on a planet. Born and raised on a starship. Troy didn't know if he could think of any fate more horrible, but he supposed they had no idea what they were missing. No real concept of home, other than the fleet.

The club was filled with fumarello smoke, which reminded Troy painfully of Starbuck. Dalton's father was a hero to so many young pilots, all wanting to be mavericks just like him. One of the many reasons they worshipped his daughter so thoroughly.

Tankards clinked together, the lights dimmed slightly as an old Leonid ballad was piped from a crystal sound system. Behind him somewhere, Troy could hear Boomer begin to sing along, softly, with the music from his colony.

He stepped up to Dalton, the pilots around her parting to let him through.

"Lieutenant Troy, sir," a stocky kid—Ensign Roman, Troy remembered—saluted him stiffly. "Awfully sorry about your grandfather, Lieutenant."

"Thank you, Ensign," Troy replied.

"He was a hero to us all, Lieutenant." This came from Zimmer, the youngest member of Apollo's squad. He had, in fact, replaced Starbuck.

"To me as well," Troy replied. It occurred to Troy that Dalton wasn't the only one whose family commanded respect, even adulation. It was something to consider, and he wasn't sure he liked it. Any respect he received, Troy wanted to be certain he earned by his own merit.

"Hey," Dalton said.

"You shouted?" Troy asked, teasing her as usual.

"Just thought you might want to talk," she said and flashed a smile that was pure joy, happy to be alive ecstasy.

Troy tested his own smile, and found it easier than he would have imagined. Dalton had that effect on him.

"Not here," he said. "Just with family, you know?"

"Okay," she agreed. She nodded her goodbyes to her friends and squad, picked up a long fluted glass of mead, and joined him. Dalton pulled him by the hand over to the table where Major Boomer, Captain Jolly and Major Sheba were trading tales of Adama. Sure to be a popular pastime for many cycles to come, Troy thought.

"Troy, Dalton, join us!" Boomer called. "Raise a glass to the Commander."

The toast was met with rousing shouts of approval. Troy and Dalton both drank deeply. Then she pulled him off to one side and leaned in to whisper in his ear.

"So your father's commander now," Dalton said. "Not that it's a great way to get promoted, but it's kind of a thrill."

If anyone else had made the comment, Troy would have been offended. But in a way, Adama was her grandfather too. He smiled, then shrugged.

"It's only an interim appointment. They could easily give the job to someone else," he replied.

"That's what I've been hearing, actually," she said softly.

Troy raised an eyebrow. "What's that supposed to mean?"

"Don't get touchy," Dalton said, frowning. "I've just been hearing all kinds of things from around the fleet. A lot of people are nominating their own candidates. I mean, who wouldn't want the commander of the fleet to come from their colony, or their little special interest group? Some of the pilots are even against Apollo becoming commander, mainly because they think that will take him away from spending time in a Viper. And without..."

She bit her lip. Let a warm breath slip out her nostrils. Troy could feel it on his cheek, and realized how close they were standing. It made him self-conscious, and he had to remind himself that she was only seventeen.

"Without my father, Apollo's the best Warrior in the fleet," she said finally, eyebrows knitted.

Troy knew her so well. Dalton was upset, of course, and trying hard not to show it.

"What do *you* think?" he asked, suddenly realizing he couldn't take anyone's feelings on the subject for granted.

"What are you, sniffing vapors?" she said, rolling her eyes, reminding him of the little girl she once was.

"The bloodline of the House of Kobol are the wisest beings humanity has ever bred," she observed. "We would be foolish not to follow your father. He might not be Adama, but he is Adama's son and certainly has much of his father's wisdom."

Troy didn't ask the question, the selfish question, that came unbidden to his mind: *What about me?* After all, he was of Kobol as well; most people from Caprica were. But his bloodline was not purely Kobollian. He wondered if Dalton would think him a good choice for Commander, if that time ever came.

"Apollo!" Boomer cried. Troy turned to see that his father had entered the room.

"Welcome, Commander, can I buy you a drink?" Jolly bellowed, so obviously excited that his old friend had been promoted. Seeing the way Apollo's squadron treated one another, Troy became even more aware of the sniping and backstabbing that took place among the younger Warriors. He wondered idly how Zimmer would fit in with his father's squad, the only unseasoned pilot amongst them.

None of Dalton's friends had ever met a Cylon fighter in battle. Never mind been face to face with one planetside! And now the Cylons were back.

"Troy," Apollo said warmly as he passed through a cloud of fumarello smoke to stand next to Dalton. "Dalton, how are you?"

"Hello, Father," Troy replied.

"Commander," Dalton said.

Troy watched as Apollo turned to Starbuck's daughter, taken aback by her formal address.

"Dalton, please," he said. "If we're on duty, okay, but otherwise, don't ever call me that again, okay?"

"Whatever you say," she grinned. "Commander."

Apollo shook his head, smiling, and Troy held up a hand for his father to shake. Apollo took it, pulled his son close, and they embraced heartily.

"Grandfather would be proud," Troy whispered.

"We'll see," was Apollo's only reply.

Athena stood on the command deck at the center of the *Galactica's*
bridge. The battlestar had been updated many times over the years, so
that all computer systems were automated, and each had both
flatscreen and holo functions. Due to the excessive noise on the bridge,
the voice response programs had to be keyed to individual persons'
voices. There were still bugs in the system, but it was working out.

The starfield lay ahead of them, vast and cold and empty, and as
she stared out at it, for the first time, Athena felt a little of the weight
she imagined the Commander must bear on his shoulders. Why not
her shoulders?

Apollo was fit to be commander, and the eldest, she argued with herself. That was reason enough. But the fact that Tigh hadn't even consulted or considered her still rankled. Now it appeared that she would
have to serve as her brother's first officer and infantry commander, the
way that Colonel Tigh, and later she herself, had served Adama.

After so many years of being completely independent of one another in the hierarchy, it might be difficult getting used to.

"Lieutenant Colonel," someone said, interrupting her musings.
Athena turned to see that it was Omega, the bridge operations officer.
Of course. The man had been communications officer on the
Galactica's deck for thirty yahren, a long time even considering that
the human life span was nearly one hundred twenty yahren. In his sev-
enties, he was one of the oldest officers still serving the fleet. The others had all retired shortly after Tigh had. But Tigh had continued to
serve on the Quorum and was now its President, with Adama dead.

The thought stopped her.

"Athena?" Omega inquired, obviously concerned for her welfare.

"I'm all right," she answered. "What is it?"

"I've Ambassador Puck for you," Omega responded. "He seems
agitated."

"Give me holo," she instructed.

On the communications array in front of Omega's chair, a six-inch
image of Ambassador Puck blossomed from nothing. It was full color,
showing the pale, stooped, pink-eyed Ambassador in great, pathetic

detail. The man was not very old, but seemed to have suffered the complaints of advancing age too soon. He wore brightly colored valcron garments, orange and blue, but it did nothing to make him appear more healthy.

"What can I do for you, Ambassador?" Athena asked, hoping to conclude the communication quickly. Puck disturbed her profoundly, not merely his appearance, but his every word or gesture.

"Lieutenant Colonel, I see your brother—our ersatz commander— is not on the bridge. I assume that this will not be as common an occurrence as many people are already predicting," Puck said, offending her with his tone as well as the accusation against Apollo.

"Commander Apollo is off duty at the moment, sir," she said. "How can I help you?"

Puck sneered dismissively, insultingly. As if he weren't aware the holo-system were functioning. Athena could not believe the man had once been a diplomat, hence his title. Non-military Quorum members were entitled to be addressed as Sire or Siress, but Puck had kept the title he'd gained when he became the Scorpius Ambassador to Caprica.

"Where is President Tigh?" Puck asked. No, demanded.

"I'm sorry, sir, I'm not in the habit of recording the comings and goings of the Quorum members," Athena snapped, instantly regretting her temper. "I assumed he was in his quarters."

"He is not," Puck fumed. "Should he appear on the bridge, perhaps craving the company of his former lackeys, you will instruct him to contact me immediately!"

Athena stood behind Omega, teeth grinding, breathing through her nose, attempting to calm herself before replying. It didn't work.

"Ambassador Puck, I believe you'll find that in dealing with any person in the fleet, but particularly with members of a military whose primary occupation is the protection of all its citizens, yourself included, it might be wisest to..."

"Don't presume to instruct me in wisdom, girl," Puck wheezed.

The holo-image disappeared.

"Lords," Omega whispered.

"That son of a daggit!" Athena growled. "I'd like to…"

"Lieutenant Colonel," Omega said, somewhat stridently. She understood his warning, looking warily around the bridge. Every one of the crew was staring up at the command deck.

One by one, she returned those stares. One by one, they self-consciously returned to work. Only when she saw Cassiopeia step off the ascensior onto the bridge did Athena allow herself to breathe again.

Who would want to be commander of this fleet? she thought.

"Hello, Cassie," Athena said as the blonde woman stepped onto the command deck.

Once upon a time, she had hated the beautiful med-tech, a former socialator who'd caught Starbuck's eye when Athena had yearned to be the object of his attentions. That was a long time ago. Since then, Cassie had borne Starbuck a daughter, then taken the Seal with another man, and been divorced from him. Athena herself had taken up with Starbuck again, lived with him for several yahren, and thrown him out when he suggested they take the Seal. She just couldn't take his proposal seriously.

Now he was dead, and neither one of them could have him.

"Athena, we should talk," Cassiopeia said.

"What about?" Athena asked. "We throwing a surprise nova-yahren party for Sheba?"

"No," Cassie replied, almost self-conscious. It was a look Athena hadn't seen on the other woman for quite some time. "It's a bit more serious than that, but it's hard to broach the subject. I don't know how you stand on it, and I don't want to upset you."

Athena tilted her head slightly, frowning. Where was all this headed?

"Well, there's no way to know how I'll react until you tell me, so go ahead," she urged.

Cassie glanced around, then took several steps further back on the command deck, out of range of the crew's hearing.

"You're familiar with the Gemon Matriarchs?" Cassiopeia asked.

"Refresh my memory," Athena replied, though she had no idea what Cassie was talking about. Like many other colonies, Gemini had exerted great environmental stress upon its people. Over many generations, it had altered them somewhat. Some of the colonies had experienced a bit of adaptive, divergent evolution.

Most Leonids had dark skin, an evolutionary change in pigmentation due to their proximity to the sun. Scorpions were pale because of their distance from the solar body, and had a light fur on their bodies, almost invisible from a distance, an adaptation to the cold. The Borellian Nomen, an aboriginal race that had been on Scorpius millennia before the colonists arrived, were much hairier, almost lupine, and bulkier due to their dedication to working the land.

Gemons, the people of Gemini, were arguably the most attractive of the Colonials. The air was a bit thinner, the sun a bit brighter. Athena didn't know if that accounted for their almost ethereal appearance, but she supposed it must in some way. Or something in the water. They were taller, thinner, with an exotically tinged skin color, almost like Kirasolis candy, she'd always thought.

But the Gemon Matriarchs? She'd never heard of them.

"Well," Cassie was saying, "you probably know that unlike the rest of the Colonies, Gemini had an unstable gender relationship among its peoples. Before the Cylons destroyed it, Gemini was a patriarchal society. The Gemon Matriarchs believe that women are far more capable than men and are pursuing that philosophy within the fleet."

"Yes, but there is no such gender imbalance among the rest of the fleet," Athena said, unsure as to why Cassie thought she would be interested in the Gemons.

"I disagree," Cassiopeia said. "Perhaps it isn't conscious, but I think women are discouraged from taking leadership roles. Look at the number of men versus the number of women in the military, for instance."

"What does this all have to do with me?" Athena asked, not willing to argue the point with Cassie on the bridge of the *Galactica*.

"Isn't it obvious?" Cassie asked, lowering her voice. "The Gemon Matriarchs are prepared to back your bid as a candidate for commander. And I'm planning to nominate you."

Athena stared at her, stunned by the message, and by the messenger.

4.

THE PROCTORS STIFFENED when President Tigh entered the children's center. A tall Gemon woman—he thought her name was Teal—approached quickly, concern clouding her face. Tigh held up a hand, waving her back and to silence.

Teal paused, frowning in confusion.

"Give me just a moment, would you?" Tigh asked.

"Yes, of course, Mr. President," Teal replied.

The room was brightly colored, a rainbow of streaks and splashes, as if the children themselves had decorated it. The smaller children shrieked and chased one another about the room, toddlers and infants batting and chewing plush, bright toys. The older boys and girls were more thoughtful. Some worked on puzzles or read books, but most of them waved plasteen blasters and posed, shouting at one another. They were Warriors, these children, who had never known the meaning of the word Cylon. Not really.

But if Apollo was right—and when had he ever been wrong?—the Cylons would soon become a reality, even for the youngest human in the fleet.

Tigh sighed heavily.

"He used to come here all the time you know," Teal said, startling him. He hadn't realized she still stood by him.

"I'm sorry?"

"Commander Adama," she explained. "He always said the children reminded him of his mission. Kept him going. He never stayed long, just watched them playing for a few minutes, and then left as quietly as he arrived."

Tigh was silent a moment, then turned to Teal, smiling.

"I know," he said. "I hope you don't mind if I come down from time to time."

Teal brightened visibly, a smile spreading across her face.

"I hope you do, President Tigh," she replied. "Maybe Commander Adama's still watching out for the children, do you think?"

Tigh turned and walked to the door, glanced back over his shoulder.

"The thought had occurred to me," Tigh observed, the memory of his friend, his presence there in the children's center, reaffirming his own mission, his strength, his purpose.

The door slid open and Tigh's smile disappeared. His exit was blocked by a figure in the doorway: the hunched, pale, quavering form of Ambassador Puck. The two men stared at one another. They had had little contact in the past, only their common attendance at Council meetings. But now it was clear that they were to be adversaries. The air between them stagnated with their mutual disregard.

For a moment, Tigh saw something flicker in the gnarled man's pink eyes, a spark of something truly dangerous. But Tigh was not afraid. Puck was just a man, after all, and there wasn't a man alive whom Tigh feared. The fleet's greatest human enemy, Baltar, was a craven coward. But a powerful one. If Tigh didn't fear Baltar, Puck was a fool for even trying to intimidate him.

"Mr. President," Puck scowled the word. "I won't even begin to wonder why you are wasting your time down here."

"Good, but I would like to ask the same of you," Tigh snipped, striding forward, his momentum forcing Puck to give way. The stooped little man had to hurry to keep up.

The door to the Children's Center slid closed behind them, the joyous sounds and bright colors giving way to the cold metal of the gangway. The moment had passed, but Tigh held close his thoughts of

Adama and the children whose innocence he so admired.

"I'm searching for *you*, Tigh," Ambassador Puck said, his voice insinuating and insulting. "It has come to my attention that you have been lobbying the other Quorum members independently for the confirmation of Lieutenant Commander Apollo. On the heels of your ill-advised temporary promotion of Adama's son, I wonder if you are not trying to subvert the entire purpose of the Quorum."

Tigh bristled.

"You would do well to remember, Puck, that I am now President of the Quorum. No thanks, I imagine, to you," he said archly. "I am within my rights. I'm fulfilling my responsibilities to the fleet by both naming an acting commander and by championing the one person I feel best for the position."

Puck smiled thinly.

"Ah, 'best for the position,' I see. So you don't claim that Apollo is the only person capable of leading the fleet at this time," Puck asked.

"Of course not," Tigh replied, frowning. "There are other fine candidates, and not all of them hail from Caprica, if that is your primary complaint."

Puck's smile grew wider. He looked at Tigh more closely as they walked, but said nothing more for a moment. They continued down the corridor, Puck shuffling after the President as best he could. After several microns of this silence, Tigh felt bad for making the old fellow scurry so and slowed a bit.

"Some people are resistant to another Caprican—another Kobollian—leading the fleet, aren't they, Tigh?" the ambassador asked.

"I'm not concerned about the bloodline myself," Tigh said coolly. "Apollo's advantage is that he was raised and trained by Adama. I'm from Leonis. I don't care where the commander comes from, as long as he or she has the kind of wisdom that Adama always displayed."

Tigh's boots rang on the metal gangway. He thought, for an instant, that he'd left Puck behind. Then a gnarled hand landed on his shoulder and he was spun around, almost violently. Ambassador Puck stood behind him, breathing heavily as if winded by their walk. Even as the stooped man spoke, Tigh felt those fingers on his shoulder again and was awed by the unexpected strength in them.

"Are you so certain Apollo has that wisdom?" Puck asked evenly.

"I..."

"Are you certain, President Tigh? Absolutely certain?" he reiterated.

Puck's eyes were a distraction, confusing Tigh for a moment. There was something almost intimidating, and certainly disquieting, about the way Puck looked at him now. As if he were a pupil or, worse yet, a prisoner.

"He has astounding intuition, and his skills develop every day," Tigh replied finally.

"But he doesn't have Adama's natural leadership or his wisdom, does he? Oh, he has the charisma, but he isn't about to be the commander Adama was, is he?" Puck asked smoothly.

"I...I don't know," Tigh admitted.

"I'm told the Gemon Matriarchs are going to nominate Lieutenant Colonel Athena," Puck snorted. "As if she would be any improvement over her brother."

"Athena?" Tigh wondered aloud. "I'd never thought of..."

"No, of course you hadn't, she took your old job, after all," Ambassador Puck said. "I wonder whether she's taken offense at your lack of consideration. Not that it matters. You see, I will vehemently oppose both nominations. Neither of Adama's children has truly earned this distinction. They are popular by virtue of their heritage, because the blood of Kobol runs in their veins."

"If you don't support them, then vote against them. Both of them," Tigh barked. "That's your prerogative as a member of the Quorum."

Puck's smile returned. "Oh, I intend to do that," the Ambassador said. "That and much more. You see, the reason I sought you out was to officially announce *my* candidacy for the position of commander. As you know, only basic military service is required for the appointment of the rank. I plan to move my quarters from the *Scorpius*

Ascendant immediately. Don't want to be accused of living in luxury, do we? Have to be a man of the people."

When Tigh merely stared in astonishment, Ambassador Puck turned, still smiling, and shuffled down the gangway laconically. Tigh watched him move away, frozen in place.

"Wonderful," Tigh whispered. "That's all I needed today."

The fleet sailed the stars in tight formation. But with one hundred seventy-nine vessels—warships, barges, domed agro-ships, luxury liners, residential carriers, forge industrial ships...and the *Galactica* of course—it was impossible to travel without being strung out in space like an asteroid field.

In the midst of the motley fleet sailed the prison barge *Icarus*. She held four hundred twenty-seven prisoners at the moment, in individual cells where possible. Among the inmates were thirteen Borellian Nomen: dangerous men. Once they had all shared a huge domicile-cell on the *Icarus*, but the wardens had quickly learned that such was a mistake. They became more dangerous, more uncontrollable in larger numbers. Even if the barge was severely overpopulated, they would never put more than two Nomen in a cell together, and even that was undesirable.

Of all the branches of the human race, the Nomen had evolved into the most genetically divergent. Their origins were shrouded in mystery, but they were decidedly human, or had been once. When the ancients had fled Kobol to found the twelve colonies, one of the planets they settled on was already inhabited. Caprica had an aboriginal people, a warrior race living without technology, subsisting on nature's gifts.

The Nomen. Born of human starfarers, they had arrived on the planet millennia earlier. Their leader, Borellus, ruled that technology was to be abandoned. They were to perfect themselves as beings, blend in with the Caprican biosphere, become the dominant lifeform and leave their human ancestry in the past. The new wave of colonists defeated them easily with advanced technology and took Caprica. The Nomen had despised all other branches of the human race since, considering themselves far superior in every way.

And yet, these thirteen, who might be the last Borellian Nomen in the universe, were still prisoners despite their superiority. This was the great burden borne by Gar'Tokk, their leader.

As always, Gar'Tokk sat in his cell in silence, staring out at the corridor through the crackling energy barrier that kept him captive. He stroked his long beard, his massive shoulders straight, head high. The Nomen looked barely human, adaptive evolution to Caprica's greater gravity giving them enormous physical power. From beneath his heavy, protruding brow and a mane of dark hair, Gar'Tokk's eyes were shrunken with hate. Rather than diminish with time, his hatred grew a little every day.

But one of the first laws of their founder, Borellus, was "Cultivate a thing and it will grow."

Gar'Tokk cherished his hate.

One of the wardens—Gar'Tokk refused to learn any of their names, for they were not people to him, only future victims— walked by and glanced into his cell. They always looked at him, nervously, then walked on. But this one stopped, just for a moment, and peered closer.

Peered past Gar'Tokk.

What is he looking at? the Nomen leader wondered. But he didn't even acknowledge the warden's presence. After a moment, the man shook his head, glanced back into the cell again, and then walked away, muttering something under his breath.

Gar'Tokk didn't move.

"Aren't you even curious as to what he thought he saw?" came a whisper, just off to Gar'Tokk's right.

With speed that belied his size, Gar'Tokk sprang from the bench and spun into a fighting stance, prepared to rip his visitor apart with his bare hands. He didn't enjoy killing any other way.

Before him shimmered a form, a human form—or at least he

thought so. But where the features would be was nothing, only blackness, as though a void had opened in the universe. The void was shaped like a man. Its edges had an odd warp to them, as if the reality around it had been bent back to allow it to appear.

"What are you?" Gar'Tokk demanded without fear. Nomen feared only cowardice in themselves.

"*Gar'Tokk,*" it whispered, and his mind suddenly filled with visions of pain, anger, and violence, of war and atrocity so vile it disturbed even the leader of the Nomen.

"*You are too proud to be a prisoner,*" it said, voice muffled and punctuated with viscous, sticky sounds, as if the thing were speaking with water or...blood in its mouth.

"*Don't you want to get out of here? You and your people...don't you want freedom again?*" it asked.

He stared at the man-shaped black abyss that hung in the air. It reminded him unpleasantly of the tarpits of Caprica. One step in the pits and a Nomen would be doomed. But...freedom?

"What do I have to do?" Gar'Tokk asked.

Freedom was worth any price.

Over the yahren since the destruction of the colonies—and before a planet had been found with the mineral resources to build new Vipers and repair other ships—the fleet had been forced to cannibalize itself many times. Though they had originally set out with more than two hundred and twenty vessels of every size and description, the fleet had thinned somewhat, and was now comprised of one hundred and seventy-nine ships. Others had been used for parts, their passengers either transferred, or allowed to settle, if they so chose, on one of the habitable planets the fleet had passed.

It was always a hardy band, those who chose to settle a new world. And yet, in a way, Sheba thought the rest of the fleet's citizens even more courageous. After all, what did they have to follow? What did they place their hopes and dreams upon, if not the vision of one man?

Adama had a purpose so righteous that it became powerful enough for all to share.

What now? Sheba had tried not to let the question slip into her mind. She loved Apollo dearly, of course. But the logic was inescapable. Without Adama to lead them...

The people might choose another commander. That was their right. But Sheba thought it just as likely that they would choose no commander at all. Meaning they might all decide to settle on the next habitable planet that came along.

And she wouldn't blame them.

She, herself, would never leave. She would follow Apollo to the end of the universe and back, and she believed wholeheartedly in Adama's dreams of Earth. But she understood the urge to settle well enough. They'd been in space nearly twenty yahren. People were tired. Time to rest. They'd earned it, hadn't they?

She smiled to herself. Her father would be ashamed of such talk. He was the legendary Commander Cain of the *Pegasus*, the only other surviving battlestar. Or at least, that's what Sheba believed. The *Pegasus* had last been seen, with a skeleton crew, launching an attack on *two* Cylon base stars, all by itself. When the debris from the destroyed base stars cleared, the *Pegasus* was gone.

But whether or not it had actually been destroyed had long been a subject of controversy. Commander Cain had been counted out many times before: reported dead, his ship destroyed, at least half a dozen times. She missed him terribly, but she would never believe he was gone forever.

She had been raised by the commander of a battlestar, and now it appeared that she was in love with one as well. She smiled, a flush coming to her cheeks. When she and Apollo had first met, they had instantly disliked one another. They were both inordinately stubborn and totally sincere about their roles as Warriors. Fate, she believed, had other plans.

When she was injured during the Battle of Gamoray, her father had ordered that she be brought aboard the *Galactica*. Otherwise they'd still be together, wherever Cain was now. Instead, she had become one of the premiere Viper pilots in the fleet. And, over time, her enmity toward Apollo became friendship and, finally, love.

"You're worrying about him, aren't you?" a deep voice whispered beside her, breaking her train of thought and bringing her back into the world. It was Troy.

They sat in the balcony overlooking the triad court aboard the luxury liner *Rising Star*. On the court, three men and one woman battered each other in a violent game that she had always thought a bit childish. But Apollo had once been one of the fleet's triad champions, and this game was in memory of Commander Adama, so she had attended.

The spectator seating area was overflowing with people, many of them having obviously had more than a few drinks before arriving for the match. Lights flashed above, and holo-cameras captured the event and transmitted it throughout the fleet.

People had to find some way to relieve the tension that had been growing with every centon since Adama's first cardiac seizure. Now that she thought about it, Sheba realized the tension had been growing even longer—since Apollo had returned to the fleet with the news of new Cylon sightings and the death of Captain Starbuck.

"Hello? Bridge to Major Sheba, do you copy?"

She glanced to her left. Troy was staring at her, impatiently awaiting an answer. Sheba rolled her eyes.

"Okay, so I'm worried about him," she responded, running her hands quickly through her short-cropped hair, sporting the henna tint that Apollo favored so much.

"What am I supposed to do?" she sighed. "He's lost his best friend and his father in less than a month, and now he's going to become commander, even though a lot of the fleet doesn't believe he's earned the job. It's got to be hard on him."

Troy looked into her eyes, searching. "I'm worried, too," he revealed. "They aren't being fair to him. Not at all. Through recon observation alone, my father has saved this entire fleet dozens of times. In battle, dozens more. It's not right that they should turn their backs on him now."

Sheba watched his face, his words and expression reminding her of the boy he'd once been. She reached out for his right hand and held it. More than likely, she would never have a son. But the closeness she had with Troy gave her just a small inkling of what it might be like to have her own children.

"Your father can take care of himself," Sheba observed, her tone more confident than she felt.

Troy only nodded slowly. "Sure, but can he do it while he's supposed to be taking care of the rest of us as well?" he asked.

Sheba was silent. Not because she doubted Apollo's abilities, but because she knew that having people second-guessing him, even having his loved ones so concerned for his well-being, would be hard for the man to bear.

She glanced down at the triad players. The Capricans were having their chips jarred badly by the Tauron team. Their heads and shoulders were padded, but the rest of their bodies were nearly bare, and vulnerable. She would never understand why more precautions weren't taken with the game. Unless part of the draw was the natural desire to see people barely clothed.

At first it was only a dry chuckle, but then Sheba began to laugh quietly.

"What is it?" Troy asked, smiling despite the gravity of their conversation.

"I was just thinking how cute your father always looked when he had to wear that ridiculous uniform," she replied.

"Cute?" Troy asked, astonished. "Why do you think I never even tried to join the triad league? Who in their right mind would be seen in public wearing that? It's little more than a thong and a genital shield!"

Sheba looked at him, eyes narrowed, a sly smile crossing her face.

"I'll bet Dalton would love to see you in a triad uniform," she said quietly, so only Troy could hear.

"Sheba!" he cried, drawing hushes and shouts from all around them, even the vendor selling heffala berries. "She's only seventeen," he protested, dropping his voice to a whisper.

"Yes," Sheba agreed, "and next yahren she'll be eighteen, and the yahren after that, nineteen. If you see my point."

"I see it, but I don't think you understand my..." he began, frowning.

"Oh, I understand perfectly," she said with a smirk. "And believe it or not, if Starbuck were still alive, I'm sure he'd understand as well."

Troy stared at her. Finally, exasperated, he brushed her off, saying, "Believe what you like. You always do."

"And I'm always right," Sheba replied. "At least, when it comes to romance."

"If that's the case, why haven't you and my father taken the Seal yet?" Troy asked, obviously attempting to antagonize her into changing the subject.

Sheba wasn't having it.

"Because I haven't asked him yet," she explained. "Now, since neither of us is watching this game, why don't we go have a drink at the Astral Restaurant? Maybe even some coneth stew?"

"Let's go," Troy agreed, and they stood, hunched over, and hurried to escape the throng of spectators before they could be pelted with heffala berries for obstructing the view of the match.

As they pushed through the arena doors, Troy ran a hand through his hair and asked: "Should we try to track down my father? He probably hasn't eaten in days and some quiet company might do him good."

Sheba was already drifting back into the miasma of anxiety she had been feeling earlier. Apollo wasn't certain himself if he should be commander, but she knew that the idea that others wouldn't support him would be hurtful.

"Let's leave him be," she suggested. "If I know your father, he's probably gone off to one of his quiet places to meditate. Or at least, that's what he calls it. I call it brooding. But I don't blame him. In two cycles, he'll take the bridge of the *Galactica* as commander for the very first time."

"His quiet places?" Troy asked. "He's shown me a few of them. There's a celestial chamber that…"

"I know all about that chamber, Lieutenant," Sheba replied, her blue eyes flashing. "It's one of our…I mean, Apollo's favorite spots."

Her cheeks flushed a second time, but more deeply.

"Wherever he is, if he's chosen solitude for the moment, we should honor his decision," she concluded.

5.

THE *GALACTICA*'S CREW AND INFANTRY were quartered on a single deck, separate and distant from the lower level where the pilots lived, close to the launch bays. Apollo had always hated this division, but he understood the necessity of having the pilots quartered near their starfighters. Now, as he moved along the corridor toward the officers' wing of the crew deck, he was torn.

As commander, he would have to abandon the pilots' quarters. The idea was distasteful to him. Yet he had no choice. He would also be expected to don the blue-and-white uniform of the battlestar's crew. But Apollo thought he might be able to circumvent that protocol. After all, he wasn't going to give up leading his squadron, so why not wear a Warrior's uniform?

He sighed heavily and continued along the corridor. The bare floor echoed his footsteps back to him. The officers' wing was deserted; everyone was either on duty or aboard the *Rising Star* for the triad match. The walls were a warm green, with lamps set into them every few metrons, more for decoration than illumination.

A small pang of guilt touched his heart as he passed Athena's quarters on the left. She was on the bridge, no doubt. He did not take his post as commander for two more cycles, which meant that she would have been on duty for three cycles—a full day—without rest.

This was not the source of his remorse, however. That had to do more with his destination. Adama's quarters were on the right, just ahead. No adornment singled out his door as belonging to the commander, which was as it should be, as far as Apollo was concerned.

Adama's things had been removed. If Apollo were confirmed by the Quorum as commander, he would be expected to take up residence in his father's quarters. He wasn't sure how he would feel about that. But it would make it significantly easier to gain entry to his father's sanctuary.

Sanctuary. Not merely a private room, but a storehouse of Kobollian knowledge and wisdom, a place for meditation and metamorphosis. The secrets of the Kobollian race were passed down to the eldest child only. That was the tradition, no matter how ill-advised Apollo had considered it. Adama had followed the Kobollian traditions religiously, and it had left Athena feeling like an outsider on more than one occasion. Apollo deeply regretted that.

"Father," Apollo whispered to himself. "See what your death has caused? And you thought nobody ever listened to you. You old fool."

He smiled, lines forming around his eyes, and shook his head gently. Adama had never truly appreciated his impact on the people. If he could witness the turmoil the fleet had been thrown into because of his death, Adama would no doubt have been astonished.

Apollo lifted his hand and placed it on the lock-sensor to the right of the door. Red light flashed over his palm, there was a pause.

In that heartbeat of a pause, a memory: standing here, in this very spot, more than thirty yahren earlier, with Athena at his side. Their father had just returned from a lengthy absence, and for the first time, the children were allowed on board the *Galactica*. Apollo had always loved his father—had seen him on the command deck, on the bridge, issuing orders, confident in his leadership abilities.

But this was different. As the door slid aside and they looked in to see their father sitting, waiting for them, both of the children entered cautiously. Apollo didn't recall if he had ever discussed it with his sister. He thought not. But to him, the greatest pride that swelled his heart was not the sight of his father commanding the ship, but the sight of him alone in his quarters. Apollo had felt then, for no reason he could explain, that this featureless room was the heart of the ship in a way its bridge or engines could never reflect.

At that moment, his love for his father had been surpassed by another emotion: Apollo had been awestruck.

The door slid open and Apollo glanced inside, at that same chair, now empty. He realized that he was still in awe of Adama. Probably always would be. Idly, he wondered if every child felt that way, and vowed to discuss it one day with Athena. In the wake of Adama's death, he already felt closer to her, though she had seemed distracted during their last few meetings, which had consisted mainly of superficial military conversation.

All of which brought him back to his destination and his guilt. On the far wall of his father's quarters stood a door that in any other compartment would have been a closet of some kind. In Adama's room, it led into the sanctuary.

Apollo approached the door and announced himself: "Apollo, son of Adama and the House of Kobol."

After a moment's hesitation, in which the sanctuary's secured computer system performed a unique voice comparison, the door slid open and the room's interior lights flickered into life.

Apollo had been coming to the sanctuary since his thirtieth novayahren. After the party had died down, Adama had become serious and instructed Apollo to meet him in his quarters. There, during the nine centon light-duty cycle, when most of the fleet was sleeping, Adama had first shown him into the sanctuary.

While the child he had once been might have enjoyed sharing that secret with his father, a secret kept from everyone including his sister, Apollo keenly felt Athena's exclusion. But the Books of the Lords of Kobol were very clear. Unless there was no second-generation heir by the time the eldest reached the age of fifty yahren, no one else was allowed within the sanctuary.

Feldergarb! Apollo struggled now with his desire to include his sister against the wishes of his dead father. It was not a decision he would make rashly.

He slid into a tall wooden chair, one of the few such antique pieces left in all the fleet. In the sanctuary, it was the only thing that did not gleam and shimmer, smooth and cold.

A red eye blinked into life on the computer station directly in front of the chair. The rest of the chamber, an oval room whose walls were dotted with star maps drawn from legend, was empty but for the room's second chair, the plasteen seat Apollo had always used.

His eyes ranged over the walls, etched with galaxies, and then lingered a moment on that red eye light on the face of the computer. An awareness of his presence. Yet not sentient. It was oddly disquieting, and yet, familiar and comforting.

The computer had always bothered him because it was so unlike any other he had seen. Almost organic in its design, sides curving up and around as if to embrace the user, glittering gold and silver face. And no screen. No screen. All of this computer's images were holo-projected. The rest of the *Galactica's* computers had holo and flatscreen modes. But this machine, more than five centuries old, was light years ahead of the others.

Ignoring the plasteen seat, he slid into Adama's antique wooden chair.

With a ripple of electronic current that seemed to buffet Apollo like a sea breeze, the holo-projector erupted with light and life. A head, shoulders, upper body, blue and white uniform, white hair. The concern-furrowed brow and sparkling blue eyes of his father, Adama.

"Hello, Apollo," Adama said, voice tinged with sympathy, and Apollo's heart nearly burst with repressed grief.

"Father!" he gasped. "By the Lords..."

But he knew. He knew.

"I'm sorry, son," Adama said. "But if you're seeing this projection,

I must be...I suppose I must be dead."

Apollo was surprised to see this hesitation in his father, a moment of self interest and humanity he never would have allowed himself in public. He was a man of the people, all his life. But here he was revealed as vulnerable. The prospect of his own death clearly saddened him.

"I'm with the light now. The Lords of Kobol have taken me," Adama's recording continued. *Morbid,* Apollo thought, *and what was that about the light?* Some religious tradition Adama had never explained to him, he assumed.

"You're to become commander now, I presume," Adama noted. "I'm very proud of you, Apollo, but now you must swallow your grief for a time while I explain to you why you must be commander of the *Galactica.* There are a handful of others within the fleet who might meet the criteria—the real criteria—but none with your battle experience."

Apollo closed his eyes briefly, sparing himself from Adama's intense gaze for a moment. His father was dead, this recording his last communication. But the pain of his absence was only exacerbated by the holo-projection, so fully fleshed did it seem.

"Since the celebration of your thirtieth novayahren, we have spent much time together in sanctuary, meditating, developing your mental skills. Concentration, meditation, inner vision. But the exercises that we have conducted, I must now tell you, would be useless to most other humans," Adama said firmly.

"Our race, our breed, are known for their wisdom; this is no secret. The people of Caprica always elected Kobollian leaders because they knew this. But it is more than merely legend or study which has made us so. We are...how to say this? Gifted? Yes, that will do. We are gifted, Apollo," he smiled wistfully.

"You must be commander of the *Galactica* because I do not believe she could survive if led by any but another Kobollian, of pure blood. As I was. As you are. Your mother and I, our parents before us, were descended from the original Kobollians in a direct line. You and

Athena, poor Zac, you all had that blood. Aboard the *Galactica*, there are only a handful of others. Troy is one of them, fortunately. Though I'm not sure he knows it.

"This is not arrogance on my part, Apollo."

Here, Adama lowered his eyes, took a breath.

"Perhaps it would be best if I explained."

"It couldn't hurt," Apollo said, mostly to himself, but also to the spirit of his dead father, whom he suspected kept watch over him still, somehow.

"Our twelve colonies, destroyed after Baltar's betrayal, were founded by the people of the planet Kobol," Adama began.

On the wall of the chamber, two star systems lit up with a spray of color. Apollo recognized the twelve-planet system of his birth, and the system that contained Kobol.

"Mythology will tell you that Kobol was not their native planet. This is true. The original planet, which the myths refer to only as Parnassus, was the font of all humanity. But as you know, without enemies like the Cylons, even with such enemies, it is human nature to incite conflict. They fought amongst themselves, tore at one another on the basis of regional origins, gender, flesh tone.

"The House of Kobol were a family of priests. They lived in seclusion, taking few acolytes but many followers. The Lords of Kobol, as the priests were called, spent every moment improving themselves. Concentration. Meditation. Inner vision.

"Over long millennia they developed mental abilities far superior to those of other men. Chief among these were clairvoyance and telepathy. Do you understand the words, Apollo? Telepathy is communication, mind to mind, without a spoken word and often across great distances. Clairvoyance is the power to call to mind visions of the future, or even the present, to see what it is impossible to see with the eyes."

When he made this holo-recording, Adama knew it would be his final communication with Apollo. He was quite serious.

"By the Lords," Apollo whispered.

"I can only imagine how you must feel," Adama soothed. "I remember how I felt when my own father revealed these things to me on the occasion of my fortieth novayahren celebration. It was centons before I believed him. I am not there to convince you, so please indulge me. Even if you can't believe me yet, continue to listen. And learn.

"Overpopulation was destroying Parnassus. They had spent centuries developing interstellar travel. Outposts were created. Colonies far and wide. There is a record of a planet called Cylon, which was discovered at the time, but whose sentient creatures were savage and antagonistic. They were a reptilian race, and their planet was given a wide berth after that. They were no threat, you see, for they had no technology to speak of.

"While this exploration was taking place, the Lords of the House of Kobol continued to evolve. Time seemed irrelevant to the Lords of Kobol, and their private writings discuss an elevation or evolution, an 'advancement to the light' which has never been explained in any greater detail. They watched their rival Houses settle colonies on planets orbiting suns hundreds of light years distant. Several of these had sentient life already, life whose evolution could be influenced.

"Earth, Apollo, is one of those planets. Its location is never specifically detailed, no coordinates are given, but..."

Behind Apollo the wall lit up again, showing the star system whose planets he had studied closely many times before. The third planet from the star called Sol was Earth. According to legend. But for the first time, Apollo understood his father's absolute confidence in the legend. He knew it existed, knew it beyond a shadow of a doubt. He simply hadn't known where to find it.

"The Lords of the House of Kobol were the first to realize that their system's star was going to go nova. They had yahren to plan their exodus. When they finally left, most of the planet's other people had left for previously established colonies. The Lords led their acolytes and many followers to a remote planet which would sustain them quite well from the fruits of the land," Adama explained.

"Kobol," Apollo whispered.

"Kobol," Adama said. "But it was not long, mere centuries, before the growing population began to squabble just as the people of Parnassus had done. The Lords of Kobol, having spent much of their solitude perfecting space travel, made a radical decision.

"They left. Simply and quickly left the planet, leaving acolytes and followers behind to forever question what had happened to the Lords themselves. Where had they gone? Their goal was to improve themselves, and humanity as a whole. Legends imply that they might have gone to Earth.

"We simply do not know. The remainder of this history does not include them, except by legendary reference to the Thirteenth Tribe. They are the Thirteenth Tribe, Apollo. When the people of Kobol spread out into space once more, inhabiting the twelve-planet system we called 'the colonies,' the first group to leave became the lost Thirteenth Tribe of Kobol.

"While many of the acolytes of the House of Kobol remained on the planet, others traveled far across space to the colonies. Specifically, to Caprica. Where they ruled. Where our family, Apollo, the pure-blooded descendants of the House of Kobol, ruled for millennia, until the Cylons came.

"This sanctuary," Adama's deep bass voice rumbled, "was built into the design of the *Galactica* when she was first constructed more than five hundred yahren ago. This was done without the knowledge of the other colonies. It was determined that there should be a Kobollian sanctuary aboard ship.

"We have no way of knowing what happened to the original Lords of Kobol, of how far they might have evolved beyond other human beings. But the descendants of their family all have the ability, through meditation, to access talents other humans could never hope to use. We all have them, you see, but humans use very little of their brains. By accessing more of the mind's potential, the descendants of the House of Kobol can master these mental powers.

"I have trained you well, Apollo. As best I knew how. You are old enough now, and have enough self-control, that you ought to be able to make great use of these abilities. Do not doubt you have them, lying dormant within you. Only use our mantra, concentration, meditation, inner vision, and new galaxies will open for you, within you. They will serve you well as you continue to lead our people toward their only hope of refuge.

"Earth."

The image of Adama flickered and disappeared. Several minutes passed before Apollo could even begin to consider what he had heard. His father's face, his voice, his eyes lingered in Apollo's mind. He raged, at first, angry that Adama had known so much more than he had ever revealed about the history of their people, that the Kobollians in general had kept such truths hidden for so long.

And yet, what was mythology and what was truth? Adama seemed to know precisely where to draw the line between the two. Apollo was not so certain. But he knew that his more than ten yahren of meditative sessions in this sanctuary were beginning to bear fruit.

In all that time, during all those sessions, he was being prepared not only to accept the truths of his heritage, but to utilize them in his role as commander.

Of course, his father's assumption that he would be commander was an obvious one, even though succession was still an open question. There were many options, and Apollo wondered if there weren't other candidates more suited for the role. But he understood why Adama had wanted him to take command, and he would do his best to fulfill his father's wishes. Not merely for Adama, but for the fleet itself.

"By the Lords," he mumbled, and the phrase, so commonly uttered all his life, now took on significance it never had before.

Questions filled his head. Where had the Lords of Kobol gone after leaving the planet they named for themselves? What of the many other colonies the citizens of Parnassus were supposed to have founded? First and foremost, however: What was the reality behind the mental abilities his father had revealed to him?

He ought to have left the sanctuary then, gone to eat something, get some kind of sustenance. Apollo couldn't recall the last time he'd eaten. But his pulse was racing, his mind reeling with questions and with excitement. A kind of excitement he had only experienced before in battle. This was the discovery of new territory, a lost world inside his own mind. Misty paths that led someplace wondrous and incredible.

As a boy, he had dreamed of the galaxies beyond, incredible creatures...and great power within himself. He had dreamed of nobility and heroics, as many children did. Those dreams had led him to become a Colonial Warrior, to emulate his father and train to be a Viper pilot. He had thought all those urges long since satisfied, but this was something entirely new.

His shoulders were burdened with the weight of many responsibilities, now. He was an adult, not a dreaming child. But how much greater would his ability to deal with such responsibility be enhanced by the talents his father claimed were his legacy?

It would surely take time to access such abilities, to master them. But that meant he had no time to waste. He was due on the command deck, to take his new position, in twelve centons: a cycle and a half. The time was now.

Sitting up straight in the wooden chair, feeling the rigid bars against his back, Apollo concentrated on that sensation. With the techniques of breathing and muscle control that Adama had taught him, he slowed his racing heart to normal pulse, then further still. Eyes locked on the red light on the computer's face, he cleared his mind as completely as he could.

His excitement lingered, but Apollo struggled to dismiss it. He had dreamed of heroics as a child, but had become a gravely serious military man. This military diligence he now applied to the meditative state. Slowly, ever so slowly, his breathing and heart beat carefully regulated and diminished, he cleared his mind of all things.

Apollo waited, breathing, concentrating, meditating.

Fully two centons passed before his mind was disturbed by a nagging thought. In all the yahren he had trained with his father, he had never experienced the abilities Adama had referred to. All he had were intuitions, gut feelings he'd learned to follow. If higher mental powers were stored away, there must be some key to unlock them. Was it physical? Or mental? Or did he simply lack what his ancestors had taken for granted?

Perhaps it required a conscious effort, he considered. A target, so to speak. Or at least, a question asked, a vacuum to be filled.

With great effort, he returned to his meditative state. Concentration, meditation, and inner vision, that was Adama's mantra, and now his own. He had always taken "inner vision" to mean some ability to fully understand himself, to see the path of his life clearly and make decisions without hesitation.

Now Apollo understood that it meant something else entirely. He closed his eyes, entered a state that was like sleep, but without the lack of awareness that usually comes with it. He attained a trance state. His eyes rolled slightly upward and he reached out with his spiritual essence.

Apollo used his inner vision, for the first time, to look beyond himself. Instantly, he was overwhelmed by a rush of sensation that made him forget the cold little room in which he sat. Voices, mumbled, images, urges, some distasteful, all visited upon him at once. His stomach roiled and he felt sick, but the floodgates had been opened and he could do nothing to close them again.

Thoughts, he realized. These were thoughts, all around him. Yet they were like a tangled skein, which he could not unwind. Nothing was distinct. But in time he would be able to differentiate among them, he was confident. Already, he recognized some of the minds in that cacophonous thought storm. His friends were there, concerned for him; he could feel that.

All but Starbuck.

No sooner had the thought of Starbuck crossed his mind than the telepathic maelstrom cleared and Apollo had the rushing sensation of frenetic motion. Traveling somewhere, momentum tearing at his fragmented reality.

Where?

He opened his eyes. But he wasn't in the sanctuary anymore. He didn't recognize his surroundings, but he was running. Blood pumped in his veins, pounded in his ears, his lungs hurt and still he ran. His boots slapped the corridor floor, and he dove to avoid a laser blast. He jumped up, glanced behind him, and saw them approaching: CYLONS!

Somewhere in the back of his mind, Apollo dimly realized that he had joined with another mind. Like a parasite, a voyeur of some kind, he was experiencing whatever this man was experiencing. And it was a mind he recognized.

In the secret sanctuary chamber, the red eye of the computer burned on, unnoticed. Apollo could only see and feel and hear what his host experienced. He could not even hear his own voice, resounding through the chamber as he cried out a name.

"Starbuck!"

6.

"Frack!" Starbuck cried. "Enough with the lasers already, I would've thought you'd be glad to see me go!"

At the turn in the corridor, he spun, took cover and fired back. Two Centurions went down hard, sparks flying as their cybernetic systems were fried. But he had no idea how many Cylons there were on this planet. The only thing he did know was that he didn't want to see any more of them for a long time.

"Is this any way to treat a guest?" he shouted. Starbuck glanced around the corner, then made a mad dash along the same corridor. He thought he recognized it from his capture, when they had dragged him by his feet, head bouncing and sliding, to a cell.

A cell where he had remained for weeks, awaiting death. The crash should have killed him; Starbuck considered his survival a miracle. During his captivity, they had fed him infrequently, allowing him water only to deal with his wounds. He had torn his tunic into long strips to serve as bandages. His crimson flight jacket covered his battered torso; his pants were in tatters. The light layer of body fat he had allowed himself to accumulate had been quickly shed.

When the Centurions had come to his cell, Starbuck hadn't been sure if it was to kill him or transport him elsewhere. Not that it mattered. He wasn't completely healed, but this would be his only chance for escape.

Feigning injury worse than he had actually suffered, a ruse he had followed since his capture, he had gotten close to the Cylon nearest him and attacked. A quick kick to the chest plate had sent the Centurion stumbling backward into the other guard, and Starbuck had rushed forward and snatched the laser from the Cylon's fist.

Those two were the first he had killed. He'd been killing Cylons for several centari now, and there seemed no end to the supply. They were slow and rambling—easy targets, for they never took cover—but there were too many of them.

He had to get out.

A klaxon sounded, pealing loudly, sound splitting his head, which still ached from some unseen injury he'd sustained in the crash. It had worried Starbuck for some time, but he didn't have the luxury of such anxiety now.

With every ounce of energy, he ran full out down the corridor. Warning lights flashed on the walls and the slapping of his boot soles seemed inordinately loud, even with the klaxons wailing. He heard a clanking, metal clamor behind him and glanced back to see an entire unit of Cylons, thirteen of them, marching across the junction he had just passed through.

They had to have seen him. But they didn't stop. Not at all.

"Now what's this all about?" he wondered aloud, slowing just a bit.

That's when four Centurions and a gold gleaming Cylon captain stomped around the corridor corner just ahead, weapons leveled at his chest. Starbuck threw himself flat on the ground, cheekbone striking metal. He returned fire, blasting at them twice, but didn't see how he might escape. Retreat was not an option. He would have to shoot it out with five Cylons. Not great odds, but he supposed he had faced worse.

Rarely alone, of course. But he'd always believed that the only way to be sure the tough jobs would be accomplished was to take them on yourself.

Starbuck cried out in anger and rolled to one side, avoiding a laser blast. He fired back and the Cylon captain fell, one of the cyborg's arms torn from its body by the laser. Dark blood spurted from the wound as circuitry sparked.

"I could use a little help here," Starbuck muttered, glancing at the ceiling, appealing to a higher power he had never truly believed in.

To his right, a door slid open with a hydraulic hiss. Starbuck turned his eyes to the ceiling again. "Thanks," he said, and rolled again just as several shots came from the Cylons, advancing now to less than twenty metrons from his position.

Standing inside the open door was a tall, robed Cylon with a transparent skull. The Warriors called them diplomats, because they were non-combatant. Starbuck didn't think he had ever been happy to see a Cylon. But he was now.

"Out of the way, buddy," Starbuck cried as he dove into the room and hit the door control. It slid shut even as the Cylon diplomat began to approach him, shrieking in a high voice.

"Here! The human is here! He has escaped! Take him now, he is here!" the diplomat cried.

"Enough of that feldergarb," Starbuck mumbled, lifted his stolen laser and blasted the diplomat's transparent skull to shards. The body fell heavily to the floor and did not move. He was happy to have that blaster. His own weapon would not have been half as effective against Cylons. He would have to make sure he held on to it.

If he lived through the day.

Starbuck blasted the control panel that would have opened the door. The Cylons began hammering on it a micron later. Another micron, and they'd blow it open.

He spun, wincing as the movement reopened a wound in his side he hoped was healed. Starbuck glanced quickly around the room, searching for some kind of defense, or another exit. Nothing but the window.

Laser fire ripped through the chamber door, singeing his hair as it tore past his face and scorched the wall.

The window would have to do.

Starbuck ran over to the portal that looked out upon the planetary surface, and blanched. The Cylon base had been built into the side of a mountain face and out the window was a sheer drop. Below there was a waterfall that rushed out of the mountainside and might have supplied some of the power to the base itself. Might even be why they chose this spot, he thought.

Another laser blast behind him and heavy Cylon fingers slid into a newly opened space between door and frame. With a shrieking of metal, the door was hauled open several centimetrons.

"I should've died in the crash," Starbuck spat. He backed up and blasted the window out over the precipice, debris tumbling down more than one hundred and fifty metrons to the small pool beneath the falls.

Without any other choice, Starbuck took two steps back and then hurled himself out the window. Even as he fell, tumbling, he saw the laser fire that followed him outside.

Time slowed. Buffeted by the air, he tumbled, lurching with his legs, trying to guide himself toward the pooling water. Which as he neared it, grew to be much larger than he'd thought.

A rumbling filled his ears that was even louder than the rush of the falls behind him. He'd thought it was his eyes, and the velocity of his fall, but Starbuck realized that the ground beneath him was shaking. The ground as far as he could see was shaking.

Temblor!

What next?

Then he hit the water, hard, the air forced from his lungs by the impact. He was under, sucking water in, trying to get his bearings. He kicked off in one direction, and agony shot through his side and his left leg. Probably fractured by the impact, he thought. His last moment of clarity before terror struck.

He was swimming down. The light filtered through the water above and Starbuck changed direction. His lungs were going to burst, he was choking on water. He tried not to open his mouth again, but the instinct was too great. Once more he inhaled a great gulp of water, the pain of it going down making his eyes bulge. His heart raced in panic.

Starbuck broke the surface, coughing, choking on water that might have been toxic to humans for all he knew. He pulled himself to the shore, the land no longer trembling, hacking the alien water up through his ragged throat. Starbuck sucked in enormous breaths of air, trying desperately to clear his mind.

It wasn't enough. In his peripheral vision, phantom images played, then darkened. The blackness swept over him. In the moment before he lost consciousness completely, he sensed someone nearby, a friend. Could almost hear the voice.

"...Apollo..." he muttered.

Then he was lost to the void, and would not wake again until the next temblor.

In the silence of his father's sanctuary, Apollo's eyes snapped open and he gasped for air, gagging on water that was not in his lungs. He breathed greedily of the oxygen filtering through the *Galactica's* venting system. Several microns passed before he realized what he'd experienced.

"Starbuck," he whispered in the private chamber.

There was no other explanation for it. He had been with Starbuck, in real time, as he made his escape from the Cylon outpost on Ochoa. He was alive! This was no prescient vision of the future; though his father had assured him those were possible as well. This had just happened.

And what of that temblor? Had the pull of Ochoa's two suns already become so disruptive? If memory served, it hadn't yet even passed into direct alignment between the dual stars. If there were temblors already, what would happen when that alignment was in synch?

"Starbuck!" Apollo said loudly, a smile stretching across his face.

The leap over the falls could have killed him, but Starbuck hadn't hesitated. If his friend were to survive, Apollo couldn't hesitate either.

He sprang from his chair and marched to the door. As it slid open, the computer and lights turned themselves off behind him.

Apollo paused, glancing back into the darkness, at the space where the image of his father had shimmered centons earlier. When he returned, he'd have to play that recording back, simply to enjoy Adama's presence. But for now, he had to see Athena. He was supposed to take command of the *Galactica* in...he glanced at his timepiece...less than a cycle! Just seven centons.

A lot to be done between now and then.

"*Baltar*," a voice spoke in the darkness.

It was the croaking voice of a man dying of disease, wracked with illness and horrible suffering. Yet it was strong. Strong and loud enough to wake Baltar from a deep sleep in his chamber.

"*Baltar!*" it croaked again, and Baltar came fully awake. In an instant, he recalled all that had befallen him, the humiliation of being replaced as base star commander by his own advisor.

"*Your wrath is righteous,*" the voice said, and there was something about it which reminded Baltar of thick-skinned slithering things.

He sat up slowly, warily, swinging his legs over the edge of his berth. Eyes narrowed, he scanned the room for some sign of the speaker, and found nothing.

"Where and what are you?" he asked. "You're not Cylon, certainly. How did you get here and what do you want with me?"

"*I've always admired that about you, Baltar,*" the voice slithered. "*You never diverge from the central question: how will anything harm or benefit you.*"

Baltar smiled thinly. "It is, after all, the only question that truly matters, don't you think?"

Silence. And in the silence, Baltar reached out and passed his hand over a sensor that would illuminate the chamber. Instantly, light flooded his shabby new quarters. For a micron, he got a glimpse of a billowing, unctuous black hole that was shaped like a man. Then the lights went out again.

"I can think of one other question you might be pleased to have the answer to," the voice said, ignoring the passing glimpse of itself Baltar had received.

"What you want of me?" Baltar suggested. "That might be good to know."

"And you shall know, soon enough," the voice answered. *"But not the question I'd considered. Actually, I thought you might like to ask me for the specific coordinates for the location of the Colonial fleet."*

Baltar stopped breathing. No dramatic intake of breath, no choke or gasp, no exclamation. Merely stopped breathing, and slowly rose to his feet. He walked in the darkness toward the spot where the black bilious creature had appeared, and stared.

After a moment, he began to breathe again.

"You know where to find the *Galactica* and her tattered vestiges of human civilization?" he asked, narrowing his eyes with skepticism.

"Indeed," the darkness said, and Baltar's heart leaped with joy. *"I can tell you precisely where to find the fleet."*

7.

TROY AND DALTON WALKED SIDE BY SIDE along the garden path, one of the few areas of *Agro-3* open to the public. This particular starship was, for all intents and purposes, an enormous greenhouse floating in space. Other than its crew quarters, bridge, and engines, the entire vessel was comprised of a large soil depository where plant life was cultivated for food, including such common delights as heffala berries and fallaga. A vast transparent shell covered the garden, its many panes absorbing and storing stellar light, radiating it down upon the garden in alternating patches of illumination.

It was hard to see the stars from inside an agro-ship. But Viper pilots saw enough of the stars.

Vegetation grew lush all along the path and throughout the garden. Greens and reds in varying shades, orange and blue here and there as well. These were the colors of food. The stuff of life. The agro-ships were vital. But even more vital was the oxygen that the vegetation produced. *Agro-3* wasn't frequented by the fleet's citizens merely because of the garden's beauty, but because of the wonderfully fresh air.

"I love it here," Dalton said, eyes ranging across the garden path. "I'm tempted to grab a handful of just about everything I see and take a bite."

Troy chuckled dryly, but turned away when she looked at him.

"What?" Dalton asked. "What's funny?"

"Nothing," Troy insisted. "I was going to say something vile, but I thought better of it."

Dalton shook her head, laughing. "You daggit," she said, and struck him in the shoulder. "What were you going to say?"

"I love the warmth of these stellar projectors," he said absently, turning his face to the shining, transparent panels on the agro-ship's dome.

"Troy!" Dalton cried, smiling even as she glared at him. "What. Were. You. Going. To. Say?"

Troy looked down at her. Despite the exercise regimen that kept her toned and muscular, and despite her stature as a pilot and Warrior, Dalton was still little more than a slip of a girl. In appearance. Troy was torn between his memory of her, and his knowledge that she had, indeed, matured.

"Sorry, Dalton, they were thoughts and words not fit for young ears," he said, several meanings hiding behind the teasing in his tone. "After all, you're only seventeen."

Dalton fumed, eyes wide, her mouth open as she prepared some new barb or taunt. Then her mouth closed, lips pressed in a grim line, eyes narrowed in real anger. Even as Troy watched, her features were altered again, softening. A kind of sadness swept over her face, and his heart crumbled at the thought that her melancholy was his doing.

She reached for his hand, held it gently, and looked up into his eyes with such genuine warmth and affection that it stopped his breath a moment. He reminded himself of the words he had just spoken—she was only seventeen.

As if she had heard him, a smile tempted the corners of Dalton's mouth.

"I won't always be seventeen, Troy," she said softly.

The moment was painful. She was a Warrior already, but just a girl even so. Still, Troy could wait. Patience was a skill he had long practiced.

"Well," he said, teasing, "may the Lords of Kobol help us when your next novayahren cycles around. May they help us all."

They stood for a moment, facing one another, each seemingly unsure what to say next. Troy became acutely aware that Dalton still held his hand. He mumbled something, trying to break the spell. He had recon duty next cycle anyway. He couldn't be venting centons into space just wandering around with Dalton.

As much as he might want to.

"I…" she began.

Before Dalton could continue, a shriek rent the air on the path ahead of them. A man's voice.

Then they heard a woman shout, "Oh, vengeful God!"

Troy spun, ran, boots pounding soil along the path, dimly aware that Dalton raced beside him, step for step. There was trouble ahead. His hand slapped to his hip where his blaster was usually slung, but off-duty Warriors were never armed.

Tree branches dipped down across the path ahead of them. Dalton sprinted under and ahead of him, while Troy had to brush the branches away from his face. When he emerged, he saw two men and a woman, a Leonid by her skin tone. One of the men was a Gemini. They were standing four or five metrons off the path in a field of mange grass, which wouldn't be in season for stews for several months.

"Warriors! Stand where you are!" Dalton snapped, her voice as full of command as any Troy had ever heard.

"Turn and face us, hands in front of you, and return to the path immediately," Troy added, calm now that he could see the citizens creating the disturbance were unarmed.

The two men responded at once, turning and marching to the path, keeping their hands visible. An agro-worker rounded a corner further up the path just in time to see them stepping back onto the soil. The woman was still standing amidst the mange grass, and the worker's face registered shock and anger simultaneously.

"You there!" he shouted, voice high and strident. "Get out of that field! You're ruining the crop, woman! Have you been sniffing plant vapors?

"Warriors!" the man said upon noticing them. "Come now, can't you get her out of there?"

"Sir, we're working on it, okay?" Dalton responded. "Why don't you relax for a moment while we take care of this?"

"Relax?" the man cried, appalled and offended by the mere suggestion. "How do you expect me to...oh, by the Lords!"

The man stood not far from the point where the woman had diverged from the path. He stared along the broken blades of mange grass, and at first Troy thought he was merely inspecting the damage. Then he noticed that the man's gaze was riveted, not at the trampled vegetation, but at a point just beyond where the Leonid woman stood. The grass was damaged there, too, somehow. But even as he approached, Troy could not quite make out...

"Troy," Dalton said suddenly, stopping short on the path in front of him. "We've got trouble."

He smelled it before he saw it. Troy suspected that's what had drawn the passing citizens' attention to it as well, the stench. Too many days in the tall grass, growing ripe.

Troy motioned for Dalton to hold her position, and she went about keeping both the agro-worker—who seemed to be a shift supervisor or in some other position of authority on the ship—and the other citizens away from the trampled field.

The agro-supervisor huffed slightly when Troy started across the field, but Dalton snapped at him and he went silent. Troy began breathing through his mouth as he crossed the last two metrons between the path and the long, gnarled black form that lay on the ground amidst broken blades of grass.

Though it was nearly impossible to believe while looking at it, logic dictated that the dead thing which lay before him had once been a human being. Mugjapes burrowed in its empty eye sockets, foraging for whatever remained of the corpse's brain tissue. Its flesh was burned beyond recognition, to the bone in some places. White fragments jutted out of its belly, and it was clear that the victim had been crushed to death before he or she had burned. Gender was impossible to determine.

Troy knelt in the soft earth next to the foul-smelling corpse. The soil shifted slightly, upsetting the lay of the dead thing, and its entire stomach collapsed in a cloud of blackened cinders that reminded him of the ash on the end of a fumarello. A burst of noxious gas floated up into his face, and Troy jerked away from the body.

"All right, Lieutenant, you've done enough," a deep voice said. "Back off from the body now, please."

Troy turned, annoyed, to find that a trio of blackshirts had joined the growing crowd on the garden path. They were the Quorum's security force, responsible for the day-to-day policing of the fleet and her citizens. But they were also largely untrained, men and women who didn't have the chops to become Warriors. Some of them were spiteful because of it.

Paris was one of those. He and Troy had entered Academy together. But Paris hadn't lasted two weeks, and he resented it. As if Troy were responsible for his failure. Troy realized that the time might be at hand when he could ignore it no longer.

"I'm sorry, Paris, were you talking to me?" Troy asked, adopting the set of the jaw and steely gaze he had seen his father use to great advantage hundreds of times over the years. Women loved his blue eyes, blue like tylium flame, he'd so often been told.

But there was only cold saligium in those eyes now.

"Step away, Troy, we have a job to do," Paris insisted. The man was larger than Troy by far. He was a Tauran, with the red-tinged skin and dark hair so common among his people. Paris was dangerous, Troy decided. A truth he had always known, but only now recognized.

"You seem to forget that this fleet is still under martial law, security chief," Dalton interrupted, shattering the standoff between the two men. "In the case of murder, the law clearly states that the military will pursue the investigation."

"Murder!" The man who had shrieked earlier, and whom they all seemed to have forgotten, gasped out the word and swooned slightly before the Leonid woman steadied him. The agro-supervisor stared out across the grass at the incinerated corpse.

"You!" Troy barked. "Get the other civilians out of here. See that they stand by for questioning. Other Warriors will arrive presently."

"Murder?" Paris scoffed, looking at Dalton with an amused smirk on his face. "You haven't even gotten a close look at the body, Ensign. What does a little girl know of murder?"

Troy winced, and glanced at Dalton.

"What do I know about murder?" she asked, rolling her eyes back in her head as if she were seriously considering the question.

Before either of the other blackshirts could react, before Paris even knew what was happening, Dalton had crossed the metron that separated them, grabbed him by the hair and forced his head down into the soil with her knee at the back of his neck. A long, thin, non-regulation shiv drew a small bead of blood from Paris's temple.

"Maybe you want me to show you?" Dalton whispered.

Troy said nothing. He was her superior officer. She was clearly way over the line, her behavior unacceptable by any standards and grounds for a service review and possible prosecution. If she'd behaved this way with a citizen, he would have ordered her off and taken her in himself if she balked. But this was different. No civilian witnesses, just a standoff between them and the blackshirts. She was a Warrior, and his friend. He would back her up, whatever move she made.

"Get off me, you..." Paris went from growl to yelp in the same breath.

"You might want to reconsider what you were about to say," Dalton advised, pressing the point closer.

The two blackshirts with Paris stared not at Dalton and their chief, but at Troy, Commander Apollo's son, who made no move to stop what was happening. Not knowing what to do, inaction had apparently appealed to them as the wisest course.

Paris said nothing. After a moment, Dalton got off his back. The shiv disappeared as quickly and mysteriously as it had materialized. Troy didn't even know where Dalton had secreted it on her uniform.

"Shame to lose your commission so soon after receiving it," Paris snarled now that he was free. "Lieutenant Troy, I expect you to arrest

Ensign Dalton immediately, or I'll have to do it."

Troy smiled, forcing the expression to take on the taint of patient amusement.

"Nobody's going to be arrested, Paris—except the murderer," Troy said. "Ensign Dalton hasn't done anything wrong as far as I can see. And let's be honest, who are the Quorum really going to believe?"

Paris grew even redder with anger and embarrassment. But he knew Troy was right. What he could not know was how sickened Troy felt at having to pull the influence of his family out for protection. His father and grandfather were legend, as was Dalton's dad. It never felt right, but sometimes that power had to be used.

Whatever weapons were in the arsenal, as Starbuck had been so fond of saying. Dalton's father had a lot of advice like that, Troy recalled.

"Why are you so sure it's murder?" Paris asked, disgusted but abandoning the nursing of his injured pride for the moment. Not forever, though, if Troy knew him at all.

"The corpse was crushed, then burned to bones and embers. Doesn't anything seem odd to you?" Troy asked, incredulous.

Paris only frowned, his fat nose wrinkling.

"None of the grass is burned, Paris," Troy explained, and then watched as the microns ticked by. He had counted to seven before he saw the light of understanding begin to flicker in the blackshirt's eyes.

"It didn't happen here," Paris said.

"Hey, not bad," Dalton taunted him. "Now why don't you do us all a favor? Get on the comm and ask Lieutenant Colonel Athena to send some infantry Warriors down here to seal off this site."

The blackshirts retreated, however reluctantly, and Troy and Dalton were finally alone again. With the body, of course.

"Who do you think it was?" she asked.

"No idea, but we're going to find out," Troy replied. "If you don't count domestic quarrels, there hasn't been an outright murder in the fleet since I was six yahren old. Some triad player on the *Rising Star*. Can't remember his name. Your father was accused, though, as I recall."

Dalton frowned, still staring at the corpse. The mugjapes had multiplied, and now they swarmed out of the skull, presumably having eaten all the brain and now looking for other juicy organs. Troy felt his gorge rise, and Dalton turned away.

"Well, at least there's a bright side to this mystery," Dalton said mildly. "They can't try to pin this one on Starbuck."

They laughed together for a moment, but the presence of the corpse, and its odor, were overwhelming.

"So we begin," Troy declared. "Search both military and Quorum records from the last few weeks for anyone who's come up missing. Somebody must have noticed the victim's disappearance."

"Yes, Lieutenant," Dalton answered, stiffly formal now. All business. And she was fracking good at it, too, Troy thought.

One of these days—if she could rein in that flashfire temper— she'd make a fine commander herself, he thought. But he'd never tell her that. She was cocky enough already.

"I can't do this," Athena said, laying a hand across her eyes and lowering her head with a sigh.

"Yes, you can," Cassiopeia insisted. "I know he's your brother, Athena. He's my friend. But Apollo is better suited for a Viper's cockpit than the command deck of the *Galactica*. He's too headstrong to be commander. Other than Starbuck, and even that's too close to call, Apollo might be the best Warrior we've ever had."

"But you'd be a better commander. You know it. We all do."

Athena threw water on her face from the basin, then looked up at her reflection on the imager. Behind her, she could see them standing, an odd assortment of more than a dozen women representing the entire fleet, including each of the twelve colonies and several additional members of the Gemon Matriarchal Society.

"Athena?" Cassiopeia pleaded. "Come on, the reporter from TransVid Information Service will be here any second. You're going off duty in five centari. You can't stay in here anymore."

Every muscle in her body was tensed, her stomach hurt and her breath came shallow and ragged. Athena had never been so overcome with anxiety. But she'd never had this kind of reason before. A fleet of Cylon base-stars would be easier to face than these women.

"It's going to tear the fleet apart," she said, and turned to them at last. "Marialis, you've got to see that. Apollo is extremely popular, with good reason, and anyone who paid attention could see that my father intended for him to become commander."

Marialis stepped forward and put one hand on Athena's shoulder. The tall, slender Gemon woman was characteristically pale, but her eyes were bright and lively. There was something charismatic about her, something that made her every comment seem inarguable. But Athena had to argue. What they were asking was so contradictory to her personality, her loyalty and sense of fairness.

Fairness. The word rang hollow in her mind. *Tigh hadn't even considered her. Was that fair?*

"Athena?" Marialis urged, and Athena glanced up at her. Their eyes locked. "The fleet is already being torn apart by this controversy. Simply because he seems to have been anointed by your father to become commander, Apollo is being attacked. Several Quorum members actively oppose his nomination. Many question his ability to command, others would simply prefer that he remain a part of their active defense.

"You are another story. A woman, yet a Caprican, a Kobollian, still Adama's child. And with the proven skill to helm the fleet," Marialis said. "Apollo is not going to be commander, Athena. The question is, are you?"

Athena felt sick, but she did not hesitate another moment. She turned and left the women's lounge, strode along the corridor back onto the *Galactica's* bridge. From the hatchway, Marialis and Cassiopeia stood and watched her closely.

Omega barely glanced at the others as he hurried to her side.

"Lieutenant Colonel, you've really got to see this," Omega said.

In her anxiety, Athena didn't register the depth of the officer's distress. Instead, she motioned for the reporter from TIS to approach. The woman, whose broad, squat body immediately identified her as hailing from Cancer, ambled in her direction with an S-cube, a simulcast sight-and-sound unit.

"Lieutenant Colonel?" Omega persisted.

"What is it?" Athena asked as she glanced nervously about the bridge. The presence of Marialis and the other women, so obviously standing by in anticipation of some event, had gotten the crew's attention. Now the Cancerian reporter tagged on her S-cube, and the front of it lit up, lens gleaming. Whispers flitted across the bridge.

They all stared at her now, including Omega. The reporter stopped just to her left, and Omega frowned as he looked at her.

"Omega, what is it?" Athena barked, and the man started as if slapped.

The aging officer looked from Athena to the reporter once more, then shook his head and backed away.

"It can wait, I guess," he said. Something in his eyes told Athena he suspected what was happening, and disapproved vehemently. But he would never say a word. His loyalty was unquestionable.

"I'm Guinevere," said the reporter, whose roundish face and dark red hair gave her a bit of a porcine appearance. "Are you ready, Lieutenant Colonel?"

"No, but let's hurry anyway," she replied. After all, the last thing she wanted was to be in the middle of this when Apollo arrived to take the bridge as commander for the first time. She supposed Guinevere would record that as well.

The reporter began, captivating every crew member on the bridge. Cassiopeia, Marialis and the others came further onto the bridge now. Even if Athena wanted to back out, it was too late. She felt as if she were in a rushing torrent of water, being carried forward against her will, without the energy to swim for shore.

"This is Guinevere reporting from the bridge of the battlestar *Galactica*," she said. "We are all acutely aware of the political turmoil the fleet has suffered since the tragic death of Commander Adama, a true visionary whose leadership some say was largely responsible for the survival of the human race.

"Our sources tell us that Commander Adama's daughter, Lieutenant Colonel Athena, is going to make a startling announcement today," the woman continued, as if she didn't know. Then: "Lieutenant Colonel, what is this great revelation?"

"Not a great revelation, but a humble announcement," Athena replied, staring directly into the lens of the S-cube, well aware that half the fleet would be watching, hearing every word even as she spoke them.

"With no disrespect meant to my brother, Lieutenant Commander Apollo, or to President Tigh, who has named him acting commander in an obvious attempt to force his choice upon the Quorum, I submit that after the yahren I have served as the first officer of the *Galactica*, I am better suited for the rigors of command," she asserted.

When she heard the collective intake of breath on the bridge, the gasps of astonishment, Athena wanted to cringe, to close her eyes and wish it all away. But she refused to let her anxiety show. The people needed to see that she was confident, even if that was a sham.

"A finer Warrior than Apollo has never lived," she continued, "but the position of commander requires more. It requires diplomacy, a facility for government, and knowledge of the workings of the fleet beyond the military. Further, it requires the ability to be objective in the face of irrationality and cautious in the confrontation of any threat. I feel that I have acquired and displayed these attributes during my active duty.

"Therefore, I respectfully place myself in nomination before the Quorum for the post of commander of the battlestar *Galactica*, and of the fleet," Athena concluded.

From the opposite edge of the command deck, Marialis seconded the nomination and Cassiopeia lent her support. The crew glared at Athena, though she saw some smiling, supportive faces. Omega's was not among them. She had never seen him so grave, so dour.

"Now, Omega, what was it you wanted me to see?" she asked,

ignoring the heavy silence that had descended upon the bridge.

"Only this," Omega said sternly, and tapped a key on his console. A holo-image sprang to life immediately, and Athena recognized Ambassador Puck. He seemed, somehow, even more stooped and frail than ever. But his words stunned her.

"It is a breach of tradition, I know," Ambassador Puck said. "So I hope you'll forgive me. Though Quorum members are traditionally silent about their deliberations regarding major political appointments, I must speak.

"Thus far, we have received more than two dozen nominations. Only a handful of these can we even begin to consider as serious candidates. Though they may fracture the public sentiment if they begin to, shall we say, campaign for support, none of them pose a serious threat to acting Commander Apollo receiving the Quorum's blessings."

Here, Puck's smile melted away into a sneer.

"You are being ignored, citizens of this great fleet, the last vestiges of humanity," Puck declared. "Even now, sources inform me that Lieutenant Colonel Athena is preparing to announce her own candidacy for nomination. To oppose her brother, perhaps.

"I would think, however, that you would all see through this deceit. A contest between brother and sister, both of whom already have your love, your loyalty, your respect, can still only end one way...with a Caprican as commander. With one of Adama's children as commander. I would suggest we all consider if Apollo and Athena are truly at odds, or have collaborated on a showman's scheme to draw all attention to themselves."

Athena stared at the holo-image of Puck, and wished he was there in the flesh. She wanted so badly to strike him or, at the very least, to have him feel the hatred in her gaze. How dare he! The decision she had made was not some lark, but the hardest choice in her life.

"My people, while it may seem out of place to you, the crossing of a line, perhaps, that should never be crossed, I cannot stand by and allow this travesty to unfold," Puck said with a scowl. "There is no law which prevents it, so I submit to you a new candidate for the post of commander. I submit...myself!

"Look hard at Athena and Apollo, my people. Are their positions based on actual accomplishment, or an accident of birth? And finally, consider what has happened in the short time since Commander Adama first fell ill. The Caprican cabal which quietly wields power over this fleet has led us, once again, into territory infested with the Cylon menace.

"It is for the Quorum to decide who will be commander," Puck concluded. "Raise up your voices, my friends, and they will listen!"

The holo-image flickered and then disappeared. The bridge was silent, and Athena could only imagine the sickening doubt now sweeping through the crew. And not only the crew, but the entire fleet!

"Oh, Father, what have I done?" she whispered to herself.

She glanced at the hallway, where Cassiopeia had stood with Marialis and the others. They were gone now, all but Cassie, who seemed as stunned as Athena. Strange, she thought, that the only ally she felt she could trust would be a woman with whom she had been at odds for nearly twenty yahren.

Athena knew what she had to do. This foolishness had to be put to rest before it went any further.

"Omega, where is Commander Apollo right now?" Athena asked, striding across the command deck to his seat.

Omega consulted his flatscreen, tapped several keys, and frowned.

"What is it now?" Athena asked in a tightly controlled voice.

"Commander Apollo is in the launch bay, Lieutenant Colonel," Omega said. "His Viper is preparing to launch."

8.

BALTAR WAS IN A RAGE, YET AGAIN. It had occurred to him, of course, that in some ways he was lucky simply to still be alive. But it was totally humiliating to have his command taken away and handed over to that simpleton, Lucifer, who for all his knowledge was less useful, in Baltar's view, than the average Centurion drone-warrior.

In his wildest musings, however, he had never imagined that it could get worse from there. Yet it had. Not only was he now, essentially, Lucifer's servant, but he, who had once cast his desires down as orders from on high, was now forced to wait like the lowest creature at the door to the command chamber. Lucifer, he had been told, was not prepared to receive him as yet.

Not prepared to receive him!

Baltar had sworn, in that moment, that when he regained the seat of command, he would personally see Lucifer ripped apart and returned to Cylon for parts recycling.

With a hydraulic hiss, the chamber door finally slid open. Baltar stood from the uncomfortable kyluminam chair and hurried forward as a golden Centurion captain exited. But the door slid shut again before Baltar could even see inside.

"Baltar, you have not been authorized to enter the command chamber," the captain intoned. Baltar had never found the Cylons' electronic voices to be as grating as he had over the past several days.

"Captain, you don't understand," Baltar importuned. "I've got to see Lucifer. He has no idea what the events on Ochoa will lead to. If the prisoner was who I think he was, we've got to…"

"You will be called when you are needed, Baltar," the Captain informed him. "If you are needed."

Baltar digested the cold finality of the Centurion's words. "I…I don't understand," he implored. "What do you mean by that? The Imperious Leader is in dire need of human counsel. Why, without me, the Cylons simply cannot understand how the human mind functions."

The Centurion captain ignored him. Its head was cocked slightly, as if it were listening carefully to something Baltar couldn't hear.

"By your command," it said, and its head rotated slightly to regard the human. For a moment, Baltar thought that the captain had just received orders to execute him.

"Lucifer has called for you, Baltar," the captain droned. Baltar's sigh of relief was audible. He didn't even try to hide it because he didn't think the Cylons would understand its significance anyway. That's why they needed him. They did nothing but follow their primary objectives and the Imperious Leader's commands. They could not understand human logic.

"It's about time," he huffed as he stepped over to stand next to the captain in front of the command chamber door. "Lucifer and I have much to discuss."

The door slid open with a familiar hiss. Baltar took one step and halted half a metron into the room. Lucifer was perched on the high seat of command. That was to be expected. What had caught him off guard were the dark, armored beings who surrounded him.

"Iblis' ghost, what are those soldiers?" he gasped.

"Oh, Baltar, do come in and meet your children!" Lucifer invited.

One of the horrible, lethal-looking creatures began to make a low snuffling noise. If Baltar didn't know better, he would have thought the thing was actually laughing.

The Battlestar *Galactica* was adorned with two long fighter bays, one on either side of her. Each bay was split in half, with the fore section acting as launch bay, and the aft section reserved for landing. The *Galactica* carried a complement of seventy-five Vipers, with the capacity to launch twenty, ten from each bay, almost simultaneously. Hostilities against the Cylons and other enemies had, over time, dealt a devastating blow to the battlestar's Viper contingent. At the lowest, their numbers had dropped to fewer than forty.

Finally, after what had been more than a decade of almost constant fear and equally frequent warfare, they had been able to take the time to rebuild, even just a little. New cadets were trained as Warriors, and thus added to the ranks of both pilots and infantry. But those trained as pilots needed Vipers to fly. Finally, they had found a planet with the mineral resources needed to build Vipers and to repair other ships in the fleet.

A huge old, creaking freighter was retrofitted and re-christened the *Hephaestus*. It had become one of the most valued ships in the fleet. Most of the older Vipers had been laboriously rebuilt, using a new pulsar system that burned cleaner Tylium samples—not as much risk of solium leaks. There had been more than forty new Azure-class Vipers built before the new Scarlet-class model, of which Apollo had the first.

Apollo pulled on his helm and fired the Scarlet Viper's engines, blue-white flame jetting from the starfighter's triple pulsar engines. He lifted a hand to signal to the crew, wrapped his hand around the navi-hilt and prepared for the thrust that would carry the Viper through the launch tube and into space. Any moment he should see the end of the launch tube open to reveal the starfield beyond.

Any moment.

When nothing happened, Apollo turned in the cockpit, craning around to get a glimpse of the launch bay. The crew should have cleared the area by now, but the launch master still stood in the bay.

Apollo waved to him, shrugging. No commlink contact, of course. Nobody knew he was leaving, and he didn't want to alert the bridge.

Again he motioned to the man, who pointed to the back of Apollo's Viper. What was it? Trouble? Mechanical problems, he assumed. He cursed, and was about to raise the canopy of his Viper when he felt the starfighter dip slightly to the left.

Apollo turned, startled by the sudden weight. As he watched, Athena pulled herself up onto the Viper's wing and walked over to the canopy to stare down at him. He sighed, annoyed with the delay but resigned to having to deal with Athena now. Apollo punched the cockpit release. The internal air was expelled with a hydraulic huff and the canopy opened even as he removed his helm and set it on his lap.

"Where exactly do you think you're going?" Athena asked.

Apollo couldn't help smiling. His sister's strident tone reminded him so much of their childhood. She had changed so much, her concerns grown so much greater, but when it came to her big brother, she dealt with him the same way: with impatient dismay.

"I'm going out on recon," he lied.

Her brown eyes darkened as she narrowed them.

"You're supposed to be on the bridge right now, taking command for the first time," Athena said. "Not to mention that you're not listed on the duty roster for recon, and you haven't cleared your launch with the bridge."

"I'm the acting commander, Athena," Apollo reminded her, quite unnecessarily he was certain. "I don't need to clear my launch with anyone."

"Cut the feldergarb, Apollo," she snapped. "Where in God's name are you going? Don't you have any idea what's been happening?"

Apollo tilted his head slightly, frowning. Something had changed in Athena's tone. He could sense her distress. If he concentrated, he suspected he would be able to see within, to the cause of her anxiety. He...but no, every centon, every centari might make the difference between life or death for Starbuck.

"Listen, Athena, I'm sorry but I've got to go," he said grimly. She started to protest and he lifted a hand to stop her. "No, really, I have to launch. I don't have time to explain, but I left a message on the comm-unit in your quarters."

"No," she said harshly. "You don't know, Apollo. Listen to me. I'm not leaving the bay until you do, so you can't launch without killing me."

"Athena, get off the ship—get out of here. You may have cost Starbuck his life already!" Apollo snapped, exasperated.

Athena stared at him as if he were sniffing plant vapors, and Apollo understood her reaction completely. As far as she was concerned, Starbuck was dead. Apollo himself had reported that nobody could have survived the crash.

"I think you'd better explain," she said.

And he did. As briefly as possible, and without revealing the existence of their father's sanctuary, he told her of the mental powers inherent in the genetic line of the Kobollians, of his clairvoyant contact with Starbuck and his determination to return to Ochoa.

"Even if I believe everything you've said, which I don't, you can't go," Athena stated when he finished.

"Athena, I'm not psychotic, or inebriated...or running away," he insisted. "Look into my eyes. Can't you see the sanity here, the determination? Do I seem any different to you now than in any other crisis we've faced?"

She did as he asked, staring hard at him. Athena shook her head slowly, trying to deny the truth of his words, of his character. But they were brother and sister. With their father's death, there was no one else who knew him as she did, no one else who knew her as he did.

"Apollo, do you have any idea how poor your timing is?" she finally said. "I love you, brother. You should know that. But I've placed myself in nomination for command."

Apollo's eyes went wide. He shook his head.

"I don't understand," he said, unable to conceal his pain at this revelation.

"I'm sorry, but for every person who supports you, there are several who are either unsure or dead opposed to you as commander," Athena said calmly. "Frankly, I think I'm a better candidate anyway. But that's not the worst."

At a loss for words, Apollo merely nodded for her to continue.

"Ambassador Puck has announced his own candidacy, and been nominated as well," she explained. "He's made it seem as if my running is just a stunt to draw attention away from other candidates, to make sure you're elected."

Apollo grimaced. "That's ridiculous. It doesn't even make sense."

"To us!" Athena snapped. "What matters is, does it make sense to the Quorum and to the individual citizens of the fleet. Sure, it's plausible enough. We contend for the appointment and people debate our individual merits, then I drop out and you win because nobody else is ever seriously considered.

"But that's not my reasoning. I truly think I'd be a better commander than you, Apollo, which doesn't mean I don't respect you and your accomplishments. But now Puck has branded my candidacy a fraud, and made us both look like scheming buriticians."

Athena paused, lip curling in anger.

"I don't want to do this," she said, "but I'm going to withdraw myself from consideration. Maybe other serious candidates will come up, but it looks like it's going to just be you and Puck. If I withdraw now, we can show that Puck is just laying out a bunch of feldergarb to draw attention to himself."

Regret piled upon regret as Apollo tried desperately to think of a way to solve all of their problems at once. He should stay, if only to talk to Athena about her resentment regarding his promotion to acting commander. He should stay to show the fleet that Ambassador Puck was a nasty, shrill little man whose intentions could only be self-serving.

Everything his father had ever taught him, the example Adama had set, told Apollo he had to stay, to fight for the fleet, for the vision, for the future. But Adama also taught him to take care of his own.

"I'm sorry, Athena," he said grimly. "I've got to go. Starbuck is going to die if I don't go after him."

"Even if your vision was accurate, think for a moment. It's a Cylon outpost, Apollo! You'll be killed as well! Then where will we be?" she cried. "Send Boomer and Sheba after Starbuck. Send anyone. You're needed here."

"With whatever mental abilities my meditations have aroused, I may be the only one capable of finding Starbuck. As for the Cylons, they've long since cleared off. The planet is tearing itself apart. There's only one thing for you to do, Athena. You've got to stay in consideration for commander. If I come back, we'll contend for it, brother against sister. If I don't come back, you'll have to make certain they pick you over Puck.

"Besides, you're right. You probably *would* make a better commander than me," Apollo admitted. "Now get off the wing. Try to leave me a message buoy with your heading, and a small refueling tanker as well. By the time I get back to fleet, I'll have long since needed to fuel up."

Athena stared at him, a grave expression etched on her face. Then her countenance began to soften, her brows coming together in a kind of melancholy frown.

"You really think he's alive, don't you?" she asked.

"I know he is," Apollo answered.

Athena climbed down off his wing and walked from the launch bay without looking back. Apollo pulled on his helm, lowered the canopy on his Viper, and fired the pulsars again. This time, when he signaled to the crew, the hatch that covered the external door of the launch tube irised open, revealing the starfield beyond.

Silently, he wished Athena luck. From the sound of things, she would need it as much as he did.

He gripped the navi-hilt and thumbed the turbo button, then felt his craft shoot forward with phenomenal speed. The initial acceleration pressed his body back into the Viper's seat.

Apollo's Viper rocketed from the *Galactica's* flank and out into space.

"I'm coming, Starbuck," Apollo whispered. "Don't die on me now."

The temperature on the surface of Ochoa continued to climb. The planet only passed precisely between the two suns of the Binary-13 system every fifty or sixty yahren. This orbit might be its last. The massive solar tides were about to finally tear the planet apart.

In the meantime, there was no night on Ochoa. Full daylight at all times, with one sun on either side of the planet. It was getting hot.

Starbuck had wanted to use his flight jacket as a pillow while he took some rest. But with his tunic destroyed, he was forced to cover his body with the jacket for fear of radiation damage to his skin. Beads of sweat poured from his brow and down his back, but he didn't dare uncover himself.

It had been at least three centons since the last major temblor, the one that had jostled him out of sleep period. He'd bathed in the small lake into which he had fallen, but he was growing hungry and didn't dare eat anything found on the planet. There was no way to know what was safe to consume.

The good news was that, despite his fall, he seemed not to have received any new injuries. He had wrenched some muscles in his leg, but the pain had been temporary.

Now he crested a small rise and looked down upon the small lake, up at the waterfall and at the shattered remains of the Cylon outpost where he'd been a prisoner less than two cycles earlier. The temblor had caused the bedrock to rupture and the mountainside to crumble down on top of the base, burying it from sight. The Cylons, he reasoned, had probably planned to destroy it after launching themselves to safety. But with the planet on the verge of self-destruction, they had wasted no time with their exodus.

The next temblor might well send the debris covered outpost sliding down the mountain in a massive avalanche. Or the one after that. There was no way to know.

"Paradise," he said quietly. "If I had a bottle of ambrosa and Athena by my side...or Cassiopeia, this would be bliss."

Starbuck paused a moment, savoring his sarcasm, aware there was no one with whom to share it. The Cylons had cleared off in shuttles and fighters less than twenty centari before the temblor that caused the last avalanche. So far, he hadn't seen anybody else. Just a few lower lifeforms, small animals with fur or scales. Nothing he recognized.

The mountain loomed high above him, the drop precipitous near the waterfall but not nearly so steep even one hundred metrons to the right. Starbuck sighed and began trudging in that direction.

If he had any chance of getting off this godforsaken rock, it lay within the shattered Cylon outpost. This meant finding a way into the buried base to look around, no matter the risk.

Starbuck reached the bottom of the mountain, and craned his neck to analyze the path that would take him to a place where he might gain entrance.

"Paradise," he said again, shaking his head as a slight smile creased his cracked lips.

Then he began to climb.

9.

ALONE IN THE PILOTS' QUARTERS, Boomer dressed in silence. The chamber was poorly lit and used mostly for sleep periods and for changing. There wasn't room for much else.

He'd had a short sleep period, followed by a refreshing sonic shower. Despite the anxiety he felt, and the uncertainty which seemed to cloud every moment of late, it felt good to slip into a clean uniform. For some reason, it renewed his sense of purpose.

Not that he had any special mission to attend to this cycle. There was a problem with the mechanism that opened and closed the canopy on his Viper. The launch crew couldn't fix it, so Boomer was going to fly it over to the *Hephaestus* to have it checked out. A lot of different things could go wrong, and he didn't savor the idea of losing his life to some kind of mechanical frizzort—and he might have to launch at any moment, since Apollo's recon had discovered Cylons in this sector of space.

In Boomer's experience, people were the most vulnerable when they were in emotional turmoil. Now, with the entire fleet in turmoil, he didn't even want to think about what might happen if the Cylons found them unprepared.

A scuffle behind him caught Boomer's attention, and he turned swiftly. He didn't like having his back to the action. Some Warriors called it paranoia, others caution, and the veterans, they called it wisdom.

It was Troy.

"Major Boomer, what a relief, I thought you might be down here," Apollo's son said.

Boomer shut his locker as Troy came further into the pilots' quarters. As a ranking officer, he could have had his own quarters, something both Apollo and Starbuck had opted to do yahren ago. But Boomer taught at the Academy. He needed to be with the younger pilots to understand them. And for them to understand him.

"Something on your mind, Lieutenant?" Boomer asked, but he knew the answer. Troy was no better than Apollo at hiding his emotions.

"We've got a problem, Boomer," Troy said, eyes intense. Boomer ignored the kid's dropping of his rank. There was nobody else there, and alone, they didn't need formality. Troy was like his own nephew.

"We've got a lot of problems," Boomer answered. "What's the latest one?"

"There's been a murder," Troy answered, nodding his head, bristling with nervous energy. "Dalton and I were on *Agro-3*—we were there when the body was discovered. The poor son of a daggit is burned beyond recognition. Dalton's mother has already started running tests, trying to identify him."

"Does Cassiopeia have any guesses, yet?" Boomer asked.

"Nothing."

"Not good. With the current political climate, this kind of thing could really send people over the edge. Obviously, we want to keep it quiet, if possible," Boomer noted. "But why tell me? Isn't this something for Athena to deal with?"

Troy looked at Boomer oddly.

"Actually, I figured my father should handle it, but I can't find him or Athena," Troy said, exasperated. "Somebody's got to start cross-referencing to any missing persons reports, but I can't give that order."

Boomer stared at him.

"What?" Troy asked, impatient. "Boomer, can't you just give the order? Give me the authority as the investigator of this case, at least until I can get the official approval."

Frowning, Boomer cleared his throat. "Troy," he said softly, "your Aunt Athena is meeting with President Tigh right now. The reason you can't find Apollo is because he's left the fleet."

"What are you talking about, left the fleet?" Troy asked, confused. "Is he on a mission?"

"I'm not sure," Boomer answered truthfully. "Athena's not telling anyone anything, and Apollo didn't talk to anyone but her before he left. Still, the rumors are already going around."

Troy stared at him, eyes narrowing.

"What rumors?" the kid asked.

"Ambassador Puck has started telling people he believes that your father has left to rendezvous with the Cylons, that he's a coward, and that he's going to betray us," Boomer said, anger renewed as he thought of it.

"Feldergarb!" Troy sneered.

"Of course it is," Boomer answered. "But Puck is very persuasive. After this move, I don't think Apollo stands a chance of becoming commander. It's up to Athena now to keep Puck from the post."

The warden was nervous. Gar'Tokk could see that quite clearly. He knew the reason for the man's anxiety as well. Normally, he sat back in his cell, in the shadows he so preferred. Not now. Now, Gar'Tokk stood with his ridged nose only centimetrons from the transparent force shield that held him captive.

Gar'Tokk stared at the warden, not to intimidate the man, but merely because he was fascinated. If the dark being who had visited him in his cell had been telling the truth, the next few moments would prove quite interesting.

The warden fidgeted, glanced at Gar'Tokk, and then turned away to continue his pacing guardianship of this prison wing. From the right, another warden appeared, and called out to the first.

"Alexei!" the new arrival barked. "Come here!"

Gar'Tokk stared hard at the new warden, even as the nervous

guard, Alexei, hurried back to his superior.

But this new arrival was not Alexei's superior, was not a warden at all. The perceptions of the Borellian Nomen were far more advanced than those of other humanoids. Which explained why Alexei could not see what Gar'Tokk saw clearly.

This new arrival was not human. In fact, in a purely physical sense, he wasn't even there at all. The shimmering energy and the wan lights of the *Icarus* were poor illumination, but it was clear that this "warden" cast no shadow. None at all.

"Yes, sir!" Alexei responded, snapping to attention as he stopped in front of the shadowless being.

The ersatz officer reached out to Alexei. When his fingers touched the warden's flesh, they seemed to melt right into the arm. Alexei cried out in alarm and pain, but only for a moment. Then he stood rigid, paralyzed, eyes rolled up, as the creature's illusion disappeared and it revealed itself to be the same enigmatic being of pure warped-darkness that had appeared to Gar'Tokk in his cell.

The leader of the Nomen watched, engrossed, as the darkness seemed to flow out of its shape and seep into the warden called Alexei. In seconds, the two had merged. Alexei's eyes were no longer white, but black and undulating, as he turned to regard Gar'Tokk. When he spoke, it was with the thick, mucous-filled voice that had whispered its plan to Gar'Tokk earlier.

"We must be swift, leader of the Nomen, for this body will not last me very long," the creature said.

Merely looking at it, Gar'Tokk could see that this was so. Already, the body of Alexei seemed to be withering, drying and aging before his eyes.

"You have no body of your own, then?" Gar'Tokk asked. He feigned idle curiosity, but thirsted for knowledge of this being who was his benefactor. Knowledge, it could never be disputed, was power.

The hands of Alexei, contorting with the agony of suddenly ancient, thin fingers and jutting knuckles, deactivated the energy shield keeping Gar'Tokk in his cell.

"What you have seen is merely a projection of myself, a part of my energy. I do have a body of my own, but it is..." Alexei's mouth widened in a malevolent grin, then widened further, far enough that it split the dying warden's lower lip.

"...otherwise engaged," he finished, blood dribbling down his chin. *"Now, release your companions and follow the plan we have agreed upon."*

Gar'Tokk stepped from his cell into the corridor, blood pumping with the exhilaration of freedom. But it might be a brief moment of liberty if he did not release his fellow Nomen and destroy the other wardens.

He watched a little longer as the gnarled limbs and sunken features of the dying warden began to tear and decay, the body's dissolution gaining speed.

"We shall speak again...soon," came the viscous voice.

"The Borellian Nomen are in your debt,..." Gar'Tokk trailed off, realizing that he did not know what to call his liberator. The pause did not go unnoticed by the creature which animated the rotting corpse before him.

"You may...call me..." it croaked, then collapsed to the floor of the corridor with a clacking of bones and a puff of dust. The skull was covered with wisps of hair and flesh thin as crawlon webs. Impossibly, the jaw moved again.

"Count Iblis," the thing said, naming itself.

Then it was gone.

The Scarlet-class Viper slid through the vacuum of space, making no sounds with its engines in the airless void. Apollo was alone. Whenever his squad was on duty, he would fly in formation with at least one other pilot, often more. Boomer, Sheba, Jolly, Giles... Starbuck. He could always count on them to watch his back.

Not now. He wasn't sure exactly what Athena would tell President Tigh about his departure, nor what she might say to his friends. He might have blown everything, including his father's intention that he become fleet commander, for nothing more than a fantasy...a daydream.

But no, that was foolish thinking. What he'd experienced was far more than a daydream. It was a genuine vision. Apollo was certain.

The problem was that the people of the fleet, and the Quorum in particular, were certain to have other ideas. Still, he wouldn't turn back. He didn't know if Starbuck was still alive, or if the planet Ochoa would still be there by the time he reached it. But he had to go, no matter what it cost him, or he might as well be dead himself.

And if Athena became commander? Well, that was fine with Apollo. He wasn't sure which of them was best for the post, truth be told, but he knew she would do a fine job. And Adama himself had said Athena was eligible. She was pure-blooded Kobollian, just as he was.

Blip!

Apollo scanned the helm readout shimmering before his eyes. The Viper's scanners had picked up something. Another ship, more than likely. It had to be. But what kind of ship? Apollo could take on a couple of Cylon fighters, but if there was a base star nearby, he could be in big trouble.

Turning his attention to the Viper's scanners, he watched as the computer tried to identify the other vessel. Ship schematics flashed across the flatscreen, twenty per micron, too fast for the eye to follow. Then two words appeared: Vessel Unknown.

Apollo tensed. What to do? His mission was vital, but they were covering new territory all the time. He and Starbuck had been to Ochoa before, but they'd come at the Binary 13 system from an entirely different vector.

This ship could be from another world in the Binary 13 system, or elsewhere in the quadrant—or a new Cylon craft they'd never seen before. Theoretically, he should give it a wide berth and hope he wasn't picked up on their scanners. But the rules of engagement had changed since the fleet had left those regions of space with which they were familiar. Now every alien race was considered a potential source of information and supplies, as well as a potential ally.

Apollo was torn. He'd been delayed enough, Starbuck could be...

Pain tore through his skull. He felt pressure in his head like it was being squeezed in a vise. Even his teeth ached. Apollo's body spasmed in the cockpit of his Viper. He threw his head back, hands grasping the sides of his face.

Then it was over.

"Frack!" he gasped. "What was that?"

But to his great surprise, he discovered that he knew exactly what he'd felt. Somehow he'd been in telepathic contact with the pilot of that other ship—an alien being in such great distress it could not even sense his own presence without hurting him.

That was it exactly. The alien had sensed him. It, too, had some kind of telepathic skill. Perhaps its race communicated that way. It knew Apollo was there, and it needed his help.

It had cried out to him. How could he ignore a direct plea for assistance? Regardless of his mission, he could not.

"Computer, manual navigation now," he said, wincing as a small remnant of the pain he'd felt jolted him again.

Apollo grasped the navi-hilt and the Viper veered from its course. A moment later, he was closing on the alien vessel. The scanner blipped several more times as he approached, trying its best to give him a readout on the ship. One lifeform, unknown. The ship itself was oddly shaped, and the computer struggled to create a schematic, but Apollo ignored it. In a moment, he would have eye contact.

Despite the urgency he felt, a small thrill began to grow in him. Before the destruction of the colonies, there was a lot of galactic exploration going on. Entire corporations were established for that purpose. Though Apollo had seen only the sector where the colonies were, and where the war with the Cylons had taken him, he knew the star-maps well.

Whenever and wherever he flew, even after the destruction of the colonies when the fleet had set out across the galaxy, he was comfortable. He knew what the nearest planets were, how fast he might get there, and what to expect upon his arrival. But they had quickly passed out of the area that had been explored or mapped by human beings.

They'd been sailing into the unknown ever since. No planet could be counted on as a safe haven. They didn't even know what solar systems might be passing beyond the reach of their scanners. The Thirteenth Tribe had wandered the universe. The Kobollians, his ancestors, had visited endless worlds, according to his father's teachings. The fleet had run across myriad pockets of human or humanoid civilization over the yahren, obviously descended from a common ancestor.

But far more often, the peoples and creatures they met were completely alien, totally unlike humans except for their reliance on some kind of organized group society.

Apollo pulled back on the navi-hilt, slowing as he neared the alien ship's location. The starfield spread out before him, its familiarity deceptive. Space was an ever-expanding mystery for his people, even though they'd called it home for so long.

Something shimmered ahead with reflected starlight. A solid object. Even from this distance, the vessel's appearance startled him. He tapped the navi-hilt right, and the Viper veered off slightly. He wanted to come up next to it rather than approach it dead on.

The Viper slid closer. Apollo let the hilt go limp, stopping the ship's forward propulsion. He stared in awed silence at the bizarre craft floating in space just ahead.

At first sight, it reminded him of an avion, what the Borellian Nomen called a bird. But something wasn't right. It didn't actually resemble a bird because it had no head, no legs, no real body to speak of. A wing, then, curved at an angle, with an imperfect disk halfway along its length.

The craft itself was green, its surface gleaming despite the dark color. Apollo glanced down at the scanners to see that the computer had no idea of the ship's composition.

There didn't appear to be a cockpit; no canopy or window of any kind. It was completely sealed. Or, at least, it had been before the attack. For surely, that is what happened. The alien ship had crossed paths with an enemy, but whether native to this area of the galaxy or perhaps even Cylon, Apollo could not know.

He guided his Viper in a circuit of the alien craft. There were openings, tubes of some kind, which he hadn't noticed before, at both sides of the disk between what he surmised were the ship's wings. Engines, he wondered?

Where the ship had been damaged, at the juncture of wing and disk, something leaked from the craft, but he couldn't get any clear view of what it might be.

"Open a short range comm-cast and hail the craft," he instructed the computer.

"Hailing on all frequencies in Kobollian, Cylon and fundamental code," the computer acknowledged.

Apollo waited, hoping for some sign. He supposed he could try some telepathic contact, but even that would be useless, he felt, if the alien race did not share some basic understandings with humankind.

The Viper continued its circuit around the alien craft. Apollo examined it closely. As he passed the opening created by the vee of the wings, he saw a green light begin to flicker in the dual tubes there. Perhaps it wasn't incapacitated after all, he thought.

"What is that?" he asked the computer. "Engines powering up?"

The green light flickered brighter, and then exploded out from the alien ship, strafing Apollo's Viper with waves of destructive energy.

He was under attack.

Starbuck stood on a pile of rubble and stared down into a chasm illuminated by artificial means. He had found a way into the Cylon outpost on Ochoa. Not much of an entrance, he thought, but it would have to do.

Careful not to twist an ankle or lose his footing entirely in the loose rock that had tumbled down the mountainside, he crept toward the opening. By his judgment, more than two centons had passed while he'd scaled the mountain to reach this point in search of an entry. He'd almost given up hope when he spotted what at first seemed as if it might be nothing more than a hole in the ground.

It was a hole, of course, but not merely in the ground. The top edge of the Cylon outpost, that had once jutted out over the waterfall below, had collapsed under the avalanche. Here was a shattered passage through that ceiling. The shaft was still lit from within, he noted with relief upon first approaching. That meant that the outpost's automatic systems were still functioning.

Hope was the only thing that could have convinced Starbuck to enter that hole. But the alternative was death. Not much of a choice. He knelt by the shaft, knees abrading on crumbled rock and earth. Starbuck slid backward into the hole, holding tightly to whatever sturdy outcropping his hands could find. They were scratched and bruised already, and they were taking more punishment. But he could not stop. If he were inside next time a temblor struck, it wasn't likely he'd ever see daylight again.

Starbuck glanced back into the shaft, which didn't seem to be more than six or seven metrons deep. If he could hang down by his hands, he ought to be able to drop into the corridor without injury and move on from there.

His legs hung inside the shaft already. With great caution, Starbuck eased his hips over the edge. He put as much weight as possible on his chest as he reoriented his hands and tried to get a suitable grip. For a moment he hesitated.

The side of the shaft crumbled beneath him, and Starbuck tumbled down nearly ten metrons. He slammed into the floor of the corridor on his back, debris biting into his shoulders and the back of his head.

For the first several moments, he did nothing but struggle to breathe again. As the shock of the jolt slowly passed, the pain set in. He ached all over, but the jabbing pain of stone jutting into him forced him to move. Painfully, Starbuck rolled over onto his belly. It was a good sign, he felt, that he was able to move at all.

With a groan, he ran a hand across the back of his head, and felt sticky dampness there. Blood.

"Frack," he said mildly as he sat up.

For a moment, he felt dizzy. Then the feeling passed. Still, Starbuck merely sat there, looking up at the hole in the ceiling through which he'd fallen. The sun shone down through it, and for the first time he recognized and accepted the idea that he was very likely to die on Ochoa. And probably quite soon.

Thoughts of his family, of his comrades and friends, began to overwhelm him. Questions, mostly. Had Dalton graduated early? Had the Cylons found the fleet after the skirmish he and Apollo had with them? What had happened to Adama, whose health was in question just before Starbuck and Apollo had reached Ochoa?

Would a rescue mission be sent for him? Did they even suspect he was still alive?

No. Clearly they'd assume he'd been killed. A natural assumption given the circumstances of his crash. They had to believe he was dead and continue on. Perhaps, he thought bitterly, he had seen the last of them all, of Apollo and Athena, Boomer and Sheba, of Troy and Cassiopeia, and Dalton. He missed Dalton most of all.

Starbuck ran his fingers through his hair, took a breath, and despair began to overwhelm him. He'd meant to get up, to move on. But there didn't seem to be much point. Rather than fool himself into thinking that he might survive, he found himself wishing he could have had one last conversation with each of them.

Not that he had any significant regrets. He had grown up a bit over the yahren, and each of them surely knew how he felt about them. Even when he didn't ever seem to find the right moment to say it out loud. But, still...

"Dalton," he sighed, and shook his head.

The corridor began to shake.

"Frack!" Starbuck snapped.

The temblor came on strong, dust and stone debris sliding through the hole above. Starbuck dove down the corridor, away from the shaft, just in time to avoid being trapped under a ton of shattered mountainside. For several microns, he sprawled on his back on the floor as the temblor continued, the entire facility quaking. He was certain it was going to crack open and spill down the side of the mountain along the waterfall.

Then it subsided. A cloud of dust rose from the newly collapsed section of corridor, and he knew he wasn't going to be getting out that way.

Starbuck climbed unsteadily to his feet, despair and injuries forgotten. He stared again at the pile of earth that had almost crushed him.

"I've got to get my pogees out of here!" he said bluntly.

He turned and started down the corridor, trying to orient himself, though he'd seen very little of the outpost when he was incarcerated there. Still, he believed there was a central ascensior shaft, similar to the central core that was the axis of every Cylon base star. If he could reach that, he could access any area of the outpost not caved in by the temblors.

The latest rumble had jarred his chips slightly, for he now recalled one thing he had seen while being moved to his cell. Somewhere in the outpost was a repair hangar for damaged Cylon starships.

Starbuck moved with renewed urgency, boots slapping the corridor as he ran, racing the planet to its own destruction.

10.

IN THE COUNCIL CHAMBER, President Tigh massaged his right temple, trying to stave off the headache that had been insidiously gnawing at him for more than a centon. Not coincidentally, that was just about the amount of time they'd been in session. Never had he imagined, in the days before he became a member of the Quorum, never mind its president, that the Twelve who were the fleet's ruling body were such a collection of spineless imbeciles.

He ought to have known it, certainly. All the years Adama had served on the Quorum should have taught him what to expect: a group of men and women so frightened of potential consequences that the very idea of making a decision that wasn't forced upon them by circumstance would terrify them into inaction.

No wonder they let martial law stand for nearly two decades, even six yahren after the last Cylon sighting! They couldn't make any decisions for themselves.

Well, at least nine of them could not. This left Tigh in a one-on-one battle against Ambassador Puck for the opinions of the Quorum. They could be counted upon to take the path of least resistance, Tigh knew. Once, that would have meant naming Apollo as the new commander. However, circumstances had rapidly changed. It would be a fight now.

So be it. Tigh was ready.

The chamber was cold, but he felt warmed by the anger burning in his gut. He was ashamed of his fellow Quorum members, and he hoped whomever was chosen to fill Adama's seat would be a bit more strong-willed. He could use an ally right now.

Athena wasn't helping.

"So, let's see if I understand this correctly, Lieutenant Colonel," Tigh said, and sighed. "Apollo has left the fleet. You either don't know his destination or you are unwilling to reveal it at this time, except to say that it is on a mission of significant importance. And you want us to leave behind a message buoy and a small fuel tanker so that he can catch up with the fleet. Have I left anything out?"

Athena shook her head. "No, President Tigh, that's about the sum of it. I'm sorry I can't tell you more, but there isn't much more to tell. Except to say that both Apollo and myself happily accept our nominations for the post of commander. I accept for him by proxy, of course."

Tigh's eyes opened wide, reflecting his exasperation. Then he looked away from Athena. The walls of the Quorum chamber were a drab white, unadorned but for the elaborate pictographic symbols which represented each of the members' lost colonies.

He'd never noticed just how uncomfortable his Quorum chair was before.

"Well!" Ambassador Puck huffed, and drew himself slowly, painfully to his feet. "I hope you're pleased with yourself, Lieutenant Colonel. Perhaps you are at that, now that your brother is no longer here to oppose you. So you don't know where he is, eh?"

Athena looked at the bent, pale man and when she spoke it was with obvious disdain.

"I can't say," she said, her words clipped, her tone harsh enough to make Tigh wince. He wanted to warn her how hard he thought Puck was willing to play, but Athena wasn't foolish. She knew.

"Or you won't say!" Puck cried shrilly, raising his arms in dramatic fashion. "Do you realize, Athena, that you could be incarcerated for your lack of cooperation, here? The Quorum could lock you up on the *Icarus* for treason! In fact, I think that's exactly what we ought to do!"

"I'm sure you do," Athena hissed. "Since that would make you the primary candidate for command. On the other hand, it would make you look particularly bad."

"Now, let's not get carried away," croaked Sire Belloch, the Gemon representative to the Quorum.

Both Puck and Athena shot withering stares at Belloch, and Tigh knew it was time for him to step in. No matter the cost to himself, or his future as President.

He stood, drawing their attention immediately. Puck did not sit in deference to Tigh's rank, but he was hunched and gaunt, and Tigh's presence was the greater of the two. As long as Puck remained quiet. For when he spoke, the Ambassador was quite a powerful presence indeed.

"My fellow Quorum members," Tigh began, "we must elect a new representative from Caprica to fill Adama's seat. Only then can we vote on the command post. In the meantime, difficult decisions must be made. It is my burden that I have the power to make some of these decisions myself." Tigh waited for the reaction as the meaning of his words sank in.

The President had powers created specifically for dire situations such as this. But these powers had rarely been invoked in the history of the colonies, and he could see that the members of the Quorum were taken aback by his words. Just as they had been by his interim appointment of Apollo as commander. Frack, Tigh thought, if that disturbed them, they might have seizures when he revealed the rest of his decisions.

"In the absence of Lieutenant Commander Apollo, I am placing Lieutenant Colonel Athena in temporary command of the *Galactica* and all military operations," Tigh declared.

"You dare much, Tigh!" Ambassador Puck warned, lifting a crooked finger as if it were a weapon aimed at Tigh.

"I do what I must to preserve the integrity and security of this fleet,

Ambassador," Tigh said coldly. "Perhaps you ought to consider doing the same?"

Puck glared at him, then turned away from the table, heading for the door. Tigh did not even give him the respect of halting his speech until the man had left the chamber.

"I also nominate Lieutenant Colonel Athena for her father's vacant post on the Quorum," Tigh stated. "Even if she is not given full command, I don't see why she should be denied this position. With the absence of Apollo, and the questions surrounding his actions, Athena is clearly the most prominent Caprican in the fleet. I would like to vote on this immediately if possible."

Silence descended upon the room as Tigh let his eyes drift from face to face, gauging their reactions. He thought he might get the vote through, and that would be a step toward securing the command for Athena—or Apollo, if he ever returned. Tigh and Athena had talked a long while about her nomination. She admitted resentment that he had not consulted her. But he *had* considered her. He had only chosen Apollo because he felt that was what Adama would have wanted.

Her father had never thought Athena was less capable than his son, but was ever more protective of her. In a way, she had been Adama's favorite, though Tigh knew she would never understand such discrimination.

"President Tigh," Sire Belloch intoned grandly. "While we appreciate your..."

The chamber door hissed open and Sheba was inside the room before it had cleared the frame.

"Athena, we've got to..."

"Major Sheba!" President Tigh barked. "This is a closed council session!"

"I'm sorry, President Tigh, but it can't wait," she said. "The *Scorpius Ascendant* has declared its independence from the fleet, and will not answer any hail until Puck is given command!"

"An outrage!" Belloch cried.

"There's more," Sheba admitted apologetically. "There are protests starting all over the fleet. Word has spread that Apollo is gone, and the rumor is that he's off to meet with Cylon agents to betray us! The people are in an uproar."

"Puck!" Tigh growled, then turned on the rest of the Quorum. "Now do you see what you are dealing with?"

"But President Tigh, even if we wish to spurn him, how will the fleet respond?" Siress Kiera asked, her logic impeccable.

"What now?" Belloch asked anxiously.

"There's more," Sheba reported.

"What is it, Sheba?" Athena asked.

"There's been a murder on *Agro-3*," Sheba told her. "Troy and Dalton are investigating, and Boomer is helping out as well."

"Murder," Athena whispered. "Well, let's pray it's the only one."

There was a green flash that blotted out the starfield for a moment. Energy blasts pounded the Viper's shield, crackling tendrils snaking around the canopy. Apollo held his breath a moment in anticipation of his death. Then he exhaled with relief as he realized the shields had held.

"That's how you want to play it," he said aloud. "Fine."

Apollo gripped the navi-hilt and thrust forward. The Viper leaped into motion from its slow orbit around the injured alien craft. It continued to fire at him as the Viper peeled away. A moment later, he started to bring the starfighter around.

He wanted to blow apart the alien ship, spread its debris across a parsec of space. But Quorum policy was to preserve alien life unless absolutely necessary. Knowledge was treasure to what remained of humanity. Knowledge of the universe, to help them survive, and knowledge of themselves and their ancestors, to get them to their final destination.

Still, he wouldn't allow himself to be killed. If he died, Starbuck died. A laser blast across the nose of the craft might give the alien pause, especially since its ship seemed to be drifting, incapable of any true space battle.

At Apollo's command, the Viper dipped, avoiding a strafing blast that might have knocked out a wing if it got through his shields. The alien craft was in the center of his starfield now, and he swept down upon it as if he meant to destroy it utterly.

His thumb caressed the button that ignited the turbolasers.

"Let's see how you like it, friend," he murmured, and then fired. A laser blast burned up the space between them, passing less than a metron above the open vee which he now realized was the front of the craft.

Apollo nudged the navi-hilt right, planning to flyby close to the craft, jarring the pilot's chips even further with a scorching dose of his tylium pulsar trail. That's what he intended, at least.

Pain ripped through his skull, like anchor spikes driven into his head, and he cried out for the second time. His hands flew from the navi-hilt for a moment and he clamped them to the back of his skull as if holding it together.

"By the Lords..." he started to say.

Then the vision hit him, visceral and real.

He had an awareness of the alien ship, but it wasn't now; it was then—sometime in the recent past. He could sense the vessel around him, tight on his wide, flat, cold body. And yet, he didn't see space from inside the vessel. He saw it as a panoramic, almost all encompassing view, aware of it, seeing it all at once, but only able to focus on one area of the space around him at any give time.

The ship sliced through the silent void, its pilot searching for any sign of another presence. No scanners, no traditional comm-link of any kind, just its mind and its awareness.

Awareness of...danger! Attack!

Three black patches of nothing blotted out the starfield ahead. Like black holes, they seemed to suck away all the available light. Their shapes could only be determined by the lack of reflection, the blacker-than-endless-space hue of their hulls. They were flat, bent ovals, like...like Cylon ships, but for their color and a dorsal fin that jutted from the rear of each ship!

These couldn't be Cylons, though. They'd never had any craft like these before! These were Apollo's thoughts, however. The alien whose memories he was witnessing had no referent for any such ships.

A red light burned brightly at the bow of each of the dark craft, tendrils of crimson energy lancing out, stroking the abyss before them. Then they fired in unison, a triple blast of devastating intensity. The alien craft turned with the speed of thought, but could not prevent one of its wing tips from being sheared off.

It shrieked in torment and began to bleed green ichor. The ship was actually little more than thin armor and transport for the creature. For the most part, the alien pilot was the same size and shape as its vessel, but for the engines and weapons systems on board. When the light-sucking starfighters had fired, slashing its wing, the alien itself had been injured.

Apollo snapped his head up, once again aware of his real surroundings. The Viper drifted in space, not far from the damaged alien craft. The alien was going to die. Bleeding to death, most of its vessel's systems shorted out, it drifted in space, crying out for help...with its mind.

Apollo had heard it and responded. But by the time he approached, the creature had become almost delirious and had fired on him as it roused from slumber, in a reflexive action. For it clearly controlled the ship through a form of telepathy.

This vision had been forced upon him the way the alien's distress signal had been, as if his head had been pried open and the information inserted there. Telepathy. The creature had the most powerful mind of any being he had ever encountered, enough to pilot its ship, to see without eyes, to fly telekinetically in the skies of its home planet—another fragment of vision Apollo had caught.

"Telepathy?" a voice asked in his head. He sensed its satisfaction as it tested the word. *"Hmm, yes, telepathy."*

The alien had spoken to him. Without asking he knew that it had plumbed his mind, his knowledge, his memories, and had essentially stolen the Kobollian language from his head. He should have felt violated. Instead, he merely felt awe.

"How did you defeat them?" Apollo asked aloud, intimidated by the sound of his voice in the Viper's cockpit, but not yet comfortable with the idea of merely thinking his communication.

"*You have a warrior's mind, my...friend, yes?*" came the reply. "*Apollo is your name? I am...the closest approximation in your language would be...Valor, I think? Is this word familiar to you?*"

"Of course," Apollo sighed. "But...Valor, how did you defeat these dark fighters? Were they Cylons? What happened?"

"*I could not defeat them. They would have destroyed me,*" Valor replied. "*Instead, I merely touched their minds and...convinced them that I had gone, that their sensors showed no ship of any kind. I don't know if they were your enemies, the Cylons. Only that they have now become the enemies of my people, whom you would call the Sky.*"

"Incredible," Apollo said. He was impressed and amazed by the extent of the alien's...Valor's mental abilities. But there were more important issues at hand.

"I hope that our people can be allies, then," Apollo offered. "We are merely passing through this area of the galaxy, but if there are Cylons, or any other predatory race in this quadrant, we would be happy to offer, and to receive, friendship.

"First, though, let's see what we can do about getting you home," he added.

"*I fear that this will not be possible. Even if you could help to ignite my engines, I will surely die before I could reach my home. It is quite a distance from here,*" Valor replied.

Apollo narrowed his eyes. The ships had drifted too far from one another for him to have a clear view of the damage. He nudged the navi-hilt forward, and tylium fire erupted once again from the trio of pulsars at the rear of the Viper. He navigated around Valor's craft as slowly as his engines would allow, maneuvered himself into a better vantage point, and killed the engine again, allowing the Viper to drift.

It truly was extraordinary. From his time connected to Valor, and the design of the craft, the blood seeping from the damaged wing, he could make several assumptions. First, the Sky could survive in deep space, for the integrity of Valor's ship had been compromised without question. Second, whatever its flesh looked like, Valor was shaped similarly to his ship's design, a wide double-wing form, close to a water-creature he had once seen called a ray. Though he sensed that it did have some kind of tendril-like extremities, he wasn't certain how useful they might be.

Finally, he believed that the Sky had no eyes at all, save mental ones. The ships reflected that, for there was no window or other portal from which to see.

Green ichor spun away from the breached wingtip in strings and droplets into the vacuum of space. Apollo studied the craft's schematics, or what his Viper's computer had been able to put together via its scanners.

"*Valor,*" he thought, communicating only with his mind for the first time. "*Can you stand more pain if it means stopping the flow of blood? It's dangerous, but I think I see a way to close the wound.*"

"*Your plan is revealed to me in your thoughts, Apollo,*" came the reply. "*I have...I can hear the phrase in your mind...'I have nothing to lose.'*"

No time to waste, then, Apollo thought. To himself, this time, not to Valor. If Valor lived, Apollo would have to inform him that very few humans had access to their innate telepathic abilities. Due to their reliance on privacy, most humans would be frightened even by the concept. Since Valor's people lived by telepathy, he wasn't sure the alien would understand. But such concerns were for later, after the Sky pilot was out of danger.

Apollo reignited his engines and pushed the navi-hilt to the right, taking a long slow arc to reorient his Viper's trajectory. After a moment, he was perpendicular to Valor's craft, canted slightly to one side. He could see the damage—and the creature's blood, seeping freely from the shattered wing.

"Computer," he ordered, "turbo laser power at two percent. Narrow beam at one half of one percent in diameter. Give me the best approximation you can to a med-tech's finite micro laser."

"Acknowledged. Laser adjustment executed. Fire at will," the computer replied.

"Prepare yourself, Valor," Apollo said aloud.

"*I will try to shield you from the pain. Otherwise you will not be able to finish and we may both die,*" Valor replied.

His aim guided by the Viper's computer, Apollo fired on the alien vessel. The powered-down laser's fine beam struck the savaged wing of the craft and slowly edged across until it touched the surface of Valor's long, ragged wound.

Pain spiked through Apollo's head, and he winced and gritted his teeth. But it was manageable. Valor was screaming the only way he knew how, venting his suffering in psychic wails of pain, but somehow he succeeded in shielding Apollo from the worst of it.

Grimly, Apollo continued. As quickly as possible, and with all the precision the computer could muster, he scorched the alien's raw flesh with his weakened turbo lasers, closing the massive wound. The crew who'd designed and built the original Vipers, and even the Scarlet-class ship he was flying, never would have imagined the laser being put to such use.

And it worked.

"Valor?" he said aloud.

There was no response, and Apollo began to feel quite alone again. There was a comfort and intimacy to telepathic contact, a warmth in the cold void. But it was gone. He couldn't sense Valor at all.

"*Valor?*" Apollo thought. "*Are you...alive? Awake? Can you hear me?*"

"*I hear you, Apollo. Thank you for my life,*" came the response. Apollo was elated.

"Not at all," he replied. "I only wish it could have been less painful for you. Now we just have to get your ship running again. Any idea how to do that?"

There was a pause as Valor considered the question. Apollo looked out of his canopy at the other ship, at the closed wound, no longer bleeding. Still, the craft was damaged and open to the void. He wondered momentarily why Valor even needed the ship at all. If his people could fly telekinetically, why would they need starships?

Rest, he reasoned. *They couldn't rest.* And, of course, they wouldn't have any weapons systems.

"Your entire craft, including the engine, is based on an entirely different technology from mine. You wouldn't even understand how my ship is built, never mind how the engine functions. However, there are certain similarities. Though my vessel is telepathically piloted, there are internal systems that have been affected by the attack, including my ignition system. Internal scans indicate that the engine is still functioning, but cannot be ignited," Valor's thoughts filled Apollo's mind.

"Here is what I propose," the alien began, and then told Apollo of his plan. *"It could kill us both. I will understand, Apollo, if you do not wish to try it. I see in your mind that this delay alone may have cost you much."*

Valor was right. Even if its plan did work, Apollo knew that he might have to return to the fleet before he could continue on to rescue Starbuck. Could he risk Starbuck's life for Valor's?

But, he knew this wasn't truly the question. The real question was, could he simply leave Valor stranded in space, merely to die more slowly now that he was no longer bleeding?

There was only one answer.

"Let's try it," he said aloud. "But let's be quick about it. Meanwhile, tell me what you can about hostile races in this quadrant."

Apollo gripped the navi-hilt and gave the pulsars quick bursts to guide the Viper around behind the Sky vessel. At the jutting point that was the ship's aft end, he could see the dimly glowing green light that confirmed the engine was still functioning. With small pulsar bursts, manipulating the retro rockets that were only used for such delicate moves, he began to turn the Viper into position.

"The only hostile presence in our quadrant is recent, Apollo. Perhaps you are right, perhaps they are the same race as those whom you call 'enemy.' I believe you named them Cylons. We have

not seen them, really—only the results of their passing. Their scouts have been in the quadrant, apparently preparing to set up one or more outposts here.

"*The Sky will not allow this,*" Valor vowed.

"It might not be as simple as that," Apollo said, watching the read-out that shimmered in the transparent energy flow of his helm. Information flashed by rapidly and he tried to take it all in while piloting his Viper.

"If you plan to battle the Cylons, for as long as our fleet is in the area you should consider us your allies," Apollo said. "Only know that we are trying to avoid them, and will do our best to help without jeopardizing the civilian population of the fleet. I wish I could do more."

"*You are about to risk your life for me, Apollo. That is more than I might ever have expected,*" Valor responded.

The Viper was in place. Apollo paused a moment, shut his eyes and prayed to God and the Lords of Kobol and to the spirit of his father, which he felt certain was still with him. Then he opened his eyes, breathed deeply to center himself, and relied on his skill and training. Concentration. Meditation. Inner vision.

"Computer, purge half our remaining tylium fuel," he instructed.

The Viper's instruments went wild with calculations, sending the information through its uplink to his helm so that the same numbers then appeared on the helm readout.

"Observation: there will not be fuel enough to reach Ochoa and return to the *Galactica,*" the computer voice crackled.

"Commence purge," Apollo instructed, chest tightening a little. It was as he suspected. He would have to return to the fleet before going after Starbuck. If Starbuck lived that long. But he might already be dead as far as Apollo knew. He could only hope his friend would hang on, stay alive. Then again, that had always been what Starbuck was best at—staying alive.

"Purge commencing," the computer confirmed.

Apollo heard the hydraulic sound of a pump somewhere in the back of the ship. Tylium fuel was being siphoned from the tanks out into space, drifting into the ten metron gap that separated the Viper's massive engine funnel and the relatively small tube that performed a similar function for Valor's Sky fighter.

"*Whether or not this works,*" Apollo thought, "*I doubt we'll see one another again.*"

"*Thank you, Apollo. I owe you an extraordinary debt,*" Valor replied.

"Just survive," Apollo muttered to himself, smiling grimly. "Otherwise I'll never be able to collect."

Apollo wiped his right hand on his jacket, wrapped his fingers around the navi-hilt, and gave it a full forward thrust. It was as if he were launching from a standstill in space. The g-force whipped him back against his chair and tylium fire blazed from the pulsars. The liquid tylium gas he'd vented ignited immediately in a momentary conflagration of incredible proportions.

As the Viper shot away, burning even more of its fuel, the blazing tylium ignited Valor's engine, which caught immediately. A thin green flame jetted from the back of the Sky craft. The engine was lit, a tiny green beacon skittering away into the void of space as Apollo's Viper hurtled ahead, slicing through the starfield at top speed.

Distantly, as if it were a dream he was rapidly forgetting upon waking, Apollo heard the psychic thanks that Valor sent. He was alive, and on his way. That was good. But Apollo's heart was heavy. Even if he made his way back to the *Galactica* at top speed, he held out little hope for Starbuck's survival. Some part of him knew his friend would be dead before he could reach him.

There was no way...

Blip!

"Huh?" Apollo muttered with a start, staring at the Viper's scanners. His helm hadn't picked up the presence of any other ship or space debris, nor any comet or asteroid.

Blip! Blip!

Two more? What could be...he started to ask, and then the question was answered. Three large patches of the starfield ahead were completely blanked out, as if the light in them had been consumed by some voracious beast. The patches were blacker than the everlasting night of the void, and Apollo knew immediately that he was facing Valor's attackers.

Valor had only survived because he could telepathically convince them he was gone. Apollo was a natural telepath, but less than a novice where the use of that ability was concerned. He had not been able to duplicate Valor's trick.

The scanners went berserk trying to log the new vessels' schematics into its system, worse than it had with Valor's ship. It couldn't seem to get a clear reading, and Apollo guessed that was for the same reason that the light of space seemed to bend around these vessels.

"Computer, try to scan the ships' interiors, see what kind of creature is flying those things!" he cried.

Apollo didn't wait. His thumb felt for the aim button on the navihilt and he held it down. His helm readout changed, showing the tracking system that was linked with the ship. It zeroed in on the middle of the attackers' ships just as all three of them fired on him.

He jerked the hilt to the right, and all three shots missed, but he didn't think he'd be as lucky with the second volley.

"Readings unclear, but vessels and passengers appear to be...Cylon," the computer croaked.

"By the Lords," Apollo growled. "If they're all like this now, the fleet doesn't stand a chance."

The center ship came into the aiming grid again, and Apollo thumbed the "fire" button. Both turbolasers blasted, sending what should have been lethal bolts at his attackers.

But Apollo had never returned the turbolasers to full power. He couldn't even scratch the Cylon fighters at the current setting, and they were bearing down on him, weapons blazing.

11.

AFTER LANDING ABOARD THE *HEPHAESTUS*, Boomer had to pop the canopy clean off his Viper just to get out of the cockpit. He climbed down and explained the situation to the serviceman who greeted him. Informed that repairs would take only a centon or so, Boomer decided to wait, rather than shuttle back to the *Galactica*.

He only wished he'd brought something to read.

"Is there a lounge on the Forge?" he asked, using the ship's nickname, which he knew her crew preferred.

"Yes, sir, Major," the serviceman responded. "Just take the ascensior one flight. You can even see the repair bay from the overlook windows."

Strange concept of a scenic view, Boomer thought with amusement. But he didn't put voice to the comment. No need to insult those who would be doing him a service. He'd been told the shipbuilders and servicemen of the Forge were paid notoriously low wages. He felt for them. After all, they were worth their weight in oregg. Where would the fleet be without them?

Boomer decided he'd have to speak with Apollo about it. Or Athena. Or whoever became commander when the confusion created by Adama's passing had settled.

He rode the ascensior in silence, just one level. When the doors hissed open, he was greeted by dim, multi-colored lights and the noxious odor of cheap fumarello smoke. At least Starbuck had sprung for expensive smokes, he thought wistfully, missing his old friend.

Tankards clanked together at the bar, and raucous laughter rolled across the room toward him. Boomer glanced at the bar, where an attractive Gemon woman, lithe and pale, suffered the comments of half a dozen blackshirts with admirable restraint. The Quorum security men had been there drinking for a while, that much was clear.

Other than the blackshirts, there were perhaps a dozen patrons in the lounge. Mostly techs and pilots, all civilian. Boomer was the only Warrior. Like him, however, the rest seemed to be waiting on their ships, or for parts they would install themselves. All but the blackshirts.

Odd.

Boomer slid into a metal chair at an unsteady table by the window. He looked out on the repair bay and admired the four Scarlet-class Vipers that were being completed on the far side of the massive chamber. His own Viper was only four yahren old, but the servicemen had stationed it near the newer starfighters, and side by side, his ship just didn't measure up.

A servitor hovered nearby, and Boomer ordered a tankard of grog he didn't want, just to be courteous. After the servitor left, Boomer sensed another presence behind him.

"Well, well, what have we here?" a deep voice asked. "One of our *new commander*'s loyal house-daggits. Tell us, Major, are all the Warriors willing to follow the vanity games of the Kobollians and wander around the universe forever?"

Boomer didn't turn right away. His eyes narrowed and he gritted his teeth, so he took a moment and a breath to calm himself. He'd always had a bit of a temper, even more so than Apollo. Finally, he turned slowly in his chair to see that the blackshirts had followed their security chief across the lounge to hedge him in. The chief looked familiar, his red-hued skin marking him as a Tauran.

"Do I know you, Chief?" he asked evenly, not rising from his chair.

"How quickly they forget, eh, Major?" the chief snarled. "You drummed me out of the Academy eight yahren ago. What were the words again? Oh yes, 'Cadet Paris would be far better at crashing Vipers than flying them.' You always were a pompous fool."

"I remember you now, Paris," Boomer said, rising to his feet angrily. "You obviously haven't learned anything in eight yahren. I could arrest you right now for sedition, the way you're talking."

Paris laughed.

"It's you and Apollo and all the others who should be arrested for sedition, Boomer," he growled. "It took Adama's death and Ambassador Puck's inspiration to make us see it, but this entire fleet has been trailing around after an old man's ravings and pride for near on two decades. We've worked as hard or harder than we would have if we'd simply colonized a habitable planet. Just to keep going, Major. You understand? Just to keep going nowhere, we've sweated to find new fuel sources, new food sources, to cannibalize ships so the traitors of the Forge can repair your warships and build new starfighters."

"That's enough, Paris!" Boomer snarled.

"You're a fool, Boomer, led by an even bigger fool who is nothing but a pale shadow of his father," Paris roared, glancing around at his friends for support and encouragement. "Adama might have been crazy, but at least the old man had pogees. In fact, I've heard Apollo left the fleet to betray us to the Cylons. He's just another Baltar, isn't he?"

Boomer had tried so hard to hold in his rage that his head throbbed. Now he let it out. His nostrils flared and he dove for the man. Paris lifted an arm to block his attack, and Boomer broke it with a lightning strike of his hand. It was a clean snap, echoing through the lounge, and Paris wailed with pain.

Then the other blackshirts came after him. Boomer taught hand-to-hand combat at Academy, among other things. But there were five of them, not including Paris, and he wasn't at all sure of his chances. A flurry of blows rained down and he dodged or blocked most of them, returning harder blows in kind. He cracked a jaw, ruptured a solar plexus, and fractured a vertebrae.

He was beyond rage now, but in the back of his mind he knew what he could get away with. These men were seditionists he was trying to arrest. Everything he did would be seen as that and nothing more. He made them hurt.

There was a brush against his side and he glanced down even as Paris snatched Boomer's blaster with his good hand. The others backed away the moment they saw that Paris had Boomer covered. They nursed their injuries, glaring at him with anger and smug satisfaction now that they truly did have the upper hand.

He ought to have known, that's what Boomer thought as Paris leveled the blaster at him, as he watched the grin spread across the security chief's face. He ought to have known something was wrong here.

Unless they were the security detail meant to be working the *Hephaestus* to begin with, the men had no reason to be there except to cause trouble. But six seemed too large a number for one detail on this ship, and if they were supposed to be on duty, what were they doing drinking grog?

Surely they hadn't come here just so Paris could have his revenge on Boomer? Eight yahren later, the idea was ridiculous.

"Time to pay, Boomer," Paris sneered. "Just as everyone who isn't loyal to the fleet, as everyone who still supports Adama's family will pay."

Boomer glared at him, tensed, and waited for an opening. "You've been sniffing plant vapors, Paris," he said grimly. "There are witnesses here, and a lot of them. You'll be locked up on the *Icarus* in a centon. All of you."

"Wrong," Paris sighed, as if even the response was beneath him. "Once Ambassador Puck takes command, we'll be hailed as heroes. Goodbye, Major Boomer."

Boomer stared down the laser sight of his blaster. He smiled. Paris frowned in return. Boomer started to chuckle slightly and reached a hand up to cover his mouth to prevent himself from laughing out loud.

"He's laughing at you, Paris," one of the other blackshirts said in surprise. "Why don't you scorch him right now?"

"He's just hiding his fear," Paris retorted angrily.

Even as Paris held the blaster a bit higher, ready to pull the trigger, Boomer lunged forward. Paris tried to blast him, and nothing happened. Shocked, the security chief looked down at the weapon, trying to determine what had gone wrong.

Boomer was on him. He grabbed the weapon, twisting it out of Paris's hand and breaking a finger or two in the process, judging by the snapping sound of it. He punched the man hard in the face, only once, and Paris went down on his knees. The blackshirt leader cradled his injured fingers and merely stared at Boomer's blaster, blood dripping from his nose onto his mouth and chin.

The other blackshirts were so astonished they hadn't even begun an attack. Boomer stepped back and covered them all, the tables turned again.

"You're all under arrest," Boomer declared. "Attempted murder of a Colonial Warrior is only one of the charges. And as for you, Paris," he added, "you should have done your research. The Forge techs have been introducing personal blasters for more than a yahren. They don't fire for anyone but their imprinted owner."

He urged them toward the exit with his sidearm.

"Now let's go," he said. "And keep quiet before you start to really annoy me. Then I'd have to shoot you before you even face the Tribunal. I don't want to hear a sound from you the whole shuttle ride to *Icarus*."

"Shuttle!" one of the blackshirts cried in alarm. "We can't go on the…"

"Enough!" Paris shouted, silencing the talkative blackshirt with angry glare.

Boomer narrowed his eyes. What was that all about?

Then the repair bay exploded with a massive concussion blast that nearly stopped Boomer's heart. The long glass windows behind him blew in, and the force of the blast knocked them all down. Glass cut through his uniform, and his temple struck a table as he fell.

Smoke and fire filled the Forge.

In the harsh light of her station within the *Galactica's* med-lab, Cassiopeia struggled to keep her mind on her work. The fleet was in an uproar. Apollo had left, for reasons apparent to no one, except perhaps Athena. Word was already leaking out about the murder on *Agro-3*—Cassie had heard about it from several sources, including her daughter, Dalton, who was one of the investigating officers.

Though he hadn't made any overt moves that might be considered treason or sedition, it was clear that Ambassador Puck's followers were prepared to do just about anything to put him in power. Already the *Scorpius Ascendant* had threatened secession. As far as Cassiopeia knew, the ship might have already left the fleet. Others might follow. There were already growing protests aboard the *Adena* and the *Delphi*.

That was just scratching the surface. She knew that the fleet was torn because she herself had questions about what the right course of action was. It wasn't merely the leadership of the fleet, or command of its battlestar. It was the future that primarily concerned all of them.

She wanted to stop. They'd been traveling so long that it was difficult for her to remember what it was like to actually live on a planet. To have a home that wasn't simply another chamber on a space vessel. Despite her position as one of the *Galactica's* crew, she wasn't a Warrior. People talked to her. And in her days as a socialator, she had become quite good at listening, trying to figure out what her clients wanted.

Cassiopeia knew that a lot of the fleet's civilian population felt they had traveled far enough. They wanted to stop, to colonize the first suitable planet. It sounded wonderful, but Cassie had been close to Commander Adama, almost part of the family. She knew the power of his vision for the future of mankind and of his belief that they would find Earth—that it was their destiny.

She didn't want to abandon that dream, or its power, which was why she had backed the Gemon Matriarchs' movement to have Athena nominated for the command post. It had felt like a small betrayal at the time, for she loved Apollo as if he were her own brother. But it was the right thing to do. Apollo's subsequent actions only reinforced the fact that Athena was the more practical, reliable of the siblings.

Still, without Adama there seemed to be no figurehead, no leader who could pull the fleet together. But someone had to step forward. Someone had to stop the escalating conflict within the fleet.

"Not me," she said softly. Cassiopeia had a job to do. Identifying the murdered man. Which was proving to be much harder than it ought to have been.

Still, she bent back to her work with diligence. Carefully, she used a scanning microlaser to extract yet another cell sample from the corpse. As she did so, the sound of soft footfalls echoed in the otherwise empty med-lab behind her. The rest of the staff had gone on meal break.

"Who's there?" Cassiopeia asked, craning her neck around the wall of her med-station.

"Hi, Cassie," Athena said, striding across the lab toward her.

She looked resplendent in her blue-and-white Warrior's uniform, so much more formal than the pilot's crimson and black. Cassiopeia had always been able to see why Starbuck cared so much for Athena. Not only had they shared much of their youth together, but she was the total opposite of Cassie herself, like oglivs and beschkurd.

"Athena," Cassiopeia said. "Nice to see you. How are you faring, given all the brouhaha?"

"The situation is escalating out of control," Athena admitted with a heavy sigh. "Though the Quorum has finally seen the light to some extent. They're afraid to openly oppose Puck because of the incredible backing that has sprung up almost out of nowhere for the man. But Tigh has named me acting commander until the vote, and I have been officially elected to the Quorum to fill my father's seat."

Cassiopeia brightened. "That's the best news I've heard in cycles," she said. "Puck must have blown a chip."

"Puck doesn't know yet," Athena said darkly. "But he can do nothing about it. It was a majority vote, as required. There are protests all over the fleet, on dozens of ships, and the *Scorpius Ascendant* is still traveling with us, but has officially separated itself from Quorum rule, or assistance. That won't last, but it doesn't look good. It's only going to get worse, I fear, at least until the Quorum chooses a commander or finds a way to show the fleet Puck's true colors. He's an arrogant, self-serving man, who seems to thrive on creating trouble."

Athena sighed, again. "Then, of course, there's this murder," she said.

"I wish I could offer some relief," Cassiopeia said. "But I'm afraid if you've come for an update on our charred friend here, I don't have much news for you."

Athena frowned. "What's wrong? Scanners giving you trouble?"

"More complicated than that, actually, and something of a mystery," Cassiopeia replied. "Come have a look."

Athena followed her to the med-station, which included a long examination table upon which the burned corpse lay. Cassiopeia was used to the presence of the dead, but it occurred to her that Athena might be disturbed by such a sight. She moved to cover the cadaver, but Athena waved her off, realizing her concern and dismissing it.

"He must have died horribly," Athena observed.

The table beneath the corpse gleamed white, as did nearly everything else at the station. The lab's harsh light gave even more illumination reflected off the highly polished surfaces. The computer station was a dark stain on the immaculate lab, as was the blackened corpse itself.

"Or is it a she?" Athena wondered aloud.

"That, at least, I've determined," Cassie replied. "Definitely a male. But I learned that from actual physical examination rather than any genetic testing. I was just taking another cell sample when you arrived. I'll show you the problem."

As Athena watched, Cassiopeia used the microlaser to cut a fresh, deep sample from the corpse, a speck of flesh, no more. She placed it on a small transparent slide and inserted the slide into the med-unit analyzer linked to the flatscreen and micronoscope.

"At first I thought the body was so burned that I could not get a proper genetic sample from the upper layers of the flesh. Then I went deeper," she explained.

Athena watched expectantly, but Cassiopeia wanted her to get a closer look.

"Come here," she beckoned. "I want you to see this."

Interest obviously piqued, Athena approached. Cassie stood aside to let the other woman, once her rival, now tentatively her friend, get a better look at the computer screen. Together, they watched as the screen began to fill with gibberish, words and numbers, combinations of letters and symbols.

"I know you're not a tech," Cassiopeia noted. "Let me assure you that what you're seeing means absolutely nothing. We are supposed to be seeing a complete genetic map, which would then be matched with one of the citizens of the fleet, all of whom have had their genetic codes recorded."

"Yet this is an otherwise adequate sample?" Athena asked, confused.

"Perfectly adequate," Cassie assured her. "In fact, in the case of that solium leak last yahren, I had two bodies in worse condition, and had no problem getting gene-matches for them."

"Then what is it, faulty equipment?" Athena asked, looking more closely at the bizarre computer readings.

"I did gene-maps and matches for ten other subjects, five living and five deceased," Cassiopeia informed her. "All the others checked out fine. It's just this one."

"So what could be causing this anomaly?" Athena asked, looking up at her.

Cassiopeia's attention was locked on the mysterious corpse on the examination table. Then she looked back at Athena.

"That's just what I'd like to know."

At the heart of a Cylon base star, not too terribly distant from the Binary 13 system, Baltar stared in astonishment at the newly designed armored creatures in Lucifer's command chamber.

Yet, coupled with this new development, he was buoyed by the knowledge that he wielded a secret power. The power of information.

Information imparted to him by a dark visitor to the base star, a creature whose voice seemed oddly familiar, a creature that called itself Count Iblis.

Count Iblis, the legendary adversary of the House of Kobol. And, if Iblis was to be believed, Baltar's own ancestor.

Baltar smiled inwardly, even as he stared at the gleaming ebony shrouds of these new arrivals. *New Cylons,* he corrected himself. For surely, that's what they were.

"Well, Baltar," Lucifer asked, his tone a mockery as always. "Don't you have anything to say to your children?"

It was the second time Lucifer had made such a reference. Baltar smiled broadly and approached the dark Centurions with confidence. They would not harm him unless Lucifer ordered it, he knew.

"Magnificent!" he crowed. "They are a crowning achievement, Lucifer. A new breed of Cylon, obviously, and far superior to the more common Centurion, I imagine. But why do you insist upon referring to them in relation to me?"

Lucifer turned slightly, sparkling electronic eyes regarding Baltar with cybernetic disdain.

"Why?" Lucifer asked. "Haven't you determined that for yourself, Baltar? Not only are these Centurions far superior and more deadly in every way to their brethren, but they are equipped with a new brain implant as well—a *Human Logic Function*, if you will."

Baltar stared in horror at the creatures, his secret advantage forgotten for the moment.

"Do you mean to say that these vile mechanoid creatures have minds modeled after my own?" Baltar asked.

"Of course," Lucifer replied. "You didn't actually believe the Imperious Leader allowed you to live because you were a great Warrior?"

He paused as Baltar grew pale and began to back away from the high seat of command.

"Oh, I see that you did," Lucifer said, without pity. "Poor fool. Centurions, execute Baltar. We shall suffer the presence of humans no longer."

12.

THE CYLON OUTPOST ON OCHOA had suffered far more damage than Starbuck had initially estimated. Though the corridor through which he had gained reentry remained substantially intact, other areas were sealed off entirely by debris from collapsed ceilings. Lights flickered, floors were split by impassable chasms, and small tremors caused the entire facility to shudder and moan—a constant reminder that its dying breath might be only microns away.

Yet, rather than becoming more desperate, Starbuck grew ever more resolute. While another might have been tempted to simply sit and await destiny, Starbuck forged ahead. He had spent a lifetime creating his own fate, and he refused to even consider the alternative.

Another rumble shivered through the base. This one felt different somehow, as if its source were not shifts in the planetary crust beneath the Cylon structure, but some other geological event taking place nearby. Images of volcanic eruption entered his mind, but Starbuck pushed them away. He had more than enough to worry about.

Starbuck strode down the corridor as quickly as he could manage. This entire area of the facility was canted to one side, and he suspected he was approaching the section which had sheared off and tumbled down the mountainside. Any minute, more of the structure might give way.

A dozen times he had been forced to change course, descending through pried open ascensior shafts and climbing hills of rubble to reach an upper level. Side corridors led him away from the central core, which was his goal. Finally, he thought he was approaching the core, and now this: a chasm five metrons across.

The temblors had pulled the facility apart in many places, but this was one of the worst. Looking up, Starbuck could see that the rift had also separated the floor on the level above—several levels, in fact. Peering into the chasm, it was clear to him that the lower level had also been torn apart, but not quite so far: two metrons at best. Fallen debris from the floors above had sifted down far enough that the rift on the lower level was partially filled with rubble.

Starbuck had no rope, no grapple, nothing with which to lower himself. The edges of the chasm were ragged, filled with frayed, sparking cables, and looked liable to erode even further at any provocation. It appeared he had come to an impasse.

But when inaction meant certain, inevitable death, Starbuck knew he had to press on. Should he die now, trying to stay alive, or later as the planet finally tore itself apart, he would be no more or less dead.

"Lords of Kobol," he muttered under his breath, "I'm not a praying man. Actually, I'm a betting man. But only a fool would wager in my favor today. So a little prayer couldn't hurt. Lords, you're closer to God than the rest of us, maybe you could help me out."

Starbuck stared at the hole, comforted, even re-energized by the sound of his own voice. "Starbuck, old buddy, you've just got to stop talking to yourself."

With only a moment's hesitation, he stepped toward the chasm and jumped. Arms up, legs bent, he fell through the gaping hole in the floor toward the debris clogged, smaller hole one level below. He meant to hit, crouch into a roll, and move away from the breach as quickly as possible. It might have worked, for the fall itself was not more than five or six metrons. He'd been a bit out of shape before getting shot down, but captivity had done wonders for reminding him, body and soul, what it was to be a Warrior.

Starbuck plummeted down through the gap. His feet slammed into the piled rubble and he thought, momentarily, that he might break an ankle or tear something else vital. Instead, the debris simply gave way beneath his weight.

He scrambled for purchase, but slid helplessly through the narrower hole along with a cascade of shattered flooring. Starbuck opened his mouth to shout his favorite expletive, but was silenced by a sudden impact to the back of his head. He fell through to the level below and was half buried by the fragments that continued to fall on top of him.

With a groan, Starbuck sat up, brushing structural shrapnel from his legs. He felt the back of his head and found only a growing lump. The lack of blood relieved him, though his earlier wound was still sticky.

"This is getting ridiculous," he said aloud, but without a smile.

Starbuck climbed to his feet and surveyed his surroundings. This level was relatively intact, the crack in the corridor floor only centimetrons wide as far as he could tell. The lights flickered and buzzed, snapped on for several seconds and then went completely dark before beginning to flicker on again.

After taking a moment to orient himself, Starbuck started down the corridor in the direction of the central core of the outpost. Once again, the structure began to shiver beneath his feet. Not significantly, but with the whispered promise of the cataclysm to come.

To his surprise, Starbuck realized that he recognized this particular corridor. It was the very level from which he had made his potentially suicidal and yet miraculous escape attempt. Which meant that if he moved away from the mountain side of the base, he would come eventually to the collapsed mountain or the wide open, sheared-off edge of the outpost. The chamber wherein he had been held captive was likely gone now, buried at the bottom of the waterfall.

But if he remembered correctly, a right turn at the next juncture should bring him to his goal. He turned, saw a broad, scarlet hydraulic door at the end of the hall.

Then the corridor went dark.

Starbuck paused, waiting for the light to return. After a moment, he had to assume it was not going to. Determined, he continued on, and tried his best to peer into the darkness. His steps were cautious, searching, yet still he stumbled several times.

He reached the door and began to search its frame with his hands, trying to find the button, lever or switch which would open it. There in the darkness, feelings of despair and helplessness began to steal over him for the first time. He had to open the door but couldn't even see where it was. His only chance of survival—and a remote chance it was—lurked on the other side. There was access to the chamber from upper levels as well, he believed. But that would require backtracking in the darkness, and trying to climb up through shattered floors or damaged ascensior tubes without the ability to see potential dangers.

"Just so you know," he whispered aloud, "this is not my idea of a good time."

Starbuck's fingers finally found a wide plate attached to the door frame. The plate was inset with a large oval button. He pressed it, praying that there was still power running through the base's systems. With a loud hiss, the door cycled open.

Eerie red light flooded in, and Starbuck blinked the darkness away. The chamber behind the door must have had emergency backup generators, he reasoned. Perfectly logical, and a total relief.

But his relief only lasted a moment. The huge chamber was blanketed by debris, its vast ceiling apparently having given way during one temblor or another. The distant wall of the hangar was blocked by mountains of rubble, and he could only assume that end had once been open to the outside.

In the dim red emergency light, he could see that there had been three Cylon fighters under repair within the facility. First glance told him all of them were at least partially covered with debris. Second glance confirmed that all had suffered damage as a result. Even if the Cylon techs had fixed the fighters before the exodus—which was unlikely since they had been left behind—the ships would not be viable now.

Silently, Starbuck put a hand to his forehead and massaged his left temple. He closed his eyes, and considered sitting down. A simple act, sitting. He could find a relatively comfortable place to rest while the world ended. There seemed to him something almost poetic about that. But he'd never been a poet.

"Cut the feldergarb, Captain," he chided himself.

Starbuck didn't have the knowledge to repair a Cylon Raider, and he was fairly certain he did not have the time either. But it occurred to him that if he could find one of the outpost's flatscreens and access it, he might be able to contact the Colonial fleet. It was possible someone could talk him through repairs minor enough to get him safely into space and keep him alive long enough for help to arrive to tow him in.

As for the hangar's blocked entry, if he had a working Raider, he could blast his way out. He didn't see much potential for survival in his plan. But it was the only plan remaining to him, and therefore, the best course of action.

On a Colonial vessel, he knew, all landing, launch and repair bays were outfitted with comm systems and computer terminals. The Cylons were not human, that much he knew. But their technology was similar enough that it seemed logical to think he might find the corresponding systems here in the hangar.

Starbuck began to search. The red light threw odd shadows. It cast a nightmarish pall over the hangar, the debris, and the damaged Raiders. Starbuck ignored everything but his search. In particular, he did his best to ignore the quiet rumble of the earth and the intermittent sliding, shifting noises that the debris made as it continued to settle. He tried not to think about what remained of the ceiling above, and the splintered mountain above that, all of it waiting to come down from a big enough jolt.

Carefully, he climbed over a small mound of debris. Ten centari of searching had turned up nothing. Now he moved around one of the damaged fighters, which didn't actually seem to be completely ruined, and saw some kind of station in the corner of the chamber. Screen, chair, broad keyboard, all somehow preserved from the catastrophic events thus far.

"By the Lords," Starbuck said aloud. *If God meant for me to die, he wouldn't keep teasing me this way.*

He scrambled down the small mound of rubble. Started for the comm station…and fell.

"Frack!" he cried as he dropped painfully to hands and knees. "Enough falling, already!"

Angrily, he stood and started across toward the station. Belatedly, he recalled something his peripheral vision had caught microns before. The silver gleam of armor, turned red in the emergency light. Starbuck turned quickly and stared at the place he had fallen, realizing for the first time what he had tripped over.

Half buried under the rubble was the outpost's only remaining Cylon.

The info-feed in Apollo's helm scrolled sensor readings, scanner reports, tactical suggestions, and a low-fuel warning, but the letters and numbers sped by faster than the eye could follow. Apollo didn't even try to take it all in.

He was busy trying to stay alive.

"Computer!" Apollo cried. "Recalibrate turbo lasers to full power and beam width! Now!"

Too late. The sleek, ebony Cylon Raiders erupted with another, far more accurate barrage of laser fire. Apollo jerked the navi-hilt to the left, giving the Scarlet-class Viper a one hundred-eighty degree tilt.

The first volley had missed him. Three Cylon Raiders were a threat, but he'd beaten such odds before. This was different. He had no way of knowing what capabilities these new fighters had, and they already had the advantage on him.

"Lasers recalibrated," the computer informed him.

He didn't even have time to fire as a Cylon laser blast burned right through the Viper's force shield and into the aft section of the ship. The force of the hit knocked him off course, and Apollo struggled with the navi-hilt to keep his bearings.

Then the Raiders were past him and already slowing, course-correcting, clearly quicker to come around than any starship he had ever seen. He had five or ten microns, no more.

"Damage report!" he demanded, but the computer was ahead of him. The holo-scanner burst to life, showing a three-dimensional image of his Viper. The fuel tanks were untouched, fortunately, but the pulsar and gyro-capacitor systems had been torched. Already he could hear the Viper hitching, and he prayed it would not simply seize up and shut down in space, leaving him a helpless target.

The onscreen scanners showed that the Viper's systems had finally constructed a readout on the Cylon vessels. They did seem to bend light around them, and thus would have appeared almost invisible against the blackness of space if not for the starfield. Yet when they'd first appeared, they had been more than simply black. They'd been like tears in the fabric of space, their absence of light the only way to actually locate them. His scanners hadn't picked them up until they'd been about to attack, as if they had literally appeared from nowhere.

What Apollo wanted to know was, how?

Blip!

Frack, they were fast, coming around again already. Apollo slammed the navi-hilt to the right. The Viper did not respond. He moved it to the left, still without response. Left and right, he tried again, but with the navigational systems damaged, at least partially, the navi-hilt was not functioning properly.

His only recourse seemed to be flight. But if he tried to outrun them, he would be out of fuel in less than a centon, and he had the feeling they were faster than his Viper. He wasn't going to get away.

Blip! Blip!

The other two had also come around to pursue him. They were far enough behind because he had stayed his course, but there were only microns for him to respond, somehow, or die.

Unless the navi-hilt wasn't completely fried! Apollo pulled back on the hilt as hard as he could, and the Viper groaned and responded, altering course ninety degrees to a vertical heading perpendicular to his previous path. The Cylons began to compensate immediately, but they were approaching too fast. They let off a barrage of laser blasts that went wide as their ships continued on past Apollo.

He brought the Viper into line again, falling into pursuit of the Cylon Raiders. The Cylons split off from one another immediately. He knew then that he would not survive, for he could not pull that maneuver again, and with the three fighters split up he had no chance of taking them all down.

"I'm not going alone," Apollo vowed, and as he considered death, he thought of Adama. "This one's for you, Father," he added.

Unable to follow either of the Raiders to the left and right, Apollo kept after the center ship. His thumb depressed the fire button on the navi-hilt and the turbolasers lashed out across space and slammed into his quarry.

At first, nothing happened. The laser blast seemed to be refracted, splintering and jumping over the surface of the Cylon ship. Then, in an instant, the refraction ceased and the blast burned through whatever kind of defensive shield these new enemy fighters had.

The Cylon ship went up in a stellar explosion.

Already, the other two had come around, and Apollo was trapped between them. With the Cylons he had fought previously, he might have tried to get them to shoot one another. He and Starbuck had managed it only weeks ago. But there had been two of them, not one damaged Viper. And these new Cylons seemed far more dangerous than the originals.

It wasn't going to work. Even from the flight patterns, he could see that they weren't flying head-on and wouldn't be foolish enough to be drawn into such a confrontation. They were easily keeping up with his Viper, closing in on an intersecting pattern.

A klaxon blared inside the Viper's cockpit. Apollo was almost out of fuel. Acting on instinct, he reached for the instrument panel and shut down the Viper's apex pulsar. Another switch and the retro-engines kicked in. They didn't do anything but slow the Viper—no way to actually put a starfighter in reverse when it's already in motion—but it was enough to get him out of the Cylons' direct line of fire.

Then they were in front of him, turning to bear down on his ship. Apollo was slowing. Unable to turn right or left, and moving too slow to avoid them with a vertical climb or downward dive, they had him dead to rights.

But Apollo had lasers, too. He fired, turbo blasts lancing out and splintering against one of the Cylon Raiders. He held the firing button down, and finally the lasers punctured the Cylon's shield. The enemy craft exploded.

Then it was over. Apollo had taken two of his attackers, despite their greater technology. But the third had him squarely in its firing sights. He was incapable of avoiding attack. Cylon lasers scorched across the space that separated the two fighters. The first blast cut right through his force shield and tore away the outer edge of his right wing. Life-support gases began venting out into the abyss.

"I'm sorry, Starbuck," Apollo whispered. "I tried."

The second shot tore something away from the Viper's underside. The third would certainly kill him. But it never came.

The starfield separating the combatants shimmered and warped. Something huge was appearing there, though whether it had just arrived or suddenly become visible, Apollo did not know. It was huge, larger than a battlestar, its crystal spires, as gossamer as a spirit, shone with incredible brightness.

Then it was whole and real and solid, and its light was so bright that Apollo had to shield his eyes. A massive ship of some kind, encrusted with crystals, flashing brilliantly enough to sear his vision.

Apollo felt faint. Then the light faded, and he slipped into unconsciousness, even as his Viper's life-support systems failed completely.

The Cylon's head and shoulders were pinned beneath a saligium beam too heavy for Starbuck to even consider moving. He had hoped to remove it and bring it with him if he ever escaped. Cylons were usually meticulous about removing their dead from the field of battle. He was sure the fleet would welcome the opportunity to do a real autopsy on one of them.

Instead, he would have to satisfy himself with tearing open the Centurion's breast plate. This sounded easier than it actually turned out to be. Still, he had finally made a breach in the Centurion's armor. With a metal bar he had recovered from the ceiling rubble, Starbuck now levered the armor open with a huge effort. The armor shrieked as its seams burst, and it peeled back to reveal the body inside.

"Give the man a tankard of grog," Starbuck said, as he stared in disgust and awe at the physical body of a Cylon Centurion.

13.

DALTON PILOTED THE SHUTTLE, following the computer's pre-plotted course. They had to stay within range of the fleet's drag-field, or they'd be left behind in no time. This way, the collective mass and inertia of the other ships created a kind of gravity well that kept the smaller ships traveling with them and allowed intra-fleet travel.

"Nervous?" Troy asked from the co-pilot's seat.

Dalton glanced at him, frowning.

"Why would I be nervous?" she asked, idly brushing her hair away from her face.

"Oh, I don't know," Troy replied, and shrugged. "You've only been a Warrior for two weeks. You haven't had any actual combat experience outside of training at Academy. Now we have a murder investigation that leads us to the worst ship in the fleet. The *Ursus* has quite a reputation, after all."

Dalton lifted her chin slightly and stared out at the fleet passing by. She could see the *Delphi*, a freighter converted into a marketplace, upon which all manner of goods were available from more than thirty different merchants. There was the *Adena*, a passenger ship known for its complement of socialators, and the *Cerebus*, which had the distinction of being the fleet's archive ship.

"Dalton?" Troy asked, apparently concerned that she had not replied.

"I'll be fine," she said.

They sat in silence for several centari. Dalton knew that, though he appeared to be teasing her, Troy's concern was genuine. They had been friends a long time. But she was a Warrior now and didn't need anyone's protection or concern. She'd proven that on *Agro-3* with that security chief, Paris. Of course, Troy had reprimanded her later for her actions. But she would do the same thing again if necessary.

Her father had taught her many things, but the lesson she valued most was this: allow your opponent to underestimate you only long enough to take advantage of his or her misconceptions.

She smiled slightly.

"What's funny?" Troy asked.

"Nothing, just thinking of my father," she replied.

"Hmm," Troy mused. "I was thinking of my father as well. I only wish I knew what all this insanity was about. Puck is stirring up a flanchette's nest all over the fleet. Apollo should be here."

"He'll be back," Dalton said, and they both fell silent at the unspoken implication of her words. Apollo would come back, they both felt certain. Starbuck, however, would never return. He was dead.

The shuttle weaved among the vessels of the fleet as it headed toward the rear. Commander Adama had cracked down on the *Ursus* several times a yahren. But every time the crime and depravity aboard the ship were cleaned up, they would simply begin again. Dalton had always assumed that the *Ursus* was actually a kind of pressure valve on the fleet. Most of the undesirable citizens ended up there. In some ways, it seemed to her a natural way to segregate them from the general population.

Morgan, the captain of the *Ursus*, never reported a crime. Whatever happened on board, he and his crew would handle it. While the Quorum might look down upon rumors and half-proven reports of violence and ubiquitous usage of mind-altering substances, there were other dilemmas to attend to. If Morgan prevented his problems from becoming the fleet's, they were more than happy to look the other way.

Adama had been more concerned about such things, but could never prove anything. Sending in Warriors would have infringed upon the duties of Quorum security. Politics. They had always disgusted Adama, and Dalton had admired Troy's grandfather for that.

This murder investigation, however, was another story. It would take them into the very bowels of the *Ursus*. Then, finally, a Warrior would learn first hand what was true and what merely rumor.

"Well," she said with a sigh, "this should be interesting, anyway. I've always wondered if the *Ursus* was just a low-class gambling barge, a poor man's *Rising Star*, or the den of depravity people have made it out to be."

"I know this much," Troy replied. "I wouldn't want to go into the Pit without my uniform."

"The Pit?" Dalton asked.

"That's what they call the lower levels of the *Ursus*," Troy explained. "I've heard it's like a pack of animals—you have to fight for your social position in the Pit."

"I can't believe Morgan actually allows such behavior," Dalton said in disgust. "It's inhuman."

"All too human, actually," Troy noted.

They were passing the *Hephaestus* when Dalton noticed fire licking at a broad, blackened area of the hull, around the landing bay.

"Troy, do you see...?" she began, but he was already on the comm-link back to the *Galactica*.

"This is Lieutenant Troy to *Galactica*," he said. "Ensign Dalton and I are on our way to the *Ursus* and have observed a fire burning on board the Forge. Should we divert?"

"No need, Lieutenant," came the reply from Major Omega. "We have emergency crews being shuttled to *Hephaestus* now. We will alert you should the situation change in any way."

Dalton stared out at the fire as they moved away from the Forge. A terrible, sick feeling began to grow within her.

"It feels like the end times," she said softly, completely cognizant of the vulnerability she revealed. But this was Troy; there was no one she trusted more.

"It's not as bad as all that," he replied, putting a hand on her shoulder, squeezing, leaving it there.

"Feels like it," she continued. "It's all falling apart. Maybe it's just entropy, the way things happen, but I never expected it to be in my lifetime. The fleet is destroying itself, and we can't rely on Adama, or one of our fathers, to save us this time."

Troy was silent, and Dalton glanced over to see him staring grim-faced out at the fleet.

"Troy?" she asked.

"I suppose we'll just have to save the fleet ourselves this time, won't we?" he asked. His expression did not change, nor did he turn to face her.

"There's the *Ursus*," he added.

"I'm afraid I still don't understand why Warriors are needed to pursue a single fugitive aboard my ship," Morgan said gruffly.

Despite the bearded man's reticence and rough demeanor, Dalton found herself coming to like him almost immediately. He had a unique charisma and a stern air of authority that was admirable.

But he clearly did not want them on board his ship.

"He isn't a fugitive," Troy argued. "I've told you, he's a potential witness to a murder. The supervisor on *Agro-3* confirmed that Terence was on duty at the estimated time of death, and we've got to…"

"Lieutenant," Captain Morgan chided, "you're disrupting my crew and my vessel, and you aren't even chasing your prime suspect? May the Lords help us all when you begin looking for him!"

"Morgan," Dalton interrupted, "let me explain."

The man looked down at her just as sternly as he had at Troy. Then Morgan seemed to soften a bit.

"That would be greatly appreciated," the burly captain said.

"The fleet is still under martial law," Dalton began, smiling cordially and using her hands as she spoke, trying to make him feel comfortable with their presence, to feel less as though they were usurping his authority.

"There has been a murder," she continued. "Of course, that is supposed to be confidential, but I'm confident we can trust you. Under martial law, a murder must be investigated by the military, rather than the civilian Quorum security forces.

"Our best lead is to the one man we believe may have witnessed the crime, an agro-worker named Terence. The last person to see Terence anywhere saw him on board your ship. If you know his location, we need your help. If not, we'll have to search the lower levels ourselves. If you'd care to help, it would be appreciated. We don't want to disrupt your running of your ship at all—if possible."

Morgan stared at Dalton, stroked his bearded chin, then moved his hard gaze back to Troy.

"It's our only purpose in coming here, Captain," Troy interjected. "Anything else we see down there is between you and your passengers."

Morgan seemed thoughtful a moment, glanced over at Dalton, and nodded slowly.

"You do remind me of your father, Ensign Dalton," the captain observed. "But only in appearance. He was never as, shall we say, *professional* a Warrior as you seem to be. A good man, however."

Dalton was taken aback by the sudden shift the conversation had taken.

"You knew my father?" she asked warily.

"Knew him well," Morgan replied, and allowed himself a small, nostalgic smile. "Trained him at Academy, actually. And Lieutenant Troy's father as well, though he was a hard one to read."

Dalton looked at Morgan again in a new light. He had been a Warrior once, that much was certain, and had trained her father at Academy when there were still colonies to defend.

She glanced around the bridge of the *Ursus*, caught the eye of more than one crewman. The bridge was cramped and dingy, much of its tech outmoded, stocked high with blasters and population-control gear. This was a war room, not the bridge of a starship. But Dalton could see in the eyes of the crew the unmistakable glint of pride, in Morgan and in the *Ursus.*

A question fought its way to her lips and she held it back only with effort. She wanted very badly to ask why Morgan was here. Why the *Ursus?* With his background, she knew he didn't have to captain a ship with such unruly, dangerous passengers.

When Dalton looked back at him, Morgan was smiling.

"I know what you're thinking," he said. "The answer is simple. Somebody's got to keep the animals in line. It isn't prison, which is where some of them belong, but at least if we keep them together they prey mostly on each other."

"Does that mean we have your cooperation?" Troy interjected.

Morgan put his hand out for Dalton to shake, ignoring Troy for a moment. Dalton liked that, and she liked Morgan. She took his wrist and he took hers and they sealed their understanding, their alliance. Morgan turned to Troy and offered him the same.

"You have more than my cooperation," he told Troy. "You have my aid. I wouldn't send Ambassador Puck into the Pit alone, and believe me, right now I'd like to flush that mugjape out an airlock!"

Dalton smiled. "You know, Captain," she said, "I think we're going to get along just fine."

A short time later, Dalton and Troy had begun their descent into the Pit. Morgan accompanied them with four of his men, all in what they called cleanup gear—helms and chestplates that made them look like Cylons.

"*You* don't wear armor?" Troy asked Morgan as the ascensior carried them down through the ship's levels.

"Can't show fear, Lieutenant," Morgan noted. "That's the first rule in dealing with lowlife scum. They live *in* fear, and live *by* it. It's the law of the wild, you've got to show them where you stand in the hierarchy, and I stand on top, my friend, always."

Dalton let her hand rest on her side, comfortably close to her sidearm. She wasn't afraid, actually. But cautious? She was that, most certainly.

The ascensior rattled and hummed as it descended, nothing like the perfectly tuned machinery on board the *Galactica*. But then, visitors to the Pit arrived and departed by a lower level shuttle bay, operated by a commercial intra-fleet service. No one used that ascensior aside from Morgan and his crew.

With a screech, the ascensior slid to a halt. The wait before the doors opened seemed interminable. When they finally slid aside, Dalton didn't hesitate before stepping out onto the lowest level of the *Ursus*, into the Pit. As she moved forward, the others behind her, she stared in disgust at what she saw.

The Pit was everything it was reputed to be. She had seen pictures, once, of a crumbling urban area on Aries that looked something like this. The Pit was wide open, the belly of some gigantic beast, its walls corroded or simply coated with some kind of byproduct from the massive chemical use of those who lived there. Open fires burned, and the stench was terrible.

"Move on," Morgan grunted behind her, and Dalton started to walk again without even realizing she had halted.

They passed people whose gender could not be determined merely by sight. Many did not register their presence, and Dalton believed most of them had chemically altered perceptions. To the right, two men fought with bloody faces and ragged fists as a crowd milled about, calling to them with insults or support.

To the left were rows of corridors and chambers Dalton had to assume were living quarters. A woman stumbled out of one open door with what appeared to be a small child in her arms. There was a blood-encrusted wound on her forehead, and she glanced up warily as they passed.

"Please...help me..." the woman croaked.

Immediately, Dalton touched fingers to her blaster and began to approach the woman.

Morgan reached her first, and the Tauron female dropped her burden and lashed out at him with a shiv. The bundle struck the sticky floor, and shattered. A wrapped up bottle of some kind.

With a swift sidestep that belied his age, Morgan disarmed the woman and knocked her to the ground. She was up in moments, and slinking back into the open doorway, cursing them all.

"Don't try to help anyone," the captain whispered to her when he rejoined the group. "They aren't all here by choice, but it's impossible to determine who is and who isn't. Trying will only get you killed."

"By the Lords," Troy hissed behind them, "somebody's got to help the ones who want help."

"When they ask for help, we help," Morgan replied, a bit testily. "If you have any other suggestions, son of Apollo, I'd be most interested to hear them. God's truth, you are your father's son."

They soon came to a far cleaner area of the Pit, which seemed no less dangerous for its greater reliance on hygiene. Here the side corridors and quarters were cared for, even decorated in some cases, though only in the most perfunctory manner.

"Is this where we'll find our agro-worker?" Troy asked, his voice barely more than a whisper.

"If he's here, this is where he'll be," Morgan admitted. "There is a Sagittarian cult here, probably the most powerful group in the Pit. Many of them actually have some functions out in the rest of the fleet. Jobs, even. I think they may even have a Warrior or two in their ranks, not living here, of course."

"But why are they still here?" Troy asked. "If they're out in the fleet, working, they have cubits. There is no discrimination based on religion in the fleet."

"What are they hiding from?" Dalton asked.

"Just what I've been wondering for quite some time," Morgan admitted. "But though they have power down here, I haven't had too many problems with them. Still, if your quarry, this Terence, came into the Pit and didn't come back, he either came as a tourist and was murdered, or he's a member of the Cult of the Serpent."

"Why the serpent? What's the significance of that?" Dalton wondered aloud.

"You can ask Tybalt. He's their leader. Any one of them would give their life for him. Don't doubt it for a moment," Morgan said, and Dalton could see that the captain was somewhat in awe of the faith Tybalt's followers placed in him.

"Is he that charismatic?" Troy asked. "What is he teaching that makes them so devout?"

"We're here," Morgan replied simply, and lifted a hand to indicate the corridor to their left.

They had seen fewer and fewer people lingering in the main chamber of the Pit. For the first time, it struck Dalton that the Pit itself was not the belly of the *Ursus*, but an enormous chamber than ran around its circumference. The chambers to their left were actually at the center of the ship. Thus, they had been gently curving around during their exploration, and now could see few people even behind them.

"They truly fear the Serpent Cult," she observed, then turned to look down the characterless, unassuming corridor. "Let's find out why, shall we?"

Troy and Dalton started forward side by side. Morgan hesitated a moment, and they both looked at him for explanation. After a moment, he offered one.

"They've got power, but they haven't caused me much difficulty. Still, I've always been curious about them. I'm sure I'm inviting trouble, but...frack, let's just jar their chips some," he said decisively.

Morgan took the lead, followed by Troy and Dalton, both of whom drew their blasters. Morgan's four crewmen trailed them in their cleanup gear. The short corridor ended in a large, oval iris door. Finally, he extracted his weapon from its holster and held it up beside his head. Silently, he motioned his cleanup men forward.

"The door," he whispered.

One of the crewmen moved forward and accessed the door's controls. There seemed to be some kind of coded tech-lock on the door, but the man simply pried off the control panel and made direct contact with the hard wiring.

The door irised open.

"In!" Troy shouted, and led the charge. Dalton was right behind him, with Morgan backing her up. The crewmen came in last, but by then, Dalton had already begun to think they had made a terrible mistake.

What greeted them when they burst in without warning was a quiet scene of domestic peace. Three men and two women sitting in a circle on the floor, a small fire burning at the center of their circle. Praying? Dalton wondered.

"Well, hello, Captain," a slender Sagittarian man said, fairly leaping to his feet with enthusiasm. "Though I'm a bit surprised, I have to admit I'm happy to see you. And you brought friends! This is a special occasion. Please, why don't you introduce us?"

"Tybalt, why don't you sit down and…" Morgan began impatiently. Troy didn't let him finish.

"Tybalt, I am Lieutenant Troy, here on a Warrior's business," Troy snapped, getting the cult leader's attention instantly. "I am conducting an investigation and am searching for a man I believe has information that would be invaluable to me."

Me? Dalton noticed the word, but didn't question it. Troy needed to get to the point quickly, and he was the superior officer, she knew. It was his place to assert authority in this instance.

"I have reason to believe that you are harboring this man, Tybalt, and I want to know where he can be found," Troy declared.

Tybalt did not respond at first. He approached Troy and Dalton cautiously, motioning for his followers to remain seated around the circle. He seemed a curious man, but not an especially dangerous one.

"Lieutenant Troy?" Tybalt asked. "That sounds so familiar, doesn't it children? But I…yes, I know it now. You're *Apollo's* son."

Suddenly, the zealot's smile disappeared. "How does it feel, Troy, to be the son of a traitorous coward? To know that he will never be commander, that Ambassador Puck will soon rule the fleet? Are you ashamed?"

Enraged, Dalton could not stop herself. She surged forward, blaster up, and jammed the nose of the weapon under Tybalt's chin.

"I think you'd better watch what you say, mindwipe!" she barked. "Nobody cares what happens down here, especially not to jettison like you. The astral winds would carry your remains all the way back to Sagittarius, if you're lucky."

Dalton stared at Tybalt, who had not stopped smiling. It was the smile that had done it. She just couldn't control her temper.

Then Morgan and Troy were beside her, pushing her weapon down, moving her away from Tybalt.

"Aren't you the little solium leak?" Tybalt said admiringly. "I like your spirit, not afraid to break some rules. You should be down here with us."

His words disturbed her. Troy had said little of the events on *Agro-3*. Maybe he knew that part of her temper was a reaction to her father's death. But she had to get control or she wouldn't be any good to him or anyone else.

"Contrary to what you may think, there are rules down here," Morgan said. "My rules. We don't know Tybalt's done anything, so far, except insult your partner."

At the word "partner," Morgan looked from Dalton to Troy and back again. She suspected he was wondering if there was more to their partnership than a Warrior's business, and she didn't blame him. She wondered it often enough herself.

With Morgan's crewmen covering Tybalt and his followers, she turned to Troy and apologized quietly. He didn't look at her immediately, and when he did, she saw that she had disappointed him somehow. It hurt her.

"Troy?" she asked.

"Dalton, I need to know that I can count on you," he whispered, pulling her aside so the others couldn't hear. "You could get us killed with this temper of yours. If you can't remember your Warrior training, then maybe you shouldn't have graduated early."

She wanted to protest, but she knew Troy was right. When she turned to face Tybalt and his followers again, her lips were pressed together in a tight line.

Troy pointed his blaster at Tybalt.

"Apparently, you're not much of a cult leader if you yourself have bought into Ambassador Puck's melodramatics," he said. "But we're not here to talk about politics."

"Oh, but you are," Tybalt sneered. "You just haven't realized it yet."

"And what does that mean?" Troy asked, moving closer to Tybalt, his weapon never wavering.

Tybalt's followers began to rise, but Morgan warned them against it, his crewmen discouraging them with a show of weaponry. Tybalt seemed about to reply, but then the smile disappeared from his face and he shook his head in exasperation.

"Just ask what you've come to ask, and then remove yourselves," Tybalt demanded. "You've no reason to be here if you're not going to arrest us. This is a private dwelling."

Dalton cleared her throat. Troy looked at her and she questioned him with her eyes. He nodded.

"We're looking for a man named Terence, an agro-worker we believe is one of your followers," she explained.

"Well!" Tybalt sighed dramatically. "Why didn't you say so before? Terence is here. He's right through there in the mealprep area."

Dalton walked through the chamber, past the circle where she now saw there were some kind of crude etchings in the floor. Some kind of ritual then. More than prayer. There was a short passage into the mealprep, perhaps two metrons, and she moved along it with blaster at the ready.

"Any sign of him, Dalton?" Troy called from behind.

"Not yet," she replied.

She stepped into the mealprep and glanced around the chamber. Nothing. No one there. She was about to turn and say exactly that, when she noticed something out of place in her peripheral vision. Something that shouldn't have been there. Dalton looked around, stared across the room at the eyes of Terence, at his face.

At his head, which sat inconspicuously on the countertop among storage containers, tilted at an angle that made the expression on Terence's face almost comical.

Dalton wasn't amused.

"Troy!" she shouted, and started back through the short hall to the main chamber.

As she entered, at a run, a hand flashed down and grabbed her wrist. Her blaster fired, searing a hole through one wall of the chamber. A large woman, one of Tybalt's followers, ripped her blaster away, almost breaking Dalton's wrist, and then batted her to the floor.

Dalton was quick to rise, ready for battle, but the blaster was now aimed at her face. She looked to Troy for action, but Troy and Morgan were also disarmed and under guard. Troy's face was bloodied and he cradled his left arm as though it might be broken. Morgan's face was red with fury rather than blood as he stared down at his crewmen.

The room was now filled with Tybalt's followers. Dalton surmised they'd taken Morgan's crew by surprise. Their cleanup gear had not prevented their throats from being cut, and even now their blood pooled on the floor. One man was still moving. A ragged, unwashed serpent cultist fell upon the dying man and drove a shiv into the back of his neck, severing the spinal cord with an audible crunch, finishing the job.

Tybalt stalked over to Troy and growled in his face like an animal. "I'll insult your father as often as I like. He's a coward and a fool. Puck will give us all we ever dreamed of.

"And you!" Tybalt cried, whirling to glare at Dalton. The madman stormed across the chamber, wheeling madly as if urged on by some unseen force. He stopped in front of Dalton and grinned obscenely.

"You're going to suffer for your affront, for your arrogance, little girl," he vowed.

Dalton looked away from his insanity. Across the room, Morgan dabbed at a head wound Dalton hadn't noticed before. Troy met her gaze, and she saw determination and fury in his face. There was a communication there, a confidence that they would survive this encounter.

A quiet, dangerous calm grew within Dalton.

Somehow, she knew, Tybalt would pay. And soon.

14.

In the shattered repair bay in the Cylon outpost on Ochoa, Starbuck gave a cursory examination to the remains of a Cylon Centurion. But he didn't really know what he was looking at. He was no med-tech like Cassiopeia.

At the thought, Starbuck realized that he missed her. They had been just friends for so many yahren—while he'd lived with Athena—that it was strange to feel her absence so powerfully. But then they'd had a daughter together, and Dalton's every breath was a link neither Starbuck nor Cassiopeia would ever deny.

"Ah, Captain," he whispered whimsically to himself, "you're getting old."

Starbuck had no implement to cut the Cylon's flesh, and he didn't want to waste time. Every second was vital if he had any chance of escape. Still, he lingered at the sight of the pried-open Centurion chest plate. Beneath it, the enemy's flesh was cold and gray, but not from death. Starbuck believed it to be the natural flesh tone of the Cylon.

It wasn't skin, exactly. Rough and ridged, it had plates or scales like those he had seen on the cold-blooded lizards of Caprica. Even more disturbing was the confirmation of something Colonial scientists had long believed: The Cylons were humanoid. Inside the armor was not some sentient blob of alien flesh controlling a robotic soldier.

The Cylon's body had arms and legs and a torso, just as a human did. He had to assume that it also had a head inside that ugly armored helmet, but the Centurion's upper torso was trapped beneath a collapsed portion of ceiling. The temptation to cut it open was limited to brief curiosity. He didn't really want to explore the internal organs of a Cylon, now or anytime.

Starbuck sighed, sat back on his haunches and stared at the alien corpse. Then he climbed to his feet.

"Love to stay and natter all day, but I'm in a bit of a hurry," he said amiably. "There you go, Starbuck, talking to yourself again."

The comm station stood in a far corner. He moved to it as swiftly as he could safely navigate the fallen debris. There was a flatscreen, not terribly different from those the Colonial fleet used. No keyboard, however, and Starbuck wasn't surprised. How would one type with armored fingers, after all?

There were characters scrolling across the screen, but Starbuck could not read them. Though he shouldn't have been, he was somewhat surprised. The Cylons had always communicated in Kobollian, and so he had assumed it was their language as well. Just another mystery to add to the many others surrounding the greatest enemy of humanity. After discovering that their armor housed humanoid reptilian forms, he was even more surprised that they had a native language other than Kobollian.

"Computer?" he asked, hoping for some response. None came.

"Comm station, respond," he said, touching the screen to be certain there was not some pressure sensitive command system. Nothing.

"Standard Kobollian, please," he requested.

"By your command," a computer voice crackled. So much did it resemble the voice of a Cylon Centurion, that Starbuck spun halfway around in alarm before recognizing it as the computer's reply.

"Narrow beam subspace communications open," he commanded, detailing the frequency and the coordinates to which he wished to direct the message. It would be sent in bursts covering a small segment of the galaxy he prayed the fleet would have reached.

It was a risk. The signal could be picked up by Cylons or another hostile race; they could use it to track the fleet. But there was likely enough vital information within the computer system that it was worth the limited risk. Only time would tell.

"*Galactica,* this is Starbuck," he began. As briefly as possible, he explained his situation, and the prospect of recovering vital Cylon tech. Then Starbuck signed off, unwilling to risk making the message any longer than necessary.

He prayed that it would be received, and that Adama would send someone for him. In the meantime, he would hope the planet stayed together a little longer and try to gather what information he could from the comm station.

"Display all biological and historical records," Starbuck ordered. The dead Cylon had inspired him. If the outpost had medical records of any kind, they could learn quite a bit about their enemies.

"There are no entries conforming to the reference 'historical records,'" the computer droned. "Biological records collating now."

Reports, documents, charts, cybernetic schematics, all scrolled up the screen at a speed too rapid for any human reader. But Starbuck didn't need to read them now. He knew he had found what he was seeking.

"Dump data to portable storage sphere," he instructed.

"By your command," the computer replied. Several seconds later, a tiny chirp informed him that the transfer was complete. He left the small green sphere in its place, protruding from the face of the comm station.

"Scan tech files for combat and navigation systems," Starbuck ordered.

"By your command."

Starbuck wanted to download all the tech files he could find, but knew the sphere wouldn't hold them all. Combat and navigational advances would be most important to the fleet, so he would begin with them.

The flatscreen was instantly cluttered with a string of what he assumed were project titles. Some he could not decipher, and realized they must be Cylon terms, untranslatable to Kobollian. Others were clearly obsolete, or useless references to galactic quadrants they had long since explored. Several, however, caught his eye immediately.

"Open file thirty seven, 'base star schematics,'" Starbuck instructed.

"By your command," the computer replied.

Starbuck began to read and, slowly, to smile.

Apollo's eyes hurt. The pain intensified as he tried to open them. He lay in a brightly lit chamber, on a flat surface that was neither berth nor med-unit. Too soft to be a table.

"Why don't you open your eyes, Apollo," a friendly, familiar voice suggested. "You're too old for guessing games. Which, as I recall, you never liked to begin with."

His breath caught in his chest. Apollo heard his heart thundering in his ears. He knew that voice, older now, more lighthearted than he remembered. But...no! It couldn't be him.

Apollo opened his eyes, blinking away the painful glaring brightness of the room. It was all white, blazing, pure light, and he remembered it. He had been there once before. Maybe more than once. But that voice!

He let his gaze drift to the right, and slowly turned his head to see a figure, all in white, whose flesh seemed to glow with celestial energy. The face was handsome, the hair dark and lush. The man looked quite a bit like Apollo, in fact. Of course he did.

"...Zac..." Apollo croaked. "...You...you're dead!"

"Apparently not," Zac replied, and smiled.

Apollo merely stared. Eighteen yahren earlier, he and his little brother had been on routine patrol. The colonies had sent all twelve battlestars out as a ceremonial vanguard to meet the Cylon fleet for what was to be the greatest peace accord in the history of humankind. After a millennium of war, the fighting was over.

Baltar had negotiated the peace.

Baltar had lied.

It was all a trap, ingeniously set, to lure in and destroy the battlestars, after which the colonies could be easily taken by the Cylons. Just before the ambush, Apollo and Zac had come upon dozens of Cylon fighters waiting for the attack signal. They had fled to warn the fleet, and the Cylons had moved in. Zac had been killed. Those on the bridge of the *Galactica* had heard his little brother's screams as he burned up in the cockpit of his Viper a micron before it exploded. Apollo had been spared the pain of that, but had been haunted every centon since by the idea that he might have somehow prevented Zac's death.

Apollo looked once again upon the shining, smiling face of his little brother. He didn't seem to have aged much, and yet there was something very...old about him. Calm in a way that Zac had never been.

"It *is* me, though, Apollo," Zac said. "Though in a way you couldn't possibly understand. And please, stop agonizing about leaving me behind. You did what you had to do, and would surely do the same thing again. There was no other choice.

"Now, why don't you sit up and we'll see if we can't get you something to eat. I imagine you're hungry," Zac suggested.

Instantly, Apollo realized he *was* hungry. Ravenous, in fact.

"How long have I been here?" he asked.

"It doesn't matter," Zac replied. "Several days by our reckoning. You were quite badly injured, nearly dead when we pulled you out of that battle with the Cylons' new starfighters. Our healing methods are swift, but you still needed to rest."

Apollo sat up, swung his legs over the edge of the table, and stood, shakily. His uniform was as white as everything else, altered somehow, though it felt the same. They were his clothes, but not his, in a way he opted not to contemplate.

"Wait," he said suddenly, panic speeding his heart. "Several *days?* Oh, Lords, no. Starbuck! There's no way he could have survived."

Apollo felt a bit unsteady on his feet, and Zac put out a hand to support him. When he took his brother's hand, vitality surged through him. Apollo stood straight, strong and refreshed, and looked upon his brother once more with awe.

"What have you done?" he asked.

"Shared with you, just a bit of myself," Zac replied, as if it were the most natural thing in the world. "As for Starbuck, don't worry. When we put you back in synch with your own universe, only moments will have passed."

"I don't understand," Apollo replied, frustration growing within him.

"No, I don't imagine you do," Zac said, amusement in his voice. "Now, sit, eat something, and I will try to answer all those questions I can hear in your mind."

"You can..." Apollo began.

Zac cut him off. "Eat," his brother said.

Confused, Apollo looked around the room. There was a table, its gleaming glass top laid with platters of food and a bottle of ambrosa. Apollo's stomach rumbled and he walked toward it immediately. The table had not been in the room a moment before, nor had the chairs on either side of it. When he slid into one of the white chairs, and Zac into the other, he could no longer hold back the question burning in his mind.

"Zac, am I dead?"

Zac actually laughed. It was a sweet sound, without any mockery, and it echoed in the room, which seemed to grow and take on new features the more Apollo looked around—almost as if the room was shaping itself based upon his own memories of his quarters on the *Galactica*.

"This is no heaven, Apollo," Zac replied. "The appearance of this food, this chamber, your clothing, is not magic. It is merely a science so advanced that you can not conceive of its workings. You see, this entire vessel—and you, for as long as you are with us—exists in a state of molecular flux. We are not technically within the reality or dimension of our birth."

Apollo nodded. "I've been here before," he said. "Once, maybe twice. But I never really had much chance to question, and when I did, I never got any real answers."

Zac relaxed, sliding a bit in his chair in a way that Apollo remembered so well from their childhood. It was a joyously painful thing to see.

"I've missed you so much, Zac," Apollo professed. "Athena has, as well. Things between us were never the same after you...well, after you were gone. And Father. Father is dead."

The moment the words were out of his mouth, Apollo froze as if paralyzed. He stared at the table, then slowly brought his gaze up to Zac's face.

"Or is he?" Apollo asked.

"Why don't you let me tell you a bit of history," Zac said. "Everything that I'm allowed to reveal, and maybe a bit more. Some of it you may already know, or suspect. In the meantime, I suggest you eat. You're going to need all your strength if you're to save Starbuck's life."

Apollo looked at his brother for a moment, still unused to the extraordinary pleasure of his company. Then, slowly at first but soon more rapidly, Apollo began to eat.

And Zac spoke to him.

"In the distant past, many millennia ago, the human race began on a planet called Parnassus. This you know. You also know of the destruction of Parnassus and the migration of the House of Kobol to a new planet, which they christened after themselves.

"You know of the disgust the Lords of Kobol felt with the rest of humanity. In truth, the Lords had already evolved far beyond their brethren. Thus, while many of their descendants and followers remained behind, the Lords of Kobol went out into the universe to contemplate the fabric of reality, to create beauty and peace, and to aid their less evolved counterparts in whatever way they might.

"Their wisdom has proven invaluable for thousands of years. They are still worshipped. The Books of the Lords of Kobol are still the philosophy by which humanity wishes it had the fortitude to live. The presence humans call God has long been sought by the Lords of Kobol, though this quest has proven fruitless thus far.

"When I died," Zac explained, stressing the last word in ironic tones, "the molecular structure that comprised my body was accelerated. The Lords of Kobol have left an ancestral memory, a genetic imprint, on all those of pure Kobollian blood. Remember Apollo, that this is science, not magic. This is no celestial home for the spirit, but a real, physical afterlife. It is not eternal, but enduring enough that eternity does not seem impossible from our perspective.

"I was transported here a moment after my death, my molecular structure was repaired, and I have been here ever since. Learning. Growing. It is a process which, even by our standards, takes quite some time. In answer to your question: yes, of course, Father is here. Somewhere. I have not seen him, nor, in truth, did I know that he has passed on. But he is of pure Kobollian blood, and so I am certain that, eventually, he will coalesce and become one of us."

One of us, Apollo thought. *What is that?*

Haven't you realized it yet? Zac asked telepathically. *We are the lost Thirteenth Tribe, Apollo. We are the Kobollians, the Lords of Kobol.*

"Then telepathy…"

"Is one of the attributes of all our people," Zac confirmed. "And make no mistake, you are one of us. When your time comes, you will rise to the next phase of your life and join us on one of these wondrous lightships.

"I know you have many other questions, but we do not have much time. If you are to save Starbuck, we cannot hold you here indefinitely. Time *will* pass, and I'm afraid he hasn't much time left. Or, rather, the planet Ochoa doesn't.

"Still, there is a part of our story you must know. Our great and ancient enemy," Zac said, the smile disappearing from his face, disturbing in its absence.

"The Cylons?" Apollo asked.

"They are the enemy, most certainly. But I speak of a time when Cylon was nothing more than a dank, lush planet overrun by dimly sentient reptiles. A time just after the planet Kobol was settled. Within the Lords of Kobol, there was a man who lacked the purity of his brothers. He was a spiteful, bitter, angry man, who wanted power more than wisdom.

"When he was censured by the other Lords, this man broke ranks. In time, he came to found his own dynasty. While we remained the House of Kobol, a portion of the population fell prey to his sharp tongue and devious wit, and with them as his followers, he founded the House of Iblis," Zac explained.

Apollo's eyes widened. His fork hovered inches from his open mouth and he stared at Zac.

"*Count* Iblis?" he asked in horror. "That can't be! What you speak of happened thousands of yahren in the past. But Iblis tried to take over the fleet only eighteen yahren ago."

"Iblis left Kobol eventually, bringing all of his followers with him," Zac continued, ignoring the interruption. "What he did after that constituted such horrors that we are forbidden to discuss it. But when Iblis died, Apollo, he was...accelerated, just as I have been. Just as all the Lords of Kobol were.

"Yet his soul was so twisted, so horrible and filled with hatred of his human brothers, that he did not become one of us," Zac said in a voice hushed by revulsion. "In all the universe, Count Iblis is totally unique. He is a leech, sucking the fear and death of countless planets into himself for his sustenance.

"I tell you all this, Apollo, because Iblis' gambit on the *Galactica* those yahren ago was his attempt to corrupt and destroy our father. Now that Adama has passed from your understanding, Iblis is going to come after you. It is important that you be prepared for this. Important that the wisdom of Kobol continue to guide the primary extant human society."

Apollo took a long draught from the bottle of ambrosa, wiped his mouth and prepared to ask Zac the first of the many questions searing his soul. The food was delicious, but his belly was filled now, and there was so much to learn in so little time.

"How do I combat Iblis, then, if he comes for me?" Apollo asked.

Zac stood and began to walk toward the door. Apollo rose and followed him.

"There is no combat," Zac explained. "Iblis cannot destroy one of us with direct physical violence...or perhaps he could, but he will not. He must triumph over your will, your wisdom. He will employ deception, cunning. That is the battle to come. If he can drive you to despair, that will be his greatest triumph."

The shining white door irised open and Zac stepped through, gesturing for Apollo to follow.

"Now, my brother, I'm afraid you must go. The rest you will have to learn instinctively, or through your own ends. Even if I could tell you more, you do not have time. Starbuck needs you. Your Viper has been repaired, and you will be returned to synch at coordinates not far from Ochoa," Zac revealed.

As they walked down a shimmering corridor, Zac turned to Apollo. "Give Starbuck and Athena my love," he said. Then they had reached the end of the short corridor, and a massive door slid open to reveal Apollo's Viper, shining white as bone, glittering with light.

"The Lords travel with you until you return to us," Zac said, and ushered Apollo toward the Viper.

"Zac, wait!" Apollo snapped. "I have so many questions. You've got to help me understand. I don't know what..."

As he propelled Apollo to the starfighter, and up onto its wing, Zac looked a bit sad. His new existence might be paradise, Apollo thought, but it isn't perfect.

"One question," Zac allowed. "Only time for one."

Apollo climbed into the cockpit of his Viper, mind reeling with the enormity of everything he did not know. It came down to one question after all, though. The question that was always foremost in his mind.

"The Lords of Kobol have explored the universe," he said. "In their wisdom, they've seeded human colonies everywhere. If you...or we... are the legendary Thirteenth Tribe, then where is our destined home-world, Zac?

"Where is Earth?" Apollo asked.

"I cannot tell you, Apollo. I'm sorry," Zac said.

"What?" Apollo asked, frustrated. "Why?"

The Viper's canopy closed. Apollo stared out at Zac, who looked away unwilling to face his brother's gaze.

Why? Apollo asked again, this time with his mind.

And this time, Zac answered.

I cannot tell you because I do not know.

15.

EVERY WARDEN ON THE *ICARUS* WAS DEAD, save for their chief, who had barricaded himself into the cell control center. The Borellian Nomen were raging, driven into a frenzied state by the taste of freedom and vengeance. Brutal as they were, however, those civilians not wearing a uniform were spared a bloody death. Gar'Tokk ordered his people to ignore them. They had other, more vital tasks to perform.

Their benefactor had asked very little in exchange for freedom. The dark creature that called itself Count Iblis wanted chaos, and the Nomen would deliver it.

Gar'Tokk screamed a battle cry in the ancient tongue of the Nomen. His fellow warriors joined in the cacaphonous whooping. Snie'Goss, one of the six Nomen he had appointed as his chieftains, appeared at his side.

"Sovereign Lord Gar'Tokk," Snie'Goss roared, "we have secured the bridge and taken the hearts of the crew. We are preparing, even now, to take this prison ship far from the fleet."

A low growl of pleasure built in his chest, and Gar'Tokk smiled.

"Excellent," he said. "I will take six Nomen and free the other prisoners as Count Iblis asked. Then we will leave the fleet. Go now, and await our return. Kill any human who tries to stop us or enter the bridge."

"Yes, Lord," Snie'Goss vowed, and executed the salute of the

Nomen, contorting his left hand into a claw and scratching lightly across his own chest.

Then he was gone.

Gar'Tokk chose six Nomen to follow him, and sent the others after Snie'Goss. He led his chosen few down a narrow corridor at a run; they pounded along behind him. Several turns later, they reached a door that was sealed tight against them. At his command, Nomen began to attack the door with their bare hands.

Two, perhaps three centari later, the frame cracked and then shattered. A space appeared between the doors and from there it was a simple matter for the Nomen, with their prodigious strength, to peel the doors away.

Laser fire tore through the opening almost immediately. One Noman was hit, badly injured, and fell to the floor of the corridor. Gar'Tokk cursed loudly, and surged into the gap.

"Halt there, Gar'Tokk!" the chief warden of the *Icarus* cried. "You are a prisoner of the Quorum. If you continue this escape attempt, you will be killed."

With surprising speed, Gar'Tokk launched himself across the cell control center, and tore out the chief warden's throat with his bare hands.

"You should have surrendered," he informed the chief's corpse as he let it fall to the metal floor of the bridge with a wet thud.

"Sovereign Lord Gar'Tokk!" one of his Nomen shouted. "I have found what you seek!"

Gar'Tokk crossed the chamber to a flatscreen readout showing the schematics of the prison barge's cell quadrants. He could barely bring himself to look at the computer. Technology had been anathema to his people for so long. But it had to be done. They had given Count Iblis their word.

"Can you do this?" he asked the Noman soldier.

The long-bearded one glanced up at his leader and nodded grimly. "If I must," he said.

"Good," Gar'Tokk confirmed. "Then do so. Shut down the

restraining field on every cell quadrant."

The Noman did as he was ordered. As Gar'Tokk and the five surviving chosen turned and moved back toward the bridge, all the prisoners on the prison barge *Icarus* flooded the ship's corridors. They were all free to do as they wished, as long as they didn't try to interfere with Gar'Tokk's control of the ship and its destination.

The *Icarus* was his.

Sheba lay on her berth, shifting uncomfortably as she failed in her attempt to get some much needed rest. The stress within the fleet was growing worse by the centari, and she was torn. She wanted to be ready the moment military action was required—and her gut told her that moment would come soon—but she'd slept only three centons in the last five cycles.

Dim light filtered across the room from the one lantern she'd left on. Just enough illumination to be certain she could be up and dressed instantly if a klaxon sounded.

With a sigh, she tried once again to get settled. On the music-link, Cancerian percussion and windsong lulled her with their swaying, intimate rhythms. Finally, Sheba closed her eyes and began to drift off to sleep.

A sound, a thump, a scuffle in the corridor outside.

"Major Sheba!" someone shouted.

There came a pounding on her door.

Microns later, when Sheba slapped the panel that caused the door to slide open, she was in uniform. Well, sans her flight jacket, which she was slipping on even as the doors parted to reveal her visitor. Ensign Zimmer was brand new, the youngest pilot in Sheba's squadron. Still, she liked the solemn Warrior, whose white-blonde hair and starship-gray eyes reminded her a bit of her father, the legendary Commander Cain.

"You woke me up, Ensign Zimmer," she lied. "I hope you've a good reason."

"Yes, Major, I…" Zimmer hesitated a moment, perhaps collecting his thoughts, and touched his forehead, the salute of a Colonial Warrior. "Lieutenant Jolly sent me for you, Major. We've got a major problem in the launch bay!"

"Let's move, then," Sheba said. She had always favored action over explanation, a philosophy she'd picked up from her father. Whether for good or ill, she had never been able to decide.

Shoulder to shoulder, Sheba and Zimmer stormed down the hallway, passing the general pilots' quarters on the way.

"Why didn't I hear a klaxon?" she asked, though she kept her eyes forward.

"What?" Zimmer mumbled. "Oh, we're not being deployed, Major."

Sheba's gait faltered. This time, she did turn to face Zimmer as they slowed a bit.

"Then what does Jolly need in such a hurry?" she asked, annoyed that she had been roused just when she might actually have gotten some sleep.

"That's just it," Zimmer tried to explain. "Even if we were deployed, we couldn't go anywhere. The entire service crew is staging some kind of demonstration in favor of Ambassador Puck. They won't *do* anything. No Vipers can launch without a crew."

A look of intense relief crossed Jolly's face as Sheba entered. He was an excellent pilot, a courageous Warrior, but she considered him the most underestimated man she had ever met. That relieved expression was part of the explanation. Jolly was a peacemaker, uncomfortable in any hostile social situation. He could fly into battle against Cylons with twelve-to-one odds against him, but was stopped cold by hostility.

On the other hand, if peace wasn't possible, if someone was going to persist in questioning the honor of Colonial Warriors, well, then Jolly might actually get angry.

When Sheba walked in, Jolly hadn't gotten angry yet, but he was getting there.

"Listen, I understand, I really do," Jolly announced to the hostile faces of the launch crew who were gathered around him. "You guys have a right to your political beliefs, and I'm not here to take that away from you, but you can't let that stop you from doing your jobs. What if we're under attack? The fleet will be destroyed if the Vipers don't launch."

"But we're not under attack, Jolly, that's the point," one man, Sheba thought his name was Virgil, declared. The others all nodded and grunted their agreement.

Sheba and Zimmer were halfway across the launch bay, walking toward the gathered crewmen, when Jolly surrendered and simply looked at her, waiting for her to intervene.

"What exactly is the point, then, Virgil?" she asked as she approached, Zimmer striding silently at her side. "Is the point that you think Commander Adama misled the fleet? That Apollo or Athena would do less than everything in their power to provide for all of us? Or is the point that Puck's slander, his attempts to prey on the fear we all have that maybe there is no Earth, no help against the Cylons, no goal to strive for...is the point that Puck's feldergarb has paid off?"

Jolly smiled slightly, not enough to antagonize the crew. For their part, the launch techs were silent, averting their gazes. Finally, Virgil looked up, standing up to Sheba with more guts than she would have given him credit for.

"I'm sorry, Major, but I don't think we're asking much. We want Puck. He's a realist, and we all agree that's what this fleet needs right now. We've had enough of dreams. Dreams are gone when you wake up, Major. We've all just woken up, is all," Virgil explained. "We just want the Quorum to vote. I don't understand why it's taking so long."

"You're an eloquent man, Virgil," Sheba observed. "Maybe you could write some of these propagandist speeches that Puck keeps making. Course, it doesn't seem like he'll need your help. All he needs are fear and desperation."

Virgil was silent, but he didn't turn away. Now some of the other techs met Sheba's angry gaze as well.

"We need Vipers out on recon. We need to be able to send out assistance if those fighting the fire on the *Hephaestus* call for it. If you're not going to do your jobs, I will have you removed from the bay, and eventually, from the *Galactica*," she warned. "It's up to you."

"I'm sorry, Major," Virgil said. "We're not going to be bullied."

"You do realize that with the fleet under martial law, you could be prosecuted as mutineers?" Sheba asked.

Several of the techs looked stunned, and it was clear that, though Virgil was unfazed, her words were news to some of them. But none broke ranks. Virgil only nodded.

"Ensign Zimmer!" Sheba snapped and turned to face the young pilot. "Pass along an order that all infantry Warriors currently aboard the *Galactica* will sign up for duty in the launch and landing bays. Bring the first watch with you when you return. Also, ask Captain Hecate to report to me immediately with her entire squadron."

Zimmer grinned broadly.

"Go!" Sheba snapped, and Zimmer turned to jog from the launch bay, the grin still on his face.

"Jolly," Sheba continued, turning to the overweight Lieutenant, "you're to take command of all starship operations immediately. Get infantry up to speed—use some of Hecate's squadron if you need help tutoring the soldiers. Then launch six Vipers from Hecate's squadron. Two on normal recon, the other four on fleet sentry duty.

"I have a feeling this is only going to get worse," Sheba added softly.

"Yes, Major," Jolly said formally.

When she turned back to the crewmen, Sheba found them simply staring at her.

"You don't have the authority to do all that," Virgil said grimly.

Sheba had dealt with the situation as objectively, and as swiftly, as she was able. But Virgil's words erased her objectivity in an instant. She stalked across the few metrons that separated them and leaned in so that her face was only centimetrons from his.

"With Major Boomer on the *Hephaestus*, I am the highest ranking Warrior pilot on this battlestar," she informed him through gritted teeth. "Do not even presume to question me, Virgil. Now, all of you, remove yourselves from this bay immediately. I will recommend charges be filed against you. I assume the Quorum will let you know soon enough."

She turned back to Jolly.

"Any one of these traitors tries to come back into this area, arrest him," she ordered.

As she and Jolly quietly conferred, Virgil and the others made their way out of the bay. Just before Virgil left, Sheba turned to him.

"By the way, Virgil," she said sharply. "Didn't Commander Apollo save your life in this bay several yahren ago?"

Virgil looked stricken, his mouth agape. He stared for endless microns at Sheba, who waited patiently for an answer. Finally, Virgil looked away.

"Yes, he did," Virgil admitted. "I'm sorry I...I can't help it!" he cried, and fled the bay.

Sheba and Jolly looked at one another, their faces contorted with confusion.

"Now what was that all about?" Jolly asked.

"I wish I knew," Sheba replied.

In the confused aftermath of the explosion, mere microns long, Boomer had exited the Forge's lounge at a run. He'd stayed low, stuck to the walls and held his blaster at the ready should Paris or any of the other blackshirts come after him. He had passed a transparent blast shield that looked down upon the repair bay. He'd known in that instant that he was trapped on the *Hephaestus*. Every functioning vessel in the bay had either been destroyed, was badly damaged, or in flames.

Black smoke billowed out from the bay toward the launch aperture, an enormous hole that looked out upon deep space and the rest of the fleet. Under normal circumstances, oxygen and gravity were kept in the bay by a combination of internal pressure and force shields generated under the same principle as the face shield on a pilot's helm.

The smoke passed through it. The fire probably could. But as the flames licked the roof of the bay, where dozens of power lines lay, Boomer knew that soon the shield would fail. He only hoped the crisis shield was in place. It was a secondary system that would seal off the bay from the rest of the ship, if crisis crews could not douse the flames themselves.

Boomer stared down at the devastated repair bay for half a centari, and then turned and ran down the corridor. He was determined to stay ahead of Paris, to reach the bridge first.

The wide door irised open at his approach. Boomer entered with his laser still drawn, ready for any resistance. He had no idea how far this conspiracy went. His revulsion at what Paris and the other blackshirts had done burned in his stomach. Boomer ignored it, concentrating instead on making sure they paid.

"Attention, please!" he cried as he ran onto the bridge. The crew turned and collectively recoiled when they saw his drawn weapon.

"The explosion in the repair bay was no accident!" he declared. "It was an act of sedition and terror against the Quorum and the military command of this fleet. Please use whatever means necessary to secure this bridge and inform your entire crew and any other residents to confine themselves to quarters.

"Until further notice, all Quorum security officers on board are to be ignored, under my authority through martial law," he instructed.

A stern Gemon man shambled across the bridge toward Boomer, one hand raised in a gesture that was both calming and some sort of protest.

"Now see here!" the man said. "I am Heimdall, captain of this ship. What have these men done that you usurp them in this way?"

Boomer narrowed his eyes in anger and surprise.

"Listen, Captain, these mugjapes are responsible for the bomb that just killed at least one dozen techs and pilots," Boomer said harshly. "They're still on this ship, with who knows how many accomplices. And we've got fire crews coming aboard who might be targets and are totally ignorant of any potential danger."

Captain Heimdall glared at Boomer.

"Let me explain something to you, Warrior," the captain sneered. "I don't care much for the military, and in particular your attitude. My crew is completely capable of dealing with the fire, and the emergency crew.

"In the meantime," the old man said, "you have no authority here because the *Hephaestus* has, as of this moment, removed itself from Colonial service."

Boomer's jaw dropped.

"What?" he cried. "What are you talking about, you can't just..."

"But I can," Heimdall replied. "And I have."

The old man pulled a blaster from behind his back even as several other crewmembers nearby also produced weapons. Boomer lifted his own blaster but did not fire.

"You people are insane," he said.

"On the contrary," Heimdall sniffed, his tone haughty, "we are simply not subject to your rules. However, since you have made such a nuisance of yourself, and since I assume Paris and his friends will do so anyway, we will be forced to execute you."

Paris!

Even before the pieces of the puzzle had all clicked together in his head, Boomer was moving. He dove to one side, behind a comm station. As he fell, he fired at the floor in front of Heimdall's feet, sending sparks flying, distracting the captain.

After several other shots from around the bridge seared his hiding place, Boomer popped up and shot Heimdall in the chest. The blast threw the old man back and he was dead before he hit the floor.

Boomer fired a few more bursts at the other armed crewmembers. But these weren't trained Warriors. Most were too distracted by the sight of their dead captain to take the offensive. Still, he was cut off from the door he had used to enter. Nearby, the ascensior tube waited, but he did not have time to call the platform to this level of the ship.

No choice. Even as the crew began to focus on him once more, Boomer crouched and blasted the ascensior tube open. He ripped off his flight jacket, fired his blaster behind his head at the crew, and ran for the devastated door. He leaped through the blaster hole and, hands wrapped in his jacket, grabbed hold of the wide vertical groove which held the ascensior level in the tube.

Then he dropped, sliding too fast, trying to evade blaster fire that burned into the tube after him. His hands burned, fingers stung and bled, and then Boomer couldn't hold on any longer. He lost his grip and tumbled through the tube. The hard landing came quickly after only a four metron fall, and though Boomer felt something tear in his shoulder, he thanked God and the Lords of Kobol for his life.

Boomer shaded his eyes and blasted the bottom level door open. A laser blast from far above seared his hip, inflicting a painful but superficial wound. Then he was out into the lower level, into the smoke and fumes of the burning repair bay. Fire crews had arrived from the *Neptune*, a crisis-control ship commissioned for military service. A female crisis officer saw Boomer and pointed, shouting at him to stay where he was.

He ran toward her, holstering his blaster so as not to present a threat.

"Take cover!" he shouted. "All of you, take cover. The ship has been taken by seditionists!"

She stared at him in horror.

"But...the fire," she stammered.

"Let it burn!" he cried. "Then they'll have to put it out themselves. We've got to get off this ship or we're dead. Your crisis shuttle is the only way off the Forge!"

Screams and laser fire erupted on the opposite side of the repair bay. Boomer and the woman turned to see that Paris and his blackshirts had arrived. In microns, they had killed a half-dozen crisis officers. Boomer let off a flurry of laser blasts at them, getting their attention.

"We can't let them reach your ship!" Boomer shouted.

"It's too far for us to get to it!" she cried back.

Paris intended to destroy the crisis ship, trapping him here. Boomer was determined to stop him, and kill him if necessary. He had to get these people off the Forge and warn Athena.

Laser fire volleyed from one end of the bay to the other.

Stalemate.

The door irised open and Athena marched into Ambassador Puck's temporary quarters aboard the *Galactica*. Colonel Tigh and Sire Belloch followed her.

"What is the meaning of this?" Ambassador Puck demanded, climbing feebly to his feet. "How dare you barge into my quarters like this?"

"Trank it, Puck!" Athena growled. "For once, know enough when to keep quiet."

Puck's face, normally so chalky, grew flushed and his eyes narrowed with fury. The Ambassador's nostrils flared, but he said nothing.

"Ambassador Puck," President Tigh began, "Sire Belloch and I have accompanied Commander Athena to this meeting so that there will be no question about what was discussed, and the results thereof."

"Please," Puck urged with caustic, false courtesy, "do continue, *Commander* Athena."

Athena smiled, refusing to allow Puck to shake her. For the first time since her father had fallen ill, she felt some kind of stability. Confidence in her direction. But then, catastrophe left very few choices.

"I've been named Interim Commander," Athena informed him. "In addition, the Quorum has voted me into my father's seat, representing Caprica."

Puck didn't react to the the news, which disappointed Athena somewhat. It was almost as if he knew, or somehow, didn't care. No matter, there was far more to discuss.

"The Quorum is dismayed, to say the least, by your tactics in seeking command of the fleet," Sire Belloch said, and Athena was astonished that the man had the nerve to speak to Puck in that way. They had all seemed so intimidated by him.

Again, catastrophe left few choices.

"The vote will not take place until the fleet is back in some semblance of order," Tigh added. "We will not be bullied by you or your supporters."

"I don't know what you're referring to," Puck said, without making any effort to convince them he spoke the truth. They all knew better.

"You're tearing this fleet apart," Athena snapped at him.

"The people know what they want," Puck replied.

"The people know what you've told them to want, after you've filled them with venomous lies about my family!" Athena shouted.

"Commander?" Puck asked, pretending shock at her behavior.

She forced herself to take a breath, to calm down, before continuing.

"There have been protests on more than one hundred ships, strikes, literal mutinies in some cases," she said grimly. "The *Scorpius Ascendant* has left the fleet, and a bomb was planted on the *Hephaestus*. The *Galactica's* own Viper crews have refused to work. They all demand you be instated as commander."

Puck smiled thinly, knowingly, dropping any pretense at last.

"Well then," he said, "I believe we have a mandate, do we not?"

"We do not," President Tigh snapped, and Puck seemed at last surprised. Finally, something he had not predicted.

"You will address the fleet on unicomm immediately," Athena ordered. "You will tell all of your supporters that there will be no vote until the fleet is functioning again. Everyone must return to their usual jobs and routines. The Cylon threat is very real, and we cannot allow ourselves this vulnerability."

"You'll also tell them that command is the Quorum's decision, not a democratic one," Sire Belloch said firmly.

Ambassador Puck turned his back on them. He hobbled, bent over, to an oval window. He stared out at the starfield, and did not face them again when he spoke.

"No," he replied. "I will not."

"I'm not sure you understand, Ambassador," Athena began.

"I understand perfectly," Puck sneered, still without facing them.

"By the Lords, man!" Belloch roared. "Your people are tearing this fleet apart. Never mind the Cylons—this alone could destroy us!"

Finally, Puck turned to them. His smile was sickening, and Athena could barely stop herself from looking away. She forced herself to meet his gaze.

"I think you know what you must do," Puck said.

Athena scowled, looked first at Sire Belloch, then at Tigh, to be certain she had their support. Neither had softened in the face of Puck's malice.

"Yes," she agreed. "We know what must be done."

Athena turned back to the door, which irised open to reveal two Warriors standing just outside.

"Corporal," Athena said to the ranking infantryman, "Ambassador Puck is under arrest, confined to his chambers until further notice. All comm access is to be diverted from these quarters immediately."

"Yes, Commander," the Corporal replied, and touched fingers to forehead. He hadn't even blinked at the order, Athena noted. Good soldier. At least some of the fleet's population hadn't lost their minds.

She exited Puck's quarters with the Ambassador's sputtered curses ringing in her ears. When the door irised shut, she turned to speak to Tigh and Belloch once more. Before she could open her mouth, there was a shout from further down the hall.

"Athena!"

Athena turned to see Sheba running toward her.

"Major?" she asked, and raised a brow to remind her friend that they were in public and had to follow protocol.

"Commander," Sheba said breathlessly, saluting as she slowed to a halt. "Sire Belloch, President Tigh. I am sorry to interrupt."

Then Sheba ignored them, turning to Athena with desperation in her eyes.

"Commander, the explosion on the *Hephaestus* was just the beginning. The Forge's crew has apparently mutinied and have announced their intention to leave the fleet," Sheba said.

"What next?" Sire Belloch raged.

"We've had a report from the crisis crew sent to control the fire," Sheba continued. "Major Boomer is there. Apparently the seditionists are Quorum security. They're trying to execute the crisis team, and Boomer with them. Dozens are dead already from the original crew—anyone who didn't go along with their plan!"

Athena's first instinct was to put up a false front, a facade of cool, unwavering control. But then she thought of her father, Adama. As commander, he was never afraid to show his passion, his anger. With that, Athena's fury spilled over.

"Fools and beasts, the lot of them!" she cried. "God help them and us!"

Sheba waited for orders. Tigh and Belloch waited to see what Athena would do.

"First, thank you for your exemplary handling of the crisis with the launch and landing crews," Athena noted.

"Now, Major Sheba, take two Vipers and a shuttle full of infantry and take back the *Hephaestus*," she commanded. "No quarter."

Athena waited for her order to be acknowledged. Sheba didn't move.

"There's more?" Athena asked.

"Isn't there always, these days?" Sheba asked. "Lieutenant Troy and Ensign Dalton have been investigating the murder on *Agro-3*. They followed a lead to the *Ursus* and went into the Pit with that ship's captain, a man named Morgan.

"They have not returned," Sheba informed her.

For a moment, Athena stopped breathing. Adama was dead. Starbuck apparently dead as well. Apollo gone, perhaps never to return. Troy was the only family she had left, and Dalton was very nearly family as well.

"Athena?" President Tigh asked in gentle tones.

"Tigh, please inform Cassiopeia about this development," Athena asked. "I'm going after them. Now."

"At least bring Captain Hecate and some of her squadron, some infantry!" Sheba urged. "You can't go into the Pit alone, Athena, not with Puck's followers so rabid. You'll be killed."

Athena started off down the hall, ignoring her at first. Then she turned.

"I'm leaving now. Send Hecate and two Vipers after me, and another shuttle of Warriors," she said, then picked up her pace.

Nearly running, she called back without turning. "You have your orders, Major."

16.

FOR JUST A MOMENT, while his mind struggled to keep up with reality, Baltar stared in horror at the ebon-armored Cylon Centurions whose minds had been patterned after his own. His children, in some perverse way.

The very creatures whom Lucifer had just ordered to execute him.

"No!" Baltar cried, disgusted by the desperation in his own voice. "Stay back."

The dark Centurions drew their blasters. Baltar bolted for the high seat of command, which had once been his own place of power. Lucifer sat atop the platform, looking down at his plight with what Baltar was certain was mockery, amusement, dismissal. But he was not ready to be dismissed.

"Lucifer, stop!" Baltar shouted. "You don't know what you're doing! I can still be of help to you! I know things...things of value!"

"We have taken all we ever wanted from you, Baltar," Lucifer's metallic voice crackled. Sparks stormed around the transparent dome that was his brain. For the first time, Baltar realized that his former advisor had been built with the smirk on his face. It was subtle, but it was real, not his imagination.

"Kill him," Lucifer ordered.

"No!" Baltar screamed, as laser blasts burned past him on the steps to the high seat. Laser fire burned his right calf, and he shrieked in pain, humiliated by his weakness but unable, as ever, to control himself.

"Lucifer!" Baltar screamed. "You need me! I can still hand the fleet over to you!"

For a moment, Lucifer did not respond. Baltar scrambled backward up the steps, using only his left leg, for his right would not answer his commands. The dark Centurions were advancing. He was going to die.

"Hold," Lucifer said behind him. Baltar exhaled, nearly fainted on the steps with the relief of that one word.

As best he could, Baltar turned to face his former advisor. The humiliation of his position, on his knees before Lucifer, whom he once commanded, was nearly lost on him now. His life was all that mattered. Drawing another breath was the only priority.

"If you could deliver the fleet, Baltar, why wouldn't you have done so already?" Lucifer asked skeptically.

"I couldn't have done it before. But I have new information," Baltar explained. "I can tell you exactly where they are."

Lucifer descended the few steps to where Baltar had begun to climb to his feet, painfully favoring his injured right leg. The cyborg advisor grabbed Baltar by the neck, hefted him to his feet by the throat. As he choked, some part of Baltar had the presence of mind to marvel at this strength in Lucifer. A strength he had never been aware of.

"Now, Baltar, if you want to live," Lucifer said softly, his glowing dead red eyes locked on Baltar's face, searching for a lie, "tell me what you know of the Colonial fleet."

Baltar smiled, despite the pain in his leg.

"Oh, I'll tell you, all right," Baltar agreed. "But only when we've concluded our negotiations."

Dust and debris sifted down from the half-collapsed ceiling. There was an almost constant low rumble now, the sound of distant thunder, and Starbuck could feel the planet Ochoa moving beneath him. It shuddered like an old engine. The last temblor had been a decisive moment for him.

Time to go. If there was any chance he was to be rescued, it wouldn't happen while he was underground, and if he stayed any longer, he'd no doubt be buried.

He had already learned much. The technology the Cylons had been building on Ochoa was extraordinary. But he had used the only accessible infosphere to download biological reference on the Cylons. He couldn't take any of the tech data with him.

Still, there was one piece of Cylon technology he couldn't leave without. If he was to get off the planet—and strangely, as if a voice were whispering in the back of his mind to hurry, he had the oddest, most inexplicable sensation that he was indeed going to survive—he couldn't leave without taking that one item with him.

Starbuck worked feverishly to move enough debris to expose the engine of a Cylon fighter. He was no service technician, but he knew enough about starships to get into the engine. And he had seen the schematics of the piece he was looking for. It seemed like nothing more than some kind of bulb, egg-shaped and somewhat transparent, though tinted with gold. One wire connected it to the rest of the engine.

He opened the engine compartment. Nothing looked familiar to him. It bore no resemblance to the engine of a Viper. But he quickly spotted the bulb he sought, partially because it looked out of place, as if it were an afterthought. And it was, he knew.

Starbuck reached for the bulb, slid his fingers along the single wire to attempt to disengage it from the engine.

The planet roared then, the ground buckled beneath his feet and surged up, throwing him backward. Starbuck struck the stone floor, which heaved but did not shatter. The Cylon fighter rocked and danced as the floor split, separating him from the ship. The noise was deafening, and Starbuck felt as though he had placed his head inside one of the *Galactica*'s engine wells.

Though he knew it would not help him, he scrabbled away from the rift in the floor and clawed at the hard ground of the repair bay, trying to get a handhold.

"Quiet!" he screamed, and laughed at his own fear and raving.

The temblor began to subside, the roar of the planet dying to the same distant thunder he had heard before. The ground still quivered like an ancient man, and Starbuck knew it might erupt again at any micron. He stood, warily, and walked back toward the Cylon fighter he had worked so long to reach. A two-metron chasm now separated him from it. He thought about trying to reach it, but two metrons might as well have been twenty, for he didn't see anything he could use to bridge the gap.

"That's my luck," he said aloud. "Maybe it's time to go, Captain Starbuck? You were sniffing plant vapors to come down here in the first place."

A terrible, thunderous crack reverberated through the vast chamber. But it didn't stop. It began a cascade of snapping noises, like the breaking of huge bones. Only after several seconds did Starbuck think to look up.

The repair bay was four levels deep. The ceiling was already shattered and collapsed in some places, revealing the stone of the mountainside above. Now the stone itself was breaking, splitting.

"Oh, frack!" Starbuck screamed.

The ceiling scraped and slid and rumbled and caved down into the chamber. Starbuck ran four steps and then dove toward the comm-station that had been so helpful to him before. A mountain of soil and stone rained down from the hole in the ceiling, pounded the floor of the chamber, and pummeled two Cylon ships to scrap.

Seconds later, the dust from the collapse began to clear. Starbuck rose to his feet and blinked back a bright glare that shone in his face from above. It took him a moment to realize it was the dual suns of Ochoa. The collapse had buried the door through which Starbuck had entered the bay, but he realized it might have provided him with an exit as well.

If he could just get up there.

He started for the wall nearest the hole in the ceiling, thinking there might be enough of a handhold if he climbed the debris and reached out. Then he noticed something else the collapse had done. It had filled the chasm that separated him from the Cylon fighter. Not completely, but enough that he could cross. Carefully.

Starbuck was so careful that it took him several centari to cross the gap. The planet rumbled beneath him, and he knew the next temblor would take the whole outpost down, and not long after that, the whole planet would go.

But if he was leaving, he wasn't going empty handed. When he reached the Cylon fighter, it was simple enough to reach in and snap the wire that connected his prize. Once again, he ventured cautiously across the gap. He reached the other side and exhaled, holding the golden bulb gingerly in his hands. Starbuck didn't know if it was fragile, but he didn't want to take any chances.

Even as he turned back toward the light, a voice echoed down from above.

"Any time you're ready, old friend."

Starbuck squinted and gazed up to see a tall figure silhouetted against the glare, framed in the wide hole in the ceiling.

"Apollo?" he asked, astounded.

Then Starbuck laughed. "I don't believe it! I must be hallucinating!" he cried.

A thin cord slipped into the hole and unraveled as it dropped down into the chamber. He recognized it immediately as a fiberline, a required part of the emergency kit stashed in every Viper.

"Is that a comm-station?" Apollo asked, and pointed to the far corner.

"Yes," Starbuck replied, reaching for the fiberline. "Wait until I tell you what I accessed with it!"

The ground shifted beneath his feet. Starbuck stuck the gold bulb inside his tunic and tested his weight on the fiberline. It jerked in his hands, and he looked up again to see that, to his astonishment, Apollo was sliding down toward him.

"Wait!" Starbuck yelled. "What are you...don't come down here! We've got to go! The planet is coming apart, Apollo! Don't..."

Apollo slid the final metron and his boots slapped the ground. His eyes were intense as he reached out to grip Starbuck's shoulder.

"I know. We may only have a few centari. But we've got problems that comm-station may be able to help us with. The Cylons are infiltrating this quadrant. They may already be ahead of the fleet, establishing new outposts. They have other enemies here, but we need to find out as much as we can about the Cylons' locations. And how many base stars and how many fighters they've got. Anything that will help," Apollo explained.

Then he embraced Starbuck. After a moment, as Apollo's sudden appearance and the news he brought began to sink in, Starbuck returned the embrace. He smiled.

"You're always trying to get me killed," he said wistfully. "I'm not sure I should be happy to see you, but I am."

Apollo held him at arm's length then, and the two men smiled at one another. Their long friendship had always been all the more interesting because of their differences.

"I thought you were dead, Starbuck. We all did. I have a lot to tell you. Good things, bad things, others you won't even believe, if I know you," Apollo said, then his smile disappeared. "Dalton graduated early."

Starbuck swelled with pride, then caught the look on Apollo's face. "What's the bad news?" he asked.

"My father is dead," Apollo replied, without hesitation.

As quickly as his spirits had risen, Starbuck's heart sank. He searched for the words, but they didn't come to him. He looked at Apollo and saw a calm there, in his eyes and even the set of his mouth. An acceptance that surprised him.

"It's all right, Starbuck," Apollo said. "In a lot of ways, he was your father, too. You don't have to say anything."

Starbuck ran a hand through his light brown hair, then scratched the back of his head idly.

"I've never been at a loss for words before," he said. "I'm sorry."

The smile returned to Apollo's face, and immediately Starbuck felt better. There was something different about him, Starbuck thought distractedly. Where once Apollo seemed always to be driven by some furious, barely-controlled anxiety, his new determination seemed almost calm. Serene.

"You know," Starbuck said. "It was the strangest thing, just a few centari ago, even though I was sure I was going to die here, I got this feeling that I'd be all right. It's almost like I knew you were coming."

"You did," Apollo replied, his smile cryptic. "I was talking to you all along, telling you I was on the way."

Starbuck stared at him, thoroughly confused. Beneath their feet, the ground trembled.

"Let's move," Apollo said, and together they ran to the comm-station.

Apollo opened a dialogue with the computer, and Starbuck admired the pure instinct with which his friend elicited just the information he needed from the Cylon records. He told Apollo about the infosphere he had with the Cylon biological data.

"I wish we had time to store that data in my Viper's computer, then come back for these records," he said.

"We don't," Starbuck said curtly. "Don't go getting any ideas."

"So, what was it you were tearing out of that starfighter?" Apollo asked as he waited for data to appear detailing the quadrant's Cylon deployment.

"When we get topside, I'll try to install it in your Viper," Starbuck said excitedly. He pulled the globe from his tunic and turned it over in his hands. Apollo frowned, examining it more closely.

"The Cylons called it a Quantum Shift-Effect generator," Starbuck explained. "If it works the way the tech specs lay it out, it should make any ship or even an entire outpost pretty much invisible, both to scanners and to the naked eye."

The data Apollo was waiting for began to scroll up the screen, but he paid no attention. He stared at Starbuck, then took the gold bulb from his hands to examine it more closely. The ground shifted under them, but neither man paid much attention.

"How?" Apollo asked as he examined the device.

"Hey, I'm no scientist," Starbuck said. "But apparently it moves the ship or base, or whatever, out of dimensional phase somehow. A quantum shift. Meaning the ship's reality becomes subjective somehow. It's still there, but it's impossible to pinpoint, blurred on a subatomic level."

Apollo stared at the globe. He seemed upset by something.

"What's the matter, Apollo?" Starbuck asked. "This is phenomenal! The Cylons would have destroyed us with this, but the way the specs read, our techs should be able to duplicate the effect, to build our own QSE generators without much trouble. Isn't that a *good* thing?"

No reaction.

"Apollo?" Starbuck said. "Hello? What's the problem?"

Finally, Apollo looked up, as if returning from some kind of trance. "What?" he mumbled. "No. No problem. It's just that I've seen something like this before, but far more advanced. Light years further. In fact, so have you."

Starbuck stared at him before a long-buried memory returned, of something which had happened many yahren before. He'd almost begun to believe it had all been a dream.

"The lightships?" he asked.

Apollo nodded. "The Lords of Kobol."

"What?" Starbuck asked. "You know, Apollo, I'm the one who's been by myself too long, having whole conversations all alone, but you're really starting to confuse me."

"The crew of the lightships, they're the Lords of Kobol, Starbuck," Apollo explained. "Somehow, this Cylon device seems related to their technology."

"How do you know all this?" Starbuck asked.

Apollo looked up at him again and seemed to register Starbuck's presence for the first time in several minutes. Then the ground rumbled beneath their feet once more, and Apollo handed the globe back to Starbuck.

"I'll tell you everything later," he replied. "For now, let's just get out of here."

After a moment, Starbuck nodded. "Sounds almost as good as if you'd offered me a bottle of ambrosa and a beautiful smile."

"I won't ask whose," Apollo jabbed.

"Good, 'cause I'm not sure what my answer would be," Starbuck replied. "You get your data yet? I think we've overstayed our welcome here, my friend."

Apollo turned to study the information on the comm-station's flatscreen. As Starbuck watched, his face grew more and more concerned.

"Not as bad as it could be," Apollo interpreted. "But the Cylon presence in this quadrant is growing rapidly."

As Starbuck watched, he leaned closer to the comm-station to provide instructions.

"Triangulate location of all base stars with Binary 13 system and overlay galactic quadrant star map," Apollo instructed the unit.

"Comm-link to all base stars in this quadrant functioning. Beaming signal to locate," the computer noted.

One by one, the positions of Cylon base stars appeared on screen. There were several smaller ones and two full-size base stars within the quadrant. But Starbuck was certain there were more on the way. The unsuspecting inhabitants of the quadrant wouldn't know it, but there were far more where that came from.

As he stared at the screen, Starbuck suddenly recalled the other piece of tech he'd found so fascinating, mainly because it wasn't Cylon in origin.

"Computer," he spoke up. "Which one of those base stars is commanded by the human called Baltar?"

Apollo looked at him curiously, but waited as the computer searched for Baltar. On the flatscreen, the base star closest to Binary 13 began to blink.

"Of course," Starbuck said drily. "He *would* be right on our tails."

"What is it, Starbuck?" Apollo asked, not taking his eyes from the informational display. "I don't like Baltar being that close, but there's something else you're not..."

Apollo's voice trailed off. He cocked his head slightly and stared at Starbuck with what could only be described as awe on his face.

"Are you all right?" Starbuck asked.

"The Cylons have a holo-cube star map showing the original colonies settled by the emigrants from Parnassus," Apollo said quietly, as the meaning of this information struck him with awe and dread.

It was Starbuck's turn to stare.

"Apollo?"

"The records indicate that Baltar was last known to possess the holo-cube," Apollo said.

Starbuck's mind reeled.

"That cube might have the location of Earth on it," Apollo whispered. "Even if it doesn't, it could give us the locations of planets where other humans once lived. Maybe live even still. Allies, Starbuck! A place to settle, a place to dig in and fight the Cylons once and for all, with our ancient kinsmen at our sides! Do you have any idea what this means?"

Starbuck laughed. "Yeah, it'd be nice, wouldn't it? Too bad we can't slip aboard that base star, steal the holo-cube from Baltar's quarters, and run back to the fleet."

The very idea of it made Starbuck laugh even louder. The planet began to quake even more vigorously, and he knew they'd run out of time.

"I think we'd better go," he said.

Apollo didn't look at him. He was staring at the flatscreen where the location of Baltar's base star blinked on and off, not far from the Binary 13 system. Not far from Ochoa. Finally, Apollo looked up at him, his face grimly determined. His eyes met Starbuck's.

"Oh, wait—no!" Starbuck snapped. "I know that look. No way, Apollo. If I live long enough to get off this planet, I'm not going on any suicide mission with you. You must have brain crystals if you think I'm infiltrating a base star!"

Apollo smiled. "It was your idea, Starbuck," he pointed out.

"I was joking!" Starbuck cried. "By the Lords, I need a fumarello."

Without blinking, Apollo produced one of the long, thin brown smokes from inside his crimson flight jacket. Starbuck stared at it a micron.

"You know, Captain, I could simply order you to accompany me," Apollo reminded him.

"Apollo, it's crazy!" Starbuck protested.

"All right, I won't order you," Apollo relented. Starbuck sighed with relief, took the fumarello and searched for a light. Apollo produced one, and as he ignited the fumarello, he smiled once more.

"Well, I guess I'll be going now," he said. Without another word, he jogged toward the fiberline.

"What?" Starbuck said, and followed at a swift pace. "Wait a centari. You came here to rescue me, remember?"

Apollo didn't turn as he responded. Instead, he began to climb the fiberline.

"I did come to rescue you, yes," he admitted. "But since I'm going to steal that holo-cube, and you don't want to go, I don't have much choice but to leave you here. I certainly can't drop you off at the fleet and then come back to rob Baltar, can I?"

Gape-mouthed, Starbuck stared up at Apollo, who was nearly halfway up the line. He scowled, grumbled under his breath, and began to climb after Apollo. "I don't like this new you."

" Did you say something, Captain?" Apollo asked, taunting him.

"You're too calm," Starbuck called up to him. "I always got away with having a bit of a temper because you were such a hothead. Now what am I going to do?"

Apollo didn't respond, but Starbuck could hear him chuckle. Then the soft sound was drowned out by the rising growl of distant thunder which was, in reality, the death throes of a planet.

Starbuck was halfway up the fiberline when the worst temblor of all began to convulse the mountain, and what remained of the Cylon outpost. The line began to sway and he nearly lost his grip. Rocks slid down through the open ceiling, pelting him as he climbed.

The temblor roared in his ears. Starbuck could not stop himself from wondering if he had lived so long, been given such hope, only to lose his life here, now. He had always thought of Commander Adama as somehow immortal. But if Adama could die, anybody could die.

"Move, Starbuck, move!" Apollo shouted above, but Starbuck barely heard him.

Behind him came a deafening crack and rumble all too familiar to Starbuck now. The ceiling caved, tons of stone and soil pouring into the bay, burying the damaged Cylon fighters for eternity. The huge chamber's lights flickered, then blinked out. The emergency generator that had kept the lights and comm-station functioning in the repair bay had been crushed.

On the fiberline, Starbuck was spared the worst of the upheaval. Still, the earth moved enough to jerk him back and forth, bouncing him in the air like a merciless puppeteer. He glanced up quickly, saw Apollo urging him forward. He looked down, and saw that the floor of the bay had been rent asunder by the temblor. Now, though, it was not a matter of two or three metrons, but a huge chasm that would swallow him with the falling debris if he let go.

Hand over hand, as fast as he could, Starbuck hauled himself up. He felt the Cylon QSE generator inside his tunic, and prayed it hadn't broken, although it now seemed not to be as fragile as he had initially believed.

"Starbuck!" Apollo roared above him.

A small stone cut his cheek, but when Starbuck looked up, Apollo was there, reaching out for him. Apollo gritted his teeth, eyes ablaze, as he crouched on the heaving mountain. As Starbuck watched, the ground undulated beneath Apollo's feet. Then it began to crack.

Starbuck's eyes went wide. He grabbed Apollo's hand and held on tight. With his other hand, he got a hold on the edge of the hole, and began to haul himself up, the stone slipping away even as he released the fiberline.

He rose to his feet, crouched a bit, trying desperately not to fall. Apollo looked at him, legs spread to keep himself from tumbling over the precipice into the chamber below. They scrambled up the mountainside, toward a plateau where Apollo's Viper sat. They were both breathing heavily. Their glanced at one another, and Starbuck saw his own desperation reflected in Apollo's gaze.

"Well, I'm glad to see there are still some things that can agitate you," Starbuck quipped.

Apollo smiled. "A lot of things agitate me, Captain. Right now, I'd just like to leave this resort planet you brought me to."

"If you insist," Starbuck replied. "Though I was just beginning to grow fond of the place."

Behind them, the ground buckled. Starbuck fell to his knees against the mountain, and Apollo nearly tumbled backward. The hole in the roof of the outpost had continued to grow, and now the mountainside behind them began to disappear. The stone was being swallowed by a growing rift that seemed to split the mountain. The stone and earth began to crumble, and then the entire mountainside simply slid away into nothing.

The noise was horrible. The roar as the splinter of Ochoa speared the ground far below was louder than anything Starbuck had ever heard. The mountain continued to convulse.

"It isn't stopping," he shouted to Apollo.

"What?" Apollo cried, over the noise.

"It isn't stopping!" Starbuck yelled. "The others were all just temblors, a centari or two. But this is it, Apollo! I think this is the end!"

Starbuck climbed toward the Viper with every last ounce of strength even as the mountain threatened to simply drop out from beneath them.

Then they had reached the starfighter. As the ground heaved, the Viper's landing tripods slipped. The canopy opened and Starbuck climbed quickly into the cramped area behind the pilot's seat. It wasn't a seat but it would serve. Apollo slid into the pilot's chair, handed Starbuck a spare helm he must have brought just for that purpose, and slipped on his own.

"Apollo," Starbuck warned, as he watched the ground crumbling, the planet opening up in a rift that led straight toward the Viper. "We need to take off now, please."

The canopy closed.

"Apollo!" Starbuck cried, as the mountain ruptured nearby the Viper.

The engines fired, Apollo grabbed the navi-hilt, and the Viper thrust up and away from the mountain even as gouts of fire arced into the air from gashes that scarred the landscape below.

Starbuck watched Ochoa until they were out of the planet's atmosphere. Only when he could no longer see the fires burning below did he exhale in relief and turn his attention back to Apollo.

"Are you sure we can't just go home?" he asked.

"Not yet," Apollo answered.

17.

A POLLO AND STARBUCK WERE FORTUNATE ENOUGH to find a second life-bearing planet within the Binary 13 system. They were forced to leave their helms on to filter oxygen from the atmosphere, but they at least had the opportunity to install the QSE generator in the Viper. Apollo wasn't at all certain it would work, but Starbuck seemed to think it would. If it didn't, their attack on Baltar's base star was going to be particularly short-lived.

In as much detail as he could afford, Apollo told Starbuck all that had transpired since he had been shot down: The death of Adama. The turmoil of the fleet. Meeting Valor of the Sky. The new Cylons. The Lords of Kobol. Much of the history he had learned he kept to himself, as well as the extent of his mental abilities and the existence of the Kobollian sanctuary on the *Galactica*.

It was not that he desired secrecy from his best friend. It was only that these were things he had never told Athena. As Adama's daughter and a woman of full Kobollian blood, he had begun to believe she had a right to know. He felt that to tell Starbuck first would be wrong.

For his part, Starbuck had said little during the conversation, except to provide some sketchy outlines of his Cylon captivity. They both agreed that the threat to the fleet was imminent, but avoidable, if they could accomplish their mission. And, of course, if the Cylons had not already discovered the location of the fleet.

Zac had been thoughtful enough to stock Apollo's Viper with a fresh uniform for Starbuck, which he'd donned immediately. The crisp bova-leather crimson flight jacket was new, and its buckles shone. From his cramped space in the back of the Viper, Starbuck put a hand on Apollo's shoulder.

"Thank you, Apollo," he said sincerely.

"A Colonial Warrior is always prepared. I had a feeling you might want a change of clothes," Apollo said, choosing not to reveal the source of the uniform just yet.

Starbuck chuckled. "I meant for coming after me," he said. "For believing I was still alive, even if it was some crazy vision that led you to me. You risked everything in coming back for me."

Apollo smiled and waved off the thanks. "No less than you would have done, for me."

"True," Starbuck boasted happily. "I just wonder what kind of a fleet we'll be coming home to. If we ever get home."

"We'll get home," Apollo insisted.

The starfield spread out before them, vast and endless. Apollo had never been bothered by the solitary nature of piloting a starfighter. But rarely had he traveled so far in a Viper by himself. It was a great comfort to have Starbuck with him now. That he lived at all, when Apollo had once believed him dead, was cause for celebration. But the camaraderie, the sense of brotherhood, was exhilarating.

There was one other thing he had left out when speaking with Starbuck: Zac. That was also something he felt Athena should know first. Whether anyone else would ever know was something Apollo was not prepared to decide as yet. He felt no sense of superiority because of the supposedly greater mental abilities of the Kobollians, but he suspected there might be those who resented what the future might hold for him and for Athena. Possibly even for Starbuck, whose parents had both been Caprican and might well have been full-blooded Kobollian.

"Starbuck?" he asked suddenly. "What do you think of the idea of Athena becoming commander of the fleet?"

"Ah!" Starbuck exclaimed in triumph. "So you *do* think we're going to die on this crazy mission!"

"Not at all," Apollo said with a laugh. It occurred to him that he never laughed so much as when Starbuck was around. "I mean, what do you think of her as commander instead of me?"

Apollo heard Starbuck shift in the space behind him, then his helm appeared in Apollo's peripheral vision. Behind the force shield that covered Starbuck's face, the captain was frowning.

"I think she'd make a fine commander," he said finally, with some reluctance. "But she's not as well suited for it as you are."

"You're my best friend," Apollo argued. "You have to say that."

"Feldergarb," Starbuck muttered. "I lived with her for how many yahren? Athena has your charisma, your confidence and drive. You both inherited that from Adama. But you have more tactical experience, more field experience, more command experience. You've had significantly more direct contact with the Cylons. There's no question that you are better suited.

"On the other hand, since you're determined to die today..." Starbuck began, then let his words trail off.

Apollo ignored him. He scanned the readouts on the flatscreen and also on the helm-scroll. They were rapidly approaching the coordinates he had retrieved regarding the Cylon base star.

"Time to see if this gadget works," he told Starbuck. "Computer! Quantum shift, now!"

The change was instantaneous.

"Incredible!" Starbuck exclaimed.

Apollo could barely voice his agreement as he watched the stars seem to expand before his eyes. The dark void of space abated somewhat, as the stellar illumination brightened. The stars had not actually grown larger, but each was surrounded by a glittering corona. Brilliant tendrils of sparkling gold light shot from each star like the branches of a tree.

And the colors...Apollo could barely stand to look at them.

"I guess it's working," Starbuck said.

Apollo didn't turn to look at him, but smiled at his friend's fondness for stating the obvious, allowing only his tone to reveal if his words were meant in appreciation or sarcasm.

"It's wonderful, and ironic. The Cylons created this technology," Apollo said softly, "but they could never have appreciated it for anything more than its martial applications."

Light swirled and danced around the Viper, or at least it appeared to do so. Apollo could not determine what was real and what was a subjective interpretation of their surroundings. Not that it really mattered. They had, after all, subtly phased out of what they had always known reality to be. In the strictest sense, what they were seeing was not real. But at the moment, neither were they.

"I feel like I've had too much ambrosa," Starbuck declared, allowing the awe to creep into his voice. "The problem is, I haven't had any."

Blip!

"There it is," Apollo said grimly.

He sensed Starbuck craning forward just behind him. The flatscreen scanner showed a computerized image of a base star. A moment later, a holographic diagram of the massive Cylon war vessel burst from the flatscreen and spun in front of them.

"Are you sure they can't see us?" Starbuck asked.

"Am *I* sure?" Apollo replied with a frown. "I didn't even see the specs on this thing. I'm only going by what you told me."

"Oh, right," Starbuck mumbled.

Then there was only silence in the Viper, broken by the tiny beeps of the starfighter's sensors as they noted the diminishing distance to the base star.

Only microns later, they had visual contact. At a distance, it seemed no more threatening than a child's plaything. But both men had seen a Cylon base star up close. The voice of dread whispered in Apollo's ear, and he knew Starbuck must hear it as well.

Seen from their altered reality, the base star was a blossom of violet brilliance. But the light itself seemed somehow tainted, almost withered. The base star was an enormous structure. The bottom half was the shape of a rounded pyramid, the top identical yet inverse, so that the peaks of the structures met in the middle, at the central core, or shaft, of the ship. Four launch and landing bays were spaced equally around the top portion of the base star. Thankfully, all seemed inactive.

"They haven't launched anything yet," Starbuck said. "That's a good sign."

Blip! Blip!

"Frack!" Apollo snarled. "Two Cylon fighters just launched. They must know we're here. This thing isn't working!"

He gripped the navi-hilt tightly, prepared to blast his way past the Cylon fighters and head full speed toward deep space. Starbuck grabbed his wrist, and Apollo turned to glare at him.

"What?" he snapped.

"Give it a micron," Starbuck suggested. Apollo relented, nearly holding his breath as he watched the Cylon fighters, with their dark, glowing auras, arc away from the base star. They kept going, past the massive warship, and away.

"Regular patrol?" Starbuck asked.

"Must be," Apollo realized, then exhaled loudly. "I guess I'm not as controlled as you thought."

"Glad to see it," Starbuck admitted. "I was beginning to wonder if you were still human."

Apollo didn't respond, but he wanted to. He wanted to say that he wasn't quite sure himself anymore. But such conversations were for another time.

"Going in," he said finally.

Slowly, carefully, he piloted the quantum-shifted Viper toward the still-open landing bay.

"Good thing we're in a Scarlet-class Viper," Apollo noted. "I know you probably miss that antique of yours, but if we were flying that, we'd never be able to pull this off. The old starhounds didn't have a hover-mode."

"If it gets us out of here alive, then I'll be impressed," Starbuck replied.

As the phased starfighter slid into the bay, into the controlled environment of the ship itself, there was a slight ripple in the QSE field. The presence of their arrival must have impinged on non-shifted reality at that moment, for Apollo saw two Cylon Centurions appear from the depths of the bay, scanning for signs of intrusion.

"Only two," Starbuck said. "We can take them, no problem."

"Yeah, if there are only two," Apollo said. "If they sound an alarm, or if there are others down here, we'll never even reach the central core."

Silence behind him. Apollo turned to see Starbuck staring at him, a look of reproach on his face.

"You know, for the person who came up with this suicide mission, you should try to work on your morale," Starbuck said. "Now open the canopy."

"What?" Apollo asked. "You can't get out until the QSE is off. We don't know what might happen."

"Just open the canopy," Starbuck urged, his expression and body language implying a condescension that had gotten him in a lot of trouble over the yahren. "Let me worry about the rest."

"Canopy open," Apollo instructed the computer.

"Opening."

Starbuck stood up as the canopy rose, stretched, and unholstered his laser. He rotated his shoulders and head, neck cracking with stiffness, and groaned.

"I'm going to have to shut down the QSE generator," Apollo said, still eyeing the Centurions tensely.

The Centurions stared out into space, right past the phased Viper. Their energy rifles were held across their chests, and the red light of awareness panned across each of their visors.

"Shut it down," Starbuck said.

Apollo gave the computer his order, and the QSE field snapped off instantly, like blowing out a candle. It left a peculiar odor behind.

The Centurions swung their weapons toward the Viper the moment it came back into phase with reality. But they were too late. Starbuck was a dead-on shot, one of the best in the fleet. His laser erupted twice, and the Cylons went down with blackened holes in their chestplates.

Starbuck leaped from the cockpit and landed hard on the metal floor. He swung his laser in an arc across the bay, prepared for a second wave of Centurions. When no response seemed forthcoming, he removed his helm and tossed it up to Apollo.

Apollo removed his own helm and tossed them both behind him. Then he climbed down onto the wing and ordered the canopy closed. He drew his laser and dropped to the floor next to Starbuck. Together, they advanced toward the back of the bay.

A large door slid open at their approach, revealing a long, wide corridor. They waited to see what would happen next. Several microns passed and nobody came into the bay to discover why the door had opened.

"How long do you think we have until that patrol returns?" Apollo asked.

"Anywhere from five to ten centons," Starbuck replied. "But there's no way to know when the guards were supposed to change shifts in here. We have to be quick, twenty-five centari, no more. Even then, there's no way to know."

"Then we go now," Apollo said.

The doors slid open once more, and the two Colonial Warriors stepped quickly through. Apollo spun left, Starbuck right, lasers at chest level to take down any Centurion who might have the misfortune to be in the corridor at that moment.

Their luck held. It was empty.

"Come on," Starbuck said, starting off to the right. "Central core is this way."

"No," Apollo argued. "Base star schematics say this way."

"When was the last time you looked at the schematics of a base star?" Starbuck asked. "Really looked."

Apollo shrugged. "Three or four yahren," he replied. After all, it had been six yahren since they'd confronted any Cylon presence at all. "What about you?" he asked.

Starbuck grimaced.

"Longer than that," the Captain said. "All right, we go your way. But if you're wrong, I'll shoot you."

"If I'm wrong, you won't have time," Apollo replied without smiling.

"Oh, so glad to see your spirits have improved," Starbuck grumbled.

Then they moved down the hall noiselessly, staying close to the wall, laser pistols up and ready to fire. A short way down the hall, they found the access hatch to the central core. It did not slide open automatically, but there was a manual latch that proved simple enough to release. Once inside, they continued to creep soundlessly across a mesh landing.

Apollo looked down. Ten or twelve metrons below was the actual core of the base star, the chamber that connected the top and bottom of the vessel. Two Centurions posted within that chamber, around which were also positioned ascensior tubes and the communications facilities, if Apollo remembered correctly. The bridge was in the lower part of the base star, oddly enough, and the command chamber, thankfully, in the top.

Apollo pointed down to indicate the Centurions, then up to urge Starbuck to begin climbing. Slowly, methodically, they began their ascent. Two levels brought them to an area Apollo believed should allow them to emerge just outside the command chamber. Apollo tried to speak to Starbuck telepathically, but the other Warrior didn't respond. Obviously, he was a long way from mastering the talents he'd discovered within himself.

"There will be guards," he whispered, his words so quiet he could barely hear them himself.

"Nothing to be done for it now," Starbuck replied in the same whisper. "But Baltar's a coward. If we can take him as a hostage, he'll do anything to save his life, including ordering them not to fire at us."

Apollo looked at him. "That makes sense," he noted. "I hadn't thought of it."

"Wait," Starbuck said a bit too loudly. He looked down at the

Cylons before continuing in a quieter tone. "You mean, you didn't have any plan at all? I thought this was what you had in mind."

"Well, I'm glad you thought of it," Apollo said with a smile. "Maybe *you* should be the commander of the fleet."

"No, thank you," Starbuck murmured.

Apollo put a hand on the latch and looked at Starbuck. When he nodded, Apollo cranked the latch down and shoved it open, diving out into the corridor. Even as Starbuck followed him, Apollo rolled and came up under a barrage of fire.

Only two guards. The Centurions apparently did duty in pairs.

Starbuck and Apollo each loosed a shot, and the Cylons went down, armor clanking.

"I'm a little upset that you say they're building better Cylons," Starbuck said. "These guys are nice and slow."

Apollo raised a finger to his lips, quieting Starbuck, and the two moved to the door of the command chamber. They had taken a risk, reasoning that the odds favored Baltar being on his "High Seat of Command" rather than in his private quarters. Now they would see if it paid off.

The doors slid open, and two other Centurions, one a gold-plated captain, started out into the corridor. Apollo agreed with Starbuck. A dozen Centurions were hard to fight, but one on one, even three on one, was fair odds because they were so slow. These two stepped past them. Starbuck cleared his throat—Colonial Warriors didn't shoot people in the back, even Cylons—and the Centurions turned, only to be blasted and crash to the floor.

"Go!" Apollo shouted, and the two of them shot into the command chamber without another thought.

The Cylon cogitator called Lucifer was on the command chair. Baltar was there, but at the foot of the steps to the seat, as if he were no longer commander. Neither of them was armed.

"What's the cog doing up there?" Starbuck asked, even as they aimed their weapons at Baltar.

"Never mind, just take him," Apollo snapped.

"My, my, what a pleasant surprise!" Baltar crowed.

"You're coming with us, traitor," Apollo growled. "Let's move, and if we see a single Centurion with a weapon, you'll die with us."

The smile left Baltar's lips. "I'm afraid you've made an error," the coward said. "None of them care what happens to me. I'm not in command anymore, you see."

Lucifer had remained silent, but now, as Baltar's words shattered Apollo's plan, he stood from his seat.

"Take them alive," he said, in a chilling, electronic voice.

From the shadowy corners of the room, six Centurions emerged. Apollo was filled with horror as he gazed upon the reptilian styled ebony armor of the new dark Centurions. He raised his laser pistol and fired several times. Behind him, Starbuck did the same.

The laser blasts were deflected, burning electric stains elsewhere in the chamber. Apollo fired again, concentrating on one dark Centurion, but the laser did not cut through whatever armor or force shield protected it.

"Apollo!" Starbuck yelled from behind him. "I think we'd better get out of here!"

Apollo heard a crack, a grunt, and then the sound of Starbuck hitting the floor.

"No!" Apollo screamed as he spun and fired at the dark Centurion standing over his friend.

Pain exploded in his skull as he was struck by something hard, and Apollo crumpled to the floor beside Starbuck. The last thing he saw was Baltar's face, strangely unsmiling. The last he heard was the dry, pervasive chuckle of Lucifer.

Then, simply, nothing.

18.

LASER IN HAND, Athena strode urgently onto the bridge of the *Ursus*, flanked by Captain Hecate of the Fourth Squadron, and three other Warriors on her squad. The crew of the *Ursus* was in turmoil, and her arrival did nothing to pacify them.

"Commander Athena!" one of the crewmen exclaimed, and the rest of them froze. They were not soldiers, and so did not salute, but it was obvious they felt they should make some gesture toward Athena, even if her command was, for the moment, temporary.

"Who has the bridge?" Athena snapped, without acknowledging their respect or their discomfort.

"I have," said a tall, powerfully built Sagittarian woman. "Until Captain Morgan returns from the Pit."

Anger flashed through Athena, but she fought it down.

"From what I'm told," she said tersely, "your captain will not be returning from the Pit. At least, not without assistance."

The first officer of the *Ursus* said nothing. The others would not meet Athena's gaze.

"My father used to say that the Pit served a purpose for this fleet. Perhaps it does. Controlled anarchy is subversive, but because it is contained, it does not disrupt society as a whole. Perhaps, in some ways, it is even productive and instructive," she suggested.

"But it is still anarchy. When this is all over, the Pit will be regulated, patrolled...ordered," Athena declared. "For now, your captain, Ensign Dalton, and Lieutenant Troy, along with several other members of your crew if my information is correct, are in dire need of our help.

"That is, if they're even still alive down there," she said, in a softer voice.

Athena stared into the eyes of the Sagittarian woman. She didn't know what she was looking for there, but had the feeling she'd found it.

"I need ten people, armed with lasers, to accompany me into the Pit immediately. I'd like you to join us as well, if there is someone else to whom you feel comfortable entrusting the ship," Athena said.

The woman, whose name was Portia, went into action immediately. Only a few centari passed before they were descending into the Pit, ten armed crew members and five Colonial Warriors. But set against the hundreds of disenfranchised denizens of the Pit, Athena still didn't like the odds. It really depended, she supposed, on how far Puck's influence had reached and how many of these people even cared about the succession of command. And, of course, how many were psychotic enough to want to kill them without any real motive.

"When we hit the bottom level, we will move swiftly through the Pit," she ordered. "Fire a warning shot if anyone gets too close. If we come under attack, do not hesitate to use your weapons. There are too many to let them get a jump on us."

"Commander?" Portia ventured. "If I may say so, I think you'll find the majority of the Pit people unthreatening. I believe the captain was taking your missing warriors to see the Cult of the Serpent. I doubt we'll run into trouble until we reach their dwellings."

"By the Lords, Portia, I hope you're right," Athena said.

The ascensior doors began to cycle open.

Cassiopeia had entirely abandoned the idea that she could get any kind of reading on the murder victim's tissue samples. Any testing that might be done, she would have to do herself. It would be investigative work, the process of elimination.

She found herself excited by the challenge.

Slowly, methodically, she began to measure bone lengths, skull size, diameter of the charred corpse's ocular orbits. She examined the bone structure for any trace of past physical trauma, or signs that would indicate the age of the victim.

It was a tedious task. But when all the numbers were recorded on computer, when she had observed all she could about the corpse itself, she hoped to be able to initially decipher what colony the dead man hailed from. From there, the same statistics might possibly be used to determine precisely who he'd been.

There was still no report of any missing person even remotely matching the description of the corpse.

"I *will* find out who you are," she vowed to the dead man. "No matter how hard you try to make it for me."

Tybalt capered madly about the Pit as he issued instructions and jabbered on unintelligibly. Troy stared at the lunatic, even as his mind careened through various escape plans, none of which seemed solid enough to use.

"He's truly insane!" Captain Morgan snarled. "Who is he talking to?"

"Himself, probably," Dalton said, as she attempted to inconspicuously loosen the fiberline that bound her wrists. "Tybalt is probably arguing with Tybalt over who gets to fire the laser blast through our brains."

Troy glared at her. That was just the kind of sentiment—gallows humor or no—that they didn't need right now. He looked around and analyzed their situation once again. Hopeless, he concluded. He might be able to slip his bonds, even rush a couple of the Serpent cultists, but not before the others blasted Morgan and Dalton.

"Troy?" Dalton asked, her voice tender now with concern for him.

"Yeah," was all he said.

"What in God's name is that?" Morgan asked suddenly.

Troy and Dalton both turned to see that the captain was staring once again at Tybalt. The fool's capering had subsided, and now he stood awkwardly, head cocked to one side like a slowbrain, listening. Paying too much attention to nothing.

Yet it wasn't nothing. Troy could see that now. In the darkened squalor of the Pit, the wide area they had been moved to from the cult's quarters, Troy could see that whatever Tybalt was listening to, or looking at, was real. There was a silhouette there, the size of a man, though it seemed to blend in with the other shadows. Troy thought if he closed his eyes and listened carefully, he might be able to hear the things that dark mist of a man was whispering to Tybalt. But he didn't get the chance.

"Lieutenant Troy!" Tybalt cried gleefully, so obviously mad now. When they'd first arrived, the man had played at sanity. But the charade had long since been dropped.

Troy looked up as Tybalt approached, nearly prancing.

"Have I got a surprise for you, Lieutenant!" Tybalt cried.

In the shadows behind the mad prophet, the dark thing had disappeared. Troy didn't think he wanted to hear about Tybalt's surprise.

"Hmmph!" Tybalt grunted. "No response? Then I suppose it really will be a surprise."

Tybalt turned to his gathered followers—whose numbers had greatly increased—and began to order them about once more. There was some kind of tech setup several metrons away, being rapidly programmed by a woman Troy had not seen before. Tall, hot lights flashed on, bathing them in painful glare, growing warmer by the micron.

A hand was shoved in front of Troy's face. A small kyluminam ball dotted with glass eyes lay in Tybalt's outstretched palm.

"Leave him alone!" Dalton snapped.

The look Tybalt gave her verged on adoration. But for this madman, Troy thought, that might be the same as lust or mere homicidal psychosis.

"My dear Ensign Dalton," Tybalt crooned, "this is not a weapon.

It is a highly advanced TransVid skyeye. This is the surprise I told you about. You see, with the tech at our disposal, we're going to splice our skyeye feed into both the TransVid system and the unicomm. Your plight will be viewed by the entire fleet."

A cold knot formed in Troy's gut.

"Do it," Tybalt cried.

The skyeye buzzed into life, the eyes emanating a light of their own. They were not eyes, though, but lenses, capturing the events in the Pit from every possible angle. The skyeye leaped into the air, rotated, and zipped from one point to another with wild abandon. Its own internal processors told it what to film for transmission.

"Salutations, friends!" Tybalt cried with glee. "I am Tybalt, high priest of the Serpent. If you don't recognize the people behind me, let me introduce them."

Tybalt nearly danced toward them, the skyeye following his every move. There was a murmur of approval from the cultists gathered round, but in the glare of the lights, Troy could not see any of their faces. He sensed something in them, a kind of hunger, that made him despair for the first time. Escape seemed hopeless.

"This is Lieutenant Troy!" Tybalt said giddily. "Handsome one, isn't he, ladies? Adopted son of the traitorous Lieutenant Commander Apollo."

"That's a lie!" Troy roared, thrusting forward, trying to reach Tybalt and failing.

Tybalt slapped him down again, put a foot on Troy's chest. The skyeye buzzed in close, hovering above him to capture every painful micron. The humiliation was worse than the pain.

"Quiet, boy," Tybalt sneered. "This isn't your show."

He spun in almost a full pirouette.

"Now! On to the lovely Ensign Dalton, daughter of that maverick Captain Starbuck, a more charming and beloved citizen, a more skilled Warrior, we can't imagine. Apollo probably shot down poor Starbuck himself, to hide his dealings with the Cylons," Tybalt cried, his voice rising to a mad pitch.

"By the Lords," Dalton fumed, "I'll kill you with my bare hands!"

"Ah, ah, ah!" Tybalt warned, waving a finger in front of Dalton's face. He turned to stare right into the skyeye.

"Young love," he said, and sighed happily. "Beautiful, isn't it?"

Troy saw Dalton's face flush, a combination of anger and embarrassment. The skyeye moved in as well. It didn't miss anything. The thought that the entire fleet was watching spurred him on.

"Tybalt, you're a murderer and a seditionist!" Troy shouted. "You have abducted Colonial Warriors. Turn yourself in now, and maybe the Quorum will be lenient because you are mentally deficient. Continue with this insanity, and you will be dealt with quite harshly," he said sternly.

Tybalt ignored him, moving on to Captain Morgan.

"Here's a man most of you won't know! Morgan, captain of the *Ursus*, benevolent warden overseeing this stinking Pit," Tybalt snarled. "Old, soft, useless. But I suppose somebody out there must love him."

Tybalt held his hand out toward the shadows, and one of his younger followers, a pretty blonde Gemon girl, rushed forward with wide, adoring eyes. She laid a laser pistol across his palm.

Without ceremony, Tybalt turned and shot Morgan through the head.

"No!" Troy and Dalton screamed in unison.

"You fracking mindwipe!" Troy shouted. "He'd done nothing to you!"

Tybalt moved in on Troy again.

"Nor have you, Lieutenant," Tybalt said amiably. "But I'll do the same to you soon enough."

The skyeye caught it all, up close. Tybalt turned his back to Troy, and the young Warrior struggled harder agains his bonds than ever before.

"Now then, this is a message for the esteemed Quorum, the Council of the Twelve," the madman announced. "You will put an end to your vacillation, and you will vote Ambassador Puck in as commander within one centon. If you do not, Ensign Dalton will die as gruesomely as the late Captain Morgan."

"Oh my God," Dalton whispered. "Troy, we've got to get out of here."

"I can afford to let her live, you see, for her father was a hero," Tybalt explained. "On the other hand, just to be certain you know I'm serious, and because his father is a greater traitor even than Baltar, Lieutenant Troy will die now."

"Frack!" Troy snapped, and thrust himself forward again, struggling with his bonds. Dalton was screaming at his side as Tybalt leveled the laser pistol, aiming at his face.

"Now, sires and siresses, for your viewing pleasure," Tybalt said happily.

"I'll kill you, Tybalt," Dalton screamed. "Don't fire, you mucoid mugjape! Don't do it!"

Tybalt looked at her and grinned. He turned his attention back to Troy, and there was the electric crackle of laser blast accompanied by a flash of light.

Troy recoiled, then stared down at himself to see that he was unhurt. Tybalt began to whimper with pain. The mad prophet cradled his scorched and withered right hand against his chest, the laser on the ground between them. Desperately, without even looking to see who had fired at Tybalt, he tried once again to slip his bonds...to no avail.

Suddenly, Dalton was free. Somehow she had done what he could not. She snagged the laser and lifted it to fire at Tybalt, but the madman had scrambled back to join his followers.

"Kill them!" Tybalt screamed. "Kill them all!"

Laser pistols were raised. Then, from further back in the shadows, came a voice.

"You people just don't get the message, do you?" the voice called. "Let them go immediately and you'll live to be incarcerated on the *Icarus*."

"Athena!" Dalton shouted.

Troy was relieved. But only for a moment. Even as Dalton shoved him into a shadowy corner among some plasteen crates, and slipped him free of the fiberline, a cultist swung one of the massive lights toward Athena and the Warriors she'd brought with her. The cultists badly outnumbered them.

The laser battle began, and the skyeye flitted about, transmitting it all over the fleet.

Boomer was worried. Maybe even a little frightened. He had arrived in the repair bay of the *Hephaestus* just in time to warn the crisis crew working there that they were in danger. They had nearly extinguished the flames, only to be set upon by seditionist Quorum security forces. The traitors had commandeered the ship, and had pinned Boomer and the crisis crew in the bay.

The stalemate wasn't going to last. The blackshirts had more weapons. Eventually, they would outflank Boomer and the techs, or just wear them down. If backup didn't arrive, Boomer knew this would end quickly, and not well.

From the things that had been said, he gathered that some of the more zealous of the seditionists had executed the entire *Hephaestus* crew and all civilians on board, except for those like Captain Heimdall who were cooperating with Paris. Once Boomer and the others were dead, the *Hephaestus* would be a pirate ship, completely in their control.

"Surrender, Major! You can't win!" Paris called from behind a crippled Viper. "You'll never reach that shuttle, and even if you do, we'll never let it out of here in one piece."

Boomer needed to buy time with some kind of distraction. He'd scanned the area behind him in the bay, the only place he could move freely without being cut down by a laser blast. He'd found nothing there that would be of use to him.

On the other hand, not far from the crippled Viper Paris and his blackshirts were using for cover, there was a large mobile fuel tank. If he was not mistaken, it would be filled with already diluted tylium, an extremely volatile substance. If he could get a clean shot at it with his laser, Boomer was certain it would explode and take the Viper with it. Some of Paris's men would undoubtedly be killed. The problem was even such an explosive diversion would not provide enough time for the entire crisis crew to board the shuttle and for the ship to launch. Boomer stared at that fuel tank and then glanced over at a group of techs shielded behind an enormous athanor, a kind of furnace used for working metals. They were too far for him to call out to without Paris hearing the exchange, so he was forced to improvise. As foolish as he felt, Boomer used hand gestures to simulate a flying starship, then pointed at the terrified crewmen. Most of them merely looked confused, one man stared at him as if he were mad, but a stout Libran woman in the back waved to get Boomer's attention and then pointed at her own chest.

Thank the Lords, Boomer thought. A pilot. He held up a hand, palm out, signalling that they should wait for him to act before moving. A plan had begun to form, even as Paris had mocked him, and now Boomer started to see it in greater detail.

"Not so perfect a Warrior now, are you, Major?" Paris called from across the bay. "More than one hundred people died on this ship today, and what did you do to save them? Nothing!"

Boomer gritted his teeth. Starbuck and Apollo, had they been with him, would have railed at the man's savagery. No matter how different they had been, there had always been some fundamental similarities in the two Warriors. But Boomer was neither Starbuck nor Apollo. He had a temper, no question, but he would not allow himself to be goaded into ill-advised action.

He crouched behind the solid saligium base-cab of a magnalift, it's latticed crane towering overhead. To his left was a series of levers that controlled the crane, an archaic yet effective system. Boomer studied these levers closely, analyzed the position of the crane and the layout of the bay. Silently, he prayed. Then he wrapped his fingers around the center lever, and pulled it toward him with every bit of his strength.

The crane fell to the side, slicing through the repair bay. Before it slammed its full weight into the floor of the bay, Boomer turned to the techs behind the athanor and screamed, "Go!" The crane crashed to the floor, separating the seditionists from the shuttle. The techs rushed out from behind the athanor and ran for their only hope of escape, crouching as they ran. The crane was tall enough to provide them decent cover, but its bridgework was no sure protection from laser fire. Even a deflected blast could be fatal.

"Kill them!" Paris screamed. "Don't let them escape!"

He stepped out from behind the crippled Viper, a broken arm dangling limply by his side. Boomer was tempted to shoot him down then and there. But he wasn't alone, and Boomer didn't want to give the other blackshirts time to take a bead on the escaping crisis team. Instead of killing Paris, he aimed at the fuel tank just behind the Viper, and blasted it.

The explosion ripped the Viper up, tossing Paris half the distance to where Boomer still hid. The man slammed to the floor with a loud snap and didn't rise. Three other blackshirts had been incinerated in the blast, and gouts of flame leaped up toward the ceiling of the bay.

It didn't last, though. Six or eight other blackshirts had taken shelter elsewhere in the bay, and after the initial horror of the explosion, had begun to fire upon the crisis team as they boarded the shuttle. Boomer heard the ship's engines power up, and felt a grim satisfaction. He popped up from behind the magnalift's base-cab and fired at the exposed blackshirts. He let off several blasts before ducking back down again.

"Major!" someone cried from the shuttle. "We're all aboard, let's go!"

Boomer lifted his head again and was forced to duck down immediately to avoid having his face scorched. About seven against one, now. No way could he make it to the ship. But he could certainly make sure the blackshirts were too busy returning his laser fire to worry overmuch about the shuttle.

"Go on!" he cried. "Go, go, go! I'll make sure you get off safely!"

"Major, we're not going to leave without you!" a deep male voice rumbled across the bay.

Boomer looked over at the shuttle and saw the man pull his head back inside as laser fire slapped a staccato rhythm against the shuttle's hull and open door. It could take a certain amount of punishment, but if the seditionists shot at the ship's fuel tanks, the shuttle might very well explode.

"This is a direct order from a Colonial Warrior: The fleet is under martial law," he said. "Launch that shuttle immediately!"

Even as he spoke, he bobbed his head up again, and succeeded in blasting two blackshirts who were firing on the shuttle. He winged one. The other went down hard and didn't move. Boomer burned with rage at them, not only because of their heinous crimes, but because they had forced him to take human lives, something he had only done once before in his career as a Warrior. It turned his stomach.

Then the shuttle rumbled and lifted off, hovered a moment, and blasted out of the repair bay. Several blackshirts tried to fire at its tanks as it departed, but Boomer laid down a heavy stream of laser fire that discouraged them.

"Happy now, Boomer?" a voice croaked nearby.

Boomer risked a glance across the bay and saw that Paris had finally risen to his feet. The security chief's broken arm was contorted further, white bone jutting from his uniform, and Boomer recalled the snap he'd heard when Paris hit the ground. How could the man even stand with that pain, Boomer thought? He hadn't even screamed when he'd hit the floor, crushing that broken arm beneath him. It was inhuman.

Yet, there he stood, laser held in his only functional hand.

Not that it really mattered. The fool was standing out in the open. One shot and Boomer could take him down. It almost seemed unfair. But after the atrocities Paris had committed, he didn't care.

"The shuttle's away, but that still leaves you here with us. Time to see who's the better man, *Major*," Paris sneered.

Boomer bounced up, aimed his laser at Paris, and was shot in the right shoulder by another of the blackshirts. Pain shrieked through him, Boomer spun backward, and his laser pistol clattered to the floor.

When he looked up, cradling his shoulder, he understood that it was over for him. While he was still shielded from the other seditionists, Paris was only twelve or thirteen metrons away, directly in front of him. Even if his aim was off after his injuries, the seditionist had a clear shot.

"Frack," Boomer said softly.

Paris smiled.

Boomer went for his laser even as Paris raised his own weapon. There wasn't enough time. Oddly, as the knowledge of his own impending death overwhelmed him, Boomer could think only of his baby sister, Persephone, who had died with the rest of his home planet, Leonis, during the Cylon destruction of the colonies. Every time he'd killed a Cylon, Boomer had remembered his sister, her gap-toothed grin, her laugh. Now, Paris staggered, aimed his laser, and Boomer thought of Persephone again.

"Goodbye," Paris said.

There was a loud roar, and both men glanced over toward the repair bay entry portal. The starfield was blocked by a speeding shuttle which pierced the invisible shield of energy that kept the void of space outside the launch aperture. The shuttle thundered into the bay, and Boomer had a moment to wonder what maniac was at the navi-hilt.

Then Paris screamed.

Boomer turned to see the seditionist spin and run for cover. But he was too slow. The shuttle pounded into Paris, crushing his bones to powder with its bulk and speed, then settled down on top of him, forward landing gear obliterating the man beneath its mass. Boomer only stared at the shuttle now, wondering what crazed impulse had inspired the crisis crew to return. For even with Paris dead, there were quite a few of the traitorous blackshirts left on the *Hephaestus*.

The seditionists appeared immediately and began firing on the shuttle. A hatch on the near side of the vessel popped open, and a squadron of Warriors dropped to the floor, one after another, lasers at the ready. The first one to hit the ground was Sheba.

"Boomer!" she called.

"Here!" he answered, then pointed to the other side of the bay. "Over there. No more than ten or twelve left, at most."

Sheba barked commands that sent the other Warriors running. Then she walked calmly over to where Boomer stood holding his wounded shoulder. She glanced at the wound and seemed satisfied that it wasn't serious.

"What took you so long, Major?" he asked.

She widened her eyes with feigned innocence. "Why Major Boomer," she said, "I just wanted to make sure we didn't arrive before you took that flesh wound. They'll never award you the Golden Cluster if you don't get shot at least once."

Boomer couldn't help but smile.

"Why, Sheba," he said, "I didn't know you cared."

19.

I N THE MOMENT BEFORE HE WOKE, Apollo had a vision. It was too real, too focused to be a dream, and it did not sift away like the sands of Cancer when he awoke. A clairvoyant episode, he was certain. What confused him were the images themselves, for they made no sense whatsoever.

The vision had shown him Baltar, firing a laser at a dead Cylon.

"One thing I have to say about Cylons," Starbuck observed, "they're very clean."

Apollo had been examining their cell for some possible means of escape ever since he and Starbuck had come around several centari ago. Now he turned and merely stared at Starbuck. The other man's gift for sarcasm never ceased to amaze him.

"No, really," Starbuck insisted. "Think about it. For a reptilian race genetically bred with human DNA, you'd think they would be really unkempt. Reptiles are kind of, well, slimy, and humans can be the biggest slobs in the known universe if they get the chance."

"You're really out of your mind, you know that?" Apollo said. "Do you think maybe you could help me try to get us out of here? Or are you going to dwell on Cylon hygiene for another centon?"

Starbuck looked askance, as if shocked by Apollo's words.

"Listen, Commander," the other Warrior said sharply, "just because I happen to be fascinated with alien species, even our enemy, doesn't mean I don't want to escape. We know from the bio-records I stole from Ochoa that the Cylons were cross-bred with human DNA, giving them their humanoid body design. I think it must be the cyborg implants that make them so fastidious. What do you think?"

Apollo stared at him.

"I think your brain has done a quantum shift, Starbuck," Apollo said sternly. "Has it occurred to you that if we don't get out of here, they're going to execute us?"

Starbuck smiled and shook his head.

"Oh, no they're not," he said happily. "If they wanted to execute us, we wouldn't be in this cell. No, they probably plan to torture us for information. And *then* kill us."

"And what part of this theory do you find so amusing?" Apollo asked, appalled by his friend's nonchalance.

"We won't be here," Starbuck replied. He raised his eyebrows several times, an expression Apollo had long since learned meant that Starbuck had some key bit of information Apollo himself had missed.

"You're wasting time," Apollo growled.

"Look down," Starbuck said.

Apollo grimaced, then looked at the floor.

"I see a floor," he said.

"You're not looking closely enough," Starbuck noted. "You're thinking in human terms. We build our vents and things in walls and ceilings. But I learned from my little shore leave on Ochoa that Cylons always build vents and water systems in the floor. The floor is a series of grated tiles, but I imagine you'll find that one or more of the corner tiles is perforated. A vent. If we can open it, it should be wide enough to squeeze through. Then if we can make it to the central core, we might actually stand a reasonable chance of getting out of here alive."

Apollo gaped at Starbuck in horror.

"You've known this all along and let me waste precious centari trying to find just such an escape route?" he demanded.

"Actually, I was a little disoriented when I came around. At first I wasn't even sure where we were. I guess I thought I was still on Ochoa," Starbuck explained, then shrugged a small apology. "Shall we look?"

The two men went to separate corners of the cell. Apollo saw the difference in the grated floor tiles immediately, now that he knew what to look for. He could barely fit the small finger of his right hand into the grate, but it wouldn't pull up.

"Try this," Starbuck said behind him. Apollo turned to see the other man holding out his laser belt and holster—something else that Zac had thoughtfully placed aboard Apollo's Viper while he was on the lightship. Immediately, he saw what Starbuck intended. He slid the buckle of the belt between two bars of the grate. When it had passed through, he gave the belt a small tug and it held. The buckle had opened slightly, as he'd suspected it would.

Apollo stood, held on to the belt, and put his weight into a powerful heave. With a shrieking of metal hinges, the grating tore from the floor and Apollo fell back against the wall.

"Well done, Commander," Starbuck said. "If I'd had that belt on Ochoa, I would have escaped a lot sooner. Now, why don't we get out of here?"

"We didn't get what we came for," Apollo argued, unlatching the buckle from the grate and handing Starbuck back his belt.

Now it was Starbuck's turn to stare. "You've got to be kidding," he said. "We don't even know where Baltar's current quarters are."

Both men looked at the crawlspace beneath the grate, their escape route. They looked at one another. Then Starbuck cursed under his breath. Apollo smiled. Then Starbuck sat on the floor and swung his legs into the vent.

"You just don't know when to thank the Lords of Kobol for your good luck and move on," Starbuck complained. "You know we're never going to find Baltar, don't you? You do realize you're going to get us killed?"

"Actually, I'm pretty confident we'll be seeing Baltar again soon,"

Apollo replied, and ignored the curious look Starbuck shot him.

From the corridor there came the electric crackle of laser fire and a loud clatter. Starbuck and Apollo whipped around to stare at the door to their cell.

"Now what do you think…" Starbuck began.

The cell doors slid open, and Baltar rushed in. Beyond the open door, they could see the prone, smoking form of a dead Cylon Centurion. Starbuck stared open-mouthed at the new arrival, then glanced at Apollo, who also seemed surprised, though not nearly as much.

Baltar smiled and tossed their confiscated laser pistols to them.

"I see you started without me," Baltar said amiably. "All well and good, but I think the corridor is the fastest route to the landing bay, don't you?"

Baltar walked back to the door, glanced out into the corridor, and then looked back in at them, urgency etched on his features.

"Well?" he prodded.

Apollo smiled at Starbuck, who stared back at him in wonder. Starbuck shrugged. They didn't have too many options. Apollo started after Baltar, and Starbuck pulled himself from the vent and followed.

"We're in the lower level," Baltar explained as they hurried along the corridor. "Walk in front of me. If we run into any Centurions, I'm bringing you prisoners to see Lucifer. We'll use the main ascensior tube, and ride it right to the bay. You'll have to kill the guards there, I'm afraid, but there should only be two of them."

Apollo did not turn to face Baltar. He wanted to keep up the appearance that the Warriors were the Great Traitor's prisoner. But he spoke harshly without looking back.

"We can't leave without the item we came for," Apollo said.

"Yes," Baltar hissed. "I was wondering what suicidal impulse had motivated your timely arrival."

"Timely how?" Starbuck asked.

"It seems my Cylon friends have spent nearly two decades using my genetic codes to create Centurions with what they call a 'human logic function,' patterned after my brain," Baltar explained archly. "It would be almost flattering, if they hadn't decided to execute me now that they don't need me any more."

"We want the holo-cube that contains the star map to the original colonies, the ones that sprang from Parnassus," Apollo revealed.

"Well, well," Baltar said. "I don't know how you even came to be aware of its existence, but rest assured I have the cube with me, along with a number of other items I believe the Quorum will appreciate."

"If you're looking for a pardon, Baltar, you can forget it," Apollo snarled as they marched down the corridor. If his senses were accurate, the ascensior tube should be off to the left of the next junction.

"A pardon?" Baltar asked. "I'd never dream of it, my dear Apollo. I just hope the fact that I've saved your lives will convince the Quorum to spare my own, misguided soul."

"What soul?" Starbuck said acidly. "And I'm a little curious about what you said before. If they'd decided to execute you, why are you still alive at all?"

"Simple," Baltar replied without hesitation. "I gave them the location of your precious fleet."

Apollo ratcheted around in the hall, ready to throttle Baltar. Starbuck moved even faster, slamming the Great Traitor against the wall so hard that Baltar's skull bounced off the saligium surface with a satisfying thud.

"What the frack are you talking about?" Starbuck roared.

"How did you even know where the fleet was?" Apollo asked, unconvinced.

"I can't tell you that," Baltar said. "But don't you think it's even more imperative that we hurry back to the *Galactica?*"

Apollo thought about Troy, about Athena and Sheba. He looked at Starbuck and saw concern for Dalton and Cassiopeia, for Boomer and all the rest of their family, their friends. Against the new Cylons he had battled, the ones Baltar had referred to as "his children," the fleet would be ill-prepared, especially with the political turmoil that ensued after Adama's death. Apollo had no way to know how disruptive that conflict had become, but he feared the worst. If the Cylons sent more than one base star, the fleet might be completely destroyed.

"I'm certain your father will appreciate the warning," Baltar added, as Starbuck released him.

While Baltar smoothed the front of his tunic with his hands, Apollo glared at him. Then, quietly, he said, "My father is dead."

Baltar looked up, his face contorted with emotion: surprise, disappointment, perhaps even some kind of sadness. Apollo couldn't read him this time.

"I'm sorry to hear that," Baltar said.

Apollo sensed that, in some perverse way, Baltar meant it. All along, he had been reaching out to Baltar with his mind, probing for some deception and finding only fear and desperation. Now he decided he didn't want to look anymore. Baltar's mind was a quagmire of devious thoughts and ugly emotions.

"Let's go," Apollo said abruptly.

As he turned, Starbuck caught his eye. Apollo nodded, almost imperceptibly, to assure his friend that he was all right. Then he walked on, toward the juncture ahead. As they approached, Apollo heard a disturbingly familiar sound: the humming of Cylon sensors. He glanced to his left to be certain Starbuck noted it as well. He had.

They turned at the juncture. A short way down the corridor, a pair of Centurions waited for the ascensior to arrive. They didn't immediately turn to recognize the presence of the humans, and Apollo at first thought to back up and wait for them to leave. Baltar poked at his back, and Apollo assumed he must know better what Cylons were capable of. The Centurions must have registered their presence by now.

"Ah, Centurions," Baltar said haughtily. "It's good that you are here. Lucifer has ordered these prisoners brought to his chambers, but I have other matters to attend to. Please transport them to his quarters immediately."

The Cylons turned to face the new arrivals. Apollo watched the red optical sensor slide back and forth across each of their visors. Baltar's words had disturbed him, but he realized he had to let it play out. Once again, he had to rely on the turncoat's knowledge of the Cylons.

"You are not our commander, any longer, Baltar," one of the Cylons said in halting, electronic tones. "We have our assigned duties to attend to."

Baltar feigned self-righteous indignation.

"Very well, continue as you wish," he said. "But be certain I will report this to Lucifer."

The Cylons said nothing. The ascensior tube opened and the Centurions stepped onto the platform. Apollo and Starbuck went in after them, and Baltar followed. Apollo was amazed that the Centurions had not noticed that he and Starbuck wore their lasers. No wonder they were such poor warriors, he thought. They can do nothing but follow orders.

Baltar gave him a warning glance as the ascensior doors hissed closed. Apollo understood. If the guards got off before the level with the landing bay, they were safe. If not, they would have to blast the Centurions right on the ascensior. Bad marksmen the Cylons may be, but in close quarters, even a bad laser shot could be deadly. They would have to act fast.

The ascensior began to rise and one of the Centurions spoke, calling out a level number indicating their destination. Baltar sighed and nodded slightly to Apollo.

"Level nine," Baltar said.

It took barely a heartbeat before the Centurions registered Baltar's words. Level nine was the landing bay. They knew he had lied. Apollo and Starbuck unholstered their lasers, turned, and fired before the Cylons could even aim their weapons. Apollo winced at the explosive roar of the lasers, too loud in the confines of the ascensior. The Centurions were thrown back and crumpled to the floor.

Baltar stepped forward with his own weapon raised, and fired directly into the helmet of one of the fallen Centurions. The faceplate turned black, melted by the blast, and inside, Apollo glimpsed a thick, scaled mouth with double rows of jagged teeth. His fascination was completely overshadowed by his anger at Baltar.

"Why did you do that?" he demanded. "He was dead already."

"Why?" Baltar asked archly, turning his back on Apollo to face the doors of the ascensior. "I've been waiting eighteen yahren to do that, Apollo."

Apollo turned to study the dead Cylons once more. Starbuck crouched over them and stared through the hole in the Centurion's faceplate. Both Warriors had been amazed by the information Starbuck had acquired on Ochoa. It explained a great many things about Cylons. But so many questions remained.

"You know, they're *really* ugly," Starbuck said, as he stood up, holstering his laser.

"I'm sure they think the same of us," Apollo replied. "What I don't understand is, if they've got human genetic material, why do they want to destroy humanity so much? The most troubling question, though, is how the original reptilian Cylon race came to be bred with humanity to begin with. It had to have happened many millennia ago, but who engineered it all?"

Baltar cleared his throat. "Gentlemen," he said in his most patronizing tone, "if you're quite through, we're about to reach the landing bay. If you behave yourselves, I might be persuaded to answer some of those questions."

Apollo's first response was doubt. There had never been a human being more prone to self-serving fabrication than Baltar. And yet, after eighteen yahren, it was only logical that he should have come to know a great deal about the Cylons.

Time would tell.

"Now, if you would both do the honors," Baltar prodded, indicating that they should step in front of him. "I want to shoot Cylons, not be shot by them."

The Warriors shared a glance and Apollo realized that once again he could sense Starbuck's thoughts. Perhaps only because they knew each other so well, or because Starbuck had precisely the same reaction to Baltar that he did.

"Coward" was the word in Starbuck's mind. No question about it.

"At least he's predictable," Apollo said aloud, and Starbuck grinned.

They moved in front of Baltar, drawing their lasers, prepared to take down any Centurions who might await them in the landing bay. The ascensior slowed, then stopped. The doors hissed open. Apollo was first through the narrow doorway, Starbuck close behind.

Apollo immediately spotted the two Centurions on sentry duty. They stood just metrons from his Viper. They weren't alone, however. Two other Cylons stood atop the Viper, apparently attempting to open the canopy without damaging the starfighter. There were several Cylon Raiders parked in the bay, including one of the sleek black models, but the landing deck was empty. Nothing to block their escape.

They had a clear view of the Cylons, but Apollo wanted to get the best shot he could. He and Starbuck slipped along next to one of the Raiders. Baltar slithered in the shadows behind them, keeping himself as far from danger as he was able while making certain they wouldn't leave without him.

"Now?" Starbuck whispered, his eyebrows rising with the question.

Apollo nodded. The Warriors stepped into the open, planted their feet and began firing their lasers. Less experienced fighters might have tried to take the Cylons on the run, to storm the Viper. But Starbuck and Apollo wanted to end it quickly, so aim was more important than the adrenaline rush of battle.

Laser fire burned past Apollo's head, singeing his hair. His second shot knocked a Centurion from the Viper's canopy. Starbuck took both the Cylons on the ground, dodging a blast that nearly struck Baltar. Apollo couldn't avoid a small twinge of regret that Baltar hadn't been hit. Then he nailed the other Cylon tech on top of the Viper, and the bay was clear.

"Starbuck, you and Baltar get that black Raider fired up," Apollo ordered. "That one probably has a QSE generator. I'll make sure they didn't do any damage to the Viper, and then we'll get out of here. Let's move!"

Starbuck started for the Raider, with Baltar following. Apollo ran for his Viper. As he was climbing up on its wing, the alarm klaxon blared in the repair bay. The dead Centurions in the ascensior had been found.

The Viper wasn't damaged. He released the canopy, climbed inside and slipped his helm on. The engines fired up instantly, and he lowered the canopy even as he began to taxi around into a launch position. He wouldn't have the speed a Viper got from one of the *Galactica's* launch tubes, but at least they would have the QSE to fall back on. Plus, any Raiders that were launched after them would have to be on their tail when they hit hyperdrive, or the Cylons would never be able to register their coordinates.

With the starfield framed in the launch aperture, Apollo thrust the navi-hilt forward and the Viper hurtled out of the base star into space. The Raider, piloted by Starbuck, was right behind him. In formation, they banked left and came around the top of the base star. Apollo was relieved to leave the Cylon war vessel behind.

"Apollo!" Starbuck cried over the comm-link. "I'm being hailed! Must be a patrol!"

Blip! Blip!

There they were, on scanners. Two Cylon Raiders returning from patrol at the most inopportune time. The Raiders swept through space, falling into line behind Starbuck's black Cylon fighter. Apollo knew he could go quantum at any moment and escape, but he wasn't certain Starbuck had determined how to use the Raider's QSE. He didn't have time to find out. Only time for one move.

"Starbuck, listen!" he snapped. "Fire on me! Do it right now! Miss, of course, but make it look like you're trying! Do it!"

Another Warrior might have argued, despite Apollo's rank. Laser fire arced from the black Raider, flashing across Apollo's left wing and rattling the Viper a bit without doing any damage.

"Good! Let them overtake you to join the fun!" Apollo ordered.

"You'll be killed," Starbuck said.

"That's when you get to play shoot-em-up, my friend," Apollo replied, enjoying Starbuck's grumbling despite the danger.

The Cylon patrol slid into formation with Starbuck's Raider, the two ships on either side. They fired on Apollo, who jerked the navi-hilt up into a vertical climb. As the two patrol Raiders followed, Starbuck allowed himself to drop back. A micron later, he blasted the two Cylon ships into shrapnel.

"Much obliged," Apollo said. "Now, have you figured out how to use that QSE system yet?"

"I've just convinced the computer to speak Kobollian," Starbuck replied over the comm-link. "Give me a micron."

Blip! Blip! Blip! Blip! Blip!

"Micron's all you've got," Apollo snapped. "Base star is launching a squad of Raiders!"

"Got it!" Starbuck cried.

"Good! Form on me, follow my coordinates, and phase to QSE on my word," Apollo instructed him. He checked his bearings on the instrument panel and his helm readouts, and set course for the fleet.

"Now!" he roared. Both ships slipped out of reality using the Quantum Shift Effect, even as they rocketed into hyperdrive. Apollo hoped Athena had left a fuel buoy behind. They were going to need it. Despite the danger, and the urgency of warning the fleet, Apollo was glad to be heading home. He hadn't even taken the precaution of setting off on a misleading course. It wouldn't have made any difference.

Thanks to Baltar, the Cylons already knew where the fleet was. He only hoped that Athena had things under control.

20.

LASER PISTOLS CRACKLED, energy arced through the filth of the Pit, and bodies dropped to the dingy floor, wounded, dying, dead. The Colonial Warriors were badly outnumbered by Tybalt's followers, the members of the Serpent Cult. Yet they were holding their own. The cultists were not trained for battle, and even though many of Athena's impromptu squad had been recruited from the crew of the *Ursus*, they were more familiar with weapons than the average citizen.

One of Captain Hecate's first shots took out the glaring light that the cultists had turned on the Warriors, and by then, both sides had ducked into whatever cover was available. Behind crates that may or may not have been some poor unfortunate's living quarters there in the Pit; in narrow corridors off the main chamber; even the shadows offered some cover.

"I wish we had lasers," Dalton hissed to Troy, where they crouched several metrons from the thick mass of cultists.

Troy knew what she meant. If they had weapons, they could trap the cultists in a crossfire. As it was, it seemed that despite their greater skill, the Warriors were certain to be eventually overrun. The sheer number of cultists would see to that.

"We've got to do something," Troy said, and looked over a short crate to get a layout of the cultist locations. Tybalt, their leader, was nowhere in sight, and Troy wondered if he had ducked out after deadly energy blasts began to fly. No matter. Tybalt was no longer their main problem. He had to take action before Athena was killed, along with other Warriors and the crew of the *Ursus.*

Troy shifted forward, balancing on the balls of his feet.

"What are you going to do?" Dalton asked, eyes narrowed.

"Try to even the odds a little," he answered. He started to rise, but Dalton stopped him, spun him to face her.

"I ever tell you you're stronger than you look?" Troy asked.

"Tell me again later, you maniac," she said. "What's wrong with you? You're likely to get your heart seared right through by your own aunt. You can't just charge out there, unarmed!"

Troy grimaced. "Listen, *Ensign,* we don't have time for this. You argue with me, somebody else dies. You'd do this yourself if I wasn't here to order you not to, not because it's the only option, but because you like the danger, you savor the risk. Well, not this time. This time you stay right here, and you back me up. If I get in trouble, you try to get me out. But you wait for my play, understand?"

Dalton glared at him, eyes smoldering underneath a brow creased with anger and concern. Troy found her irresistibly attractive at that moment. He wanted to kiss her then, but pushed away the temptation. It wasn't the time or the place.

Apparently, Dalton didn't agree. She grabbed the back of his neck and pulled his mouth to hers. Their kiss was brief, but more than a gesture of friendship.

"Don't die," she said simply.

"Never was very good at dying," Troy replied.

Then he launched himself up and over the crate, eyes roving, instantly taking in the layout. Straight ahead were two cultists fighting side by side behind a massive piece of sound equipment. He ran for them. Six strides and he was also shielded by their cover.

Troy wrapped his left arm around the neck of the closest cultist, gripped the man's laser with his right hand and swung his aim to one side. When Troy squeezed, the cultist's laser discharged, killing his comrade. He tried to wrest the laser out of the man's hands, but received an elbow to the gut for his trouble. He staggered back, looked up to see the man leveling the weapon at him, and reacted as fast as he could.

Troy erupted from his crouched position, his left leg whipping up and around, hips pivoting. His left foot knocked the laser from the cultist's hand and he heard the man's wrist snap. He followed through on the kick with enough force to catch the man in the chin with the tip of his foot. The cultist went down hard, and Troy went for his fallen laser.

His attack had not gone unnoticed, and Troy had to roll out of the line of fire behind the sound equipment. He hoped it wouldn't simply explode if hit. Momentarily safe, he glanced back for Dalton, but couldn't see her anywhere. He was glad. Better that she remained under cover.

After the next laser volley slammed into his temporary shield, Troy stood straight up into the line of fire and began blasting. There was no other way to do it. He took down two cultists immediately, evening the odds a little more. He couldn't see Athena beyond the lights glaring down on him, but the skyeye danced in the air above, broadcasting his actions around the fleet, the same way it had been intended to broadcast his execution.

A female cultist ducked out of a narrow hallway and got off a shot that zipped close by his head. When she appeared again, he winged her in the left arm. He spun to face a new threat to his right, but never got to fire again.

His hair was jerked roughly back and the muzzle of a laser pistol jammed painfully against his right temple.

Tybalt!

"Enough! Cease fire!" Tybalt cried. After a couple of errant shots crackled through the murky chamber, silence descended.

"Let him go, Tybalt!" Athena demanded.

Troy leaned forward as much as he was able without losing a piece of his scalp. Athena was left with half a dozen men and women, only two of whom looked to be actual Warriors. One he recognized as Captain Hecate. The cultists weren't much better off.

Tybalt included, there couldn't have been more than eight or ten left alive and conscious.

"Athena, don't listen to anything he says," Troy shouted. "He's insane! He slaughtered our only witness to the murder on *Agro-3*. They're a cult of lunatics."

"We're nothing of the sort," Tybalt said gleefully. "We're merely a special interest group, looking out for our special interest, which, as I've said, is the appointment of Ambassador Puck to the position of commander."

"Feldergarb!" Troy said, pleading with Athena with his gaze. "Shoot him, Athena. He's nothing more than a terrorist, and probably a Cylon spy as well."

"Be careful what you say, boy," Tybalt sneered into Troy's ear, grinding the laser against his temple anddrawing blood. "It's your father who's working with the Cylons."

"Oh, then why *are* you in the Cult of the Serpent, Tybalt?" Troy shouted, loud enough for the others to hear and for the skyeye to transmit throughout the fleet. "It's well known that the Cylons are reptilian. Could it be that they are the serpents you worship?"

"That's not it at all!" Tybalt cried, but there was an air of desperation in his tone now. "All of you back away, or Apollo's son dies. We're going to leave the Pit, now. Just the two of us."

Tybalt began to move to one side, but two of his own followers barred his path.

"Is it true, Tybalt?" one of them, a Tauran woman, asked plaintively. "Are the serpents you have us praying to some kind of Cylon gods?"

"How dare you?" Tybalt raged at the woman. He had begun to sweat. "It's the Kobollians who are in league with the Cylon evil! Haven't you been listening?"

"Maybe they have been listening," Athena said, and stepped closer to the lighted area where Tybalt had Troy captive. Her laser was held with both hands, and her aim, Troy knew, was excellent. He held his breath a moment, waiting to see if the other cultists would kill her indiscriminately. But they were confused now, unsure of their leader. Just as Troy had hoped.

The skyeye hovered in place, recording the tension.

"Let Captain Troy go, Tybalt," Athena said, a hard look on her features. "Or I will be forced to kill you."

"I'm a hero!" Tybalt cried. "I'm a patriot!"

From somewhere behind Troy, in the shadows, Dalton's voice rang out. "You're nothing more than a pet daggit to Cylon masters!" she snarled.

Troy watched the faces of Tybalt's followers go slack with horror as the accusations and Tybalt's behavior began to sway them.

"No! No! I'm a patriot!" Tybalt screamed.

"Is it true, Tybalt?" the Tauran woman asked, staring at him with disgust now, and disappointment.

"They've poisoned you!" he shouted. "They've poisoned you all!"

Tybalt took the laser away from Troy's temple, leveled it at the Tauran woman, and fired, killing her instantly.

"Troy! Down!" Athena roared from the shadows.

Troy dove away from Tybalt. Before he hit the ground, Athena had fired a laser blast that scorched a gaping hole in the cult leader's chest. The skyeye caught it all.

Troy rose and dusted himself off, and Dalton rushed to his side. The surviving cultists quietly surrendered, and now Athena also approached.

"See!" Troy said to Dalton. "I told you I wouldn't die."

Dalton punched him hard, in the shoulder, and Troy winced.

"From now on, you save the crazy stunts for me," she snapped.

"What's this?" Athena asked with obviously feigned ignorance. "I thought Troy was the superior officer here."

Dalton cleared her throat and pointed to the skyeye, which was still broadcasting. Athena pulled her laser and blasted it to scrap. Troy stared at her a moment. He had never known his aunt to be so impulsive. Athena smiled and then the three of them were laughing with relief.

"So, what was all that stuff about Cylons?" Athena asked. "Do you really think that's what the cult was about?"

Troy shrugged. "I don't know, but it was all I could think of to set his followers against him. It sure seemed like a sore spot, though."

"I wonder," Athena said cryptically.

Using concentration, meditation, and the focus of his inner vision, and aided after a time by the Viper's scanners, Apollo had no trouble locating the message buoy the fleet had left behind for him. Figuring out their course coordinates had been a simple matter, once he'd downloaded the coded information onto his Viper flatscreen. He'd double-checked them with the information Baltar had given the Cylons, and it disturbed him to discover that the traitor's information about the fleet's location was accurate.

Now they were fueling up using the small reserve tanker that had been yoked to the buoy. Apollo had taken on a little more than half the fuel in the tanker, with Starbuck now refueling his stolen dark Raider. Apollo decided it was time for Baltar to begin making himself useful.

"All right, Baltar," he said over the comm-link. "We've put up with your silence this far, but it's time to answer some questions, or you're going for a short spacewalk."

For a moment, there was no answer. Then Baltar's voice filled Apollo's cockpit.

"What is it you want to know, Apollo?" he asked. "Or is it Commander Apollo now?"

It was Apollo's turn to pause. For he didn't actually know the answer to Baltar's question. He had been commander at the time of his departure from the *Galactica*, but only on an interim basis. The final decision had yet to be made. But Baltar didn't need to know that.

"Commander will do," he replied. "And you can begin by telling us what was behind your implications on the base star. How did the Cylons end up becoming genetically altered with human DNA?"

"An excellent question," Baltar said. "And one I fear I can only provide a partial answer for. Obviously, this happened millennia ago, and so the story may be subject to the pitfalls of all ancient history. Perhaps it's nothing more than a legend."

"Just get on with it," Starbuck barked over the comm.

Apollo could hear Baltar sigh. "I'm not sure which of you is the more impatient," he said. "As I was saying, many millennia ago, an outsider visited the planet Cylon, which at that time was home to a rather truculent, warlike race of sentient reptilian creatures. These were the true Cylons. I've never seen one, but I'm told they still exist on the Cylon homeworld.

"This outsider was filled with an anger and savagery that the Cylons admired. He also introduced to them technology, which kept them in his debt, and in fear of him, for decades. During that time, he experimented with them, promising to make them the fiercest, most perfect warriors the universe had ever seen. He vowed that the Cylons would become conquerors, and because of that promise, they allowed him to do whatever he pleased.

"There were, according to the history, or the myth if you prefer, many generations of Cylons before those we are currently familiar with came into being. But, over time, the Cylon race was artifically evolved into a bipedal form to make better use of the technology this outsider had introduced to them. Human DNA was used for this purpose.

"But this outsider hated all of humanity. It was his goal that the Cylons should have, as their primary edict, the extermination of humankind. He hated all human instincts and tried to breed those aspects out of his Cylon mutants. He began a cloning process from pure genetic material that made Cylon females unnecessary and, as such, they died out. And he introduced the cybernetic implants that are now part of every Cylon Centurion. Eventually, the Cylons could feel no emotions…with the exception of hate."

Baltar stopped speaking, and for a moment Apollo could say nothing.

"I'm all set, Apollo," Starbuck announced.

"Apollo?"

"Hmm? Oh, yes, let's get under way, then," Apollo muttered, turning Baltar's words over and over in his head. It made a terrible kind of sense, certainly offering one possible explanation for the terrible scourge of humanity that the Cylon race had become. But there were so many gaps in the story.

"Baltar? Why haven't we ever heard of this alien outsider, if his race was so advanced? And where did he get the human DNA with which to conduct his experiments?" Apollo asked, bewildered.

There was a dry chuckle over the comm-link.

"I'm sorry, dear Commander," Baltar said. "I thought I'd made that clear. The outsider took the DNA from himself. According to the legend, he *was* human."

The ascensior doors swept open and Athena stepped onto the bridge. Immediately, she sensed a distance from her crew. After a moment, she identified its cause: Respect. They had always respected her, but after witnessing the manner in which she dealt with the crisis in the Pit, they looked upon her as a Warrior instead of merely an administrator.

It felt good.

As she mounted the command deck, something else occurred to Athena. She had no first officer, no one to provide the support that Colonel Tigh had offered her father so long, and that she had offered Adama when Tigh retired from military service.

Fortunately, Omega was always there. Of all the officers she had known throughout the fleet, never had she met anyone as calm and organized. As Athena approached, Omega stood from his station and offered her the fingers to forehead salute of the Colonial Warrior.

"Commander Athena," he said by way of welcome.

"Thank you, Omega," she replied. "Status report, please, fleet-wide. Your discretion as to priority."

"We seem to have regained some semblance of peace,

Commander," Omega began. "But it is tenuous at best, and tensions could flare again at any moment. The fleet awaits the Quorum's vote. "Major Boomer saved the lives of nine crisis crewmen aboard the *Hephaestus*. Everyone else aboard, crew and passengers, were killed. Major Boomer himself has been transported back to the *Galactica* and is in med-unit for treatment. Major Sheba remains aboard the Forge to see to cleanup, restaffing and to determine how long before the repair bay will be functional again. Aside from human life, we lost four new Scarlet-class Vipers, and two older fighters as well.

"Protests aboard the *Galactica*, the *Rising Star*, the *Celestra* and several other ships have been dispersed without violence, though the flight crews still refuse to work. You're familiar with the situation on the *Ursus*, of course. However, the oddest news is that the prison barge *Icarus* is no longer with the fleet."

Athena blinked.

"I'm sorry," she said. "What do you mean, 'no longer with the fleet'?"

"Sometime in the last centon, during the height of the confusion, the ship seems to have slipped away. It did have hyperspeed capacity, and we can only suppose that the prisoners somehow managed to wrest control of the vessel, and they have now abandoned the fleet," Omega explained in an apologetic tone, as if he had personally been responsible for the loss of the *Icarus*.

"Review all scanner recordings from the past hour," Athena instructed. "I want to know what their heading was on departure. Then give me a long-range scan along that heading. If we have to send patrols, we will. I want to know where they think they're going."

"Yes, Commander," Omega replied, and glanced at Sergeant Bree, who was stationed nearby. The woman turned to her flatscreen and keyboard and began working immediately on her task. Athena admired Omega's control of the bridge—he hadn't needed to voice the command.

"One more thing," Omega said. "The *Scorpius Ascendant* still maintains that it has seceded from the fleet. Her captain, Patroclus, insists that he will take commands only from Ambassador Puck."

At the mention of Puck's name, Athena's anger intensified. She was furious with the man for not at least doing his best to defuse the tension within the fleet. It was infantile behavior, completely irresponsible. And catering to it would, she had no doubt, be tantamount to simply handing the fleet over to the man.

"Commander?" a deep, soothing voice intoned behind her.

Athena turned to see that President Tigh had come onto the bridge along with Sire Belloch and several other members of the Quorum.

"I have called an emergency Council session," Tigh informed her. "I hate to take you from the bridge, but it shouldn't take long."

She nodded, turned to Omega, who stood awaiting her instructions. Athena felt the reins of control over the fleet whipping by her, just out of reach. But she knew she must grab them, gain control and hold the fleet together. If things got out of hand again, a full-fledged rebellion could result.

"Contact Captain Patroclus of the *Scorpius Ascendant*," she said sternly. "Inform the captain that he and his crew must pledge fealty to the Quorum immediately. If they do not, they will be left with two choices: leave the fleet forever, or be obliterated along with their vessel."

Omega stared at her, and Athena could feel the eyes of the entire crew. As if she had taken no notice of their response, she moved to join President Tigh, who also stared. She heard Omega's nearly whispered commands behind her, and looked up into Tigh's face to see that the President was dismayed, but impressed.

"Shall we go?" she asked, a note of defiance in her voice. She was commander, at least for the moment, and she would damn well do what she felt was best.

"Indeed," Tigh replied. "We have much to do."

A door irised open to give them access to a long corridor that would take them, eventually, to the Quorum chambers. Athena was in no great hurry to see Puck again, but she assumed Tigh would have made an exception to the ambassador's confinement for this meeting.

Tigh didn't look at her as they strode side by side.

"You don't approve?" Athena asked after the door to the bridge had irised closed behind them.

"Your father could be stern, but he would never have issued so extreme an ultimatum," Tigh observed quietly, without turning his gaze on Athena.

"No, he wouldn't have," she agreed. "But I do not command the loyalty Adama did. Nor do I have his limitless patience."

Far behind them in the corridor, the door to the bridge irised open once more. Athena and Tigh turned together, curious to see who might be following them.

Omega leaned his lanky frame through the door.

"Commander Athena!" he said excitedly. "We've got a Viper on scanners Scarlet-class, and it's not one of our patrols!"

Tigh and Athena exchanged a glance. "Apollo!" they said in unison. Omega glanced back to the bridge, and now looked into the corridor again.

"That's confirmed, Commander," he said. "We've got him on comm-link now."

"Tell him I'll meet him in the landing bay," she said instantly, then turned to Tigh. "You'll have to start the meeting without me."

As Athena hurried down the corridor, she was at once elated that her brother had returned, alive, and concerned as well. It remained to be seen if his return at that particular moment would serve to unite or further divide the fleet.

21.

APOLLO'S VIPER HAD ALREADY LANDED when Athena stepped out of the ascensior tube into the landing bay. The canopy was up, and he was just pulling off his helm. She strode briskly toward the starfighter as he climbed out onto the wing. As she went, she congratulated the substitute service techs, mostly Warriors themselves, who were filling in for the crews who had refused to work.

As Apollo climbed down, he received hearty greetings from the infantry Warriors in the bay, and a bear-like embrace from Lieutenant Jolly. As she approached, Athena could see the questions etched on Apollo's face, but rather than ask them, he merely expressed his heartfelt pleasure at returning to the fleet and seeing his comrades. So much for the horrible rumor of his collaboration with the Cylons.

The Warriors moved away to allow Athena access to her brother. Apollo smiled at her, and despite the tension that had existed between them at the time of his departure, brother and sister embraced warmly.

"I missed you," he said.

"And I you," she replied. "We all missed you, Apollo."

"Where's the regular crew?" he asked, glancing around the landing bay.

"They walked off the job," she replied. "They'll come back if and when Puck is appointed commander."

Apollo frowned. "It's gotten that bad?"

"Worse than you could imagine," she answered grimly.

When Apollo didn't offer any immediate response, Athena took the opportunity to ask a question that had been on her mind since Omega announced Apollo's return.

"Did you find him, Apollo?"

Apollo's dour expression finally cracked, and he offered a slight smile. For the second time in only a few centari, a wave of relief and joy washed over Athena.

"We've got more troubles than you know," Apollo told her, his austere countenance returned. "A lot to discuss, a lot to do, and little time to do it. But I want to show you something first."

Athena raised an eyebrow as Apollo set off across the bay to a computer station normally used by service techs. Already on flatscreen was a continuous short range scan of the stellar region immediately surrounding the fleet.

"See anything?" he asked, and nodded toward the screen.

"Nothing," she replied.

"Tell the bridge not to sound any alarms or fire on the ship that's coming in, no matter what it looks like to them," Apollo asked.

Athena looked at him quizzically. She glanced at the screen, which was still empty, and then back at her brother. *What ship?* she wanted to ask. But she'd play along. Over the comm, she repeated Apollo's instructions to Omega.

Apollo altered the comm wavelength, and said, simply, "You're clear for landing, Captain."

Whatever Athena was expecting, it wasn't this. In an eyeblink, a ship appeared on the flatscreen, already well within scanning range. So close, in fact, that she realized it must be just about to land!

Athena turned and stared across the bay, out at the starfield, where the jet black Cylon Raider rocketed toward them.

"By the Lords," she whispered. "I have a feeling this is going to be quite a story."

"I have a great deal to tell you that is important to both of us, personally," Apollo said. "But for now, we've got to think of the fleet."

As he told her about the impending Cylon attack, a horrible dread began to fill Athena.

"We'll never be able to fight off a base star," she said. "Not with the fleet in such disarray."

"We don't have a choice," Apollo said. "Decisive action is called for now, and I've got a few ideas that may give us an edge. In the meantime, the fleet must be put on alert, and the service techs brought back to work."

As the Cylon Raider landed, Athena watched it closely. Her pleasure at the knowledge that Apollo and Starbuck were alive was tainted by the daunting task that lay before them: keeping thousands of people alive, and one hundred seventy-odd starships from being destroyed.

The Raider's canopy opened, and Starbuck climbed out. He looked thinner, and a bit tired, but his smile got to her the same way it always did. Athena had never doubted that she loved Starbuck. But he had been such a rogue, so adamant about not wanting to commit, that when he had finally suggested they take the Seal, Athena found it impossible to take the offer as genuine.

After she'd thrown him out, Athena had regretted it immediately, knowing that he would likely try to reconcile with Cassiopeia. Seeing him now, Athena wondered if it was too late to try again.

"Athena!" Starbuck called amiably. "I hope you're prepared for visitors."

They embraced. Starbuck held her tight a moment, kissed her hair, her forehead, and then released his hold. Athena didn't want to let go, but she moved back half a step and looked into his sparkling eyes.

"If you mean *yourself*, of course I am," she said. "If you mean Cylons...well, that's another story."

They shared another long look, and Starbuck grinned even wider.

"What's funny?" she asked.

"Just wondering if you cried at my funeral," he confessed.

"Yes," she said, one eyebrow raised. "With relief. You complicate my life, Captain. I'm not fully convinced it's a good thing you're back in it."

"We'll have to work on that," Starbuck said.

"Work on it later," Apollo interrupted, and Athena stood away from Starbuck at last. She wanted to have a conversation with Starbuck, but it would keep. It had kept, in fact, for nearly two decades. Another day or two wouldn't hurt.

"Jolly!" Apollo called, and the corpulent Warrior strode promptly to join them. "Find that tech chief, Virgil, and bring him here immediately. At laser point, if necessary."

"Yes, Commander," Jolly said, happy to be taking some kind of action at last. Then he faltered and looked at Athena. "Sorry, Commander," he stammered. "I mean, what should...oh, boy."

"Go to it, Jolly," Athena said, and the Lieutenant hurried away.

Apollo and Athena looked at one another. She knew her brother was just as uncomfortable as she was.

"Well," Starbuck said. "This is going to be interesting."

"No doubt about that," Apollo said, and laid a hand on his sister's shoulder. Athena was glad of the firm grip, a gesture that told her he was as dedicated to working through this crisis as she was, no matter the outcome.

"There's a part of the story I left out," Apollo revealed. "Something we may be able to use against the Cylons. Or, I suppose I should say, some*one*."

Even as she frowned, Athena saw that both Starbuck and Apollo were looking back toward the Cylon Raider. She began to turn. Before she saw him, she heard his voice.

"Hello, Athena," he said, his deep voice as arrogant, as insinuating, as she recalled. Baltar's hair was whiter, but otherwise, he had not changed at all.

"God help us all," she whispered.

"I told you he was in league with the Cylons!" Ambassador Puck sneered, pointing. "He's led them right to us!"

Apollo stared at Puck in horror. He had not known the man well previous to his departure, but the Ambassador seemed to have deteriorated somehow. He had become fanatical and dangerous. Any other man who had made such an accusation would already be sprawled on the ground with a welt on his face. But madness was its own punishment.

It was President Tigh who took up Apollo's defense.

"Ambassador, please restrain yourself or I will have you removed from this session," Tigh said. "Apollo has already explained how the Cylons came to know our location, and how Baltar returned with them. Given the evidence of the new Cylon Raider, and the fact that your recent behavior has made the entire Quorum skeptical of anything you might have to say, we will continue to follow Apollo's suggestions."

"He's already dealt with the work stoppage in the launch and landing bays," Athena observed. "Baltar has been granted conditional clemency, as long as he continues to be useful to us. The entire fleet is on alert, all pilots ready to fly except Major Sheba, who is still on the *Hephaestus*. Even the *Scorpius Ascendant* has abandoned its insurrection, at least for the time being. The greater enemy seems to have interrupted the succession controversy."

Apollo smiled inwardly. He was proud that his sister had taken their father's seat on the Quorum. Administration had never been Apollo's forte, and she deserved the seat far more than he.

"We don't know how much time we have," Tigh noted. "The base star is slower than the fighters, but it could be no more than a centon. Yet, the question of succession still hangs over us. I propose that we take our vote now, appoint a new commander, and move into this situation with that person in place. Athena and Puck will have to abstain, of course. Apollo, would you step outside a moment?"

"No, sir," Apollo replied.

"I'm sorry?"

"I request that this vote not be taken now," he stated. "If you don't appoint Ambassador Puck, and for the sake of the entire fleet, I pray that you do not...well, you'll have the fleet at each other's throats again in a micron—even with the threat of the Cylons. It will cripple us."

Tigh glanced around the room, apparently waiting to see if any of the other Quorum members would argue with Apollo's logic. None seemed prepared to, other than Puck of course. But, though his face had flushed with anger, Puck said nothing.

"Point well taken," Tigh said finally. "But where does that leave us? You were Interim Commander before you left to rescue Starbuck. In your absence, Athena was named to that post."

"And from what I'm told, particularly after the events on the *Ursus*, she's performed admirably and received a great deal of support in that role," Apollo observed. "I withdraw any claim to the title. I abdicated it to go after Starbuck, anyway. But I'll help in any way I can."

"Will you be a candidate once again when this is all over?" Sire Belloch asked bluntly.

Apollo began to shake his head, but Athena spoke up before he could answer.

"Yes," she said quickly. "Yes, he will."

He looked at his sister and, for a moment, understood her more completely than ever before. It was as if, for the briefest of moments, their minds touched, communicated in a way far more profound than mere telepathy. Then it was gone. Athena looked a bit surprised, as if she had somehow sensed it as well. Of course she had, Apollo realized. She was full-blooded Kobollian, just as he was. His mental abilities were developing slowly, but they *were* developing.

"Yes," he agreed. "At that point, you may consider me a candidate."

"Fine," President Tigh said, noncommittally. "Athena, for the duration of the current crisis, you remain in command."

Athena stood quickly. "Let's move, then," she said. "We haven't a moment to spare. Apollo, will you join me on the bridge, or do you want to go to the launch bay to talk to your pilots?"

"I'll be heading to the launch bay," Apollo replied. "First, however, I'd like a few moments with you. I realize time is at a premium. But this can't wait."

Athena raised an eyebrow, surprised by his words. She didn't argue, however.

"Yes, go save your precious fleet," Ambassador Puck hissed.

Apollo glared at the hunched, pale old man. The venom in him was appalling.

"When the Cylons are gone, and it is all over, the people will still believe in me," he said. "I promised them a world to live on, a life without Cylons. If you appoint any other commander, the fleet will destroy itself. That is, of course, if the Cylons do not destroy us all first."

"So, how long do you really think we have?" Athena asked.

She strode down the corridor beside her brother. Athena felt a return to the closeness she had always enjoyed with Apollo during their youth. A unity of purpose and a confidence in one another's abilities that had been missing ever since their career paths in the military had diverged. Yet there still seemed to be something keeping them apart. Apollo had never been good at keeping secrets.

"Probably half a cycle, maybe less," he replied.

They came to a halt in the hallway outside their father's quarters. The last time they had been inside that chamber together, they had stood together in an embrace over his still-warm corpse.

"So, what is it you want to tell me, Brother?" Athena asked.

In response, Apollo placed his hand on the pressure pad outside the chamber, and the door to the commander's quarters hissed open. He nodded to indicate that she should precede him, and Athena entered. Apollo remained silent as he walked into the room behind her. When the door closed, she turned to him.

"All right, we're here," she said curtly, hands on hips. "Now I want to know why we're here."

Apollo sighed deeply.

"I have much to tell you, Athena," he said. "Much that I don't want anyone else to hear, particularly right now. I have enough faith in you that I think you will believe me, no matter how outrageous what I say may sound at first.

"However," Apollo added, then paused a moment, as if summoning courage. "However, before I share with you all the things you must know, things it is your right to know, I must apologize to you, both for myself, and for our father."

Athena felt a cold tingle at the base of her skull.

"For what?" she asked gravely.

"For keeping secrets," Apollo replied.

He turned, put his hand on a nondescript wall panel, and a portion of the chamber wall hissed open: a hidden door. Athena's eyes went wide and her right hand flew to her mouth in surprise. The irony of her thoughts regarding Apollo only moments before echoed in her head.

"You're better at keeping secrets than I ever imagined," she said, almost to herself.

Apollo entered the newly revealed chamber, and as Athena followed, the room erupted with light and the flickering illumination of a computer station. The room was like nothing she'd ever seen. The star charts on the walls seemed at once alien and yet comfortingly familiar to her. Once inside, Apollo turned to her again with regret in his eyes.

"I'm sorry, Athena," he said. "I always thought Father should have brought you here, but he said it was for the eldest only. I've known about it for ten yahren. He was far more deeply tied to the Book of the Word, and to the Lords of Kobol, than we ever knew. He could not break tradition, no matter how dearly he loved you."

Athena was silent for a moment. Then she merely nodded in acceptance. Her father had always known so much more than everyone else—about the Thirteenth Tribe, their search for Earth, and the meaning of the Book of the Word. Secrets danced in Adama's eyes; Athena had seen them there as a baby, and every day until they fled with his soul. Despite the secrecy, she felt a great relief now, in knowing. Or, at least, to begin to know.

"Thank you for showing me, Apollo," she said, and saw how surprised he was at her lack of anger. "Now isn't the time for ire or resentment. Just...tell me."

So he did. Apollo told her everything he could in the brief time they had. He told her of the Lords of Kobol, of their father's teachings, of Zac and the lightships. When he finished, tears flowed freely on Athena's face. Her father was not truly dead. She might never see him again, but Apollo had actually confirmed that, whether there existed a heaven, an afterlife where all souls would go upon their final rest, the House of Kobol had found a plane of existence somewhere beyond the mortal plane.

"Zac," she said, and smiled through her tears. "Our baby brother is still alive, out there somewhere."

Apollo nodded, but did not share her smile.

"We must defeat the Cylons and return the fleet to some semblance of order," he insisted. "We must be prepared for the threat that Zac warned me about, a threat that may appear at any time but thankfully has yet to show its evil countenance."

Athena frowned and searched her brother's eyes.

"Count Iblis," Apollo said.

"He's one of *them*," Athena said instantly, before Apollo could continue. "No—not actually one of them, but similar. That explains much."

Then Apollo smiled widely. Athena looked at him oddly.

"What?" she asked.

"You always were the more intuitive one," he said. "I was right— Father should have been training you all along.

"Iblis is going to try to test me, to corrupt me. I don't know when, but I must be prepared," Apollo said. "Still, before I can concern myself with Iblis, we must protect the fleet from the Cylons. That's the other reason I brought you here. I believe that this chamber is somehow a blind spot to any kind of scan, electronic or telepathic. This is the only truly private place in the fleet."

Once again, Apollo revealed much. Athena could barely contain it all. He told her of the Cylon Human Logic Function, and of his many reckless ideas as to how the fleet might defend itself against these Cylons. Then, less than a centon after they had entered the sanctuary,

Apollo produced a small shape from within his tunic.

"A holo-cube?" Athena asked.

"A star map with the coordinates of every colony founded by the people of Parnassus. Including, I believe, both Kobol and Earth. Since the location of Kobol, at the center of the magnetic sea, was secret, only those aware of the location of Kobol can decipher the locations of the other colonies," he explained. "We should be able to triangulate the coordinates, using Kobol and other known points of reference."

"My God," Athena gasped. She reached out and Apollo handed her the holo-cube. It was warm to the touch. She examined it a moment and handed it back.

"Now all we have to do is stay alive to use it," Apollo said.

Dalton entered the launch bay and stopped, frozen in her tracks. Troy was at her side, paralyzed with delight and astonishment. But she had all but forgotten him in that moment. As happy as he was to have Apollo returned to the fleet safely, it just wasn't the same for Dalton.

Starbuck, her father, was dead.

And then...

"Father!" she shrieked, her voice high and quavering.

She ran to him, tears flowing freely, and threw her arms around him.

"God..." she sobbed. "You...we thought...everybody said...oh, Father, you're really here!"

Starbuck held her tightly, and when she glanced up at him, biting her lip to fight the tears, she saw that he was crying too.

"I'm really here," he answered. "And I've never been happier, or more proud in my life. My little girl's a Warrior."

Dalton stepped back to show off her uniform. She spun, laughing deliriously. Then she stepped forward and punched her father in the arm.

"Ow!" Starbuck cried. "What was that for?"

"First of all, don't you ever go and die on me again!" she instructed. "Secondly, I'm hardly a little girl!"

They embraced again.

"You'll always be my little girl," he whispered in her ear.

Dalton hugged him even tighter, glanced past Starbuck's shoulder and saw Apollo and Troy, laughing together. Despite that they were not related by blood, father and son had never looked more alike. Troy might have been sired by someone else, but Apollo had been the one to shape the man he had become.

The man Dalton loved.

"We're a family again," she whispered happily.

Sheba looked up in surprise as Apollo's Viper slipped into the ravaged repair bay of the *Hephaestus*. Several members of the cleanup crew glanced up as well and then went back to their work. There was a great deal to be done to get the Forge back into service.

The Viper's canopy opened slowly, and Apollo slid his helm off as Sheba mounted the wing. She found, to her surprise, that she could barely catch her breath. She was a Warrior, and it was as a Warrior that she had first met Apollo. Their relationship was founded on mutual admiration first, and affection second. But now all she felt was the nearly overwhelming pleasure of seeing the man she loved return to her alive.

Apollo swung his legs over the side of the cockpit onto the wing, and took Sheba into his arms. She returned his embrace, entwined her fingers in the hair at the nape of his neck. Their eyes met, and Apollo kissed her with a passion devoid of the protocol that had always come between them in public. Apparently, for once, he didn't care who saw them.

Sheba loved him all the more for it.

"Troy's right," he said breathlessly as he broke off their kiss. "It's about time we got married."

Sheba stared at Apollo, at the wide grin on his face and the light cavorting in his eyes. Then she began to smile.

"It's going to take some planning," she replied. "And first we have to…"

"Yes," he nodded, the grin disappearing, "beat the Cylons."

Apollo slipped down off the wing and surveyed the hard work of the repair crew. Sheba followed. She noticed that his eyes roved far and wide over the bay. After a moment, he seemed satisfied, though she could not determine what he had found so much to his liking in such catastrophe.

"How is it coming along?" he asked without turning.

"Well, we're slaved to the *Galactica*," Sheba answered. "There might be some danger still of the ship's hull losing its integrity, so we didn't want to risk life unnecessarily. Plus, it will take time to find a reliable crew, to cull them together from the rest of the fleet."

Apollo seemed to contemplate something a moment, then turned to take Sheba's hand in his own. He gazed into her eyes, and she found something in his own that was somehow different. More assured. Apollo had always been perceptive, yet brash. There was a new sagacity about him that Sheba found comforting.

"All this can wait, Sheba," he said finally. "The Forge is a target now. Without a crew, she can't defend herself. And Blue Squadron needs your services, of course. You and the crew are to return to the *Galactica* until the Cylons have been defeated."

Sheba glanced at the wreckage, up at the hull, and back at Apollo. She opened her mouth to argue, but found that she could not. He was right. And yet there had been none of his usual impatience in the words. Only empathy and wisdom.

She nodded, and called to the crew to board the shuttle immediately.

"Aren't you coming?" Sheba asked, when they were all aboard.

"I have some quick modifications I need to make to my Viper," he replied. "You go on. Boomer's going to need you to make sure Starbuck stays in line."

Sheba frowned. "You're not flying with Blue Squadron during the battle?"

Apollo smiled. "I'll be there when you need me," he said. "Now get moving."

Sheba stepped into the shuttle, then ducked her head back out. She looked at Apollo in wonder, only now truly realizing that he had proposed the Seal to her, that they were to be married. He was exactly the same man he had always been, and yet in several almost intangible ways, he had changed dramatically.

"You know," she pointed out. "I never thought I would say this, but you're beginning to remind me of your father."

At that, Apollo laughed heartily.

Athena stood at the center of the command deck, on the bridge of the *Galactica*. For the moment, she was the commander of the entire fleet. And yet, she felt that part of her was with Apollo aboard the *Hephaestus*, and part of him there with her. They were in synch. A team.

A klaxon pealed through the battlestar, and Athena winced at its screeching wail. The volume bothered her, but she was not startled. She had expected it. Now that the battle had come, she was almost relieved.

Omega turned to make his report, his face tense with anxiety. Athena held up a hand.

"I know," she said. "The Cylons. How many base stars?"

"Two, still far out of attack range!" Omega replied. "And at least eighty Raiders, closing on us now. The way they're swarming, it's difficult to get a precise count."

"Launch all Viper squadrons immediately," she instructed him. "And may God and the Lords of Kobol be with us all."

22.

"GAR'TOKK!" the Noman called Snie'Goss cried. "Two Colonial Vipers have appeared on our scanners. They are hailing us. They order us to follow them back to the fleet or they will destroy the ship."

The leader of the Nomen sniffed, scratched the bridge of his ridged nose, and a growl rolled up from deep within his chest.

"We are armed, are we not?" Gar'Tokk asked.

"This prison barge has light laser weapons, mainly for defense, though it's not a warship," Snie'Goss replied. "They would be sufficient to destroy two Vipers whose pilots do not expect a lethal attack."

Gar'Tokk turned to regard Snie'Goss, eyes narrowed.

"Well, then?" he snarled.

"Yes, Lord," the Noman soldier assented and withdrew. Several moments later, the Icarus fired its lasers and two Colonial pilots were incinerated with their starfighters.

The *Icarus* trailed far behind the rest of the fleet. The hundreds of prisoners on the barge still railed against the Borellian Nomen, begging them to find the nearest habitable planet and plot a course there. Gar'Tokk stood on the bridge and stared out at the vastness of the starfield. No more ships were within visual or scanner range. But he knew the fleet was there.

Iblis had told him so.

The inferior human prisoners roared their displeasure in the corridor just off the bridge, held back by Nomen guards Gar'Tokk himself had posted. They did not understand why he did not share their desire to fly as far from the fleet as possible.

Gar'Tokk felt no need to explain to them that he, too, wished for a new beginning. He wanted to start a new life, forge a new path for his people. The Nomen had struck off on their own millennia ago, abandoning the safety of human civilization for the untamed cosmos. The time had come again to brave the unknown once more.

But there were debts to be paid before the Borellian Nomen could be free. The debt of honor was paramount to the Nomen. Just as a Noman would die before abandoning the bloodtrail, a debt of honor was placed before all else, no matter the sacrifice.

Iblis had freed Gar'Tokk from prison. Whatever Iblis was, whatever kind of creature existed within that man-shaped void, he knew of the honor of the Nomen. And he had taken full advantage of it.

The image of that quivering mass of darkness, a shimmering indigo pool, a man covered in the black blood of the universe, gave Gar'Tokk pause. But the debt had to be paid.

"I will come to you again and seek your aid," Iblis had said. *"Until then, follow on the course I have given you. It won't be long, I promise you."*

Thus, the *Icarus* waited in the cold heart of space, a weapon, waiting to be aimed. Gar'Tokk was uncertain as to Iblis' intended target. But it mattered not. The weapon would fly true.

The klaxon sounded through the *Galactica*. Starbuck hurried down the corridor toward Launch Bay One, Warriors crowding him on all sides. Bootsoles pounded thunderous rhythm, but the women and men were grim-faced and silent. The fleet was in turmoil, the odds were discouraging at best, and though there were eighty-seven active duty Viper pilots and something like thirty-five reserves aboard the battlestar, there were only seventy-one Vipers in service.

After his reunion with Dalton, Starbuck had tried to rest. After all

he'd been through, sleeping only when he'd been knocked unconscious aboard the Cylon base star, he'd thought the dreams would
begin the moment his head hit the pillow. Instead, nervous energy
thrumming through his body, he'd been unable to do more than
close his eyes.

Within the bay, the pilots were already gathering into their squadron
divisions. Launch order was determined by which squadrons were
accounted for at what time. Already, each of the battlestar's twin bays
had launched a full squadron of Vipers. Pilots spread out across the
massive chamber, and Starbuck saw the members of Blue Squadron
swarming nervously, apparently next in line for launch.

They waited only for him to arrive.

Starbuck shoved past two young pilots he thought he recognized as
members of Captain Hecate's squadron, along with Dalton.

"Watch out for my daughter," he hissed at them as he passed, and
didn't bother to wait for their response. Dalton was as capable as any
of the fleet's younger pilots, more so than most of them, in fact.
Starbuck was proud of her, and he wouldn't have dreamed of trying
to prevent Dalton from defending the fleet. But he was her father, after
all. He worried.

Boomer and Sheba stood with Jolly, young Zimmer, a female
Lieutenant named Eva, who had only recently transferred to Blue
Squadron, and Troy, of course.

"About time you got here!" Boomer snapped as Starbuck joined
them.

"I moved as fast as I could," Starbuck said with a shrug. "Guess
I'm getting old."

"Starbuck, I'm not sure you should be flying," Sheba admitted.
"You're running on fumes and you look about as stable as core tylium right now."

"Oh, thank you so much, Major," Starbuck said archly. "How kind
of you to notice."

Sheba scowled, but said nothing more. Starbuck was relieved. With
Apollo detained, Major Sheba was the squadron's commanding offi-

cer. She and Boomer shared rank, but Sheba had been promoted before him and actually had more combat experience.

"There's another problem," Jolly interjected, just before the squadron had to run for their ships. "What's Starbuck going to fly?"

"What?" Starbuck asked, as they all turned to regard him. "Sure, my sweet antique was incinerated with Ochoa, but if there's a shortage of ships it's the less experienced pilots who should be grounded, not me."

Sheba stared at the floor. Starbuck looked to Boomer for support, but his old comrade glanced elsewhere. Jolly shrugged in apology for bringing up the subject at all. But Starbuck didn't blame him. Jolly had run the launch and landing bays while the crews were on strike. He knew what the shortage was, and what it meant. Already, more than half the Vipers had launched. The battle was under way. Pilots were dying out there, while they argued.

"I'm sorry Starbuck," Sheba said. "You're fatigued, and you have no Viper assignment right now. It's really not my choice. If any pilots come in with injuries, you can fly whatever's functional. If you were in top form, I would try to appropriate another ship for you, or even ask a member of Blue Squadron to stand down. But...I'm sorry, Starbuck."

"It's all right, Sheba," Starbuck said. "I understand. You've got to do what's best for the squadron and the fleet."

He stood and watched as they ran for their Vipers. When the last of the Warriors had launched from the bay, Starbuck gazed out through the launch aperture at the laser blasts flashing back and forth between Cylon Raiders and Colonial Vipers and felt a terrible hopelessness overcome him. It was a dread that chilled his bones. Several Cylon Raiders were hit and obliterated in sequence, in a string of explosions that seemed almost celebratory. Seconds later, a Viper was hit, skewed at an odd angle and collided with a Raider. Both ships were destroyed.

Who had been in that Viper? Not knowing the answer, not being able to affect the battle, or its outcome, fired Starbuck into a rage. He had never felt so alone, so useless.

The panorama spread before him was daunting. The Vipers were outnumbered three to one, and the base stars were suspended in space at a distance, awaiting the outcome Lucifer must have felt was assured.

Starbuck frowned. How could the Cylons be so confident? They couldn't possibly know about the fleet's turmoil. There must be some other reason they were content not to endanger the base stars in direct conflict. After all, three-to-one odds weren't all that unusual, or that uneven, when dealing with Cylons. Why...

"Idiot!" Starbuck cried, and slapped himself on the forehead. "I must still be half asleep!"

Of course he knew why the Cylons were confident. They had Raiders decked out with QSE generators! Starbuck didn't know how many, but he figured the quantum-phased Raiders would already be trying to get close to the *Galactica*. Fortunately, while using the Quantum Shift Effect, the Raiders' weapons wouldn't be able to damage any other ship. Apollo assumed they would be used to pop in and out of the battle and make sneak attacks on Viper squadrons. But if they moved in for the kill while shifted, and then phased back into reality and attacked the *Galactica*'s weakest points, they could conceivably destroy her!

Starbuck had to do something. He turned to run for the comm station on the far side of the bay, to warn Athena of what he knew must be the Cylon plan. A dark shape loomed in his peripheral vision, and Starbuck continued his turn until he was staring at the object.

He smiled.

It was time to see if he could fly the stolen Cylon Raider without Baltar as his more experienced co-pilot.

"Starbuck, are you out of your mind? Have you been sniffing plant vapors, or something?" Athena cried into the comm-link. "Return that Raider to the *Galactica* immediately! The rest of the Warriors will have no choice but to treat you as a target! Your own comrades are going to kill you if you don't come back!"

"Listen," Starbuck replied over the comm, "it's too complicated to explain right now, but I've got to be out there. I'll be phased most of the time. Just tell them not to shoot me!"

"How are the other pilots supposed to know it's you? If they hesitate and they're wrong, it'll cost lives, and maybe cost us the fleet itself!" Athena shouted, her voice an accusation.

"It's a risk we have to take, Athena," Starbuck replied, and then his tone softened. "Tell them not to hesitate. If they see a black Raider firing on other Raiders, they'll know it's me. Otherwise, they shouldn't hesitate at all...Commander."

Athena closed her eyes a moment, then sighed deeply. "Be careful, Captain Starbuck," she said. "If you live through this, you'll probably get the Golden Cluster, but you're also going to be a *Lieutenant* again."

"I can live with that," Starbuck replied, and then the comm hissed dead air.

Athena stared out at the starfield. Omega barked battle reports to her at regular intervals, but she didn't really need them. She could see with her own eyes how badly they were faring. The odds had never been stacked quite so high against them. In the past, the fleet had faced the Cylons with the unity that their common humanity and a horrible enemy provided. But now?

By the Lords, she should not even entertain such thoughts. But hope and faith could not combat truth for very long. The way the battle seemed to be heading as she watched the squadrons of Vipers and Raiders make pass after pass, as she watched humans and Cylons die...Athena had to admit that it appeared the Cylons would win easily.

Involuntarily, she closed her eyes, and said a silent prayer.

"Athena!"

Her eyes snapped open, and Athena turned to see Cassiopeia burst from the corridor onto the bridge. Her hair was wild, her eyes wide and intense. She mounted the command platform without any attention to protocol.

"Athena," she said again, and tried to catch her breath.

Cassiopeia blinked, paused, and dropped her eyes to the floor. "Commander," she corrected. "We've got to talk."

"Three more Cylons down!" Omega barked. "Red Squadron's lost half its Vipers now. Major Tristan's Viper is crippled, he's headed for a rough landing."

"Have the rest of Red Squadron form up under Sheba," Athena snapped, then turned to survey the battle once more.

"Commander!" Cassiopeia urged.

"Not now, Cassie!" Athena said, and held up a hand to show that Cassiopeia should go.

"Athena, listen!" Cassie pleaded.

Her abandonment of protocol was not lost on Athena. Still, she had obligations.

"Not. Right. Now," she insisted.

Cassiopeia strode across the command deck, grasped Athena's shoulders and forcibly spun her around so that the women were face to face. Athena shoved Cassie's hands away, but for the first time, she saw the desperation and the fear, in Cassiopeia's eyes.

"What is it?" she asked, though the battle still raged within earshot, and her mind was there.

"It took forever, but I've figured out who that dead man was that Troy and Dalton found on *Agro-3*," Cassie said. "I don't know how to explain it, Athena, and you're never going to believe it, but..."

"Fire in landing bay two!" Omega shouted. "Crisis agents on the way."

Athena glanced at Omega and then back at Cassie.

"It can wait," Athena said, with only a trace of apology in her voice.

"No!" Cassiopeia said frantically. "It can't wait. I don't understand it, but it's...Athena, the corpse—I've identified it. Impossible as it seems, it's Ambassador Puck!"

For a moment, Athena could only stare.

"How?" she muttered, then turned back to Omega. "Have the sentries guarding Ambassador Puck enter his chambers and bring him to the bridge immediately."

Omega relayed the orders through the comm-link headset he wore. After a moment, his face went slack.

"Ambassador Puck is no longer in his quarters," he informed her.

"How can this be?" Athena asked, and turned to Cassiopeia, though she knew the med-tech would have no better answer than she did. "If that corpse is Puck, then who was confined to Puck's quarters?"

"And how could he just disappear?" Cassie replied.

The answer occurred to Athena with sudden clarity. She remembered her conversation with Apollo in their father's Sanctuary, and realized there was only one possible answer.

"Iblis," Athena whispered.

"Count Iblis?" Cassiopeia asked, horrified.

Athena nodded.

Together, she and Cassiopeia turned to gaze out at the starfield, where the hopeless battle raged on. Desperately, she tried to put together the disparate pieces of a puzzle she had only just become aware of.

I should tell Apollo, she thought. Then it dawned on her that it was possible, even likely, that Apollo already knew.

Cold rage burned inside Dalton. The horror and fury, the despair and grief she had felt when she first lost a good friend to the Cylons only centari earlier had now abated. There was only dread and hate and numbness now, her nerves cut off from the horror. Sixteen Warriors. Sixteen pilots. Sixteen friends had died, and the Cylons kept coming, the odds only seeming to grow worse.

Laser blasts arced across space on every side. Klaxons blared in the cockpit of her Viper, warning her that she was too close to a Cylon Raider, or one of the other Vipers. Ships whipped by too fast for her to even recognize friend or enemy in some cases. Unlike in previous attacks, the Cylons had not dispersed to harry the rest of the fleet. They were concentrating on the *Galactica*, taking the Vipers on in direct conflict. Their goal was clear: eradication of the obstacle the Vipers presented.

The Cylons were confident and merciless.

In the icy fire of her rage, Dalton had forged her own confidence from a determination to win or die. Any mercy that might once have lived within her had been expunged.

"Ensign Dalton, you're a bit young to have so many suitors!" Captain Hecate said over the comm-link. "There are a couple trying to court you right now."

Dalton checked her scanners. Two Raiders on her tail, and a cross-fire dead ahead. She thrust the navi-hilt forward and dove as two ships flashed past one another above. The pair of Raiders followed her move, but not fast enough. Captain Hecate sprayed laser fire across the void and both Cylon fighters exploded into shrapnel.

"I owe you, Captain!" Dalton cried, even as she drew her own sights down on an enemy fighter.

"You can buy me a tankard of grog when it's all over," Hecate replied.

Dalton began to smile, but the expression was frozen on her face by a cry of alarm from Hecate. She craned her neck to see out through the canopy, and could only watch as the leader of her squadron died in a collision with a Raider.

"Troy!" Dalton cried over the comm. "We've got to figure a way to even the odds, and fast!"

Starbuck put the stolen Cylon Raider into QSE mode the moment he launched from the *Galactica*. Being shot down by his own people was not an idea that intrigued him. He'd planned to hit and run. Using the QSE generator, he could make sneak attacks on two or three Raiders at a time, then disappear and reappear elsewhere, so that the Cylons would never know whether he was with them or against them.

But if he was correct about the Cylons' scheme to use their own QSE-phased dark Raiders against the battlestar, Starbuck's own plan was useless. His priorities had to change. Stopping the QSE-equipped dark Raiders would be his only goal, if there were any to be stopped.

The quantum-shifted Raider roared out into space and Starbuck stared at the battle scene in awe and astonishment. While thus phased into another reality, any solid object, like a star or space vessel, took on a brilliant aura. He and Apollo had seen them before, when first approaching Baltar's base star. So when he launched, Starbuck expected to see the multi-colored auras of dozens of non-phased Vipers and Raiders, and the aura-trails left by the passage of those ships, and of the fleet itself. He also expected to see instantly if the other QSE-equipped Raiders were nearby. After all, they shared the same alternate, phased reality.

They were there, all right. Five dark Raiders, shifted out of reality and into the same dimension Starbuck's ship now occupied. Five to one, and nobody else would even know this smaller, yet vital, battle was raging.

But there was something else out in space around the fleet, something he would never have imagined. For beyond the small area where the battle raged, beyond the fleet and beyond the two Cylon base-stars which hung back from the fight, there were visitors.

Observers.

In a single glance Starbuck counted ten Kobollian lightships. Immobile. Watching. Other than the Cylons flying the QSE-equipped Raiders, nobody else knew the lightships were there. Apollo had been right. This quantum technology was somehow similar to the scientific level upon which the Lords of Kobol functioned. Only far more primitive and uncontrollable.

No doubt Apollo would have spouted some philosophical feldergarb to explain why the Lords of Kobol didn't take part in the actual battle. Starbuck didn't care what their reasoning was. They were content to hover there and do nothing more than monitor a battle that would decide the final fate of the human race.

Not Starbuck.

"Lousy slaggers," he grumbled. "We'll win without your help."

Then, against the kaleidoscopic auras and stellar striations that were in themselves a tempting distraction, Starbuck saw the five QSE-shifted dark Raiders begin their attack run toward the *Galactica*. They had apparently launched only a centari or so before from one of the base-stars. If they had come earlier, he would not have been prepared. Luck was with him.

He navigated the Raider as best he could and piloted it underneath the battlestar, where he could lie in wait for the quantum-phased Cylon Raiders. He watched his scanners and noted that the phased ships appeared more prominently there than those not on the same quantum plane.

As Starbuck was looking at the Raider's flatscreen, a new blip appeared, just as distinctly as those phased Cylon ships. But this wasn't a Raider, it was a QSE-phased Viper.

Starbuck smiled. Apollo had just launched from the *Hephaestus*. He wasn't sure exactly what Apollo's plan was, but he knew it would be good. Starbuck only prayed it would be good enough to turn the tide.

Already, the appearance of the shifted Viper seemed to have disrupted the dark Raiders' plans. They turned away from their attack course on the *Galactica* and toward Apollo's Viper. His past experience with Cylons told him there was a good chance they wouldn't even realize it if he joined their ranks.

Of course, these new Cylons had the much-vaunted "human logic function." On the other hand, they'd based that program on Baltar's mental processes. And as far as he could tell, Baltar's internal logic functions were as alien to the rest of humanity as the Cylons were.

"Now things are getting really interesting," Starbuck said to himself. "Time to play Cylon."

23.

THE TWIN BASE STARS STILL HUNG BACK OMINOUSLY, refraining from direct engagement in the battle. Troy gauged the remaining Cylon forces at somewhere between one hundred thirty and one hundred sixty Raiders.

There were fifty-one Vipers still in combat. Many of the dead pilots had been his friends, but the battle allowed him no time to mourn.

By now, the odds should have changed. In earlier battles, the ratio of Raiders to Vipers had been altered in favor of the Colonial Warriors not long after the fighting began. This battle was different. The ratio had not changed much. The Warriors were holding their own, nothing more.

Dalton was right. Something had to be done to turn the tide.

"Major Sheba, this is Lieutenant Troy," he barked into the comm-link.

"Go ahead, Troy," Sheba replied.

"I've got an idea," he said. "Do you trust me?"

Troy didn't want to explain too much of his plan to Sheba on the comm. He had to assume the Cylons were able to monitor Colonial communications. Sheba was the highest ranking officer still in the battle. But she was also his friend, and, as his father's lover, the only maternal figure in his life since his mother had died when he was six.

"Of course I do," Sheba replied. "Just don't get yourself killed.

Someone has to stand with your father when we take the Seal."

"What?" Troy gasped. Then his face stretched into a broad smile. "It's about time."

He glanced out across the starfield at Sheba's Viper. In that instant, a Cylon laser blast sizzled across the nose of her starfighter and the Viper shuddered.

"Sheba!" Troy cried.

"I'm okay!" she replied. "Shields held up fine. If you've got an idea, Troy, don't waste another second."

"On my mark, you, Jolly and Zimmer draw some attention and then make a run for open space over the *Galactica*," he told her, and hoped he was vague enough that the Cylons wouldn't see his intentions, even if they were listening.

"You've got it, Lieutenant," Sheba replied.

Two Raiders were moving in on Troy's Viper from behind.

"Major Boomer, this is Troy," he said, giving the navi-hilt a jolt to the left to avoid Cylon laser fire. "I need your help to pull something off."

"You've got it, Troy. But first we've got to— "

Troy heard Boomer whisper a curse, and then the electric crackle of laser fire.

"Sorry," Boomer said. "Got a little busy. Why don't I give you a little breathing room now?"

A micron later, the Cylons on Troy's tail were incinerated, and Boomer's Viper swung into place behind him. Another Viper joined Boomer, and Troy knew who its pilot was without asking.

"You've been listening," he said aloud.

"Don't even think you're going anywhere without me, you mug-jape!" Dalton snapped at him.

"Not at all," Troy replied. "I need you both. Form on me."

With Boomer and Dalton following, Troy piloted his Viper toward the open landing bay on the side of the *Galactica* that faced the battle. As he had suspected, the Cylons ignored them, assuming they were out of the fight.

At the last micron, Troy thrust the navi-hilt forward and to the right and dodged beneath the *Galactica*. Without missing a beat, Boomer and Dalton followed.

"Shut them down," Troy said into the comm, even as he killed his Viper's engines.

A moment later, all three ships were jerked harshly to the right, carried along within the gravitational field of the battlestar's wake. Eventually, they would drift out of it, but Troy wasn't going to wait that long.

"Sheba, go!" he barked into the comm.

In the silence, in the darkness, Boomer, Dalton and Troy waited. Troy gazed out through the canopy at the starfield, the monolithic structure of the *Galactica* looming in the upper edges of his peripheral vision. The battle was above and behind them, and only open space lay ahead.

A sudden burst of laser fire split the starfield, and was quickly followed by several more. A Viper buzzed over the battlestar and zipped across the void dead ahead. It was Sheba, under fire. Two more Vipers followed, and Troy knew they must be Jolly and Zimmer. A micron later, the starfield was filled with Cylon Raiders, eleven or twelve in all, though Troy wasn't certain of the count. He didn't know what Sheba had done to get their attention, but it had obviously worked.

"Go!" Troy roared.

He fired his pulsars and the Viper erupted from beneath the *Galactica*. Troy held down the fire button on the navi-hilt and lasers ripped across space into a crowded field of Cylon starfighters.

Nearby, Boomer swore at the Cylons and Dalton screamed with savage delight. The ambush took microns. The Cylons never stood a chance.

"Troy?" Sheba asked over the comm.

"Yes, Major, we got them all!" he cried. "Let's see if they'll fall for it again!"

"Troy," Sheba said again. "We lost Zimmer."

The excitement drained out of Troy in an instant. But not the fury.

Not the knowledge that, grim as it was, they had improved the odds. And they had to do whatever it took to keep improving them.

"You want to run it again?" Sheba asked.

"We have to," Troy responded bluntly.

The battle continued. The dying went on.

Starbuck kept his vision focused on the phase-shifted Cylon Raiders. Even in the shifted reality they flew through, the ebony starfighters seemed to absorb light and color. They appeared as indigo stains on the blackness of space, and that was how Starbuck followed them. In the colorful swirls of the quantum shift, they were fluid darkness made solid. But if they were solid, they could be shot.

His focus was so intense, Starbuck didn't see the approaching Viper until the last second. Then it was blocking his view, filling the starfield, and he was nearly face to face with a Colonial Warrior. Panic overcame him for a moment: he was in a Cylon Raider—the Viper pilot would shoot him down! Lasers burned across empty space and Starbuck closed his eyes.

As he opened them, the Viper flew straight through his stolen Raider. Starbuck sucked in his breath, then shivered, unnerved. He was phased, of course. He'd been in no danger. Still, the experience made him wonder about the QSE technology, about what dimension he was in, exactly.

Then the phase-shifted Raiders had come into firing range of Apollo's Viper, and Starbuck had to act. It struck him again how odd it was to be fighting this mini-battle literally within the greater conflict, invisible to all but the Lords of Kobol, who ringed the battle in their lightships, and merely watched. The QSE-shifted Cylons either did not see them, or did not pay any attention to their presence because they knew the Lords would not intervene.

But if that was so, then *how did they know?*

Questions spun through Starbuck's head, but he pushed them away. Such contemplation was for idle consideration, not for battle.

Apollo's phased Viper stayed on its heading, moving directly for the distant, unmoving base stars. The dark Raiders were in a vee formation, winging toward Apollo's ship. Their lasers began to fire, and Apollo didn't even waver, didn't try to avoid them. Several shots were true, but the Viper's shields held up.

Then Starbuck was in place.

"Sneaky lizards," he said aloud. "Let's see how you like it when your own little subterfuge is turned back on you."

Starbuck fired. His lasers burned right through two of the dark Raiders. The ships exploded in a rainbow of color, and Starbuck assumed the debris from the ships had returned to their normal dimension when the QSE unit was destroyed.

"You learn something new every day," he observed drily.

Two of the remaining trio of Raiders continued firing upon Apollo's Viper. The other began to bank around, obviously intending to turn and face Starbuck in his stolen Cylon ship. Starbuck ignored him, staying on Apollo's trail. An instant later, he had destroyed the third dark Raider.

"So much for the vaunted Human Logic Function," Starbuck said and smiled. Since Baltar didn't have a shred of decency, of courage or loyalty, Starbuck reasoned, these HLF-programmed Cylons must already be completely confused by the Warriors' behavior.

In truth, the very thing Lucifer had been so certain would give his dark Centurions the edge over the human Warriors had made them obsolete. They might be better pilots than the previous model Centurions. They might be faster, more intelligent, and have better aim. But they had even less of a chance at predicting human behavior than their predecessors. In fact, all that extra thought was only slowing them down.

Starbuck found the irony delicious.

The errant dark Raider had come around and was angling to get the drop on him. Meanwhile, Starbuck tried to get the last QSE-phased Raider that was harrying Apollo dead in his sights. He was too late. The Raider had gotten up right behind Apollo's Viper. As

Starbuck watched, the phased ship fired its lasers—

—And the deadly beams passed right through the Viper. Apollo had simply phased back into reality, and the quantum-shifted laser blasts no longer existed in the same dimension as his Viper. But that trick would only work once. Now the Raider on Apollo's tail also unphased, and the chain reaction continued. Starbuck shut down his own QSE generator, and so did the Raider trailing him.

The situation had suddenly become impossible. Back in reality, they were beyond the thick of the battle, but there were still many Raiders and Vipers nearby. Starbuck had a dark Raider coming right up on him. In microns, the Cylon would have him. He could escape, but to do so would mean leaving Apollo without any backup.

Apollo kept on flying straight for the nearer of the two base stars. It hadn't begun firing on him yet—the Cylons would never expect a Viper to attack a base star; what harm could it do?—but it would when he got too close.

Starbuck knew what he had to do. Whatever Apollo had in mind, he had to back him up. Apollo was Starbuck's superior officer, his best friend, practically his brother. If it cost him his life, so be it.

The base star loomed ahead. Closer than he'd realized. They were almost upon it. Starbuck manuevered so the Raider trailing Apollo was directly in his line of fire. He let loose a laser blast and scored a direct hit on the Cylon vessel, which exploded half a micron later. Starbuck was flying so close behind the Cylon that his stolen Raider was buffeted by the detonation. An odd wailing alarm sounded, and he knew that the Cylon trailing him had him in its own sights.

He was dead.

Lasers flashed behind him…then another explosion. He stared down at the Raider's scanners to see that two Vipers had picked up the trail. They had destroyed his attacker, but now it was certain that they would try to take him down as well.

Apollo's mission, whatever it was, seemed safe for the moment. Starbuck had to watch out for himself. He initiated the QSE without hesitation. Laser blasts cut through his ship, cut through him, but they could no longer touch him.

Starbuck exhaled loudly. After a moment, he stared at Apollo's Viper as it grew closer to the nearer of the two base stars. Now that Apollo was safe, Starbuck had the luxury to wonder exactly what his friend's plan was. What kind of odds did a single Viper have against a base star? Did he think he could take out the command core of the base star without being obliterated himself?

Unless there was some kind of secret weapon he hadn't told anyone about, Starbuck didn't have any idea what Apollo had in mind. He could only watch as the Viper continued on, its nose pointed directly at the narrow core where the two cylindrical pyramids of the base star met at its center.

Then Apollo's Viper was under fire, closing quickly on the base star. But the Warrior's ship did not turn away or fire its own weapons. It just didn't make any sense to Starbuck.

And then it did.

He began to scream Apollo's name.

Boomer was ecstatic. In three runs, Troy's plan had already pared down the Cylon forces considerably. The odds were changing fast. Soon it was just going to be a battle of attrition. Morale was rising quickly as well, and it had a measurable effect on the efficiency of the pilots.

"Boomer!" Sheba cried over the comm-link. "Do you have any idea what Apollo's doing?"

He glanced down at the flatscreen, where his scanners showed the entire battle in progress.

"What do you mean? I didn't even think Apollo was out here with us," Boomer replied.

"Check the ship heading toward that base star!" Sheba shouted, panic in her voice. "I've tried to hail him, but he won't respond."

Boomer looked at the scanners again, focused on the Viper that seemed on a collision course with the base star. It was a Scarlet-class starfighter. As far as he knew, the only one that wasn't destroyed on the *Hephaestus* was Apollo's.

"Oh my God," Boomer said softly.

Troy heard the exchange between Boomer and Sheba. His Viper was angled toward the base stars, and he could actually see the Scarlet-class Viper in the distance, a small speck hurtling toward the core column that connected the top and bottom halves of the base star.

At battle speed, the Viper collided with the vulnerable column. The resulting explosion was enormous, far larger than such a collision would have warranted. Apollo must have had a payload of solonite on board. The impact set off the solonite and combined with the explosion of the tylium fuel tanks to obliterate most of the base star.

And Apollo with it.

"Father?" Troy whispered.

Then he, too, screamed Apollo's name.

24.

"My God, Apollo! What have you done?" Starbuck shouted, even as the explosion of the base star sent a shudder through the stolen Cylon Raider he piloted. The Raider was quantum-phased, but even shifted outside conventional reality, Starbuck could feel the brunt of the detonation.

He felt sick, and suddenly very cold.

He wasn't sure if he could get a comm-link while phased, but he tried anyway.

"Athena," he said weakly. "Athena, it's Starbuck. Did you see that?"

Nothing. Just the hiss of communication from some other reality. For the first time, there was something almost frightening about the QSE. Starbuck didn't want to be phased anymore. He was a good distance from any of the Vipers, or from attacking Cylon Raiders as well. He shut the generator off and shifted, became substantial once more.

"Athena, it's Starbuck," he said again.

"Starbuck!" Athena said quickly. "It's not what you think! That wasn't..."

Then another voice broke in.

"Starbuck!" Apollo shouted. "I guess we're even now, huh?"

He stared at the comm-link, anger rising within him.

"Apollo, you son of a lupus!" he shouted.

"Sorry, buddy," Apollo said. "Had to be done. All the Viper's systems, including the QSE, were remote-slaved. I packed it with solonite and piloted it from here. The Cylons didn't even try to stop the ship, Starbuck. Did you see it? They didn't see it as a threat because they never imagined a human would pull a suicide run. Baltar taught them too well, I think."

"That's just what I was thinking," Starbuck replied. "But I'm still going to beat the frack out of you."

The keening alarm in the Raider blared in the cockpit.

"What's that?" Apollo said on the comm. "What's wrong?"

Starbuck stared at the scanners.

"Vipers!" he replied. "Three of them!"

"I'll warn them off," Athena interrupted. "Starbuck, you're the only dark Raider left out there. I'll…"

Too late! Laser fire blazed past Starbuck on all sides. The Raider was rocked by several tangential hits. A direct hit, and he'd be dead.

"Hey!" he shouted, jerking the steering column of the Raider back and forth to draw attention to himself. "Warriors, hold your fire, this is Captain Starbuck!"

Another tangential shot burned through his shields and melted a section of his wing, throwing his navigation off a second. Then the firing stopped.

"That's got them, Starbuck!" Athena said. "You've been identified. Now how about giving your fellow Warriors a hand?"

"I don't know," Starbuck said, more to himself than to Athena. "I've been known to hold a grudge."

"Even against your own daughter?" Athena asked.

Then he heard Dalton's voice over the comm.

"Sorry, Father," she said. "I'm glad I didn't kill you."

Starbuck banked around and fired on the first Cylon ship that came into his sights.

"Not as glad as I am," he mused.

The *Galactica*'s bridge was in an uproar. With one base star destroyed, hope had surged into every member of the crew. The air was thick with it. And not only hope, but unity. Messages were coming in from every ship in the fleet, suggesting battle tactics. Several captains had offered to engage the Cylons directly, even at the cost of their vessels, their crews and passengers—their own lives.

Athena politely declined. They hadn't reached that point yet. As far as she was concerned, they never would.

"Apollo," she said into the comm. "We still have a base star to deal with."

"I'm working on it," he responded. "I've got an alternate plan right now."

"What is it?" she asked.

"You really don't want to know, Commander," he replied.

She considered that, and decided not to pursue it.

"There's something else you should know," she said. "I don't know quite how it fits in with the Cylon attack, but I can't shake the feeling this is all connected somehow. It has to be.

"The murdered man on *Agro-3*," she continued. "Cassiopeia figured out who he was."

This time when Apollo replied, his voice wasn't on the comm-link. It was whispered directly into her brain, as intimate as if he were standing right beside her. Even more so.

"*I know,*" he thought to her.

Athena had no way to even describe this communication to herself.

"Apollo—did you just...?"

"*Yes,*" came the answer. "*I've been practicing. Getting better at this. And I know that Ambassador Puck died before I ever left the fleet. It's Iblis, and he's going to come for me soon. I can...I can feel him.*"

As suddenly as he had entered her mind, Athena felt Apollo withdraw.

"God and the Lords of Kobol be with you, Brother," she said aloud. "I love you."

Around her, the crew was silent.

Now Troy knew how Dalton had felt when Starbuck, who had been presumed dead, turned up alive again. But Troy had been lucky. For him the trauma of such an experience—of believing his father dead only to have him appear, alive once more—had lasted only microns.

"Troy!" Dalton cried over the comm-link.

"I know!" he replied. "One base star down, one to go!"

The odds had improved considerably. There were forty-six Vipers left, and under one hundred Raiders. Two to one. Troy knew from his training that, against Cylons, those were excellent odds. The balance of the conflict would shift, now. They would lose fewer and fewer Vipers. It was only a matter of time.

Or it would have been, if not for the remaining base star. With its dark Raiders destroyed, its secret weapon come to naught, the destructive force of the base star began to close on the *Galactica*. The Colonial battlestar had already sustained damage in the battle. The Vipers were ineffectual against such a huge vessel.

Athena would have to command the *Galactica* to face the base star head on. But that would mean leaving the fleet unprotected. If the battlestar were destroyed, the fleet could not sustain itself for very long. It was the endgame.

Apollo stood alone on the darkened bridge of the *Hephaestus*. He stared out at the starfield, at the exploding starfighters and the flash of laser blasts. Behind the Forge ship, the rest of the fleet's ships huddled close to one another and awaited for the outcome.

Without warning, pain flared in his mind. He cried out and his knees buckled. Apollo reached out for the command seat to steady himself. The bridge was gone. He could see only what was in his mind....

The *Galactica breaking apart, burning. Cylon Raiders harrying the non-combatant fleet ships. The* Rising Star *exploding. Athena screaming on the bridge of the dying battlestar. Troy obliterated in the destruction of his Viper. Agro domes shattered. Then, only debris. Debris that had once been the fleet.*

On his hands and knees on the bridge of the Forge, Apollo retched painfully. Nothing came up but bitter bile. Teeth set, grinding against one another, he pulled himself to his feet once more.

What had he seen? A clairvoyant vision of the future, some prescient curse, or merely a warning about what might be coming? He didn't have enough understanding of the mental abilities of the Kobollian bloodline to even begin to comprehend the vision. But he was even more determined that there was only one possible course of action.

In the silence of the vast ship, Apollo moved to the navigational controls. The *Hephaestus* was slaved to the *Galactica*, in effect being towed by the battlestar's computers. The Forge was close behind the warship, and Apollo could see clearly the many battle wounds the *Galactica* had received. Already, Athena had begun to turn the battlestar to face the oncoming base-star.

The risk was too great.

"This is Apollo, override command key, 'Serina,'" he said aloud. "Disengage slave-link to *Galactica*."

"Slave-link disengaged," the computer replied.

Apollo sat down in front of the navigational systems of the *Hephaestus*, and took control.

Sheba's targeting systems sighted on a Cylon Raider that was pursuing Boomer. She thumbed the fire button on her navi-hilt. Lasers burned through the void and razed the Cylon vessel from the starfield. A large dark form moved into the edges of her peripheral vision, and Sheba craned her neck around to investigate.

The *Hephaestus* had broken rank with the rest of the fleet. The huge Forge ship was moving on a direct course to intercept the Cylon base star's attack on the *Galactica*. Sheba shook her head. It didn't make any sense. The *Hephaestus* had shields, but no weaponry. More important, it was a ghost ship. The few surviving crewmen had been shuttled off the vessel. The only person left on the Forge was...

"Apollo," Sheba whispered to herself, then spoke into her comm-link.

"Major Sheba to Commander Athena," she said hurriedly, firing off a laser blast that destroyed yet another Cylon Raider. "Do you see this?"

Sheba stared out at the Forge ship again, the air inside the Viper cockpit suddenly too warm, too close.

"I see it, Major," Athena replied over the comm. "But short of firing on him ourselves, there's nothing we can do to stop Apollo. Your orders have changed, Sheba. Do whatever you can to safeguard the *Hephaestus* so she reaches her target. Any action you may wish to take is by your prerogative."

Klaxons blared inside Sheba's Viper. Scanners flashed on flatscreen and in holographic projections. She felt cold inside. Apollo had asked her to marry him less than two centons ago. Now he was going to die. Athena had left room in her orders for Sheba to take action. She would have to do just that.

"Troy, Dalton, Boomer and Jolly, keep the Raiders off the Forge as much as you can!" she ordered.

The Vipers could discourage Raider attacks, try to keep the *Hephaestus's* shield integrity high as long as possible. Of course, once the base star began to attack the *Hephaestus*, the Vipers would have to give way. Then it would be time for prayer. The Forge ship had strong enough shields to protect it from the base star's weaponry for half a centari, no more. Three or four concentrated blasts on the same area of the shield and it would be over.

Fortunately, the Cylons hadn't taken notice of the *Hephaestus* yet. Even when they did, their response would not be immediate. There would be confusion over what one of the unarmed fleet vessels was doing away from the rest of the Colonial ships. They would be on guard, certainly, but particularly with Baltar as the template, they would never believe an entire starcruiser's crew and passengers would sacrifice their lives for the rest of the fleet. Never.

And they would be right.

But it wasn't the entire populace of the Forge. The Cylons had no way of knowing there was only one man aboard.

"Starbuck!" Sheba cried. "Form on me! We've got another mission to take care of!"

"Funny, Major," Starbuck's voice came over the comm. "I was already headed in your direction."

Sheba smiled. She ought to have known. And he'd decided to act even before Sheba had. For yahren, a secret part of her had envied the closeness between Starbuck and Apollo. There was no danger so great that either man would not risk it for the other. Yet in this most dire of moments, when Apollo needed to be rescued from himself, Sheba finally came to see the friendship of the two Warriors as an extraordinary gift between them. As well as to her. It was a great comfort to know that Apollo would always have Starbuck to back him up.

Starbuck's stolen Cylon Raider slid into formation next to Sheba's Viper. Together, the two who loved Apollo most raced for the ravaged landing bay of the *Hephaestus*, determined to save him from his own sacrifice.

A few microns with the computer, and Apollo had been able to divert almost all power aboard the Forge to the external shields. Life support was at minimal levels, and only dim emergency lights shone in the shadowy corridors and on the bridge. The starfield provided more illumination for Apollo's sharp eyes than the weak backup lights and the glow of flatscreens.

Apollo stared at the base star, growing in the starfield. He knew the klaxons should have been going off. But he had shut down those systems already. There was only quiet on the bridge. On the entire ship, in fact.

The son of Adama breathed slowly, at peace with himself and with the destiny he had faith would be his. Zac had told him that he would advance, that he would become a new lifeform not bound by the mechanics of conventional reality. He would see Zac again—perhaps quite soon. The thought was not unpleasant. Yes, he would be leaving so many loved ones behind, and responsibilities as well, but there was no other choice.

Soon, he hoped, he would see his father again.

His bittersweet musing was suddenly interrupted as a wave of nausea swept over Apollo. This was not trauma brought upon by some psychic vision, however. It was disgust, revulsion as he sensed a horrible presence.

Apollo was not alone on the Forge.

"Ah, you are sensitive, aren't you?"

The voice was familiar, yet there was something new in its timbre, some damp echo. It slithered in the shadows, like its master.

Apollo turned slowly. Dread grew within him, and yet, somehow he knew that it was unnatural. It was being forced upon him by his visitor, by the ancient enemy of the House of Kobol. Finally, his eyes found the dark shape, blacker than the shadows, its human form undulating with nightmare images. It wasn't a man, or even a spirit. It was the absence of spirit, an abyss where a human soul once thrived. A black hole, torn from the fabric of heaven, hungrily devouring light and love and hope.

"Count Iblis," Apollo said warmly. "Welcome."

The blackness shimmered, red eyes burning like embers where a face should have been. Then it changed, slowly altered itself until it wore an ethereal mask of the face Apollo remembered from their previous meeting.

"I'm glad you recognize me, Apollo," the ancient evil replied. *"We can speak plainly, then."*

"Oh, by all means, do," Apollo said. "And of course I recognized you. Though I might not have if my brother hadn't warned me of your coming."

"Brother?" Iblis asked, and his voice seemed even farther away.

"Yes, Zac," Apollo answered. "Ah, but I forget. You never had the pleasure of knowing Zac, did you? He's one of the Lords now."

A low growl issued from the man-shaped void, and the darkness seemed to convulse several times. Apollo felt a small, secret triumph. Iblis would not take him unaware, at least. There was some cold comfort in that.

"*You are more knowledgeable than I expected,*" Iblis whispered. "*A worthy opponent. I am glad. When your father died, I had thought the dynasty was at an end.*"

Apollo sighed and turned away from Iblis. He looked out at the starfield again, at the looming base star that nearly blotted out the stellar light.

"If you've got a point, you'd better make it," he said. "I'm going to be dead in a centari and then you'll have to go play your tricks on somebody else."

Apollo didn't blink. But an instant later, he could no longer see the starfield. The blackness that was Iblis had materialized in front of him. Cinder-eyes burned centimetrons from his face and he could feel a painful cold emanating from the creature.

"*You risk much, son of Adama,*" Iblis hissed. "*Don't ever think you can dismiss me so simply. And I do not play...tricks. You're going to die momentarily, that is true. But I can save you. I can save the fleet entire, to a person.*"

"Let me guess," Apollo sneered. "You save us from the Cylons, and then you become our commander. Just as you wanted to be when you murdered Ambassador Puck and took his place. Just as you wanted to be when you first vied for power against my father eighteen yahren ago.

"I'm not sure why you'd come to me," Apollo continued. "After all, I'm not the commander now. Athena is. And only the Quorum can turn power over to you."

"*My goal is simpler, now, Apollo,*" Iblis said softly, his tone almost soothing. "*All I ask, in return for the safety of the entire fleet, is your pledge of fealty to me. Swear your oath of allegiance to me, and the fleet will be spared.*"

For a moment, Apollo did not understand. Why had Iblis seemingly abandoned his goal of commanding the fleet? Why would he?

Then Apollo remembered his conversation with Zac, and knew that Iblis had never abandoned his true goal. The fallen angel had never wanted power over the fleet. He wanted only to corrupt the House of Kobol, to taint the line, to tempt the pure-blooded descendants of his ancient enemies. Yet there was something else, something Apollo felt he was missing.

"If I agreed," Apollo began, and he could actually feel the loathsome excitement that rose in Iblis at his words.

"*If* I agreed," he repeated, "how would you defeat the Cylons?"

A ragged raw hole, like a wound, seemed to form beneath the burning eyes. Iblis had smiled.

"*I would not need to defeat them,*" was the Count's only response.

It was enough. Apollo knew. Finally, he understood. Baltar had told them of a man, a human who had genetically and technologically manipulated the Cylon race millennia ago, his only goal the extermination of his own race, which he despised.

"I should have known," Apollo whispered. "It could only have been you."

"*Indeed,*" Iblis said proudly. "*It could be no other. They* **are** *my creatures, my beautiful creations. And yet like any benevolent god, I have left them to their own devices. They have almost forgotten me, but they are still in my power. They are puppets, and I hold their strings. In the end, Apollo, you are all merely puppets to me.*

"*Come now, you are prepared to throw away your life, to die for your people. I offer you life for yourself and eternal peace for them. Pledge fealty to me, and humanity may flourish again without fear of the Cylon threat. You have no choice but to believe me.*"

"Oh, I believe you," Apollo replied. "Let me tell you what else I believe. I know you would kill me, if you could. For whatever reason, you cannot. Or you are unwilling because I am of pure Kobollian blood and you are afraid of what I would then become. I don't pretend to understand.

"I also believe that the House of Iblis did not split off from the House of Kobol because of your hatred for your brethren. I think they threw your pogees out of there," Apollo spat, finger jabbing the air in front of Iblis. "I think you were excommunicated. Dismissed. I think they found you *unworthy.*"

"*You test my patience, Apollo, and tempt fate as well,*" Iblis roared, the calm arrogance of microns earlier now shattered, the humanoid mask dissipating like smoke.

"You test *my* patience!" Apollo snapped back. "I defy you, Count Iblis. The Cylons have done their best to eradicate humanity from the universe, but here we are! We still survive! And we'll continue to do so. As long as the fleet lives, the Cylons have lost and so have you!

"It's happening to you again, Iblis," he cried. "But this time, it is *I* who find you unworthy. *I* dismiss you! Go, now, and pray that those Lords who were once your brothers never falter in their wisdom, or they will certainly destroy you."

Apollo turned his head away from Iblis and stared down at the flatscreen showing the *Hephaestus* closing on the base star. He could see Vipers and Raiders blasting at one another outside the Forge. Then the base star began to fire on the massive vessel, and he knew time had run out. A few centari, probably less, and he would be dead.

"You've lost, Iblis," he said softly.

The air was suddenly sucked from his lungs as Iblis departed, creating a vacuum in his wake. Apollo could hear the roar of the spectre's fury, diminishing until it faded completely. All the electrical systems on the bridge shorted at once, and a small fire started at the dead navigation station where Apollo sat. With the base star blotting out the starfield, the darkness was almost complete. Systems were down, breathing was difficult, and the race was on to see if the base star would be able to destroy the Forge before the two vessels collided.

Apollo sat in the darkness, meditating and waiting for death.

Behind him, the door to the corridor hissed open. Shocked, Apollo turned, prepared for some new, perhaps more physical threat from Iblis. Instead, silhouetted by the emergency lights in the corridor, he saw Starbuck and Sheba.

"No!" he shouted, even as he stood and rushed toward them.

"What in the name of God are you two doing here?"

"We're here for you, Apollo," Sheba said. "Did you really think I'd let you get out of marrying me that easily?"

"We've only got a centari, maybe less!" Apollo said as he rose to greet them.

"Then we'd better hurry," Starbuck said. He grabbed Apollo's arm, pulled him into the corridor, and then all three of them were running together for the ascensior tube.

On the bridge of the prison barge *Icarus*, the escaped Borellian Nomen sat at the stations of crew members they had recently slain. Gar'Tokk, the Nomen leader, paced the bridge impatiently. He awaited word from their benefactor, Count Iblis. Honor dictated that they should perform whatever tasks he required of them until their debt was repaid. Thus, they remained motionless in space as Gar'Tokk prayed for a call to action.

He was bored. There was life to be lived, freedom to be exploited.

"Yes, my ally, freedom. Thanks to my kindness." Iblis spoke to Gar'Tokk's mind as he materialized on the bridge. The man-shaped darkness seemed to surge toward Gar'Tokk, as if trying to break through an invisible barrier of some kind. Best not to think about it, the Nomen leader decided.

"Finally," Gar'Tokk remarked. "I am pleased you have come. We would like to discharge our debt as soon as possible. Only then may we begin to live again as a tribe set aside from the human cattle."

"We are beings of like minds, Gar'Tokk," Iblis hissed. *"That's why I chose you to assist me. You may power up the engines of your former prison now. Forge ahead, and when you come upon the* Hephaestus, *you will fire on her."*

Gar'Tokk frowned.

"This ship is not armed," he observed. "We have no weaponry to fire at any ship."

Without warning, Iblis changed. The temperature on the bridge dropped drastically. Even Gar'Tokk, leader of a people long since adjusted to the harshest of climates, felt the cold. The darkness that was Count Iblis seemed to boil with it.

"*Do you take me for a fool?*" Iblis roared, and the power aboard the *Icarus* flickered twice. "*This is a prison barge! Unlike other ships in the fleet, it is armed with laser cannon for defense. They are not enough to destroy a battlestar, but certainly sufficient to attack the humans' Forge ship.*"

Gar'Tokk merely nodded. He did not like the change in Iblis, but honor demanded that he act. He gestured for the other Nomen to follow Iblis's instructions. Then he turned and watched the starfield for signs of the fleet. Count Iblis was beside him, and Gar'Tokk felt fury radiating from him, along with a kind of sickness. He realized that he didn't want to be near his benefactor, as if some of the putrescence that had eaten into Iblis would become a part of him as well.

It was only a matter of microns before the fleet came into view.

"They're under attack!" one of the Nomen crew shouted. "Gar'Tokk, it is the Cylons!"

"Do I not have eyes, Snie'Goss?" Gar'Tokk snapped, and rounded on Iblis, his anger overwhelming whatever disgust or anxiety the creature might have inspired.

"We are to attack the *Hephaestus* now, Count Iblis?" Gar'Tokk growled. "You want us to aid the Cylons in the destruction of the human fleet?"

The burning scarlet auras that served as the creature's eyes grew brighter.

"*That is precisely what you will do, Gar'Tokk. Nomen custom and honor dictate that you aid me in my goal. My goal is the destruction of the fleet,*" Iblis said.

"You are a Cylon then?" Gar'Tokk sneered.

"*Not a Cylon, but an enemy of the humans, just as they are. Just as you are,*" Iblis replied. "*Now do as I have asked, and your honor debt will be paid. Attack the* Hephaestus."

Gar'Tokk stared at Iblis, then turned to look out at the starfield, where Cylon Raiders and Colonial Vipers danced around each other, and around the Forge ship *Hephaestus*, which seemed to be headed directly for the Cylon base star. His gaze drifted across the other Borellian Nomen, his most trusted followers, whom he had chosen to crew the ship.

Then he turned back to Iblis.

"No," he said flatly.

"*What?*" Iblis roared. "*You have a debt of honor to me, Gar'Tokk! All of you do! I demand that you repay it now!*"

"The humans are inferior," Gar'Tokk said, and felt the confused and suspicious gaze of the other Nomen heavy on him. "They imprisoned us; they are our enemies. I would gladly destroy the entire fleet, had I but the power to do so. Then the Nomen would settle somewhere and begin the new human race. The true human race."

Gar'Tokk bared his teeth and growled as he continued, showing his disdain for Iblis, but also showing the other Nomen that his decision was backed by his strength. By his blood and life.

"*I did not take you for a coward, Gar'Tokk,*" Iblis taunted him.

"And only one without power descends to the level of infantile insults," Gar'Tokk retorted. "As I said, I would gladly destroy the humans. But the Cylons are the most disgusting of races, the most inferior. They are lower than humanity by far. Not content to be little more than muck-dwelling reptiles, they remake themselves as soulless machines.

"The Borellian Nomen will never ally themselves with the Cylons!" he roared. "We would sooner stand side by side with our hated captors, the revolting humans, and fight the Cylons to the death."

Gar'Tokk spun to face the other Nomen, and as he saw the pride in the way each of them stood, the glory shining in their eyes, he knew what he had to do. He turned to face Iblis again.

"We reject you, Iblis," Gar'Tokk said. "There will be no freedom for the Nomen now. Not yet. We will surrender ourselves to the humans, and thus, owe you nothing."

As he watched the red eyes blaze even brighter in the creature's liquid darkness, Gar'Tokk felt a tremor of something unfamiliar pass through him. After a moment, he realized it was fear.

"*You have made a very dangerous enemy this day, Gar'Tokk,*" Iblis whispered. "*The time will come when you shall regret it.*"

Then Iblis was gone. Slowly, the prison barge swung into line with the rest of the fleet. The other prisoners screamed and cried for Nomen blood, but the Nomen were savage and well armed.

Gar'Tokk stared at the space where Iblis had been. Silently, he vowed that he would see Iblis dead.

If such a being could be killed.

Aboard the remaining Cylon base star, the cognitor Cylon commander called Lucifer stared coldly at a scanner displaying the impending collision.

In keeping with his programming, Lucifer sighed. He opened the dataport on the comm-station in front of him and knelt in front of it. A long, thin sensorline jutted suddenly from his right eye and plunged into the dataport.

After a moment, the light in the clear dome that was Lucifer's brain went out. The red gleam in his eyes faded.

Many parsecs away, in the fourth quadrant of the Cyranus galaxy, aboard a base-star that was home to the Cylon Imperious Leader, new Centurions and cogitators were being created. In a clone-tank, connected by sensorline to the base star's computer systems, a dormant cogitator's eyes began to burn red.

"Go, go, go!" Starbuck shouted, and leaped into the stolen Cylon Raider behind Apollo.

Sheba's Viper hovered a moment, then burned out of the Forge's landing bay. Starbuck watched through the Raider's lowering canopy. Apollo fired up the Cylon ship's engines.

"We're not going to make it!" Starbuck cried.

"We'll make it!" Apollo snapped. "Get strapped in!"

Starbuck craned his neck to look out the massive bay doors. The base star was right on top of them. Collision was imminent.

"We're not going to make it!" he snarled again.

"This was your idea, Captain!" Apollo retorted.

"It'll be *Lieutenant*, if your sister has her way!" Starbuck muttered.

The Cylon Raider lifted off the deck just as the front of the *Hephaestus* made contact with the base star. The ship began to shatter and collapse around them. Starbuck winced, waiting for the fuel tanks to rupture, waiting for the explosion that would destroy the base star, and the Forge ship with it.

"Come on, come on!" Apollo urged the ship around to face open space. He glanced over at Starbuck, who opened his mouth to speak.

"Don't say it!" Apollo shouted, then shoved the steering column forward.

The stolen Cylon dark Raider surged forth, throwing them both back against their seats. The starfighter shot out into space, barely manuevering around falling debris.

Starbuck howled with triumph!

"Told you we'd make it!" he cried.

Behind them, the base star and the *Hephaestus* erupted together in a devastating explosion. The Raider was propelled uncontrollably forward at extraordinary speed. Apollo struggled to regain control of the ship. Slightly disoriented, Starbuck glanced out at the starfield to find that they were on a collision course with the *Galactica*.

"Apollo!" he shouted.

"I've got it, Starbuck, just give me a…"

"Apollo!"

The battlestar instantly grew huge, blotting out the stars. All that, just to die now, Starbuck thought. Apollo still hadn't realized the danger.

"Apollo!" Starbuck cried a third time, then reached over and grabbed Apollo's head and forced him to look up.

"By the…" Apollo whispered. "Computer! Engage QSE now!"

The Raider phased out of reality and sailed harmlessly through the *Galactica*, the two ships occupying the same space—but in different dimensions—for several microns. When they had cleared the battlestar, Starbuck stared at his best friend.

"What?" Apollo said. "Don't tell me you forgot about the QSE generator. You're the one who discovered the thing."

"Of course not," Starbuck replied gruffly. "I just wanted to see how you performed under pressure. Call it a test. To make sure you're fit for command."

Apollo smiled. "Right. Of course."

Starbuck looked back out at the starfield and saw the lightships that ringed the battle scene once more. Apollo had noticed them, but didn't appear to be surprised by their presence.

"Those guys have got real pogees, just sitting there watching," Starbuck commented. "A lot of help they were."

"They weren't here to help," Apollo replied. "They're waiting."

"Waiting for what?" Starbuck asked.

"For Count Iblis to make a fatal error," Apollo said, as if it were a completely understandable explanation.

"Count Iblis?" Starbuck asked, and stared at Apollo. "By the Lords, Apollo, what does Iblis have to do with anything?"

Apollo's grave features split into a wide grin. The grin turned into a dry chuckle, which blossomed into hearty laughter. Starbuck continued to stare at him blankly.

"Tell you what, old friend," Apollo said. "We get back to the officer's lounge, and I'll tell you about it over a tankard of grog."

Starbuck sighed and shook his head.

25.

THE DOOR TO THE QUORUM'S INNER SANCTUM was tightly closed. Representatives from TransVid gathered in the huge stellar chamber outside the sanctum, alongside high-ranking officers and representatives from each ship in the fleet.

Near the center of this gathering, Apollo stood, anxiously shifting his stance from time to time. Sheba was on his left, her right arm slung low across his back, protocol ignored as she showed her love and support of the man she was to marry. On Apollo's right, Troy tapped a foot against the floor in time with some unconscious rhythm. Apollo noticed and smiled at the realization that his son was more anxious than he was.

Troy turned and exchanged a knowing smile with Dalton, who stood behind them. Apollo couldn't help but notice their affection. When he looked away, he realized that Starbuck and Cassiopeia had noticed the flirtation between their daughter and his son as well.

Despite his anxiety, Apollo felt better than he had in some time. Starbuck still lived in an odd emotional flux between Cassiopeia and Athena, but the two women seemed to have become accustomed to it over the yahren. More than ever before, they were, all of them, a family. Adama's family. Beyond that, nobody wished to discuss Starbuck's fidelity, or lack thereof.

Boomer and Jolly were there as well, and the rest of his squadron.

Zimmer and Giles were gone, however, killed in battle like so many others. Grief would go hand in hand with hope as they began to rebuild. Sheba grasped his hand, squeezed it gently, and leaned over to whisper to him.

"I don't think I've ever seen you this nervous," she said quietly. Apollo only smiled. She was right. The odd thing was, he supported Athena's bid for the position of commander. He remained a candidate because she demanded it, but after her performance during his absence, and during the Cylon attack, he knew she had more than enough support. And yet the uncertainty that they had all lived with since his father's death had Apollo on edge.

He eagerly anticipated the end of it all. It was a chapter in the history of the human race that he would be pleased to see finished.

Sheba squeezed his hand again. To his right, Troy muttered, "Here they come."

The door to the Quorum sanctum opened and the Council of Twelve began to file out. Though with Puck's death, they were now eleven. Athena and President Tigh came last, side by side. When Tigh mounted the podium, Athena stood close by him. Athena searched the assemblage for a moment, and when she saw her brother, she smiled. Apollo found himself smiling in return. He was happy for her.

"Before I begin, I wish to thank all of you for your patience in this matter," Tigh noted.

Behind him, stellar light filtered in. The starfield seemed unusually bright. Apollo knew that the address was being transmitted over unicomm to the entire fleet, interrupting even the normal TransVid programs.

"I will let your new commander address the current state of our fleet, and our hopes for the future," Tigh announced. "I will, however, note that we have begun to rebuild. Already, the *Adena* has been chosen as our new Forge ship and will soon be building new Scarlet-class Vipers to replace those lost to Cylon tyranny.

"Nothing, of course, can replace the many Warriors we lost in that battle. But retired pilots have offered their services anew, both in action and in helping to speed the training of Academy cadets. We will never be caught so unprepared again.

"The *Icarus* has been surrendered to the Quorum by Gar'Tokk of the Borellian Nomen. Despite their actions in the attempted escape, their subsequent surrender and their efforts to return the other prisoners to their cells have convinced us to begin discussions that may lead to the Nomen leaving the fleet to found their own colony wherever they choose. The debate over whether our laws even apply to them as a species continues, and will not be addressed by the Quorum today.

"The Pit on the *Ursus* will be monitored far more closely from now on. If its people do not want our assistance, they do not have to accept it. But the Pit will be clean and orderly, and the people will receive frequent visits from a medical team on call for the ship."

Tigh paused, regarded the audience, and cleared his throat.

"Finally," he said, "before we name our new commander, the Quorum has asked me to announce that we have elected a new member to fill the position left by the death of Ambassador Puck. As you all know, that position must be filled by a native of Scorpius. In a unanimous decision, we now name to our empty seat one of the most courageous Warriors in our history, the offspring of a Warrior, a commander, whose exploits are near legendary.

"Major Sheba," Tigh said, and smiled.

Apollo turned to look at her, his eyes wide. Sheba was quite taken aback by the announcement. Her mother had been of Scorpius, but her father, Cain, was from Gemini. She kissed him, held him tight, and then hugged Troy as well.

"Major Sheba—if you accept the position, would you kindly join us on the podium?" Tigh suggested.

She hesitated only a moment, squeezed Apollo's hand one final time, then moved to join Tigh, Athena, Belloch, Siress Kiera and the others who made up the Quorum.

"Now, after much deliberation, and quite a bit of discussion as to what the obligations of the commander of this battlestar, and of this fleet, ought to be, the Quorum has decided, once more unanimously, on a new commander."

Tigh looked straight at him.

"Congratulations, Apollo," he said.

A great roar of cheers filled the chamber. Apollo was stunned. Troy put a hand on his shoulder and Starbuck clapped him on the back and said something Apollo couldn't quite hear, but which sounded like, "I told you so."

Uncertain what he was feeling, Apollo looked to the podium to see Athena. Her smile was so wide she might have been laughing. There was a glow of happiness about her that he hadn't seen in a long time.

"I will ask Commander Apollo to address you all in a moment," Tigh said, trying to calm the crowd. "Before I do, I want to add that Lieutenant Colonel Athena, who did such an extraordinary job as Interim Commander, has been promoted to full colonel. She will work very closely with Commander Apollo, so that he may continue to serve the fleet as a Warrior and pilot. God knows, nobody is going to keep him from flying his Viper."

A ripple of laughter ran through the chamber.

"In Apollo's absence, or during a battle in which he is taking active part, Colonel Athena will act as commander," Tigh concluded. "Now, Commander Apollo, if you will?"

Tigh gestured for Apollo to join the Quorum on the podium. Immediately, he strode forward. When he reached the podium, he threw his arms around his sister. Athena held him tight.

"Father would be very proud," she said.

"Of you as well," Apollo said. "And I think he would be particularly happy with this arrangement."

"I still have a lot to learn," she confessed in a whisper. "In his sanctuary, we can learn together."

Apollo kissed Athena, and moved to address the waiting crowd.

"Thank you," he said. "Your faith in me means more than you can possibly imagine, particularly after all that has happened in recent days. We are already rebuilding, but there is much more to do. Issues to be raised. The question of colonization is not over. Let it be clear from this moment: I believe in my father's vision, in the Thirteenth Tribe of man and the existence of Earth. But I will not force that vision upon you. You must all embrace it as you did under my father's command. To survive together as a people, we must thrive together, as a people.

"When I left the fleet after Adama's death, I was on a quest. I believed firmly that Captain Starbuck was alive. On my journey, and during my subsequent time with Captain Starbuck, I learned a great deal about humanity, and about our enemies, the Cylons. We have already begun to explore the origins and creation of the Cylons. With biological records obtained by Captain Starbuck, we may be able to discover new ways to combat them. And the Quantum Shift Effect technology we have taken from the Cylons will allow us to combat them, or any other opponent, more effectively.

"I also learned that the galactic quadrant into which we are headed has its own sentient races. One of these, the Sky, have made themselves our ally already. The Cylons have begun to spread their evil in this new quadrant, so we have not yet left them behind, as we once believed. But we are also no longer alone in our struggle. Who can say what other new allies may be out there?

"Working together, we will forge ahead, searching for a place to begin life anew, to truly build the foundations for the future of the human race.

"Now, I wish to show you something," Apollo said cryptically, as he reached into his formal uniform jacket and withdrew the holocube. He placed it on the flat surface of the rostrum before him.

"As you may have heard, Baltar, the Great Traitor himself, is aboard the *Galactica* right now," Apollo announced. "Without his aid, Starbuck and I might have been executed by the Cylons. This does not excuse his crimes. Baltar is the greatest criminal humanity has ever known. But rather than execute him, we have determined to learn whatever he has discovered about the Cylons in his eighteen yahren of collaboration with them.

"One thing Baltar retrieved from Cylon hands is this holo-cube," Apollo stated. He depressed a small indentation on the cube, and a three-dimensional star map blossomed in mid-air. It showed an entire galaxy, and was at least fifteen metrons high, nearly reaching the ceiling of the chamber. On the star map, twenty planets were lit up brighter than the rest, blinking.

"We have reason to believe," Apollo said softly, "that the blinking planets you see here are those colonies originally settled by our ancient ancestors, the people of the planet Parnassus. Those planets included Kobol and Earth. My father found Kobol, at the center of the magnetic sea. We believe we can use the location of Kobol to triangulate the coordinates of every one of these colonies."

The chamber was silent. If Apollo had to guess, he would have said the entire fleet was silent at that moment.

"Even if we never reach Earth," he concluded, "reason dictates that on at least one of these planets we will find other humans, people who share a common ancestry with us. Allies. A world upon which we might happily settle. A people who will aid us in our fight against the Cylons.

"More than ever before, we have hope. Not merely a dream or a vision, but...a destination!" he shouted triumphantly.

The fleet cheered for a long time. When they had calmed somewhat, Apollo took on a slightly more somber tone.

"Let's rejoice, yes," he said. "But let us also not forget what has happened to us in recent days, or the enemies who still lurk in the dark abyss of space.

"Ever since the death of Commander Adama, we have wallowed in conflicting opinions, dreams and visions, complaints and demands," Apollo declared. "This discord made us ripe for attack. Our vulnerability was exploited by Count Iblis, and it nearly cost all our lives at Cylon hands. Many of you are not responsible for your actions of late, having been manipulated by the subtle mental powers of Iblis.

"But we are not excused. We will all account for our actions and take the lessons offered by what Iblis has done. He could only take advantage of emotions that already existed. Remember that in days to come. Watch for the signs, the temptation to turn hope and faith into hatred and mistrust. Spurn him when he again rears his head, as he surely will. Perhaps it will be another eighteen yahren, perhaps only centons.

"It is my hope, my prayer, that we will be ready for him."

A captive in his quarters aboard the *Galactica*, Baltar lay on his berth in darkness. He could not sleep for the hatred that burned within him. He had escaped the Cylons' betrayal, that much was true. And he would do whatever he had to in order to stay alive. Why else would he have saved Apollo and Starbuck? But there would be a limit as to how long he would remain a captive.

One day, he would be exonerated. He would regain power amongst his people. They had followed him once, and they would do so again. Baltar had a charisma, a gift that could not be denied.

His eyes had begun to droop when he felt an odd sensation. At the end of his berth, the darkness began to undulate, the shadows spilling out into the form of a man. A man with burning embers for eyes.

"Ah, Baltar, my favorite son," the inhuman vision whispered. *"The fools have isolated you...just as I planned."*

GLOSSARY OF TERMS

altered—intoxicated and/or under the influence of drugs

ambrosa—extremely valuable, rare, sweet alcoholic beverage

anchor spikes—nails

apex pulsar—the top, center engine on the back of a Viper

ascensior—similar to an elevator

avion—bird

base star—a Cylon equivalent to a Colonial Battlestar

berth—bed

beschkurd—a green, leafy vegetable common to most
     Colonial planets

bova—large, livestock animal kept in herds

brain crystals—outlawed chemical weapon causing portions of
     the brain to wither and harden as if frozen

buritician—a member of the hereditary nobility of the Colonies

centari—equivalent to nearly one minute; one hundred microns

Centurion—a Cylon Warrior

centimetron—1/100th of a metron, or about 1/2 an inch

centon—equivalent to an hour; one hundred centari

chancery—casino

cogitator—a Cylon diplomat; e.g. Lucifer

commander's court—military court

coneth stew—a spicy vegetable dish made with bova meat

crawlon—spider

cubit—oregg coin used for money

cycle—work details and duties are divided into two eight-hour
     periods and one nine-hour period, or cycle, per ship's day

Cyranus—galaxy containing the Twelve Colonies

daggit—similar to a lupus, but more domesticated; a house pet

fallaga—a plant found on Qorax.

felgercarb—bulls**t

fiberline—thin, strong rope

flanchette—a stinging insect

flatscreen—computer screen

flexi-weave—a type of fabric
frack—an expletive
frizzort—mishap, error, malfunction
fumarello—similar to a cigar, but smaller
fundamental code—a language of sounds and/or gestures and images, which are believed to have significance to most sentient lifeforms
furlon—a leave of absence
grog—an alcoholic beverage, similar to rum
gyro-capacitor—the energy transference system used in starships
helm—the helmet worn by Colonial pilots
heffala berries—a fruit native to Caprica, grown aboard the Colonial fleet's agro-ships.
hydronic mushies—artificially grown, nutritious vegetable
imager—high-tech mirror
info-sphere—data storage capsule
kirasolis—a sticky, caramel-like candy
kyluminan—a lightweight, plasteen/saligium alloy
launch aperture—energy-shielded opening in a starship bay through which smaller ships take off and land.
lupus—wolf-like animal
magnalift—hi-tech crane
mealprep—kitchen
metron—approximately one meter
micron—equivalent to a fraction of a second; 1/100th of a centari
micronoscope—a powerful electronic microscope
mindwipe—fool or idiot. Someone whose use of altering substances has had adverse effects on his or her brain functions.
mucoid—slimy, sticky
mugjape—maggot-like creatures; the larval stage of skreeters
musiclink—fleet equivalent to radio
navi-hilt—Colonial Viper steering column; also controls turbolasers
novayahren—birthday
ogliv—prickly skinned, sweet fruit

oregg—precious metal, equivalent to gold
plasteen—an indestructible plastic
pogees—testicles
pulsar—space vessel propulsion engine
pyramid—a game of chance played with cards
saligium—a heavy metal alloy used mainly for construction
S-cube—simulcast sight-and-sound unit; similar to a videocamera
Seal—marriage
sensorline—physical connection between two tech systems
servitor—waiter
skreeter—bothersome but essentially harmless insect
skyeye—spherical, many lensed, hovering camera
slagger—slothful person
socialator—man or woman trained and educated to be the perfect
    companion, both sexually and socially
solonite—a powerful synthetic explosive made from solium
solium—a dangerously explosive byproduct of the tylium refinement
    process; in gaseous form, also poisonous
support vapors—life-support system aboard starships
sylvanus—metal used for adornment, similar to brass
"trank it"—calm down
TransVid—television
temblor—earthquake
triad—a contact sport, native to the Colonies, wherein two two-
    player teams compete in a triangular court.
Tribunal—court hearing
tulipian buds—exotic appetizier or side dish made from vegetables
tylium—an extremely unstable, rare mineral, but found in large
    quantities when found at all. Refined tylium is used as fuel
    to power Colonial space-faring vessels.
Qorax—a planet in the fourth quadrant of the Cyranus Galaxy
valcron—a simple fabric used for clothing, bedding, etc.
week—ten days
yahren—equivalent to a year; two hundred fifty days

ABOUT THE AUTHORS

Richard Hatch has enjoyed two decades of international recognition as an actor. He starred in such televised series as *The Streets of San Francisco*—for which he won Germany's Bravo Award, the equivalent of an Emmy—and *Battlestar Galactica*, for which he received a Golden Globe Award nomination. Hatch has recently plotted and written a popular new series of *Battletar Galactica* comic books. He lives in southern California, where he also lectures on acting and positive approaches to life.

Christopher Golden is the author of fifteen books, including the epic fantasies *Of Saints and Shadows* and *Angel Souls and Devil Hearts*. He has also authored the popular *Hellboy: The Lost Army*, and the best-selling trilogy *X-Men: Mutant Empire*. His short stories have appeared in such collections as *Forbidden Acts*, *The Ultimate Spider-Man*, *The Ultimate Silver Surfer*, *The Ultimate Hauntned House*, and *Untold Tales of Spider-Man*. Golden lives in Massachusetts with his wife and two sons.

 ™

Continues its epic voyage in search of planet Earth and the home of the mysterious lost colony, The Thirteenth Tribe, *in the exciting, surprise-filled sequel. Look for it in your local bookstore in 1998.*